ST. MARTIN'S

MINOTAUR

MYSTERIES

HIDE AND SEEK

"One of the year's ten best mysteries." —*The Hartford Courant*

"First-rate plotting, dialogue and characterization . . . All the right tackle beneath the kilt . . . Remarkable for its flinty-eye view of the flower of cities. . . . Highly recommended."
—*The Literary Review*

"This is classic mystery, with a cleverly constructed plot, plenty of likely suspects, and a complex, admirable hero. All this and unusual parts of Scotland that tourists rarely—if ever—see."
—*St. Louis Post-Dispatch*

"It's not too difficult to stuff a book with seamy bits . . . What is hard is to write about them so well that the book becomes an abiding pleasure. But this is what Ian Rankin has done."
—H.R.F. Keating

"Solidly drawn characters, keen psychological insights and an intriguing, well-knit plot make Rankin a newcomer to watch."
—*Kirkus Reviews*

"Suspenseful, riddling . . . exemplary . . . Rankin writes with wit, passion, and persuasive know-how."
—*The Sunday Times* (London)

"This compact, well-written, and fast-paced novel is sure to please readers of the genre." —*Library Journal*

St. Martin's Paperbacks Titles
by Ian Rankin

THE INSPECTOR REBUS SERIES:

DEAD SOULS

IAN RANKIN

St. Martin's Paperbacks

Previously published in Great Britain by Orion Books Ltd

DEAD SOULS

Copyright © 1999 by Ian Rankin.
Excerpt from *Set in Darkness* copyright © 2000 by Ian Rankin.

ISBN: 0-312-97420-5

Printed in the United States of America

St. Martin's Press hardcover edition / October 1999
St. Martin's Paperbacks edition / August 2000

10 9 8 7 6 5 4

To my long-suffering editor,
Caroline Oakley

DEAD SOULS

The world is full of missing persons, and their numbers increase all the time. The space they occupy lies somewhere between what we know about the ways of being alive and what we hear about the ways of being dead. They wander there, unaccompanied and unknowable, like shadows of people.

ANDREW O'HAGAN, *The Missing*

Once I caught a train to Cardenden by mistake . . . When we reached Cardenden we got off and waited for the next train back to Edinburgh. I was very tired and if Cardenden had looked more promising, I think I would have simply stayed there. And if you've ever been to Cardenden you'll know how bad things must have been.

KATE ATKINSON, *Behind the Scenes at the Museum*

PROLOGUE

From this height, the sleeping city seems like a child's construction, a model which has refused to be constrained by imagination. The volcanic plug might be black Plasticine, the castle balanced solidly atop it a skewed rendition of crenellated building bricks. The orange street lamps are crumpled toffee-wrappers glued to lollipop sticks.

Out in the Forth, the faint bulbs from pocket torches illuminate toy boats resting on black crêpe paper. In this universe, the jagged spires of the Old Town would be angled matchsticks, Princes Street Gardens a Fuzzy-Felt board. Cardboard boxes for the tenements, doors and windows painstakingly detailed with coloured pens. Drinking straws could become guttering and downpipes, and with a fine blade—maybe a scalpel—those doors could be made to open. But peering inside . . . peering inside would destroy the effect.

Peering inside would change *everything*.

He shoves his hands in his pockets. The wind is stropping his ears. He can pretend it is a child's breath, but the reality chides him.

I am the last cold wind you'll feel.

He takes a step forward, peers over the edge and into darkness. Arthur's Seat crouches behind him, humped and silent as though offended by his presence, coiled to pounce. He tells himself it is papier-mâché. He smooths his hands over strips of newsprint, not reading the stories, then realises he is stroking the air and withdraws his hands, laughing guiltily. Somewhere behind him, he hears a voice.

In the past, he'd climbed up here in daylight. Years back, it would have been with a lover maybe, climbing hand in hand, seeing the city spread out like a promise. Then later, with his wife and child, stopping at the summit to take photos, making sure no one went too close to the edge. Father and husband, he would tuck his chin into his collar, seeing Edinburgh in shades of grey, but getting it into perspective, having risen above it with his family. Digesting the whole city with a slow sweep of his head, he would feel that all problems were containable.

But now, in darkness, he knows better.

He knows that life is a trap, that the jaws eventually spring shut on anyone foolish enough to think they could cheat their way to a victory. A police car blares in the distance, but it's not coming for him. A black coach is waiting for him at the foot of Salisbury Crags. Its headless driver is becoming impatient. The horses tremble and whinny. Their flanks will lather on the ride home.

"Salisbury Crag" has become rhyming slang in the city. It means skag, heroin. "Morningside Speed" is cocaine. A snort of coke just now would do him the world of good, but wouldn't be enough. Arthur's Seat could be made of the stuff: in the scheme of things, it wouldn't matter a damn.

There is a figure behind him in the darkness, drawing nearer. He half-turns to confront it, then quickly looks away, suddenly fearful of meeting the face. He begins to say something.

"I know you'll find it hard to believe, but I've . . ."

He never finishes the sentence. Because now he's sailing out across the city, jacket flying up over his head, smothering a final, heartfelt cry. As his stomach surges and voids, he wonders if there really is a coachman waiting for him.

And feels his heart burst open with the knowledge that he'll never see his daughter again, in this world or any other.

Part One
LOST

We commit all sorts of injustices at every step without the slightest evil intention. Every minute we are the cause of someone's unhappiness . . .

1

John Rebus was pretending to stare at the meerkats when he saw the man, and knew he wasn't the one.

For the best part of an hour, Rebus had been trying to blink away a hangover, which was about as much exercise as he could sustain. He'd planted himself on benches and against walls, wiping his brow even though Edinburgh's early spring was a blood relative of midwinter. His shirt was damp against his back, uncomfortably tight every time he rose to his feet. The capybara had looked at him almost with pity, and there had seemed a glint of recognition and empathy behind the long-lashed eye of the hunched white rhino, standing so still it might have been a feature in a shopping mall, yet somehow dignified in its very isolation.

Rebus felt isolated, and about as dignified as a chimpanzee. He hadn't been to the zoo in years; thought probably the last time had been when he'd brought his daughter to see Palango the gorilla. Sammy had been so young, he'd carried her on his shoulders without feeling the strain.

Today, he carried nothing with him but a concealed radio and set of handcuffs. He wondered how conspicuous he looked, walking such a narrow ambit while shunning the attractions further up and down the slope, stopping now and then at the kiosk to buy a can of Irn-Bru. The penguin parade had come and gone and seen him not leaving his perch. Oddly, it was when the visitors moved on, seeking excitement, that the first of the meerkats appeared, rising on its hind legs, body narrow and wavering, scouting the territory. Two more had appeared from their burrow, circling, noses to the ground. They paid little attention to the silent figure seated on the low wall of their enclosure;

passed him time and again as they explored the same orbit of hard-packed earth, jumping back only when he lifted a handkerchief to his face. He was feeling the poison fizz in his veins: not the booze, but an early-morning double espresso from one of the converted police boxes near The Meadows. He'd been on his way to work, on his way to learning that today was zoo patrol. The mirror in the cop-shop toilet had lacked any sense of diplomacy.

Greenslade: "Sunkissed You're Not." Segue to Jefferson Airplane: "If You Feel Like China Breaking."

But it could always be worse, Rebus had reminded himself, applying his thoughts instead to the day's central question: who was poisoning the zoo animals of Edinburgh? The fact of the matter was, some individual was to blame. Somebody cruel and calculating and so far missed by surveillance cameras and keepers alike. Police had a vague description, and spot-checks were being made of visitors' bags and coat pockets, but what everyone really wanted—except perhaps the media—was to have someone in custody, preferably with the tainted tidbits locked away as evidence.

Meantime, as senior staff had indicated, the irony was that the poisoner had actually been good for business. There'd been no copycat offences yet, but Rebus wondered how long that would last . . .

The next announcement concerned feeding the sea-lions. Rebus had sauntered past their pool earlier, thinking it not overly large for a family of three. The meerkat den was surrounded by children now, and the meerkats themselves had disappeared, leaving Rebus strangely pleased to have been accorded their company.

He moved away, but not too far, and proceeded to untie and tie a shoelace, which was his way of marking the quarter-hours. Zoos and the like had never held any fascination for him. As a child, his roll-call of pets had seen more than its fair share of those listed "Missing in Action" or "Killed in the Line of Duty." His tortoise had absconded, despite having its owner's name painted on its shell; several budgies had failed to reach maturity; and ill-health had plagued his only goldfish (won at the fair in Kirkcaldy). Living as he did in a tenement flat, he'd never been tempted in adulthood by the thought of a cat or dog. He'd tried horse-riding exactly once, rubbing his inside legs raw in the process and vowing afterwards that the closest he'd come in future to the noble beast would be on a betting slip.

But he'd liked the meerkats for a mixture of reasons: the resonance of their name; the low comedy of their rituals; their instinct for self-preservation. Kids were dangling over the wall now, legs kicking in the air. Rebus imagined a role reversal—cages filled with children, peered at by passing animals as they capered and squealed, loving the attention. Except the animals wouldn't share a human's curiosity. They would be unmoved by any display of agility or tenderness, would fail to comprehend that some game was being played, or that someone had skinned a knee. Animals would not build zoos, would have no need of them. Rebus was wondering why humans needed them.

The place suddenly became ridiculous to him, a chunk of prime Edinburgh real estate given over to the unreal . . . And then he saw the camera.

Saw it because it replaced the face that should have been there. The man was standing on a grassy slope sixty-odd feet away, adjusting the focus on a sizeable telescopic lens. The mouth below the camera's body was a thin line of concentration, rippling slightly as forefinger and thumb fine-tuned the apparatus. He wore a black denim jacket, creased chinos, and running shoes. He'd removed a faded blue baseball cap from his head. It dangled from a free finger as he took his pictures. His hair was thinning and brown, forehead wrinkled. Recognition came as soon as he lowered the camera. Rebus looked away, turning in the direction of the photographer's subjects: children. Children leaning into the meerkat enclosure. All you could see were shoe-soles and legs, girls' skirts and the smalls of backs where T-shirts and jerseys had ridden up.

Rebus knew the man. Context made it easier. Hadn't seen him in probably four years but couldn't forget eyes like that, the hunger shining on cheeks whose suffused redness highlighted old acne scars. The hair had been longer four years ago, curling over misshapen ears. Rebus sought for a name, at the same time reaching into his pocket for his radio. The photographer caught the movement, eyes turning to match Rebus's gaze, which was already moving elsewhere. Recognition worked both ways. The lens came off and was stuffed into a shoulder-bag. A lens-cap was clipped over the aperture. And then the man was off, walking briskly downhill. Rebus yanked out his radio.

"He's heading downhill from me, west side of the Members' house. Black denim jacket, light trousers . . ." Rebus kept the description going as he followed. Turning back, the photographer saw him and broke into a trot, hindered by the heavy camera bag.

The radio burst into life, officers heading for the area. Past a restaurant and cafeteria, past couples holding hands and children attacking ice-creams. Peccaries, otters, pelicans. It was all downhill, for which Rebus was thankful, and the man's unusual gait—one leg slightly shorter than the other—was helping close the gap. The walkway narrowed just at the point where the crowd thickened. Rebus wasn't sure what was causing the bottleneck, then heard a splash, followed by cheers and applause.

"Sea-lion enclosure!" he yelled into his radio.

The man half-turned, saw the radio at Rebus's mouth, looked ahead of him and saw heads and bodies, camouflaging the approach of any other officers. There was fear in his eyes now, replacing the earlier calculation. He had ceased to be in control of events. With Rebus just about within grabbing distance, the man pushed two spectators aside and clambered over the low stone wall. On the other side of the pool was a rock outcrop atop which stood the female keeper, stooping over two black plastic pails. Rebus saw that there were hardly any spectators behind the keeper, since the rocks obstructed any view of the sea-lions. By dodging the crowd, the man could clamber back over the wall at the far side and be within striking distance of the exit. Rebus cursed under his breath, lifted a foot on to the wall, and hauled himself over.

The onlookers were whistling, a few even cheering as video cameras were hoisted to record the antics of two men cautiously making their way along the sharp slopes. Glancing towards the water, Rebus saw rapid movement, and heard warning yells from the keeper as a sea-lion slithered

up on to the rocks near her. Its sleek black body rested only
long enough for a fish to be dropped accurately into its
mouth, before turning and slipping back into the pool. It
looked neither too big nor too fierce, but its appearance had
rattled Rebus's quarry. The man turned back for a moment,
his camera bag sliding down his arm. He moved it so it
was hanging around his neck. He looked ready to retreat,
but when he saw his pursuer, he changed his mind again.
The keeper had reached for a radio of her own, alerting
security. But the pool's occupants were becoming impatient. The water beside Rebus seemed to flex and sway. A
wave foamed against his face as something huge and ink-
black rose from the depths, obliterating the sun and slapping itself down on the rocks. The crowd screamed as the
male sea-lion, easily four or five times the size of its offspring, landed and looked around for food, loud snorts
belching from its nose. As it opened its mouth and let out
a ferocious wail, the photographer yelped and lost his balance, plunging into the pool and taking the camera bag with
him.

Two shapes in the pool—mother and child—nosed towards him. The keeper was blowing the whistle strung
around her neck, for all the world like the referee at a Sunday kickabout faced with a conflagration. The male sea-
lion looked at Rebus a final time and plunged back into its
pool, heading for where its mate was prodding the new
arrival.

"For Christ's sake," Rebus shouted, "chuck in some
fish!"

The keeper got the message and kicked a pail of food
into the pool, at which all three sea-lions sped towards the
scene. Rebus took his chance and waded in, closing his
eyes and diving, grabbing the man and hauling him back
towards the rocks. A couple of spectators came to help,
followed by two plain-clothes detectives. Rebus's eyes
stung. The scent of raw fish was heavy in the air.

"Let's get you out," someone said, offering a hand. Rebus let himself be reeled in. He snatched the camera from
around the drenched man's neck.

"Got you," he said. Then, kneeling on the rocks, starting
to shiver, he threw up into the pool.

Next morning, Rebus was surrounded by memories.

Not his own, but those of his Chief Super: framed photographs cluttering the tight space of the office. The thing with memories was, they meant nothing to the outsider. Rebus could have been looking at a museum display. Children, lots of children. The Chief Super's kids, their faces ageing over time, and then grandchildren. Rebus got the feeling his boss hadn't taken the photos. They were gifts, passed on to him, and he'd felt it necessary to bring them here.

The clues were all in their situation: the photos on the desk faced out from it, so anyone in the office could see them with the exception of the man who used the desk every day. Others were on the window-ledge behind the desk—same effect—and still more on top of a filing cabinet in the corner. Rebus sat in Chief Superintendent Watson's chair to confirm his theory. The snapshots weren't for Watson; they were for visitors. And what they told visitors was that Watson was a family man, a man of rectitude, a man who had achieved something in his life. Instead of humanising the drab office, they sat in it with all the ease of exhibits.

A new photo had been added to the collection. It was old, slightly out of focus as though smeared by a flicker of camera movement. Crimped edges, white border, and the photographer's illegible signature in one corner. A family group: father standing, one hand proprietorially on the shoulder of his seated wife, who held in her lap a toddler. The father's other hand gripped the blazered shoulder of a young boy, cropped hair and glaring eyes. Some pre-sitting tension was evident: the boy was trying to pull his shoulder from beneath his father's claw. Rebus took the photo over to the window, marvelled at the starched solemnity. He felt starched himself, in his dark woollen suit, white shirt and black tie. Black socks and shoes, the latter given a decent polish first thing this morning. Outside it was overcast, threatening rain. Fine weather for a funeral.

Chief Superintendent Watson came into the room, lazy progress belying his temperament. Behind his back they called him "the Farmer," because he came from the north and had something of the Aberdeen Angus about him. He was dressed in his best uniform, cap in one hand, white A4 envelope in the other. He placed both on his desk, as Rebus replaced the photograph, angling it so it faced the Farmer's chair.

"That you, sir?" he asked, tapping the scowling child.

"That's me."

"Brave of you to let us see you in shorts."

But the Farmer was not to be deflected. Rebus could think of three explanations for the red veins highlighted on Watson's face: exertion, spirits, or anger. No sign of breathlessness, so rule out the first. And when the Farmer drank whisky, it didn't just affect his cheeks: his whole face took on a roseate glow and seemed to contract until it became puckish.

Which left anger.

"Let's get down to it," Watson said, glancing at his watch. Neither man had much time. The Farmer opened the envelope and shook a packet of photographs on to his desk, then opened the packet and tossed the photos towards Rebus.

"Look for yourself."

Rebus looked. They were the photos from Darren Rough's camera. The Farmer reached into his drawer to pull out a file. Rebus kept looking. Zoo animals, caged and behind walls. And in some of the shots—not all of them, but a fair proportion—children. The camera had focused on these children, involved in conversations among themselves, or chewing sweets, or making faces at the animals. Rebus felt immediate relief, and looked to the Farmer for a confirmation that wasn't there.

"According to Mr. Rough," the Farmer was saying, studying a sheet from the file, "the photos comprise part of a portfolio."

"I'll bet they do."

"Of a day in the life of Edinburgh Zoo."

"Sure."

The Farmer cleared his throat. "He's enrolled in a photography night-class. I've checked and it's true. It's also true that his project is the zoo."

"And there are kids in almost every shot."

"In fewer than half the shots, actually."

Rebus slid the photos across the desk. "Come on, sir."

"John, Darren Rough has been out of prison the best part of a year and has yet to show any sign of reoffending."

"I heard he'd gone south."

"And moved back again."

"He ran for it when he saw me."

The Farmer just stared the comment down. "There's nothing here, John," he said.

"A guy like Rough, he doesn't go to the zoo for the birds and the bees, believe me."

"It wasn't even his choice of project. His tutor assigned it."

"Yes, Rough would have preferred a play-park." Rebus sighed. "What does his lawyer say? Rough was always good at roping in a lawyer."

"Mr. Rough just wants to be left in peace."

"The way he left those kids in peace?"

The Farmer sat back. "Does the word 'atonement' mean anything to you, John?"

Rebus shook his head. "Not applicable."

"How do you know?"

"Ever seen a leopard change its spots?"

The Farmer checked his watch. "I know the two of you have a history."

"I wasn't the one he made the complaint against."

"No," the Farmer said, "Jim Margolies was."

They left that in the air for a moment, lost in their own thoughts.

"So we do nothing?" Rebus queried at last. The word "atonement" was flitting about inside his skull. His friend the priest had been known to use it: reconciliation of God and man through Christ's life and death. A far cry from Darren Rough. Rebus wondered what Jim Margolies had been atoning for when he'd pitched himself off Salisbury Crags . . .

"His sheet's clean." The Farmer reached into his desk's deep bottom drawer, pulled out a bottle and two glasses. Malt whisky. "I don't know about you," he said, "but I need one of these before a funeral."

Rebus nodded, watching the man pour. Cascading sound of mountain streams. *Usquebaugh* in the Gaelic. *Uisge*: water; *beatha*: life. Water of life. *Beatha* sounding like "birth." Each drink was a birth to Rebus's mind. But as his doctor kept telling him, each drop was a little death, too. He lifted the glass to his nose, nodded appreciation.

"Another good man gone," the Farmer said.

And suddenly there were ghosts swirling around the room, just on the periphery of Rebus's vision, and chief amongst them Jack Morton. Jack, his old colleague, now three months dead. The Byrds: "He Was a Friend of Mine." A friend who refused to stay buried. The Farmer followed Rebus's eyes, but saw nothing. Drained his glass and put the bottle away again.

"Little and often," he said. And then, as though the whisky had opened some bargain between them: "There are ways and means, John."

"Of what, sir?" Jack had melted into the windowpanes.

"Of coping." Already the whisky was working on the Farmer's face, turning it triangular. "Since what happened to Jim Margolies . . . well, it's made some of us think more about the stresses of the job." He paused. "Too many mistakes, John."

"I'm having a bad patch, that's all."

"A bad patch has its reasons."

"Such as?"

The Farmer left the question unanswered, knowing perhaps that Rebus was busy answering it for himself: Jack Morton's death; Sammy in a wheelchair.

And whisky a therapist he could afford, at least in monetary terms.

"I'll manage," he said at last, not even managing to convince himself.

"All by yourself?"

"That's the way, isn't it?"

The Farmer shrugged. "And meantime we all live with your mistakes?"

Mistakes: like pulling men towards Darren Rough, who wasn't the man they wanted. Allowing the poisoner open access to the meerkats—an apple tossed into their enclosure. Luckily a keeper had walked past, picked it up before the animals could. He'd known about the scare, handed it in for testing.

Positive for rat poison.

Rebus's fault.

"Come on," the Farmer said, after a final glance at his watch, "let's get moving."

So that once again Rebus's speech had gone unspoken, the one about how he'd lost any sense of vocation, any feeling of optimism about the role—the very existence—of policing. About how these thoughts scared him, left him either sleepless or scarred by bad dreams. About the ghosts which had come to haunt him, even in daytime.

About how he didn't want to be a cop any more.

Jim Margolies had had it all.

Ten years younger than Rebus, he was being tipped for accelerated advancement. They were waiting for him to learn the final few lessons, after which the rank of detective inspector would have been shed like a final skin. Bright, personable, a canny strategist with an eye to internal politics. Handsome, too, keeping fit playing rugby for his old school, Boroughmuir. He came from a good background and had connections to the Edinburgh establishment, his wife charming and elegant, his young daughter an acknowledged beauty. Liked by his fellow officers, and with an enviable ratio of arrests to convictions. The family lived quietly in The Grange, attended a local church, seemed the perfect little unit in every way.

The Farmer kept the commentary going, voice barely audible. He'd started on the drive to the church, kept it up

during the service, and was closing with a graveside per-
oration.

"He had it all, John. And then he goes and does something like that. What makes a man . . . I mean, what goes
through his head? This was someone even older officers
looked up to—I mean the cynical old buggers within spit-
ting distance of their pension. They've seen everything in
their time, but they'd never seen anyone quite like Jim Margolies."

Rebus and the Farmer—their station's representatives—
were towards the back of the crowd. And it was a good
crowd, too. Lots of brass, alongside rugby players, church-
goers, and neighbours. Plus extended family. And standing
by the open grave, the widow dressed in black, managing
to look composed. She'd lifted her daughter off the ground.
The daughter in a white lace dress, her hair thick and long
and ringlet-blonde, face shining as she waved bye-bye to
the wooden casket. With the blonde hair and white dress,
she looked like an angel. Perhaps that had been the intention. Certainly, she stood out from the crowd.

Margolies' parents were there, too. The father looking
ex-forces, stiff-backed as a grandfather clock but with both
trembling hands gripping the silver knob of a walking-stick.
The mother teary-eyed, fragile, a veil falling to her wet
mouth. She'd lost both her children. According to the Farmer, Jim's sister had killed herself too, years back. History
of mental instability, and she'd slashed her wrists. Rebus
looked again at the parents, who had now outlived both
their offspring. His mind flashed to his own daughter, wondering how scarred *she* was, scarred in places you couldn't
see.

Other family members nestled close to the parents, seeking comfort or ready to offer support—Rebus couldn't tell
which.

"Nice family," the Farmer was whispering. Rebus almost
perceived a whiff of envy. "Hannah's won competitions."

Hannah being the daughter. She was eight, Rebus
learned. Blue-eyed like her father and perfect-skinned. The
widow's name was Katherine.

"Dear Lord, the sheer waste."

Rebus thought of the Farmer's photographs, of the

way individuals met and interlaced, forming a pattern which drew in others, colours merging or taking on discernible contrasts. You made friends, married into a new family, you had children who played with the children of other parents. You went to work, met colleagues who became friends. Bit by bit your identity became subsumed, no longer an individual and yet stronger somehow as a result.

Except it didn't always work that way. Conflicts could arise: work perhaps, or the slow realisation that you'd made a wrong decision some time back. Rebus had seen it in his own life, had chosen profession over marriage, pushing his wife away. She'd taken their daughter with her. He felt now that he'd made the right choice for the wrong reasons, that he should have owned up to his failings from the start. His work had merely given him a reasonable excuse for bailing out.

He wondered about Jim Margolies, who had thrown himself to his death in the dark. He wondered what had driven him to that final stark decision. No one seemed to have a clue. Rebus had come across plenty of suicides over the years, from bungled to assisted and all points in between. But there had always been some kind of explanation, some breaking point reached, some deep-seated sense of loss or failure or foreboding. Leaf Hound: "Drowned My Life in Fear."

But when it came to Jim Margolies . . . nothing clicked. There was no sense to it. His widow, parents, workmates . . . no one had been able to offer the first hint of an explanation. He'd been declared A1 fit. Things had been fine on the work front and at home. He loved his wife, his daughter. Money was not a problem.

But something had been a problem.

Dear Lord, the sheer waste.

And the cruelty of it: to leave everyone not only grieving but questioning, wondering if they were somehow to blame.

To erase your own life when life was so precious.

Looking towards the trees, Rebus saw Jack Morton standing there, seeming as young as when the two had first met.

Earth was being tossed down on to the coffin lid, a final

futile wake-up call. The Farmer started walking away, hands clasped behind his back.

"As long as I live," he said, "I'll never understand it."

"You never know your luck," said Rebus.

3

He stood atop Salisbury Crags. There was a fierce wind blowing, and he turned up the collar of his coat. He'd been home to change out of his funeral clothes and should have been heading back for the station—he could see St. Leonard's from here—but something had made him take this detour.

Behind and above him, a few hardy souls had achieved the summit of Arthur's Seat. Their reward: the panoramic view, plus ears that would sting for hours. With his fear of heights, Rebus didn't get too close to the edge. The landscape was extraordinary. It was as though God had slapped his hand down on to Holyrood Park, flattening part of it but leaving this sheer face of rock, a reminder of the city's origins.

Jim Margolies had jumped from here. Or a sudden gust had taken him: that was the less plausible, but more easily digested alternative. His widow had stated her belief that he'd been "walking, just walking," and had lost his footing in the dark. But this raised unanswerable questions. What would take him from his bed in the middle of the night? If he had worries, why did he need to think them out at the top of Salisbury Crags, several miles from his home? He lived in The Grange, in what had been his wife's parents' house. It was raining that night, yet he didn't take the car. Would a desperate man notice he was getting soaked . . . ?

Looking down, Rebus saw the site of the old brewery, where they were going to build the new Scottish parliament. The first in three hundred years, and sited next to a theme park. Nearby stood the Greenfield housing scheme, a compact maze of high-rise blocks and sheltered accommodation. He wondered why the Crags should be so much more impressive than the man-made ingenuity of high-rises, then reached into his pocket for a folded piece of paper. He checked an address, looked back down on to Greenfield, and knew he had one more detour to make.

Greenfield's flat-roofed tower blocks had been built in the mid-1960s and were showing their age. Dark stains bloomed on the discoloured harling. Overflow pipes dripped water on to cracked paving slabs. Rotting wood was flaking from the window surrounds. The wall of one ground-floor flat, its windows boarded up, had been painted to identify the one-time tenant as "Junky Scum."

No council planner had ever lived here. No director of housing or community architect. All the council had done was move in problem tenants and tell everyone central heating was on its way. The estate had been built on the flat bottom of a bowl of land, so that Salisbury Crags loomed monstrously over the whole. Rebus rechecked the address on the paper. He'd had dealings in Greenfield before. It was far from the worst of the city's estates, but still had its troubles. It was early afternoon now, and the streets were quiet. Someone had left a bicycle, missing its front wheel, in the middle of the road. Further along stood a pair of shopping trolleys, nose to nose as though deep in local gossip. In the midst of the six eleven-storey blocks stood four neat rows of terraced bungalows, complete with pocket-handkerchief gardens and low wooden fences. Net curtains covered most of the windows, and above each door a burglar alarm had been secured to the wall.

Part of the tarmac arena between the tower blocks had been given over to a play area. One boy was pulling another along on a sledge, imagining snow as the runners scraped across the ground. Rebus called out the words "Cragside Court" and the boy on the sledge waved in the direction of one of the blocks. When Rebus got up close to it, he saw that a sign on the wall identifying the building had been defaced so that "Cragside" read "Crap-site." A window on the second floor swung open.

"You needn't bother," a woman's voice boomed. "He's not here."

Rebus stood back and angled his head upwards.

"Who is it I'm supposed to be looking for?"

"Trying to be smart?"

"No, I just didn't know there was a clairvoyant on the premises. Is it your husband or your boyfriend I'm after?"

The woman stared down at him, made up her mind that she'd spoken too soon. "Never mind," she said, pulling her head back in and closing the window.

There was an intercom system, but only the numbers of flats, no names. He pulled at the door; it was unlocked anyway. He waited a couple of minutes for the lift to come, then let it shudder its way slowly up to the fifth floor. A walkway, open to the elements, led him past the front doors of half a dozen flats until he was standing outside 5/14 Cragside Court. There was a window, but curtained with what looked like a frayed blue bedsheet. The door showed signs of abuse: failed break-ins maybe, or just people kicking at it because there was no bell or knocker. No nameplate, but that didn't matter. Rebus knew who lived here.

Darren Rough.

The address was new to Rebus. When he'd helped build the case against Rough four years before, Rough had been living in a flat on Buccleuch Street. Now he was back in Edinburgh, and Rebus was keen for him to know just how welcome he was. Besides, he had a couple of questions for Darren Rough, questions about Jim Margolies . . .

The only problem was, he got the feeling the flat was empty. He tried one half-hearted thump at both door and window. When there was no response, he leaned down to peer through the letterbox, but found it had been blocked from inside. Either Rough didn't want anyone looking in, or else he'd been getting unwelcome deliveries. Straightening up, Rebus turned and rested his arms on the balcony railing. He found himself staring straight down on to the kids' playground Kids; an estate like Greenfield would be full of kids. He turned back to study Rough's abode. No graffiti on walls or door, nothing to identify the tenant as

"Pervo Scum." Down at ground level, the sledge had taken a corner too fast, throwing off its rider. A window below Rebus opened noisily.

"I saw you, Billy Horman! You did that on purpose!" The same woman, her words aimed at the boy who'd been pulling the sledge.

"Never did!" he yelled back.

"You fucking did! I'll murder you." Then, tone changing: "Are you all right, Jamie? I've told you before about playing with that wee bastard. Now get in here!"

The injured boy rubbed a hand beneath his nose—as close as he was going to get to defiance—then made his way towards the tower block, glancing back at his friend. Their shared look lasted only a second or two, but it managed to convey that they were still friends, that the adult world could never break that bond.

Rebus watched the sledge-puller, Billy Horman, shuffle away, then walked down three floors. The woman's flat was easy to find. He could hear her shouting from thirty yards away. He wondered if she constituted a problem tenant; got the feeling few would dare to complain to her face . . .

The door was solid, recently painted dark blue, and boasting a spy-hole. Net curtains at the window. They twitched as the woman checked who her caller was. When she opened the door, her son darted back out and along the walkway.

"Just going to the shop, Mum!"

"Come back here, you!"

But he was pretending not to have heard; disappeared around a corner.

"Give me the strength to wring his neck," she said.

"I'm sure you love him really."

She stared hard at him. "Do we have any business?"

"You never answered my question: husband or boyfriend?"

She folded her arms. "Eldest son, if you must know."

"And you thought I was here to see him?"

"You're the police, aren't you?" She snorted when he said nothing.

"Should I know him then?"

"Calumn Brady," she said.

"You're Cal's mum?" Rebus nodded slowly. He knew Cal Brady by reputation: regal chancer. He'd heard of Cal's mother, too.

She stood about five feet eight in her sheepskin slippers. Heavily built, with thick arms and wrists, her face had decided long ago that make-up wasn't going to cure anything. Her hair, thick and platinum-coloured, brown at the roots, fell from a centre parting. She was dressed in regulation satin-look shell suit, blue with a silver stripe up the arms and legs.

"You're not here for Cal then?" she said.

Rebus shook his head. "Not unless you think he's done something."

"So what *are* you doing here?"

"Ever have any dealings with one of your neighbours, youngish lad called Darren Rough?"

"Which flat's he in?" Rebus didn't answer. "We get a lot of coming and going. Social Work stuff them in here for a couple of weeks. Christ knows what happens to them, they go AWOL or get shifted." She sniffed. "What's he look like?"

"Doesn't matter," Rebus said. Jamie was back down in the playground, no sign of his friend. He ran in circles, pulling the sledge. Rebus got the idea he could run like that all day.

"Jamie's not in school today?" he asked, turning back towards the door.

"None of your bloody business," Mrs. Brady said, closing it in his face.

Back at St. Leonard's police station, Rebus looked up Calumn Brady on the computer. At age seventeen, Cal already had impressive form: assault, shoplifting, drunk and disorderly. There was no sign as yet that Jamie was following in his footsteps, but the mother, Vanessa Brady, known as "Van," had been in trouble. Disputes with neighbours had become violent, and she'd been caught giving Cal a false alibi for one of his assault charges. No mention anywhere of a husband. Whistling "We Are Family," Rebus went to ask the desk sergeant if he knew who the community officer was for Greenfield.

"Tom Jackson," he was told. "And I know where he is, because I saw him not two minutes ago."

Tom Jackson was in the car park at the back of the station, finishing a cigarette. Rebus joined him, lit one for himself and made the offer. Jackson shook his head.

"Got to pace myself, sir," he said.

Jackson was in his mid-forties, barrel-chested and silver-haired with matching moustache. His eyes were dark, so that he always looked sceptical. He saw this as a decided bonus, since all he had to do was keep quiet and suspects would offer up more than they wanted to, just to appease that look.

"I hear you're still working Greenfield, Tom."

"For my sins." Jackson flicked ash from his cigarette, then brushed a few flecks from his uniform. "I was due a transfer in January."

"What happened?"

"The locals needed a Santa for their Christmas do. They have one every year at the church. Underprivileged kids. They asked muggins here."

"And?"

"And I did it. Some of those kids . . . poor wee bastards. Almost had me in tears." The memory stopped him for a moment. "Some of the locals came up afterwards, started whispering." He smiled. "It was like the confessional. See, the only way they could think to thank me was to furnish a few tip-offs."

Rebus smiled. "Shopping their neighbours."

"As a result of which, my clear-up rate got a sudden lift. Bugger is, they've decided to keep me there, seeing how I'm suddenly so clever."

"A victim of your own success, Tom." Rebus inhaled, holding the smoke as he examined the tip of his cigarette. Exhaling, he shook his head. "Christ, I love smoking."

"Not me. Interviewing some kid, warning him off drugs, and all the time I'm gasping for a draw." He shook his head. "Wish I could give it up."

"Have you tried patches?"

"No good, they kept slipping off my eye."

They shared a laugh at that.

"I'm assuming you'll get round to it eventually," Jackson said.

"What, trying a patch?"

"No, telling me what it is you're after."

"Am I that transparent?"

"Maybe it's just my finely honed intuition."

Rebus flicked ash into the breeze. "I was out at Greenfield earlier. You know a guy called Darren Rough?"

"Can't say I do."

"I had a run-in with him at the zoo."

Jackson nodded, stubbed out his cigarette. "I heard about it. Paedophile, yes?"

"And living in Cragside Court."

Jackson stared at Rebus. "That I didn't know."

"Neighbours don't seem to know either."

"They'd murder him if they did."

"Maybe someone could have a word . . ."

Jackson frowned. "Christ, I don't know about that. They'd string him up."

"Bit of an exaggeration, Tom. Run him out of town maybe."

Jackson straightened his back. "And that's what you want?"

"You really want a paedophile on your beat?"

Jackson thought about it. He brought out his pack of cigarettes and was reaching into it when he checked his watch: ciggie break over.

"Let me think on it."

"Fair enough, Tom." Rebus flicked his own cigarette on to the tarmac. "I bumped into one of Rough's neighbours, Van Brady."

Jackson winced. "Don't get on the wrong side of that one."

"You mean she has a *right* side?"

"Best seen when retreating."

Back at his desk, Rebus put a call in to the council offices and was eventually put through to Darren Rough's social worker, a man called Andy Davies.

"Do you think it was a wise move?" Rebus asked.

"Care to give me some clue what you're talking about?"

"Convicted paedophile, council flat in Greenfield, nice view of the children's playground."

"What's he done?" Sounding suddenly tired.

"Nothing I can pin him for." Rebus paused. "Not yet. I'm phoning while there's still time."

"Time for what?"

"To move him."

"Move him where exactly?"

"How about Bass Rock?"

"Or a cage at the zoo maybe?"

Rebus sat back in his chair. "He's told you."

"Of course he's told me. I'm his social worker."

"He was taking photos of kids."

"It's all been explained to Chief Superintendent Watson."

Rebus looked around the office. "Not to my satisfaction, Mr. Davies."

"Then I suggest you take it up with your superior, Inspector." No hiding the irritation in the voice.

"So you're going to do nothing?"

"It was your lot wanted him here in the first place!"

Silence on the line, then Rebus: "What did you just say?"

"Look, I've nothing to add. Take it up with your Chief Superintendent. OK?"

The connection was broken. Rebus tried Watson's office, but his secretary said he was out. He chewed on his pen, wishing plastic had a nicotine content.

It was your lot wanted him here.

DC Siobhan Clarke was at her desk, busy on the phone. He noticed that on the wall behind her was pinned up a postcard of a sea-lion. Walking up to it, he saw someone had added a speech balloon, issuing from the creature's mouth: "I'll have a Rebus supper, thanks."

"Ho ho," he said, pulling the card from the wall. Clarke had finished her call.

"Don't look at me," she said.

He scanned the room. DC Grant Hood reading a tabloid, DS George Silvers frowning at his computer screen. Then DI Bill Pryde walked into the office, and Rebus knew he had his man. Curly fair hair, ginger moustache: a face just made for mischief. Rebus waved the card at him, and watched Pryde's face take on a look of false wounded innocence. As Rebus walked towards him, a phone began sounding.

"That's yours," Pryde said, retreating. On his way to the phone, Rebus tossed the card into a bin.

"DI Rebus," he said.

"Oh, hello. You probably won't remember me." A short laugh on the line. "That used to be a bit of a joke at school."

Rebus, immune to every kind of crank, rested against the edge of the desk. "Why's that?" he asked, wondering what kind of punch-line he was walking into.

"Because it's my name: Mee." The caller spelled it for him. "Brian Mee."

Inside Rebus's head, a fuzzy photograph began to develop—mouthful of prominent teeth; freckled nose and cheeks; kitchen-stool haircut.

"Barney Mee?" he said.

More laughter on the line. "I never knew why everyone called me that."

Rebus could have told him after Barney Rubble in *The*

Flintstones. He could have added: because you were a dense wee bastard. Instead, he asked Mee what he could do for him.

"Well, Janice and me, we thought . . . well, it was my mum's idea actually. She knew your dad. Both my parents knew him, only my dad passed away, like. They all drank at the Goth."

"Are you still in Bowhill?"

"Never quite escaped. I work in Glenrothes though."

The photo had become clearer: decent footballer, bit of a terrier, the hair reddish-brown. Dragging his satchel along the ground until the stitching burst. Always with some huge hard sweet in his mouth, crunching down on it, nose running.

"So what can I do for you, Brian?"

"It was my mum's idea. She remembered you were in the police in Edinburgh, thought maybe you could help."

"With what?"

"It's our son. Mine and Janice's. He's called Damon."

"What's he done?"

"He's vanished."

"Run away?"

"More like a puff of smoke. He was in this club with his pals, see—"

"Have you tried calling the police?" Rebus caught himself. "I mean Fife Constabulary."

"Thing is, the club's in Edinburgh. Police there say they looked into it, asked a few questions. See, Damon's nineteen. They say that means he's got a right to bugger off if he wants."

"They've got a point, Brian. People run away all the time. Girl trouble maybe."

"He was engaged."

"Maybe he got scared."

"Helen's a lovely girl. Never a raised voice between them."

"Did he leave a note?"

"I went through this with the police. No note, and he didn't take any clothes or anything."

"You think something's happened to him?"

"We just want to know he's all right . . ." The voice fell

away. "My mum always speaks well of your dad. He's remembered in this town."

And buried there, too, Rebus thought. He picked up his pen. "Give me a few details, Brian, and I'll see what I can do."

A little later, Rebus visited Grant Hood's desk and retrieved the discarded newspaper from the bin. Turning the pages, he found the editorial section. At the bottom, in bold script, were the words "Do you have a story for us? Call the newsroom day or night." They'd printed the telephone number. Rebus jotted it into his notebook.

The silent dance resumed. Couples writhed and shuffled, threw back their heads or ran hands through their hair, eyes seeking out future partners or past loves to make jealous. The video monitor gave a greasy look to everything.

No sound, just pictures, the tape cutting from dancefloor to main bar to second bar to toilet hallway. Then the entrance foyer, exterior front and back. Exterior back was a puddled alley boasting rubbish bins and a Merc belonging to the club's owner. The club was called Gaitano's, nobody knew why. Some of the clientele had come up with the nickname "Guisers," and that was the name by which Rebus knew it.

It was on Rose Street, started to get busy around ten thirty each evening. There'd been a stabbing in the back alley the previous summer, the owner complaining of blood on his Merc.

Rebus was seated in a small uncomfortable chair in a small dimly lit room. In the other chair, hand on the video's remote, sat DC Phyllida Hawes.

"Here we go again," she said. Rebus leaned forward a

little. The view jumped from back alley to dancefloor. "Any second." Another cut: main bar, punters queuing three deep. She froze the picture. It wasn't so much black and white as sepia, the colour of dead photographs. Interior light, she'd explained earlier. She moved the action along one frame at a time as Rebus moved in on the screen, bending so one knee touched the floor. His finger touched a face.

"That's him," she agreed.

On the desk was a slim file. Rebus had taken from it a photograph, which he now held to the screen.

"All right," he said. "Forward at half-speed."

The security camera stayed with the main bar for another ten seconds, then switched to second bar and all points on the compass. When it returned to the main bar, the crush of drinkers seemed not to have moved. She froze the tape again.

"He's not there," Rebus said.

"No chance he got served. The two ahead of him are still waiting."

Rebus nodded. "He should be there." He touched the screen again.

"Next to the blonde," Hawes said.

Yes, the blonde: spun-silver hair, dark eyes and lips. While those around her were intent on catching the eyes of the bar staff, she was looking off to one side. There were no sleeves to her dress.

Twenty seconds of footage from the foyer showed a steady stream entering the club, but no one leaving.

"I went through the whole tape," Hawes said. "Believe me, he's not on it."

"So what happened to him?"

"Easy, he walked out, only the cameras didn't pick him up."

"And left his pals gasping?"

Rebus studied the file again. Damon Mee had been out with two friends, a night in the big city. It had been Damon's shout—two lagers and a Coke, this last for the designated driver. They'd waited for him, then gone looking. Initial reaction: he'd scored and slunk off without telling them. Maybe she'd been a dinosaur, not something to brag about. But then he hadn't turned up at home, and his parents had started asking questions, questions no one could answer.

Simple truth: Damon Mee had, as the timer on the camera footage showed, vanished from the world between 11:44 and 11:45 p.m. the previous Friday night.

Hawes switched off the machine. She was tall and thin and knew her job; hadn't liked Rebus appearing at Gayfield cop shop like this; hadn't liked the implication.

"There's no hint of foul play," she said defensively. "Quarter of a million MisPers every year, most turn up again in their own sweet time."

"Look," Rebus assured her, "I'm doing this for an old friend, that's all. He just wants to know we've done all we can."

"What's to do?"

Good question, and one Rebus was unable to answer right that minute. Instead, he brushed dust from the knees of his trousers and asked if he could look at the video one last time.

"And something else," he said. "Any chance we can get a print-out?"

"A print-out?"

"A photo of the crush at the bar."

"I'm not sure. It's not going to be much use though, is it? And we've decent photos of Damon as it is."

"It's not him I'm interested in," Rebus said as the tape began to play. "It's the blonde who watched him leave."

That evening, he drove north out of Edinburgh, paid his toll at the Forth Road Bridge, and crossed into Fife. The place liked to call itself "the Kingdom" and there were those who would agree that it was another country, a place with its own linguistic and cultural currency. For such a small place, it seemed almost endlessly complex, had seemed that way to Rebus even when he'd been growing up there. To outsiders the place meant coastal scenery and St. Andrews, or just a stretch of motorway between Edinburgh and Dundee, but the west central Fife of Rebus's childhood had been very different, ruled by coal mines and linoleum, dockyard and chemical plant, an industrial landscape shaped by basic needs and producing people who

were wary and inward-looking, with the blackest humour
you'd ever find.

They'd built new roads since Rebus's last visit, and
knocked down a few more landmarks, but the place didn't
feel so very different from thirty-odd years before. It wasn't
such a great span of time after all, except in human terms,
and maybe not even then. Entering Cardenden—Bowhill
had disappeared from road-signs in the 1960s, even if locals
still knew it as a village distinct from its neighbour—Rebus
slowed to see if the memories would turn out sweet or sour.
Then he caught sight of a Chinese takeaway and thought:
both, of course.

Brian and Janice Mee's house was easy enough to find:
they were standing by the gate waiting for him. Rebus had
been born in a prefab but brought up in a terrace much like
this one. Brian Mee practically opened the car door for him,
and was trying to shake his hand while Rebus was still
undoing his seat-belt.

"Let the man catch his breath!" his wife snapped. She
was still standing by the gate, arms folded. "How have you
been, Johnny?"

And Rebus realised that Brian had married Janice Playfair, the only girl in his long and trouble-strewn life who'd
ever managed to knock John Rebus unconscious. The narrow low-ceilinged room was full to bursting—not just Rebus, Brian and Janice, but Brian's mother and Mr. and Mrs.
Playfair, plus a billowing three-piece suite and assorted tables and units. Introductions had to be made and Rebus
guided to "the seat by the fire." The room was overheated.
A pot of tea was produced, and on the table by Rebus's
armchair sat enough slices of cake to feed a football crowd.

"He's a brainy one," Janice's mother said, handing Rebus a framed photograph of Damon Mee. "Plenty of cer-
tificates from school. Works hard. Saving to get married."

The photo showed a smiling imp, not long out of school.

"We gave the most recent pictures to the police," Janice
explained. Rebus nodded: he'd seen them in the file. All
the same, when a packet of holiday snaps was handed to
him, he went through them slowly: it saved having to look
at the expectant faces. He felt like a doctor, expected to
produce both immediate diagnosis and remedy. The photos

showed a face more careworn than in the framed print. The impish smile remained, but noticeably older: some effort had gone into it. There was something behind the eyes, disenchantment maybe. Damon's parents were in a few of the photos.

"We all went together," Brian explained. "The whole family."

Beaches, a big white hotel, poolside games. "Where is it?"

"Lanzarote," Janice said, handing him his tea. "Do you still take sugar?"

"Haven't done for years," Rebus said. In a couple of the pictures she was wearing her bikini: good body for her age, or any age come to that. He tried not to linger.

"Can I take a couple of the close-ups?" he asked. Janice looked at him. "Of Damon." She nodded and he put the other photos back in the packet.

"We're really grateful," someone said: Janice's mum? Brian's? Rebus couldn't tell.

"You said his girlfriend's called Helen?"

Brian nodded. He'd lost some hair and put on weight, his face jowly. There was a row of cheap trophies above the mantelpiece: darts and pool, pub sports. He reckoned Brian kept in training most nights. Janice . . . Janice looked the same as ever. No, that wasn't strictly true. She had wisps of grey in her hair. But all the same, talking to her was like stepping back into a previous age.

"Does Helen live locally?" he asked.

"Practically round the corner."

"I'd like to talk to her."

"I'll give her a bell." Brian got to his feet, left the room.

"Where does Damon work?" Rebus asked, for want of a better question.

"Same place as his dad," Janice said, lighting a cigarette. Rebus raised an eyebrow: at school, she'd been anti-tobacco. She saw his look and smiled.

"He got a job in packaging," her dad said. He seemed frail, chin quivering. Rebus wondered if he'd had a stroke. One side of his face looked slack. "He's learning the ropes. It'll be management soon."

Working-class nepotism, jobs handed down from father to son. Rebus was surprised it still existed.

"Lucky to find any work at all around here," Mrs. Playfair added.

"Are things bad?"

She made a tutting sound, dismissing the question.

"Remember the old pit, John?" Janice asked.

Of course he remembered it, and the bing and the wilderness around it. Long walks on summer evenings, stopping for kisses that seemed to last hours. Wisps of coal-smoke rising from the bing, the dross within still smouldering.

"It's all been levelled now, turned into parkland. They're talking about building a mining museum."

Mrs. Playfair tutted again. "All it'll do is remind us what we once had."

"Job creation," her daughter said.

"They used to call Cowdenbeath the Chicago of Fife," Brian Mee's mother added.

"The Blue Brazil," Mr. Playfair said, giving a croaking laugh. He meant Cowdenbeath football club, the nickname a self-imposed piece of irony. They called themselves the Blue Brazil because they were rubbish.

"Helen'll be here in a minute," Brian said, coming back in.

"Are you not eating any cake, Inspector?" added Mrs. Playfair.

On the drive back to Edinburgh, Rebus thought back to his chat with Helen Cousins. She hadn't been able to add much to Rebus's picture of Damon, and hadn't been there the night he'd vanished. She'd been out with friends. It was a Friday ritual: Damon went out with "the lads," she went out with "the girls." He'd spoken with one of Damon's companions; the other had been out. He'd learned nothing helpful.

As he crossed the Forth Road Bridge, he thought about the symbol Fife had decided upon for its "Welcome to Fife" signs: the Forth Rail Bridge. Not an identity so much as an admission of failure, recognition that Fife was for many people a conduit or mere adjunct to Edinburgh.

Helen Cousins had worn black eyeliner and crimson lipstick and would never be pretty. Acne had carved cruel lines into her sallow face. Her hair had been dyed black and fell to a gelled fringe. When asked what she thought had happened to Damon, she'd just shrugged and folded her arms, crossing one leg over the other in a refusal to take any blame he might be trying to foist on her.

Joey, who'd been at Guiser's that night, had been similarly reticent.

"Just a night out," he'd said. "Nothing unusual about it."

"And nothing different about Damon?"

"Like what?"

"I don't know. Was he maybe preoccupied? Did he look nervous?"

A shrug: the apparent extent of Joey's concern for his friend . . .

Rebus knew he was headed home, meaning Patience's flat. But as he stop-started between the lights on Queensferry Road, he thought maybe he'd go to the Oxford Bar. Not for a drink, maybe just for a cola or a coffee, and some company. He'd drink a soft drink and listen to the gossip.

So he drove past Oxford Terrace, stopped at the foot of Castle Street. Walked up the slope towards the Ox. Edinburgh Castle was just over the rise. The best view you could get of it was from a burger place on Princes Street. He pushed open the door to the pub, feeling heat and smelling smoke. He didn't need cigarettes in the Ox: breathing was like killing a ten-pack. Coke or a coffee, he was having trouble making up his mind. Harry was on duty tonight. He lifted an empty pint glass and waved it in Rebus's direction.

"Aye, OK then," Rebus said, like it was the easiest decision he'd ever made.

He got in at quarter to midnight. Patience was watching TV. She didn't say much about his drinking these days: silence every bit as effective as lectures had ever been. But she wrinkled her nose at the cigarette smoke clinging to his clothes, so he dumped them in the washing basket and took a shower. She was in bed by the time he got out. There was a fresh glass of water his side of the bed.

"Thanks," he said, draining it with two paracetamol.

"How was your day?" she asked: automatic question, automatic response.

"Not so bad. Yours?"

A sleepy grunt in reply. She had her eyes closed. There were things Rebus wanted to say, questions he'd like to ask. What are we doing here? Do you want me out? He thought maybe Patience had the same questions or similar. Somehow they never got asked; fear of the answers, perhaps, and what those answers would mean. Who in the world relished failure?

"I went to a funeral," he told her. "A guy I knew."

"I'm sorry."

"I didn't really know him that well."

"What did he die of?" Head still on the pillow, eyes closed.

"A fall."

"Accident?"

She was drifting away from him. He spoke anyway. "His widow, she'd dressed their daughter to look like an angel. One way of dealing with it, I suppose." He paused, listening to Patience's breathing grow regular. "I went to Fife tonight, back to the old town. Friends I haven't seen in years." He looked at her. "An old flame, someone I could have ended up married to." Touched her hair. "No Edinburgh, no Dr. Patience Aitken." His eyes turned towards the window. No Sammy . . . maybe no job in the police either.

No ghosts.

When she was asleep, he went back through to the living room and plugged headphones into the hi-fi. He'd added a record deck to her CD system. In a bag under the bookshelf he found his last purchases from Backbeat Records: Light of Darkness and Writing on the Wall, two Scottish bands he vaguely remembered from times past. As he sat to listen, he wondered why it was he was only ever happy on rewind. He thought back to times when he'd been happy, realising that at the time he hadn't felt happy: it was only in retrospect that it dawned on him. Why was that? He sat back with eyes closed. Incredible String Band: "The Half-Remarkable Question." Segue to Brian Eno: "Everything Merges with the Night." He saw Janice Playfair the way

she'd been the night she'd laid him out, the night that had
changed everything. And he saw Alec Chisholm, who'd
walked away from school one day and never been seen
again. He didn't have Alec's face, just a vague outline and
a way of standing, of composing himself. Alec the brainy
one, the one who was going to go far.

Only nobody'd expected him to go the way he did.

Without opening his eyes, Rebus knew Jack Morton was
seated in the chair across from him. Could Jack hear the
music? He never spoke, so it was hard to know if sounds
meant anything to him. He was waiting for the track called
"Bogeyman"; listening and waiting . . .

It was nearly dawn when, on her way back from the
toilet, Patience removed the headphones from his sleeping
form and threw a blanket over him.

There were three men in the room, all in uniform, all wanting to hit Cary Oakes. He could see it in their eyes, in the
way they stood half-tensed, cheekbones working at wads
of gum. He made a sudden movement, but only stretching
his legs out, shifting his weight on the chair, arching his
head back so it caught the full glare of the sun, streaming
through the high window. Bathed in heat and light, he felt
the smile stretch across his face. His mother had always
told him, "Your face *shines* when you smile, Cary." Crazy
old woman, even back then. She'd had one of those double
sinks in the kitchen, with a mangle you could fix between
them. Wash the clothes in one sink, then through the mangle into the other. He'd stuck the tips of his fingers against
the rollers once, started cranking the handle until it hurt.

Three prison guards: that's what they reckoned Cary

Oakes was worth. Three guards, and chains for his legs and arms.

"Hey, guys," he said, pointing his chin at them. "Take your best shot."

"Can it, Oakes."

Cary Oakes grinned again. He'd forced a reaction: of such small victories were his days made. The guard who'd spoken, the one with the tag identifying him as SAUNDERS, did tend towards the excitable. Oakes narrowed his eyes and imagined the moustached face pressed against a mangle, imagined the strength needed to force that face all the way through. Oakes rubbed his stomach; not so much as an ounce of flab there, despite the food they tried to serve him. He stuck to vegetables and fruit, water and juices. Had to keep the brain in gear. A lot of the other prisoners, they'd slipped into neutral, engines revving but heading nowhere. A stretch of confinement could do that to you, make you start believing things that weren't true. Oakes kept up with events, had magazine and newspaper subscriptions, watched current affairs on TV and avoided everything else, except maybe a little sport. But even sport was a kind of novocaine. Instead of watching the screen, he watched the other faces, saw them heavy-lidded, no need to concentrate, like babies being spoon-fed contentment, bellies and brains filled to capacity with warmed-over gunk.

He started whistling a Beatles song: "Good Day Sunshine," wondering if any of the guards would know it. Potential for another reaction. But then the door opened and his attorney came in. His fifth lawyer in sixteen years, not a bad average, batting .300. This lawyer was young—mid-twenties—and wore blue blazers with cream slacks, a combination which made him look like a kid trying on his dad's clothes. The blazers had brass-effect buttons and intricate designs on the breast pocket.

"Ahoy, shipmate!" Oakes cried, not shifting in his chair.

His lawyer sat down opposite him at the table. Oakes put his hands behind his head, rattling the chains.

"Any chance of removing those from my client?" the lawyer asked.

"For your own protection, sir." The stock response.

Oakes used both hands to scratch his shaved head.

"Know those divers and spacemen? Use weighted boots, necessary tool of the trade. I reckon when I lose these chains, I'm going to float up to the ceiling. I can make my living in freak shows: the human fly, see him scale the walls. Man, imagine the possibilities. I can float up to second-floor windows and watch all the ladies getting ready for bed." He turned his head to the guards. "Any of you guys married?"

The lawyer was ignoring this. He had his job to do, opening the briefcase and lifting out the paperwork. Wherever lawyers went, paper went with them. Lots of paper. Oakes tried not to look interested.

"Mr. Oakes," the lawyer said, "it's just a matter of detail now."

"I've always enjoyed detail."

"Some papers that have to be signed by various officials."

"See, guys," Oakes called to the guards, "I told you no prison could hold Cary Oakes! OK, so it's taken me fifteen years, but, hey, nobody's perfect." He laughed, turning to his lawyer. "So how long should all these . . . details take?"

"Days rather than weeks."

Inside, Oakes's heart was pumping. His ears were hissing with the intensity of it, the swell of apprehension and anticipation. *Days . . .*

"But I haven't finished painting my cell. I want it left pretty for the next tenant."

Finally the attorney smiled, and Oakes knew him in that instant: working his way up in Daddy's practice; reviled by his elders, mistrusted by his peers. Was he spying on them, reporting back to the old man? How could he prove himself? If he joined them for drinks on a Friday night, loosening his tie and mussing up his hair, they felt uncomfortable. If he kept his distance, he was a cold fish. And what about the father? The old man couldn't have anyone accusing him of nepotism, the boy had to learn the hard way. Give him the shitty-stick cases, the no-hopers, the ones that left you needing a shower and change of clothes. Make him prove himself. Long hours of thankless toil, a shining example to everyone else in the firm.

All this discerned from a single smile, the smile of a

half-shy, self-conscious drone who dreamt of being King
Bee, who perhaps even harboured little fantasies of patri-
cide and succession.

"You'll be deported, of course," the prince was saying
now.

"What?"

"You were in this country illegally, Mr. Oakes."

"I've been here nearly half my life."

"Nevertheless. . . ."

Nevertheless. . . . His mother's word. Every time he had
an excuse prepared, some story to explain the situation,
she'd listen in silence, then take a deep breath, and it was
like he could see the word forming in the air that issued
from her mouth. During his trial, he'd rehearsed little conversations with her.

"Mother, I've been a good son, haven't I?"

"Nevertheless. . . ."

"Nevertheless, I killed two people."

"Really, Cary? You're sure it was only two . . . ?"

He sat up in his chair. "So let them deport me, I'll come
straight back."

"It won't be so easy. I can't see you securing a tourist
visa this time, Mr. Oakes."

"I don't need one. You're behind the times."

"Your name will be on record . . ."

"I'll walk across from Canada or Mexico."

The lawyer shifted in his seat. He didn't like to hear
this.

"I have to come back and see my pals," nodding towards
the guards. "They'll miss me when I'm gone. And so will
their wives."

"Fuck you, slime." Saunders again.

Oakes beamed at his lawyer. "Isn't that nice? We have
nicknames for each other."

"I don't think any of this is very helpful, Mr. Oakes."

"Hey, I'm the model prisoner. That's the way it works,
right? I learned a fast lesson: use the same system they used
to put you where you are. Read up on the law, go back
over everything, know the questions to ask, the objections
that should have been made at the original trial. The lawyer
they had representing me, I'll tell you, he couldn't have

presented a school prize, never mind my case." He smiled again. "You're better than him. You're going to be all right. Remember that next time your pop is chewing you out. Just say to yourself: I'm better than that, I'm going to be all right." He winked. "No charge for my time, son."

Son: as if he was fifty rather than thirty-eight. As if the knowledge of the ages was his for the dispensing.

"So I get a free flight back to London?"

"I'm not sure." The lawyer looked through his notes. "You're from Lothian originally?" Pronouncing it *loathing*.

"As in Edinburgh, Scotland."

"Well, you might end up back there."

Cary Oakes rubbed at his chin. Edinburgh might do for a while. He had unfinished business in Edinburgh. Was going to leave it till the heat had died down, but nevertheless . . . He leaned forward over the table.

"How many murders did they pin on me?"

The lawyer blinked, sat there with palms flat on the table. "Two," he said at last.

"How many did they start with?"

"I believe it was five."

"Six actually." Oakes nodded slowly. "But who's counting, eh?" A chuckle. "They ever catch anyone for the others?"

The lawyer shook his head. There were beads of perspiration at his temples. He'd be making a detour home for a shower and fresh clothes.

Cary Oakes sat back again and angled his face into the sun, turning his head so every part felt the warmth. "Two's not much of a tally, is it, in the scheme of things? You kill your old man, you'll only be one behind."

He was still chuckling to himself as his lawyer was led out of the room.

Younger runaways tended to take the same few routes: by bus, train or hitching, and to London, Glasgow or Edinburgh. There were organisations who would keep an eye open for runaways, and even if they wouldn't always reveal their whereabouts to the anxious families, at least they could confirm that someone was alive and unharmed.

But a nineteen-year-old, someone with money to hand ... could be anywhere. No destination was too distant—his passport hadn't turned up. He took it with him to clubs as proof of age. Damon had a current account at the local bank, complete with cashcard, and an interest-bearing account with a building society in Kirkcaldy. The bank might be worth trying. Rebus picked up the telephone.

The manager at first insisted that he'd need something in writing, but relented when Rebus promised to fax him later. Rebus held while the manager went off to check, and had doodled half a village, complete with stream, parkland and pit-head, by the time the man came back.

"The most recent withdrawal was a cash machine in Edinburgh's West End. One hundred pounds on the fifteenth."

The night Damon had gone to Gaitano's. A hundred seemed a lot to Rebus, even for a good night out.

"Nothing since then?"

"No."

"How up to date is that?"

"Up to the close of play yesterday."

"Could I ask you a favour, sir? I'd like tabs kept on that account. Any new withdrawals, I'd like to know about them pronto."

"I'd need that in writing, Inspector. And I'd probably also need the approval of my head office."

"I'd appreciate it, Mr. Brayne."

"It's Bain," the bank manager said coldly, putting down the phone.

Rebus called the building society and endured the same rigmarole before learning that Damon hadn't touched his account in more than a fortnight. He made one last call to Gayfield police station and asked for DC Hawes. She didn't sound too thrilled when he identified himself.

"What's the word on Gaitano's?" he asked.

"Everyone calls it Guiser's. Pretty choice establishment. Two stabbings last year, one in the club itself, one in the alley out back. Been quieter this year, which is probably down to a stricter door policy."

"You mean bigger bouncers."

"Front-of-house managers, if you please. Locals still complain about the noise at chucking-out time."

"Who owns it?"

"Charles Mackenzie, nicknamed 'Charmer.' "

A couple of uniforms had talked to Mackenzie about Damon Mee, and he'd offered up the security tape which had languished in Gayfield ever since.

"Know how many MisPers there are every year?" Hawes said with a sigh.

"You told me."

"Then you should know that if there's no suspicion of foul play, they're not exactly a white-hot priority. God knows there are times I've felt like doing a runner myself."

Rebus thought of his night-time car-rides, long, directionless hours, just filling in the blank spaces of his life. "Haven't we all?" he said.

"Look, I know you're doing this as a favour . . ."

"Yes?"

"But we've done all we can, haven't we?"

"Pretty much."

"So what's the point?"

"I'm not sure." Rebus could have told her that it had to do with the past, with some debt he felt he owed to Janice Playfair and Barney Mee—and to the memory of a friend he'd once had called Mitch. Somehow, he didn't think explaining it to an outsider would help. "One last thing," he asked instead. "Did you get me a still of that woman?"

Gaitano's was little more than a solid black door with a neon sign above it, flanked either side by pubs and with a hi-fi shop across the road. There were valve amplifiers and an outsized record deck in the shop window. The deck had an outsized price-tag to match. One of the pubs was called The Headless Coachman. It had changed its name a couple of years back and was touting for tourists.

Rebus pushed the door-buzzer to Gaitano's and a woman opened it for him. She was the cleaner, and Rebus didn't envy her the job. Glasses had been cleared from the tables, but the place still looked like a wreck. There was an industrial vacuum cleaner on the carpet which encircled the dance floor. The floor was littered with cigarette stubs, cellophane, the occasional empty bottle. She'd finished cleaning the foyer, but was only halfway through the main dance area. There were mirrors on all the walls, and in the right light the place would look many times its actual size. In bare white light and with no music, no punters, it looked and felt desolate. There was a fug of stale sweat and beer in the air. Rebus saw a security camera in one corner and gave it a wave.

"Inspector Rebus."

The man walking towards him across the dancefloor was about five feet four inches and as thin as a swizzle-stick. Rebus placed him in his mid-fifties. He wore a powder-blue suit and open-necked white shirt to show off his suntan and gold jewellery. His hair was silver and thinning, but as well-cut as the suit. They shook hands.

"Do you want a drink?"

He was leading Rebus towards the bar. Rebus looked at the row of optics.

"No thank you, sir."

Charmer Mackenzie went behind the bar and poured himself a cola.

"Sure?" he said.

"Same as you're having," Rebus said. He examined one of the bar stools for cigarette ash, then pulled himself up on to it. They faced one another across the bar.

"Not your normal tipple?" Mackenzie guessed. "In my trade, you get a nose for these things." And he tapped his nose for effect. "The kid hasn't turned up then?"

"No, sir."

"Sometimes they get a notion . . ." He shrugged, dismissing the foibles of a generation.

"I've got a photograph." Rebus reached into his pocket, handed it over. "The missing person is second row."

Mackenzie nodded, not really interested.

"See just behind him?"

"Is that his doll?"

"Do you know her?"

Mackenzie snorted. "Wish I did."

"You haven't seen her before?"

"Picture's not the best, but I don't think so."

"What time do the staff clock on?"

"Not till tonight."

Rebus took the photo back, put it in his pocket.

"Any chance of getting my video back?" Mackenzie asked.

"Why?"

"Those things cost money. Overheads, that's what can cripple a business like this, Inspector."

Rebus wondered how he'd merited the nickname "Charmer." He had all the charm of sandpaper. "We wouldn't want that now, would we, Mr. Mackenzie?" he said, getting to his feet.

Back at the office, he played the tape again, watching the blonde. The way her head was angled, strong jawline, mouth open slightly. Could she be saying something to Damon? A minute later, he was gone. Had she said she'd meet him somewhere? After he'd gone, she'd stayed at the bar, ordering a drink for herself. At dead on midnight, fifteen minutes after Damon had vanished, she'd left the nightclub. The final shot was from a camera mounted on the club's exterior wall. It showed her turning left along Rose Street, watched by a few drunks who were trying to get into Gaitano's.

Someone put their head round the door and told him he had a call. It was Mairie Henderson.

"Thanks for getting back to me," he said.

"I take it you've a favour to ask?"

"Quite the reverse."

"In that case, lunch is on me. I'm in the Engine Shed."

"How convenient." Rebus smiled: the Engine Shed was just behind St. Leonard's. "I'll be there in five minutes."

"Make it two, or all the meatballs will have gone."

Which was a joke of sorts, in that there was no meat in the meatballs. They were savoury balls of mushroom and chickpea with a tomato sauce. Though a one-minute walk from his office, Rebus had never eaten in the Engine Shed. Everything about it was too healthy, too nutritious. The drink of the day was organic apple juice, and smoking was strictly forbidden. He knew it was run by some sort of charity, and staffed by people who needed a job more than most. Typical of Mairie to choose it for a meeting. She was seated by a window, and Rebus joined her with his tray.

"You look well," he said.

"It's all this salad." She nodded towards her plate.

"Lifestyle still suit you?"

He meant her decision to quit the local daily paper and go freelance. They'd helped one another out on occasion, but Rebus was aware he owed her more brownie points than she owed him. Her face was all clean, sharp lines, her eyes quick and dark. She'd restyled her hair to early Cilla Black. On the table beside her sat her notebook and cell-phone.

"I get the occasional story picked up by the London papers. Then my old paper has to run its own version the next day."

"That must annoy them."

She beamed. "Have to let them know what they're missing."

"Well," Rebus said, "they've been missing a story that's right under their noses." He pushed another forkful of food into his mouth, having to admit to himself that it wasn't at all bad. Looking around the other tables, he realised all the other diners were women. Some of them were tending to kids in high chairs, some were involved in quiet gossip. The restaurant wasn't big, and Rebus kept his voice down when he spoke.

"What story's that?" Mairie said.

Rebus's voice went lower. "Paedophile living in Green-field."

"Convicted?"

Rebus nodded. "Served his time, now they've plonked him in a flat with a lovely view of a kids' play-park."

"What's he been up to?"

"Nothing yet, nothing I can pin him for. Thing is, his neighbours don't know what's living next door to them."

She was staring at him.

"What is it?" he said.

"Nothing." She munched on more salad, chewing slowly. "So where's the story?"

"Come on, Mairie . . ."

"I know what you want me to do." She pointed her fork at him. "I know why you want it."

"And?"

"And what has he done?"

"Christ, Mairie, do you know what the reoffending rate is? It's not something you cure by slapping them in prison for a few years."

"We've got to take a chance."

"*We?* It's not us he'll be after."

"All of us, we've all got to give them a chance."

"Look, Mairie, it's a good story."

"No, it's your way of getting to him. Does this all come back to Shiellion?"

"It's got bugger all to do with Shiellion."

"I hear they've got you down to give evidence." She stared at him again, but all he did was shrug. "Only," she went on, "the knives are out as it is. If I do a story on a paedophile living in Greenfield of all places . . . it'd be in-citement to murder."

"Come on, Mairie . . ."

"Know what I think, John?" She put down her knife and fork. "I think something's gone bad inside you."

"Mairie, all I want . . ."

But she was on her feet, unhooking her coat from the back of the chair, collecting her phone, notebook, bag.

"I don't have much of an appetite any more," she said.

"Time was, you'd have gnawed a story like this to the bone."

She looked thoughtful for a moment. "Maybe you're right," she said. "I hope to God you're not, but maybe you are."

She walked the length of the restaurant's wooden floorboards on noisy heels. Rebus looked down at his lunch, at the untouched glass of juice. There was a pub not three minutes away. He pushed the plate away. He told himself Mairie was wrong: it had nothing to do with Shiellion. It was down to Jim Margolies, to the fact that Darren Rough had once made a complaint against him. Now Jim was dead, and Rebus wanted something back. Could he lay Jim's ghost to rest by tormenting Jim's tormentor? He reached into his pocket, found the sliver of paper there, the telephone number still perfectly legible.

I think something's gone bad inside you.

Who was he to disagree?

Four years before, Jim Margolies had been passing through St. Leonard's, seconded to help with a staff shortfall. Three of the CID were down with flu, and another was in hospital for a minor op. Margolies, whose usual beat was Leith, came highly recommended, which made his new colleagues wary. Sometimes a recommendation was made so a station could offload dead weight elsewhere. But Margolies had proved himself quickly, handling a paedophile inquiry with dedication and tact. Two boys had been interfered with on The Meadows during, of all things, a children's festival. Darren Rough was already in police files. At twelve, he'd interfered with a neighbour's son, aged six at the time. He'd had counselling, and spent time in a children's home. At fifteen, he'd been caught peeping in at windows at the student residences in Pollock Halls. More counselling. Another mark in his police file.

The schoolboys' description of their attacker had taken police to the house Rough shared with his father. At nine in the morning, the father was drunk at the kitchen table. The mother had died the previous summer, which looked to be the last time the house had been cleaned. Soiled clothes and mouldy dishes were everywhere. It looked like nothing ever got thrown out: burst and rotting binbags stood inside the kitchen door; mail was piled high in a corner of the front hall, where damp had turned it into a single sodden mass. In Darren Rough's bedroom, Jim Margolies found clothing catalogues, crude penned additions made to the child models. There were collections of teen magazines under the bed, stories about—and pictures of—teenage girls and boys. And best of all from the police point of view, tucked under a corner of rotting carpet was Darren's "Fantasy League," detailing his sexual proclivities and wish lists, with his Meadows exploit dated and signed.

For all of which the Procurator Fiscal was duly grateful. Darren Rough, by now twenty years old, was found guilty and sent to jail. A crate of beer was opened at St. Leonard's, and Jim Margolies sat at the top of the table.

Rebus was there, too. He'd been part of the shift team interviewing Rough. He'd spent enough time with the prisoner to know that they were doing the right thing locking him up.

"Not that it ever helps with those bastards," DI Alistair Flower had said. "Reoffend as soon as they're out."

"You're suggesting treatment replaces incarceration?" Margolies had asked.

"I'm suggesting we throw away the fucking key!" To which there had been cheers of agreement. Siobhan Clarke had been too canny to add her own view, but Rebus knew what she'd been thinking. Nothing was said of the complaint Rough had made. Bruising to his face and body: he'd told his solicitor Jim Margolies had given him a beating. No witnesses. Self-inflicted was the consensus. Rebus knew he'd felt like giving Rough a couple of slaps himself, but Margolies had no history of aggression against suspects.

There'd been an internal inquiry. Margolies had denied

the accusation. A medical examination had been unable to determine whether Rough's bruises were self-inflicted. And that's where it had ended, with the faintest of blots on Margolies' record, the faintest doubt hanging over the rest of his career.

Rebus closed the case file and walked back to the vault with it.

Mairie: *I think something's gone bad inside you.*

Rough's social worker: *Your lot wanted him here.*

Rebus went to the Farmer's office, knocked on the door, entered when told.

"What can I do for you, John?"

"I had a word with Darren Rough's social worker, sir."

The Farmer looked up from his paperwork. "Any particular reason?"

"Just wanted to know why Rough had been given a flat with a view of a kiddies' playground."

"I bet they loved you for that." Not sounding disapproving. Social workers rated only a rung or two above paedophiles on the Farmer's moral stepladder.

"They told me that we wanted him here in the first place."

The Farmer's face furrowed. "Meaning what?"

"They suggested I ask you."

"I haven't the faintest idea." The Farmer sat back in his chair. "*We* wanted him here?"

"That's what they said."

"Meaning Edinburgh?"

Rebus nodded. "I've just been through the file on Rough. He was in a children's home for a while."

"Not Shiellion?" The Farmer was looking interested.

Rebus shook his head. "Callstone House, other side of the city. Just for a short spell. Both parents were alcoholic, neglecting him. There was nowhere else for him to go."

"What happened?"

"Mother dried out, Rough went back home. Then, later on, she was diagnosed with liver disease, only nobody bothered moving Rough."

"Why?"

"Because by that time, he was looking after his father."

The Farmer looked towards his collection of family
snaps. "The way some people live . . ."

"Yes, sir," Rebus agreed.

"So where's this leading?"

"Only this: Rough comes back to Edinburgh, apparently
because we want him here. Next thing, the officer who put
him away ends up walking off Salisbury Crags."

"You're not suggesting a connection?"

Rebus shrugged. "Jim goes out to dinner at some
friends' with his wife and kid. Drives home. Goes to bed.
Next morning he's dead. I'm looking for reasons why Jim
Margolies would take his own life. Thing is, I'm not finding
any. And I'm also wondering who'd want Darren Rough
back here and why."

The Farmer was thoughtful. "You want me to talk to
Social Work?"

"They wouldn't talk to me."

The Farmer reached for paper and a pen. "Give me a
name."

"Andy Davies is Rough's social worker."

The Farmer underlined the words. "Leave it with me,
John."

"Yes, sir. Meantime, I'd like to take a look at Jim's
suicide."

"Mind if I ask why?"

"To see if it *does* tie in with Rough." And maybe, he
could have added, to satisfy his own curiosity.

The Farmer nodded. "On the subject of Shiellion . . .
when do you give evidence?"

"Tomorrow, sir."

"Got your spiel rehearsed?"

Rebus nodded.

"Remember the secret of a good court appearance,
John."

"Presentation, sir?"

The Farmer shook his head. "Make sure you take plenty
of reading matter with you."

That evening, on his way home, he dropped in to see his
daughter. Sammy had moved out of her first-floor colony

flat into a newish ground-floor flat in a brick-built block off Newhaven Road.

"Downhill all the way to the coast," she'd told her father. "And you should see this thing with the brakes off."

Referring to her wheelchair. Rebus had wanted to put his hand in his pocket for a motorised one, but she'd waved away the offer.

"I'm building up my muscles," she'd said. "And besides, I won't be in this thing for long."

Perhaps not, but the road back to full mobility was proving hard going. She was receiving physic only twice a week, spending the rest of her time concentrating on home exercises. It was as if the accident had affected both her spine and her legs.

"My brain tells them what to do, but they don't always listen."

There was a little wooden ramp at the main door to her block. A friend of a friend had constructed it for her. One of the bedrooms in the flat had been turned into a makeshift gym, a large mirror placed against one wall, and parallel bars taking up most of the available space. The doorways were narrow, but Sammy had proved adept at manoeuvring her wheelchair in and out without grazing knuckles or elbows.

When Rebus arrived, Ned Farlowe opened the door. He had a job subbing for one of the local freesheets. The hours were short, which gave him time to help Sammy with her workouts. The two men still didn't trust one another—did fathers ever really come to trust the men who were sleeping with their daughters?—but Ned seemed to be doing his damnedest for Sammy.

"Hi there," he said. "She's working out. Fancy a cuppa?"

"No thanks."

"I'm just making some dinner." Ned was already retreating to the long, narrow kitchen. Rebus knew he'd only be in the way.

"I'll just go and . . ."

"Fine."

The smells from the kitchen were like those in the Engine Shed: aromatic and vegetarian. Rebus walked down the hall, noting grazemarks on the walls where the wheel-

chair had connected. Music was coming from the spare bedroom, a disco beat. Sammy was lying on the floor in her
black leotard and tights, trying to get her legs to do things.
Her face was flushed with effort, hair matted to her forehead. When she saw her father, she rested her head against
the floor.

"Turn that thing off, will you?" she said.

"I could just watch."

But she shook her head. She didn't like him watching
her at work. This was *her* fight, a private battle with her
own body. Rebus switched off the tape machine.

"Recognise it?" she asked.

"Chic, 'Le Freak.' I went to enough bad discos in the
seventies."

"I can't imagine you in flares."

"Distress flares."

She had pushed herself up to sitting. He made just the
one step forward to help her, knowing if he got any closer
she'd shoo him away.

"How's your claim for disability going?"

She rolled her eyes, reached a hand out for a towel,
started wiping her face. "I thought I knew all about bu-
reaucracy. Thing is, I'm going to get better."

"Sure."

"So there are all kinds of complications. Plus my job at
SWEEP's still open."

"But the office is three floors up." He sat on the floor
beside her.

"I can work from home."

"Really?"

"Only I don't want to. I don't want to become dependent
on just these four walls."

Rebus nodded. "If there's anything you need . . ."

"Got any disco tapes?"

He smiled. "I was more Rory Gallagher and John Mar-
tyn."

"Well, nobody's perfect," she said, wrapping the towel
around her neck. "Speaking of which, how's Patience?"

"She's fine."

"I talk to her on the phone."

"Oh?"

"She says I speak to her more than you do."

"I don't think that's true."

"Don't you?"

Rebus looked at his daughter. Had she always had this edge to her? Was it something to do with the accident?

"We get along fine," he said.

"On whose terms?"

He stood up. "I think your dinner's nearly ready. Want me to help you into the chair?"

"Ned likes to do it."

He nodded slowly.

"You didn't answer my question."

"I'm a policeman. Usually *we* ask the questions."

She draped the towel over her head. "Is it because of me?"

"What?"

"Ever since . . ." She looked down at her legs. "It's like you blame yourself."

"It was an accident." He wasn't looking at her.

"It pushed the two of you back together. Do you see what I'm saying?"

"You're saying I'm busy blaming myself for your accident, while you're busy blaming yourself for Patience and me." He glanced towards her. "Does that just about sum it up?"

She smiled. "Stay and have something to eat."

"Don't you think I should head home to Patience?"

She lifted the towel from her eyes. "Is that where you're going?"

"Where else?" He gave her a wave as he left the room.

9

Being down Newhaven Road, he stopped off at a couple of waterfront bars, a pint in one, nip of whisky in the other. Plenty of water in the whisky. It was dark, but he could see streetlights across the Forth in Fife. He thought of Janice and Brian Mee, who had never left their home town. He wondered how he'd have turned out if he'd stayed. He thought again of Alec Chisholm, the boy who had never been found. They'd scoured the countryside, sent men down into disused coal-shafts, dredged the river. A long hot summer, the Beatles and the Stones on the café juke-box, ice-cold bottles of Coke from the machine. Glass coffee cups topped with frothed milk. And questions about Alec, questions which showed that none of them had ever really known him, not deep down, not the way they thought they knew each other. And Alec's parents and grandparents, walking the streets late at night, stopping to ask strangers the same thing: have you seen our boy? Until the strangers became acquaintances, and they ran out of people to stop.

Now Damon Mee had stepped away from the world, or had been yanked out of it by some irresistible force. Rebus got back in his car and drove along the coast, came up on to the Forth Bridge, and headed into Fife. He tried telling himself he wasn't escaping—from Sammy's words and Patience and Edinburgh, from all the ghosts. From thoughts of paedophiles and suicide leaps.

When he got to Cardenden, he slowed the car, finally coming to a stop on the main drag. There seemed to be flyers in every shop window: Damon's picture and the word MISSING. There were more taped to lamp-posts and the bus shelter. Rebus started the car again and headed for Janice's house. But there was no one at home. A neighbour supplied the information Rebus needed, information which sent him straight back to Edinburgh and Rose Street, where he found Janice and Brian sticking more flyers on to lampposts and walls, pushing them through letterboxes. Photocopied sheets of A4. Holiday photo of Damon, and handwritten plea: DAMON MEE IS MISSING: HAVE YOU SEEN HIM? Physical description, including the clothes he'd been wearing, and the Mees' telephone number.

"We've covered the pubs," Brian Mee said. He looked tired, eyes dark, face unshaven. The roll of sellotape he held was nearly finished. Janice leaned against a wall. Looking at the pair of them was far from like stepping into the past—present worries had scarred them.

"The one place they don't want to know," Janice said, "is that club."

"Gaitano's?"

She nodded. "Bouncers wouldn't let us in. Wouldn't even take flyers from us. I stuck one on the door but they took it down." She was almost in tears. Rebus looked back along the street towards the flashing neon sign above Gaitano's.

"Come on," he said. "Let's try the magic word this time."

And when he got to the door, he flashed his ID and said, "Police." The three were ushered inside while someone got on the phone to Charmer Mackenzie. Rebus looked to Janice and winked.

"Open Sesame," he said. She was looking at him as if he'd done something wonderful.

"Mr. Mackenzie's not here," one of the bouncers said.

"So who's in charge?"

"Archie Frost. He's assistant manager."

"Lead me to him."

The bouncer looked unhappy. "He's having a drink at the bar."

"No problem," Rebus said. "We know our way."

Bass music was pulsing, the club's interior dark and hot. Couples were hitting the dancefloor, others smoking furiously, knees pumping as they scanned the dimness for action. Rebus leaned towards Janice, so his mouth was an inch from her ear.

"Go round the tables, ask your questions."

She nodded, passed the message along to Brian, who was looking uncomfortable with the noise.

Rebus walked towards the bar, walked through beams of indigo light. There were people waiting for drinks, but only two men actually drinking at the bar. Well, one of them was drinking. The other—who looked thirsty—was listening to what was being said to him.

"Sorry to butt in," Rebus said.

The speaker turned to him. "You will be in a minute."

Maybe twenty or twenty-one, black hair pulled back into a ponytail. Stocky, wearing a suit with no lapels and a dazzling white T-shirt. Rebus pushed his warrant card into the face, identified himself.

"Been taking charm-school lessons from your boss?" he asked. Archie Frost said nothing, just finished his drink. "I want a word, Mr. Frost."

"They don't look like polis," Frost said, nodding towards where Janice and Brian Mee were working the room.

"That's because they're not. Their son went missing. Disappeared from here, in fact."

"I know."

"Well then, you'll know why I'm here." Rebus brought out the photograph of the mystery blonde. "Seen her before?"

Frost shook his head automatically.

"Take a closer look."

Frost took the photo grudgingly, and angled it towards the light. Then he shook his head and tried handing it back.

"What about your pal?"

"What about him?"

The "pal" in question, the young man without a drink, had half-turned from them, so he was watching the dance-floor.

"He's not in here much," Frost said.

"All the same," Rebus persisted. So Frost stuck the photo in front of his friend's nose. An immediate shake of the head.

"I'm going to take this around your punters," Rebus

said, lifting the photo from Frost's hand, "see if their memories are any better." He wasn't looking at Frost; he was
looking at his companion. "Do I know you from somewhere, son? Your face looks familiar."

The young man snorted, kept his eyes on the dancing.

"I'll let you get back to your business then," Rebus said.
He did a circuit of the room, following behind Janice and
Brian. They'd left flyers on most of the tables. A couple
had already been crumpled up. Rebus fixed the culprits with
a stare. He wasn't faring any better with his own picture,
but saw that ahead of him Janice and Brian had seated
themselves at a table and were deep in conversation with
two girls there. Eventually, he caught up with them. Janice
looked up at him.

"They say they saw Damon," she yelled, fighting the
music.

"He was getting into a taxi," one of the girls repeated
for the newcomer's benefit.

"Where?" Rebus asked.

"Outside The Dome."

"Other side of the road," her friend corrected. They were
wearing too much make-up, trying for a look they'd probably call "sophisticated," trying to look older than their
years. Soon enough, they'd be reversing the process. They
wore incredibly short skirts. Rebus could see Brian trying
not to stare.

"What time was this?"

"About quarter past twelve. We were late for a party."

"You're sure about the date?" Rebus asked. Janice
looked at him accusingly, not wanting this fragile bubble
to burst.

One girl got a diary out of her handbag, tapped a page.
"That's the party."

Rebus looked: it was the same date Damon had disappeared. "How come you noticed him?"

"We'd seen him in here earlier."

"Just standing at the bar," her friend added. "Not dancing or anything."

A couple of young men, still in their day-job suits, had
peeled off from an office party and were approaching, ready
to ask for a dance. The girls tried to look disinterested, but

a glower from Rebus sent the suitors back in the direction they'd come.

"We were after a taxi ourselves," one girl explained. "Saw them waiting across the road. Only they got lucky, we ended up walking."

" 'They'?"

"Him and his girl."

Rebus looked to Janice, then handed over the photo.

"Yeah, that looks like her."

"Blonde out of a bottle," the other agreed.

Janice took the photo from them, looked at it herself.

"Who is she, John?"

Rebus shook his head, telling her he didn't know. Glancing towards the bar, he saw two things. One was that Archie Frost was watching him intently over the rim of a fresh glass. The other was that his non-drinking friend had gone.

"Maybe they've run off together," one of the girls was saying, trying hard to be helpful. "That would be romantic, wouldn't it?"

Janice and Brian hadn't eaten, so Rebus took them to an Indian on Hanover Street, where he explained the little he knew about the woman in the photograph. Janice kept the photo in one hand as she ate.

"It's a start, isn't it?" Brian said, pulling apart a nan bread.

Rebus nodded agreement.

"I mean," Brian went on, "we know now he left with someone. He's probably still with her."

"Only he didn't go off with her," Janice said. "John's already told us, Damon left on his own."

In fact, Rebus hadn't even gone that far. They only had the girls' word for it that Damon had left the club at all . . .

"Well," Brian stumbled on, "thing is, he wouldn't want his mates seeing them together, not when he was supposed to be engaged."

"I can't believe it of Damon." Janice's eyes were on Rebus. "He loves Helen."

Rebus nodded. "But it happens, doesn't it?"

She gave a rueful smile. Brian saw a look passing between them, but chose to ignore it.

"Anyone want any more rice?" he asked instead, lifting the salver from its hotplate.

"We should be getting home," his wife said. "Damon might have tried phoning." She was getting to her feet. Rebus gestured towards the photo, and she handed it back. It was smudged, creased at the corners. Brian was looking down at the food still on his plate.

"Brian . . ." Janice said. He sniffed and got up from his chair. "Get the bill, will you?"

"This is on me," Rebus said. "They'll stick it on my tab."

"Thanks again, John." She held out her hand and he took it. It was long and slender. Rebus remembered holding it when they danced, remembered the way it would be warm and dry, unlike other girls' hands. Warm and dry, and his heart pounding in his chest. She'd been so slender at the waist, he'd felt he could encircle her with just his hands.

"Yes, thanks, Johnny." Brian Mee laughed. "You don't mind me calling you Johnny?"

"Why should I mind?" Rebus said, still looking into Janice's eyes. "It's my name, isn't it?"

10

First thing, Rebus looked through the newspapers, but he didn't find anything to interest him.

He headed down to Leith police station, where Jim Margolies had been stationed. He'd told the Farmer he was looking for a connection between Rough's reappearance and Jim's death, but he wasn't particularly confident of finding one. Still, he really *did* want to know why Jim had done it, had done something Rebus had thought about doing more than once—taking the high walk. He was met in Leith by a wary Detective Inspector Bobby Hogan.

"I know I owe you a favour or two, John," Hogan began. "But do you mind telling me what it's all about? Margolies was a good man, we're missing him badly."

They were walking through the station, making for CID. Hogan was a couple of years younger than Rebus, but had been on the force for longer. He could take retirement any time he wanted, but Rebus doubted the man would ever want it.

"I knew him, too," Rebus was saying. "I'm probably just asking myself the same question all of you have been asking."

"You mean why?"

Rebus nodded. "He was headed for the top, Bobby. Everyone knew it."

"Maybe he got vertigo." Hogan shook his head. "The notes aren't going to tell you anything, John."

They had stopped outside an interview room.

"I just need to see them, Bobby."

Hogan stared at him, then nodded slowly. "This makes us even, pal."

Rebus touched him on the shoulder, walked into the room. The manila file was sitting on the otherwise empty desk. There were two chairs in the room.

"Thought you'd like some privacy," Hogan said. "Look, if anyone wonders . . ."

"My lips are sealed, Bobby." Rebus was already sitting down. He examined the folder. "This won't take long."

Hogan fetched a cup of coffee, then left him to it. It took Rebus precisely twenty minutes to sift through everything: initial report and back-up, plus Jim Margolies' history. Twenty minutes wasn't long for a CV. Of course, there was little about his home life. Speculation was for after-work drinks, for cigarette breaks and coffee-machine meetings. The bare facts, set down between double margins, gave no clues at all. His father was a doctor, now retired. Comfortable upbringing. The sister who'd committed suicide in her teens . . . Rebus wondered if his sister's death had been at the back of Jim Margolies' mind all these years. There was no mention of Darren Rough, no mention of Margolies' short time at St. Leonard's. His last night on earth, Jim had been out to dinner at some friends' house.

Nothing out of the ordinary. But afterwards, in the middle of the night, he'd slipped from his bed, got dressed again, and gone walking in the rain. All the way to Holyrood Park . . .

"Anything?" Bobby Hogan asked.

"Not a sausage," Rebus admitted, closing the file.

Walking in the rain . . . A long walk, from The Grange to Salisbury Crags. No one had come forward to say they'd seen him. Inquiries had been made, cabbies questioned. Perfunctory for the most part: you didn't want to linger over a suicide. Sometimes you could find out things that were better left undisturbed.

Rebus drove back into town, parked in the car park behind St. Leonard's and went into the station. He knocked on Farmer Watson's door, obeyed the command to enter. Watson looked like the day had started badly.

"Where have you been?"

"I had a bit of business down at D Division, looking at Jim Margolies' file." Rebus watched the Farmer pace behind his desk. He cradled a mug of coffee in both hands. "Did you speak to Andy Davies, sir?"

"Who?"

"Andy Davies. Darren Rough's social worker."

The Farmer nodded.

"And, sir?"

"And he told me I'd have to speak to his boss."

"What did his boss say?"

The Farmer swung round. "Christ, John, give me time, will you? I've got more to deal with than your little . . ." He exhaled, his shoulders slumping. Then he mumbled an apology.

"No problem, sir. I'll just . . ." Rebus headed for the door.

"Sit down," the Farmer ordered. "Now you're here, let's see if you can come up with any clever ideas."

Rebus sat down. "To do with what, sir?"

The Farmer sat too, then noticed that his mug was empty. He got up again to fill it from the pot, pouring for Rebus too. Rebus examined the dark liquid suspiciously. Over the years, the Farmer's coffee had definitely improved, but there were still days . . .

"To do with Cary Dennis Oakes."

Rebus frowned. "Should I know him?"

"If you don't, you soon will." The Farmer tossed a news-paper in Rebus's direction. It fell to the floor. Rebus picked it up, saw that it was folded to a particular story, a story Rebus had missed because it wasn't the one he'd been look-ing for.

KILLER IS SENT "HOME."

"Cary Oakes," Rebus read, "convicted of two murders in Washington State, USA, will today board a flight back to the United Kingdom after serving a fifteen-year sentence in a maximum-security prison in Walla Walla, Washington. It is believed that Oakes will make his way back to Edin-burgh, where he lived for several years before going to the United States."

There was a lot more. Oakes had flown to the States toting a rucksack and a tourist visa, and then had simply stayed put, taking a series of short-term jobs before em-barking on a mugging and robbery spree which had cli-maxed with two killings, the victims clubbed and strangled to death.

Rebus put down the paper. "Did you know?"

The Farmer slammed his fists down on the table. "Of course I didn't know!"

"Shouldn't we have been told?"

"Think about it, John. You're a cop in Wallumballa or whatever it's called. You're sending this murderer back to *Scotland*. Who do you tell?"

Rebus nodded. "Scotland Yard."

"Not realising for one minute that Scotland Yard might actually be in another country altogether."

"And the brainboxes in London decided not to pass the message on?"

"Their version is, they got their wires crossed, thought Oakes was only travelling as far as *their* patch. In fact, his ticket only goes as far as London."

"So he's their problem." But the Farmer was shaking his head. "Don't tell me," Rebus said, "they've had a whip-round and added the fare to Edinburgh?"

"Bingo."

"So when does he get here?"

"Later on today."

"And what do we do?"

The Farmer stared at Rebus. He liked that *we*. A problem shared—even if with a thorn like Rebus—was a problem that could be dealt with. "What would you suggest?"

"High-visibility surveillance, let him know we're watching. With any luck he'll get fed up and slope off somewhere else."

The Farmer rubbed at his eyes. "Take a look," he said, sliding a folder across the desk. Rebus looked: sheets of fax paper, about twenty of them. "The Met took pity on us at the last, sent what they'd been sent by the Americans."

Rebus started reading. "How come he's been released? I thought in America 'life' meant till death."

"Some technicality to do with the original trial. So arcane, even the American authorities aren't sure."

"But they're letting him go?"

"A retrial would cost a fortune, plus there's the problem of tracing the original witnesses. They offered him a deal. If he gave it up, signed away the right to any retrial or compensation, they'd fly him home."

"In the news story, 'home' had inverted commas."

"He hasn't spent much time in Edinburgh."

"So why here?"

"His choice, apparently."

"But why?"

"Maybe the fax will tell you."

The message of the fax was clear and simple. It said Cary Oakes would kill again.

The psychologist had warned the authorities of this. The psychologist said, Cary Oakes has little concept of right and wrong. There were lots of psychological terms applied to this. The word "psychopath" wasn't used much any more by the experts, but reading between the lines and the jargon, Rebus knew that was what they were dealing with. Antisocial tendencies . . . deep-seated sense of betrayal . . .

Oakes was thirty-eight years old. There was a grainy photo of him included with the file. His head had been shaved. The forehead was large and jutting, the face thin and angular. He had small eyes, like little black beads, and

a narrow mouth. He was described as above-average intelligence (self-taught in prison), interested in health and fitness. He'd made no friends during his incarceration, kept
no pictures on his walls, and his only correspondence was
with his team of lawyers (five different sets in total).

The Farmer was on the telephone, finding out Oakes's
flight schedule, liaising with the Assistant Chief Constable
at Fettes. When he'd finished, Rebus asked what the ACC
thought.

"He thinks we should ca' canny."

Rebus smiled: it was a typical response.

"He's right in a way," the Farmer continued. "The media
will be all over this. We can't be seen to be harassing the
man."

"Maybe we'll get lucky and the reporters will scare him
off."

"Maybe."

"It says here he was originally questioned about another
four murders."

The Farmer nodded, but seemed distracted. "I don't need
this," he said at last, staring at his desk. The desk was a
measure of the man: always carefully ordered, reflecting the
room as a whole. No piles of paperwork, no mess or clutter,
not so much as a single stray paperclip on the carpet.

"I've been at this job too long, John." The Farmer sat
back in his chair. "You know the worst kind of officers?"

"You mean ones like me, sir?"

The Farmer smiled. "Quite the opposite. I mean the ones
who're biding their time till pension day. The clock-
watchers. Recently, I've been turning into one. Another six
months, that's what I was giving myself. Six more months
till retirement." He smiled again. "And I wanted them quiet.
I've been praying for them to be quiet."

"We don't know this guy's going to be a problem.
We've been here before, sir."

The Farmer nodded: so they had. Men who'd done time
in Australia and Canada, and hardmen from Glasgow's
Bar-L, all of them settling in Edinburgh, or just passing
through. All of them with pasts carved into their faces.
Even when they weren't a problem, they were still a problem. They might settle down, live quietly, but there were

people who knew who they were, who knew the reputation they carried with them, something they'd never shake off. And eventually, after too many beers down the pub, one of these people would decide it was time to test himself, because what the hardman brought with him was a parameter, something you could measure yourself against. It was pure Hollywood: the retired gunslinger challenged by the punk kid. But to the police, all it was was trouble.

"Thing is, John, can we afford to play a waiting game? The ACC says we can have funding for partial surveillance."

"How partial?"

"Two teams of two, maybe a fortnight."

"That's big of him."

"The man likes a nice tight budget."

"Even when this guy might kill again?"

"Even murder has a budget these days, John."

"I still don't get it." Rebus picked up the fax. "According to the notes, Oakes wasn't born here, doesn't have family here. He lived here for, what, four or five years? Went to the States at twenty, he's been almost half his life there. What's for him back here?"

The Farmer shrugged. "A fresh start?"

A fresh start: Rebus was thinking of Darren Rough.

"There has to be more to it than that, sir," Rebus said, picking up the file again. "There has to be."

The Farmer looked at his watch. "Aren't you due in court?"

Rebus nodded agreement. "Waste of time, sir. They won't call me."

"All the same, Inspector . . ."

Rebus got up. "Mind if I take this stuff?" Waving the sheets of fax paper. "You told me I should take something to read."

11

Rebus sat with other witnesses, other cases, all of them waiting to be called to give evidence. There were uniforms, attentive to their notebooks, and CID officers, arms folded, trying to be casual about the whole thing. Rebus knew a few faces, held quiet conversations. The members of the public sat there with hands clasped between knees, or with heads angled to the ceiling, bored out of their minds. Newspapers—already read, crosswords finished—lay strewn around the room. A couple of dog-eared paperbacks had attracted interest, but not for long. There was something about the atmosphere that sucked all the enthusiasm out of you. The lighting gave you a headache, and all the time you were wondering why you were here.

Answer: to serve justice.

And one of the court officers would wander in and, looking at a clipboard, call your name, and you'd creak your way to the court, where your numbed memory would be poked and prodded by strangers playing to a judge, jury, and public gallery.

This was justice.

There was one witness, seated directly across from Rebus, who kept bursting into tears. He was a young man, maybe mid-twenties, corpulent and with thin strands of black hair plastered to his head. He kept emptying his nose loudly into a stained handkerchief. One time, when he looked up, Rebus gave him a reassuring smile, but that only started him off again. Eventually, Rebus had to get out. He told one of the uniforms that he was going for a ciggie.

"I'll join you," the uniform said.

Outside, they smoked furiously and in silence, watching the ebb and flow of people from the building. The High

Court was tucked in behind St. Giles' Cathedral, and occasionally tourists would wander towards it, wondering what it was. There were few signs about, just Roman numerals above the various heavy wooden doors. A guard on the car park would sometimes point them back towards the High Street. Though members of the public could enter the court building, tourists were actively discouraged. The Great Hall was enough of a cattle market as it was. But Rebus liked it: he liked the carved wooden ceiling, the statue of Sir Walter Scott, the huge stained-glass window. He liked peering through the glass door into the library where the lawyers sought precedents in large dusty tomes.

But he preferred the fresh air, setts below him and grey stone above, and the inhalation of nicotine, and the illusion that he could walk away from all this if he chose. For the thing was, behind the splendour of the architecture, and the weight of tradition, and the high concepts of justice and the law, this was a place of immense and continual human pain, where brutal stories were wrenched up, where tortured images were replayed as daily fare. People who thought they'd put the whole thing behind them were asked to delve into the most secret and tragic moments of their past. Victims rendered their stories, the professionals laid down cold facts over the emotions of others, the accused wove their own versions in an attempt to woo the jury.

And while it was easy to see it as a game, as some kind of cruel spectator sport, still it could not be dismissed. Because for all the hard work Rebus and others put into a case, this was where it sank or swam. And this was where all policemen learned an early lesson that truth and justice were far from being allies, and that victims were something more than sealed bags of evidence, recordings and statements.

It had probably all been simple enough once upon a time; the concept still was fairly simple. There is an accused, and a victim. Lawyers speak for both sides, presenting the evidence. A judgment is made. But the whole thing was a matter of words and interpretation, and Rebus knew how facts could be twisted, misrepresented, how some evidence sounded more eloquent than others, how juries could decide from the off which way they'd

vote, based on the manner or styling of the accused. And
so it turned into theatre, and the cleverer the lawyers became, the more arcane became their games with language.
Rebus had long since given up fighting them on their own
terms. He gave his evidence, kept his answers short, and
tried not to fall for any of the tried and tested tricks. Some
of the lawyers could see it in his eyes, could see that he'd
been here too often before. They detained him only briefly,
before moving on to more amenable subjects.

That was why he didn't think they'd call him today. But
all the same, he had to sit it out, had to waste his time and
energy in the great name of justice.

One of the guards came out. Rebus knew him, and offered a cigarette. The man took it with a nod, accepting
Rebus's box of matches.

"Fucking awful in there today," the guard said, shaking
his head. All three men were staring across the car park.

"We're not allowed to know," Rebus reminded him,
with a sly smile.

"Which court are you in?"

"Shiellion," Rebus said.

"That's the one I'm talking about," the guard said.
"Some of the testimony . . ." And he shook his head, a man
who'd heard more horror stories than most in his working
life.

Suddenly, Rebus knew why the man across from him
had been crying. And if he couldn't put a name to the man,
at least now he knew who he was: he was one of the Shiellion survivors.

Shiellion House lay just off the Glasgow Road at Ingliston Mains. Built in the 1820s for one of the city's Lord
Provosts, after his death and various family wranglings it
had passed into the care of the Church of Scotland. As a
private residence it was found to be too big and draughty,
its isolation—distant farms its only neighbours—driving
away most of its residents. By the 1930s it had become a
children's home, dealing with orphans and the impover-
ished, teaching them Christianity with hard lessons and
early rises. Shiellion had finally closed the previous year.
There was talk of it becoming a hotel or a country club.
But in its later years, Shiellion had garnered something of

a reputation. There had been accusations from former residents, similar stories told by different intakes about the
same two men.

Stories of abuse.

Physical and mental abuse to be sure, but eventually
sexual abuse too. A couple of cases had come to the attention of the police, but the accusations were one-sided—the
word of aggressive children against their quietly spoken
carers. The investigations had been half-hearted. The
Church had carried out its own internal inquiries, which
had shown the children's stories to be tissues of vindictive
lies.

But these inquiries, it now transpired, had been fixed
from the start, comprising little more than cover-ups. Something *had* been happening in Shiellion. Something bad.

The survivors formed a pressure group, and got some
media interest. A fresh police investigation was imple-
mented, and it had led to this—the Shiellion trial; two men
up on charges ranging from assault to sodomy. Twenty-
eight counts against either man. And meantime, the victims
were readying to sue the Church.

Rebus didn't wonder that the guard was pale-faced. He'd
heard whispers about the stories being retold in court number one. He'd read some of the original transcripts, details
of interviews held at police stations up and down the country, as children who'd been held in Shiellion were traced—
adults now—and questioned. Some of them had refused to
have anything to do with it. "That's all behind me," was
an oft-used excuse. Only it was more than an excuse: it was
the simple truth. They'd worked hard to lock out the nightmares from their childhood: why would they want to relive
them? They had whatever peace would ever be available to
them in life: why change that?

Who would face terror across a courtroom, if they could
choose to avoid it?

Who indeed.

The survivors' group comprised eight individuals who
had chosen the more difficult path. They were going to see
to it that after all these years justice was finally done. They
were going to lock away the two monsters who'd ripped
apart their innocence, monsters who were still there in the

world whenever they woke from their nightmares. Harold Ince was fifty-seven, short and skinny and bespectacled. He had curly hair, turning grey. He had a wife and three grown children. He was a grandfather. He hadn't worked in seven years. He had a dazed look to him in all the photographs Rebus had seen.

Ramsay Marshall was forty-four, tall and broad, hair cut short and spiky. Divorced, no children, had until recently been living and working (as a chef) in Aberdeen. Photographs showed a scowling face, jutting chin.

The two men had met at Shiellion in the early 1980s, formed a friendship or at the very least an alliance. Found they shared a common interest, one that could, it seemed, be carried out with impunity in Shiellion House.

Abusers. Rebus was sickened by them. They couldn't be cured or changed. They just went on and on. Released into the community, they'd soon revert to type. They were control junkies, weak-minded, and just awful. They were like addicts who couldn't be weaned off their fix. There were no prescription drugs, and no amount of psychotherapy seemed to work. They saw weakness and had to exploit it; saw innocence and had to explore it. Rebus had had a bellyful of them.

Like with Darren Rough. Rebus knew he'd snapped in the zoo because of Shiellion, because of the way it wasn't going away. The trial had last two weeks so far, heading into week three, and still there were stories to be told, still there were people crying in the waiting room.

"Chemical castration," the guard said, stubbing out his cigarette. "It's the only way."

Then there was a cry from the courthouse door: one of the ushers.

"Inspector Rebus?" she called. Rebus nodded, flicked his cigarette on to the setts.

"You're up," she called. He was already moving towards her.

Rebus didn't know why he was here. Except that he'd interviewed Harold Ince. Which was to say, he'd been part of the team interviewing Ince. But only for one day—other work had pulled him away from Shiellion. Only for one

day, early on in the inquiry. He'd shared the sessions with
Bill Pryde, but it wasn't Bill Pryde the defence wanted to
examine. It was John Rebus.

The public gallery was half-empty. The jury of fifteen
sat with glazed expressions, the effect of sharing someone
else's nightmare, day in, day out. The judge was Lord Justice Petrie. Ince and Marshall sat in the dock. Ince leaned
forward, the better to hear the evidence, his hands twisting
the polished brass rail in front of him. Marshall leaned
back, looking bored by proceedings. He examined his shirt-
front, then would turn his neck from side to side, cracking
it. Clear his throat and click his tongue and go back to
studying himself.

The defence lawyer was Richard Cordover, Richie to his
friends. Rebus had had dealings with him before; he'd yet
to be invited to call the lawyer "Richie." Cordover was in
his forties, hair already grey. Medium height and with a
muscular neck, face tanned. Health club regular, Rebus
guessed. Prosecution was a fiscal-depute nearly half Rebus's age. He looked confident but careful, browsing
through his case notes, jotting points down with a fat black
fountain pen.

Petrie cleared his throat, reminding Cordover that time
was passing. Cordover bowed to the judge and approached
Rebus.

"Detective Inspector Rebus . . ." Pausing immediately
for effect. "I believe you interviewed one of the suspects."

"That's right, sir. I was present at the interview of Harold Ince on October the twentieth last year. Others present
included—"

"This was where exactly?"

"Interview Room B, St. Leonard's police station."

Cordover turned away from Rebus, walked slowly towards the jury. "You were part of the investigation team?"

"Yes, sir."

"For how long?"

"Just over a week, sir."

Cordover turned to Rebus. "How long did the investigation last in total, Inspector?"

"A matter of some months, I believe."

"Some months, yes . . ." Cordover went as if to check

his notes. Rebus noticed a woman seated on a chair near the door. She was a CID detective called Jane Barbour. Though she sat with arms folded and legs crossed, she looked as tense as Rebus felt. Normally, she worked out of Fettes, but halfway through Shiellion she'd been put in charge: after Rebus's time; he hadn't had any dealings with her.

"Eight and a half months," Cordover was saying. "A decent period of gestation." He smiled coldly at Rebus, who said nothing. He was wondering where this was leading; knew now that the defence had some bloody good reason for bringing him here. Only he didn't yet know what.

"Were you pulled from the inquiry, Inspector Rebus?" Asked casually, as if to satisfy curiosity only.

"Pulled? No, sir. Something else came up—"

"And someone was needed to deal with it?"

"That's right."

"Why you, do you think?"

"I've no idea, sir."

"No?" Cordover sounded surprised. He turned towards the jury.

"You've no idea why you were pulled from that inquiry after just one—"

The prosecution counsel was on his feet, arms spread. "The detective inspector has already stated that the word 'pulled' is an inaccuracy, Your Honour."

"Well then," Cordover went on quickly, "let's say you were *transferred*. Would that be more accurate, Inspector?"

Rebus just shrugged, unwilling to agree to anything. Cordover was persistent.

"Yes or no will do."

"Yes, sir."

"Yes, you were transferred from a major inquiry after one week?"

"Yes, sir."

"And you've no idea why?"

"Because I was needed elsewhere, sir." Rebus was trying not to look towards the fiscal-depute: any glance in that direction would have Cordover scenting blood, scenting someone who needed rescuing. Jane Barbour was shifting in her seat, still with arms folded.

"You were needed elsewhere," Cordover repeated in a flat tone of voice. He returned to his notes. "How's your disciplinary record, Inspector?"

The fiscal-depute was on his feet. "Inspector Rebus is not on trial here, Your Honour. He has come to give evidence, and so far I can't see any point to the—"

"I withdraw the remark, Your Honour," Cordover said airily. He smiled at Rebus, approached again. "You conducted how many interviews with Mr. Ince?"

"Two sessions over a single day."

"Did they go well?" Rebus looked blank. "Did my client co-operate?"

"His answers were deliberately obtuse, sir."

" 'Deliberately'? Are you some kind of expert, Inspector?"

Rebus fixed his eyes on the advocate. "I can tell when someone's being evasive."

"Really?" Cordover was making for the jury again. Rebus wondered how many miles of floor he covered in a day. "My client is of the opinion that you were 'a threatening presence'—his words, not mine."

"The interviews were recorded, sir."

"Indeed they were. And videotaped, too. I've watched them several times, and I think you'd have to agree that your method of questioning is *aggressive*."

"No, sir."

"No?" Cordover raised his eyebrows. "My client was obviously terrified of you."

"The interviews followed every procedure, sir."

"Oh, yes, yes," Cordover said dismissively, "but let's be honest here, Inspector." He was in front of Rebus now, close enough to hit. "There are ways and ways, aren't there? Body language, gestures, ways of phrasing a question or statement. You may or may not be expert at divinating obtuse answers, but you're certainly a ruthless questioner."

The judge peered over the top of his glasses. "Is this leading somewhere, other than to an attempt at character assassination?"

"If you'll bear with me a moment longer, Your Honour." Cordover bowed again, consummate showman. Not for the

first time, Rebus was struck by the utter ridiculousness of
the whole enterprise: a game played by well-paid lawyers
using real lives as the pieces.

"A few days ago, Inspector," Cordover went on, "were
you part of a surveillance team at Edinburgh Zoo?"

Oh, hell. Rebus knew now *exactly* where Cordover was
leading, and like a bad chess-player put against a master,
he could do little to forestall the conclusion.

"Yes, sir."

"You ended up in pursuit of a member of the public?"

The fiscal-depute was on his feet again, but the judge
waved him aside.

"I did, yes."

"You were part of an undercover team trying to catch
our notorious poisoner?"

"Yes, sir."

"And the man you chased . . . I believe it was into the
sea-lion enclosure?" Cordover looked up for confirmation.
Rebus nodded dutifully. "Was this man the poisoner?"

"No, sir."

"Did you suspect him of being the poisoner?"

"He was a convicted paedophile . . ." There was anger
in Rebus's voice, and he knew his face had reddened. He
broke off, but too late. He'd given the defence lawyer
everything he wanted.

"A man who had served his sentence and been released
into the community. A man who has not reoffended. A man
who was enjoying the pleasures of a trip to the zoo until
you recognised him and chased after him."

"He ran first."

"He ran? From *you*, Inspector? Now why would he do
a thing like that?"

All right, you sarky bastard, get it over with.

"The point I'm making," Cordover said to the jury, approaching them with something close to reverence, "is that
there is prejudice against anyone even *suspected* of crimes
against children. The Inspector happened to catch sight of
a man who had served a single custodial sentence, and immediately suspected the worst, and *acted* on that suspicion—quite wrongly, as it turned out. No charges were
made, the poisoner struck again, and I believe the innocent

party is considering suing the police for wrongful arrest."
He nodded. "Your tax money, I'm afraid." He took a deep
breath. "Now, it may be that we can all understand the
Inspector's feelings. The blood rises where children are involved. But I'd ask you: is it morally right? And does it
contaminate the entire case against my clients, seeping
down through the tools of the investigation, coming to rest
with the very officers who conducted the inquiry?" He
pointed towards Rebus, who felt now that he was in the
dock rather than the witness box. Seeing his discomfort,
Ramsay Marshall's eyes were twinkling with pleasure.
"Later, I shall produce further evidence that the initial police investigation was flawed from the outset, and that Detective Inspector Rebus here was not the only culprit." He
turned to Rebus. "No more questions."

And Rebus was dismissed.

"That was a tough one."

Rebus looked up at the figure walking slowly towards
him. He was lighting a cigarette, inhaling deeply. He offered one over, but she shook her head.

"Have you come across Cordover before?" Rebus asked.

"We've had our run-ins," Jane Barbour said.

"Sorry I couldn't . . ."

"Not much you could have done about it." She exhaled
noisily, clutching a briefcase to her chest. They were outside the court building. Rebus felt gritty and exhausted. He
noticed she was looking pretty tired herself.

"Fancy a drink?"

She shook her head. "Things to do."

He nodded. "Think we'll win?"

"Not if Cordover has anything to do with it." She
scraped the heel of one shoe across the ground. "I seem to
be losing more than I'm winning lately."

"You still at Fettes?"

She nodded. "Sex Offences."

"Still a DI?"

She nodded again. Rebus remembered a rumour about a
promotion. So Gill Templer remained the only female chief
inspector in Lothian. Rebus studied her from behind his
cigarette. She was tall, what his mother would have called

"big-boned." Shoulder-length brown hair fashioned into waves. Mustard-coloured two-piece with a light silk blouse. She sported a mole on one cheek and another on her chin. Mid-thirties . . . ? Rebus was hopeless with ages.

"Well . . ." she said, ready to leave but looking for an excuse not to.

"Goodbye then." A voice sounded behind them. They turned and watched Richard Cordover walking to his car. It was a red TVR with personalised plate. By the time he was unlocking the car, he seemed to have forgotten about them.

"One cold bastard," Barbour muttered.

"Must have saved him a few bob."

She looked at Rebus. "How's that?"

"He could skip the TVR's air-conditioning option. Sure about that drink? There's something I wanted to ask you . . ."

They bypassed Deacon Brodie's—too many "clients" drank there—and headed for the Jolly Judge. Rebus had once had a drink there with an advocate who drank advocaat. Now Rangers had signed a Dutch manager called Advocaat and the jokes were being dusted off . . . He bought a Virgin Mary for Barbour and a half of Eighty for himself. They sat at a table below the stairs, well out of the way.

"Cheers," she said.

Rebus raised his glass to her, then to his lips.

"So what can I do for you?"

He put down the glass. "Just some background. You used to work MisPers, didn't you?"

"For my sins, yes."

"What did you do exactly?"

"Collect, collate, stick them all into filing cabinets and computer memories. A bit of liaison, punting our MisPers to other forces and receiving theirs in return. Lots of meetings with the various charities . . ." She puffed out her cheeks. "Lots of meetings with families, too, trying to help them understand what had happened."

"Job satisfaction?"

"Up there with sewing mailbags. Why the interest?"

"I've got a missing person."

"How old?"

"He's nineteen. Still lives at home; his parents are worried."

She was shaking her head. "Needle in a haystack."

"I know."

"Did he leave a note?"

"No, and they say he'd no reason to leave."

"Sometimes there aren't reasons, not any that would make sense to the family." She straightened in her chair. "Here's the checklist." She counted fingers as she spoke. "Bank accounts, building society, anything like that. You're looking for withdrawals."

"Done."

"Check with hostels. Local, plus the usual cities—anything between Aberdeen and London. Some of them have charities who deal with the homeless and runaways: Centrepoint in London, for example. Get a description out. Then there's the National Missing Persons Bureau in London. Fax any details to them. You might ask the Sally Army to keep their eyes open too. Soup kitchens, night shelters, you never know who'll turn up."

Rebus was jotting in his notebook. He looked up, watched her shrug.

"That's about it."

"Is it a big problem?"

She smiled. "Thing is, it's not a problem *at all*, not unless you're the one who's lost somebody. A lot of them turn up, some don't. Last estimate I saw said there could be as many as a quarter of a million MisPers out there. People who've just dropped out, changed their identity, or been dumped by the so-called 'caring' services."

"Care in the community?"

She gave her bitter smile again, drank some of her drink, checked her watch.

"I can see Shiellion must have come as a welcome break."

She snorted. "Oh yes, like a camping trip. Abuse cases are always a breeze." She turned thoughtful. "I had a double rapist a few weeks back, he ended up walking. Crown cocked it up, prosecuted it as a summary case."

"Maximum sentence three months?"

She nodded. "He wasn't up for rape this time, just indecent exposure. The Sheriff was furious. By the time remand was taken into account, the bastard had under two weeks to serve, so the Sheriff put him back on the streets." She looked at Rebus. "Psych report said he'd do it again. Probation and community service, with a bit of counselling thrown in. And he'll do it again."

He'll do it again. Rebus was thinking of Darren Rough, but of Cary Oakes too. He checked his own watch. Soon Oakes would be touching down at Turnhouse. Soon he'd be a problem . . .

"Sorry I can't be more help about your MisPer," she said, beginning to stand. "Is it someone you know?"

"Son of some friends." She was nodding. "How did you know?"

"No offence, John, but you probably wouldn't be bothering otherwise." She lifted up her briefcase. "He's one out of quarter of a million. Who's got the time?"

12

There were reporters waiting inside the terminal building. Most carried mobile phones with which they kept in touch with the office. Photographers chatted to each other about lenses and film speeds and the impact digital cameras would eventually have. There were three TV crews: Scottish, BBC and Edinburgh Live. Everyone seemed to know everyone else; they were all pretty relaxed, maybe even looking a bit tired by the wait.

The flight was subject to a twenty-minute delay.

Rebus knew the reason why. The reason was that the Met officers at Heathrow had taken their time transferring Cary Oakes. Oakes had spent over an hour in Heathrow. He'd visited the toilet, had a drink in one of the bars, bought a newspaper and a couple of magazines, and taken a telephone call.

The telephone call had intrigued Rebus.

"He was paged," the Farmer had informed him. "Someone got a call through to him."

"Who would that be?"

The Farmer had shaken his head.

Now Oakes was bound for Edinburgh. Detectives had accompanied him on to the flight, then had left again, keeping their eyes on the plane right up until it left London air space. Then they'd called their colleagues at Lothian and Borders HQ.

"He's all yours," was the message.

The ACC (Crime) was putting the Farmer in charge. The Farmer didn't usually stray from his office: he was happy to delegate; trusted his team. But tonight . . . tonight was a bit special. So he was seated alongside Rebus in the squad car. DC Siobhan Clarke sat in the back. It was a marked car: they wanted Oakes to know about it. Rebus had been out to recce the scene, reporting back with news of the journos.

"Anyone we know?" Clarke asked.

"Usual faces," Rebus said, accepting another piece of chewing gum from her. This was the bargain they'd made: he wouldn't smoke so long as she bought the gum. His reconnaissance had been an excuse for a ciggie.

The dashboard clock said the plane would be touching down any minute. They heard it before they saw it: a dull whine, lights flashing in the dark sky. They had one window down, stopping the car from steaming up.

"Could be the one," the Farmer stated.

"Could be."

Siobhan Clarke had all the paperwork beside her; she'd been doing her reading on Cary Dennis Oakes. She wasn't sure that they were serving any purpose here other than curiosity. Still, she *was* curious.

"Shouldn't take long," she said.

"Don't bet on it," Rebus said, opening his door again. He was digging in his pocket for a cigarette as he made towards the terminal doors.

He circumvented the huddle of pressmen and made for a No Entry sign. Showing his ID, he made his way towards the arrivals hall. He'd already had a word, and Customs and Immigration were waiting for him. He knew what happened with international transfers: there were no checks at Heathrow. Often, there were no checks at Edinburgh either: it depended on staff rotas; the cutbacks had bitten hard. But there'd be the full panoply of checks tonight. Rebus watched as the passengers from the Heathrow flight filtered into the terminal and began the wait for baggage. Businessmen mostly, carrying briefcases and newspapers. Half the flight carried hand-luggage only. They made their way briskly through Customs, cars waiting in the car park, families waiting at home.

Then there was the man wearing casual clothes: denims and trainers, red and black check shirt, white baseball cap. He carried a sports holdall. It didn't look particularly full. Rebus nodded to the Customs officer, who stepped out and stopped the man, bringing him over to the counter.

"Passport, please," the Immigration officer said.

The man dug into his shirt-breast pocket and produced a new-looking passport. It had been applied for over a month back, when the Americans had known they'd be freeing him. The Immigration officer flipped through it, finding little but empty pages.

"Where are you travelling from, sirs?"

Cary Oakes's eyes were on the man in the background, the man who'd arranged all this.

"United States," he said. His voice was an odd mix of transatlantic inflexions.

"And what were you doing there, sir?"

Oakes smirked. He had the face of a weathered schoolboy, the classroom joker. "Passing time," he said.

The Customs officer had decanted the contents of his bag on to the counter. Washbag, change of clothes, a couple of razzle mags. A manila folder was full of drawings and photos clipped from magazines. They looked like they'd been pinned to a wall for a long time. There was a good luck card, too, telling him to "fly high and straight" and signed by "your buddies on the wing." Another folder contained trial notes and newspaper court reports. There were two paperback books, one a Bible, the other a dictionary. Both looked well-used.

"Travel light, that's my motto," Oakes informed them.

The Customs officer looked to Rebus, who nodded, keeping his stare fixed on Oakes. Everything was put back into the bag.

"This is actually pretty low-key," Oakes said. "And don't think I don't appreciate it. Quiet life's going to suit me for a while." He was nodding to himself.

"Don't plan on sticking around," Rebus said quietly.

"I don't think we've been introduced, Officer." Oakes thrust out a hand. Rebus saw that the back of it was dotted with ink tattoos: initials, crosses, a heart. After a moment, Oakes withdrew the hand, laughing to himself. "Not so easy to make new friends, I guess," he mused. "I've lost the old social skills."

The Customs officer was zipping the holdall. Oakes grabbed its handles.

"Now, gentlemen, if you've had your fun . . . ?"

"Where are you headed?" the Immigration man asked.

"A nice hotel in the city. Hotels for me from now on. They wanted to put me in some palace out in the country, but I said no, I want lights and action. I want some *buzz*." He laughed again.

"Who's they?" Rebus couldn't help asking.

Oakes just grinned and winked. "You'll find out, partner. Won't even have to do much detecting." He hefted the bag and slung it over his shoulder, whistling as he walked away, joining the throng headed for the exit.

Rebus followed. The reporters outside were getting their photos and footage, even if Oakes had slid the baseball cap down over his face. Questions were hurled at him. And then an overweight man was pushing his way through, cigarette dangling from his mouth. Rebus recognised him: Jim Stevens. He worked for one of the Glasgow tabloids. He grabbed Oakes by the arm and said something into his ear. They shook hands, and then Stevens was in charge, manoeuvring Oakes through the huddle, proprietorial hand on his shoulder.

"Oh, Jim, for Christ's sake," one of the other reporters cried.

"No comment," Stevens said, the cigarette flapping at one corner of his mouth. "But you can read our exclusive serialisation, starting tomorrow."

And with a final wave, he was through the doors and off. Rebus made for another exit, got into the car beside the Farmer.

"Looks like he's made a friend," Siobhan Clarke commented, watching Stevens put Oakes's bag into the boot of a Vauxhall Astra.

"Jim Stevens," Rebus told her. "He works out of Glasgow."

"And Oakes is now his property?" she guessed.

"So it would seem. I think they're heading into town."

The Farmer slapped the dashboard. "Should have guessed one of the papers would nab him."

"They won't hang on to him forever. Soon as the story's done . . ."

"But till then, they've got their lawyers." The Farmer turned to Rebus. "So we can't do *anything* that could be construed as harassment."

"As you wish, sir," Rebus said, starting the engine. He turned to the Farmer. "So do we head home now?"

The Farmer nodded. "Just as soon as we've tailed them. Let Stevens know the score."

"There's a cop car after us," Cary Oakes warned.

Jim Stevens reached for the cigarette lighter. "I know."

"Welcoming committee at the airport, too."

"He's called Rebus."

"Who is?"

"Detective Inspector John Rebus. I've had a few run-ins with him. What did he say to you?"

Oakes shrugged. "Just stood there trying to look mean. Guys I met in prison, they'd have given him a nervous breakdown."

Stevens smiled. "Save it till the recorder's running."

Oakes had the passenger-side window open all the way, angling his head into the fierce cold air.

"Does smoking bother you?" Stevens said.

"No." Oakes moved his head to and fro, as if under a hair dryer. "Clever of you to have me paged at Heathrow."

"I wanted to be the first to make you an offer."

"Ten grand, right?"

"I think we can manage ten."

"Exclusive rights?"

"Got to be, for that price."

Oakes brought his head back into the car. "I'm not sure how good I'll be."

"You'll be fine. You're a Scot, aren't you? We're born storytellers."

"I guess Edinburgh's changed."

"You've been away a while."

"Oh, yes."

"Do you still know anyone here?"

"I can think of a couple of names." Oakes smiled. "Jim Stevens, John Rebus. That's two, and I've only been in the country half an hour." Jim Stevens started to laugh. Oakes rolled the window back up, leaned down to switch off the music. Turned in his seat so Stevens had his full attention. "So tell me about Rebus. I'd like to get to know him."

"Why?"

Oakes's eyes never left the reporter's. "Someone takes an interest in me," he said, "I take an interest back."

"Does that put me in the frame too?"

"You never know your luck, Jim. You just never know your luck."

Stevens had wanted Oakes out of Edinburgh. He'd wanted him in seclusion for as long as it took to do the interviews. But Oakes had told him on the phone: it has to be Edinburgh. It just has to be. So Edinburgh it was; a discreet hotel in a New Town terrace. Stevens had to smile at "New Town": everywhere else in Scotland, it meant the likes of Glenrothes and Livingston, places built from nothing in the fifties and sixties. But in Edinburgh, the New Town dated back to the eighteenth century. That was about as new as the city liked things. The hotel would have been a private residence at one time, spread over four floors. Understated elegance; a quiet street. Oakes took one look at it and decided it wouldn't do. He didn't say why, just stood on the steps outside, taking in the air, while Stevens made a couple of frantic calls on his mobile.

"It would help if I knew what you wanted."

Oakes just shrugged. "I'll know when I see it." He waved a little wave towards where the police car had parked, its lights still on.

"Right," Stevens said at last. "Back in the motor."

They headed down Leith Walk, towards the port of Leith itself.

"This still a rough part of town?" Oakes said.

"It's changing. New developments, Scottish Office. New restaurants and a couple of hotels."

"But it's still Leith, right?"

Stevens nodded. "Still Leith," he conceded. But when they hit the waterfront and Oakes saw their hotel, he started nodding straight away.

"Atmosphere," he said, looking out across the docks. There was a container ship tied up there, arc lights on as men worked around it. A couple of pubs, both with restaurants attached. Across the basin was a permanent mooring, a boat which had become a floating nightclub. New flats being built across there too.

"Scottish Office is just down there," Stevens said, pointing.

"How long do you think they'll keep this up?" Oakes asked, watching the police car come to a stop.

"Not long. If they try it on. I'll phone our lawyers. I need to call them anyway, get your contract sorted."

"Contract." Oakes tried out the word. "Long time since I've had a job."

"Just talking into a microphone, posing for a few pictures."

Oakes turned to him. "For ten thou, I'll do fucking re-enactments for you."

Some of the colour slid from Stevens' face. Oakes was watching him intently, measuring the reaction.

"That probably won't be necessary," Stevens said.

Oakes laughed, liking that "probably."

Inside the hotel, he approved of his room. Stevens couldn't get one next door, had to settle for down the hall. Stuck the rooms on plastic and said they'd need them for a few days. He found Oakes lying on the bed in his room, shoes still on, holdall on the bed beside him. He'd taken one item from it: a battered Bible. It lay on the bedside table. Nice touch: Stevens would use it in his intro.

"You a religious man, Jim?" Oakes asked.

"Not especially."

"Shame on you. Bible'll teach you a lot of things. I got my first taste in prison. Time was, I'd no time for the Good Book."

"Did you go to church?"

Oakes nodded, seeming distracted. "We had Sunday service in the jail. I was a regular." He looked to Stevens. "I'm not a prisoner, right? I mean, I can come and go?"

"Last thing I want is for you to feel like a prisoner."

"Makes two of us."

"But there are a few rules, so long as *I'm* paying your way. If you go out, I want to know. In fact, I'd like to tag along."

"Afraid the competition will hook me?"

"Something like that."

Oakes turned his head, grinned. "Supposing I want a woman? You going to be sitting in the corner while I hump her?"

"Listening at the door will be fine," Stevens said.

Oakes laughed, wriggled on the mattress. "Softest bed I ever had. Smells nice too." He lay a moment longer, then swung swiftly to his feet. Stevens was surprised at the turn of speed.

"Come on then," Oakes told him.

"Where?"

"Out, man. But don't fret, I'm not going more than fifty yards."

Stevens followed him outside, but stayed by the hotel, could see where Oakes was headed.

The police car; lights still on; three figures inside. Oakes peered through the windscreen, headed for the driver's side, tapped on the glass. The one he now knew as Rebus wound down the window.

"Hey," Oakes said by way of greeting, nodding his head to the other two—young woman, and a senior-looking man with a huge scowl on his face. He gestured towards the hotel. "Nice place, huh? Any of you ever stay someplace

like that?" They said nothing. He leaned one arm on the
roof of the car, the other on the door panel.

"I was . . ." All at once he looked a little shy. "Yeah,"
knowing now how to put it, "I was real sorry to hear about
your daughter. Man, that's got to be a bitch." Looking at
Rebus with liquid, soulless eyes. "One of the killings they
pinned me for, girl would have been about the same age. I
mean, same age as your daughter. Sammy, that's her name,
right?"

Rebus pushed open his door so hard, it propelled Oakes
back almost to the water's edge. The other man—Rebus's
boss—was calling out a warning; the young woman was
coming out of the car behind Rebus. Rebus himself was up
in Cary Oakes's face. Jim Stevens was sprinting from the
hotel.

Oakes had his hands raised high over his head. "You
touch me, it's assault."

"You're a liar."

"Say again?"

"They didn't charge you with anybody my daughter's
age."

Oakes laughed, rubbed his chin. "Well, you've got
something there. Guess that gives you the first round, huh?"

The woman officer was gripping one of Rebus's arms.
Jim Stevens was panting after the short jog. The chief
stayed sitting in the car, watching.

Oakes bent a little to peer in. "Too important for all this,
huh? Or no stomach for it? Your call, man."

Stevens grabbed him by the shoulder. "Come on."

Oakes shrugged free. "Nobody touches me, that's rule
one." But he allowed himself to be steered back across the
road towards the hotel. Stevens turned round, found Rebus
staring at him hard, knowing who'd told Oakes about him,
about his family.

Oakes started laughing, laughed all the way to the hotel's glass doors. He stood on the inside, looking out.

"That Rebus," he said quietly. "He's not exactly what
you'd call a slow burner, now is he?"

Back at Patience's flat in Oxford Terrace, Rebus poured
himself a whisky and added water from a bottle in the

fridge. She came through from the bedroom, eyes slanted in the sudden light, a pale yellow nightdress falling to her ankles.

"Sorry if I woke you," Rebus said.

"I wanted a drink anyway." She took grapefruit juice from the fridge door, poured herself a large glass. "Good day?"

Rebus didn't know whether to laugh or cry. They took the drinks into the living room, sat together on the sofa. Rebus picked up a copy of *The Big Issue*: Patience always bought it, but he was the one who read it. Inside, there were fresh appeals for MisPer information. He knew if he turned on the TV and went to Teletext, there was a listing for missing persons. He'd watched it from time to time, scanning a few pages. It was run by the National MisPer Helpline. Janice had said she'd contact them . . .

"What about you?" he asked.

Patience tucked her feet beneath her. "Same old story. Sometimes, I almost think a robot could do the work. Same symptoms, same prescriptions. Tonsils, measles, dizzy spells . . ."

"Maybe we could go away." She looked at him. "Just for a weekend."

"We tried it, remember? You got bored."

"Ach, that was the country."

"So which romantic interlude did you have in mind? Dundee? Falkirk? Kirkcaldy?"

He got up for a refill, asked her if she wanted one. She shook her head, her eyes on his empty glass.

"Second one today," he said, making for the kitchen.

"What's brought this on anyway?" She was following him.

"What?"

"The sudden notion of a holiday."

He glanced towards her. "I went to see Sammy yesterday. She said she speaks to you more than I do."

"A bit of an exaggeration . . ."

"That's what I said. But she has a point all the same."

"Oh?"

He poured less water into the glass this time. And maybe a drop more whisky too. "I mean, I know I can be . . .

distracted. I know I'm a pretty lousy proposition." He closed the fridge, turned to her and shrugged. "That's about it, really."

Kept his eyes on the glass as he spoke, wondering why it was that as he said the words, a holiday snap of Janice Mee flashed across his mind.

"I keep thinking you'll come back," Patience said. He looked at her. She tapped her own head. "From wherever it is you've gone."

"I'm right here."

She shook her head. "No you're not. You're not really here at all." She turned away, walked back through to the living room.

A little later, she went to bed. Rebus said he'd stay up a bit longer. Flipped TV channels, finding nothing. Went to Teletext, page 346. Stuck the headphones on so he could listen to Genesis: "For Absent Friends." Jack Morton sitting on the arm of the sofa as screen after screen of missing persons appeared. No sign of Damon yet. Rebus lit a cigarette, blew smoke at the television, watching it dissolve. Then remembered this was Patience's flat, and she didn't like smoking. Back into the kitchen to extinguish his guilty pleasure. After Genesis, he switched to Family: "Song for Sinking Loves."

Something's gone bad inside you.

It was your lot wanted him here.

Saw two men in the dock, their lawyer working on the jury. Saw Cary Oakes leaning into the car.

He'll do it again.

Saw Jim Margolies take that final flight into darkness. Maybe there was no way to understand any of it. He turned to Jack. Often he'd phoned Jack—didn't matter what time of night it was, Jack never complained. They'd talk around subjects, share worries and depressions.

"How could you do that to me, Jack?" Rebus said quietly, drinking his drink as the room filled with ghosts.

It was late, but Jim Stevens knew his editor wouldn't mind. He tried the mobile number first. Bingo: his boss was at a dinner party in Kelvingrove. Politicos, the usual movers and shakers. Stevens's boss liked all that crowd. Maybe he was the wrong man for a tabloid.

Or maybe, all these years down the road, it was Jim Stevens who was out of touch. He seemed surrounded by journalists younger, brighter, and keener than him. These days, you could be washed up at fifty. He wondered how long it would be till the cheque for services rendered was being countersigned at his editor's desk, how long before the young bloods in the office were having a whip-round to see off "good old Jim." He knew the drill, even knew the speeches they'd make—stuff any self-respecting sub would block and delete. He knew because he'd been there himself, back in the days when *he'd* been a young blood and the old-timers had been complaining about falling standards and the changing world of journalism.

Soon as Jim had heard about Cary Oakes, he'd taken his boss aside for a private word, then had checked flight schedules, brown-nosing Heathrow Information so they'd page the prodigal son.

"It's yours, Jim," his editor had said, but with a warning finger. "Could be the cream on the cake. Just make sure it doesn't turn sour."

Now the boss was giving him a couple of snippets of gossip from the dinner party. He'd obviously had a few drinks. They wouldn't stop him heading into the newsroom afterwards. Twelve-hour days: a while since Jim Stevens had worked any of those.

"So what can I do you for, Jim?"

At last. Stevens took a deep breath. "I've got us settled in at the hotel."

"How does he seem?"

"All right."

"Not a slavering monster or anything?"

"No, pretty quiet really." Stevens deciding his boss needn't know about the blow-up with Rebus.

"And ready to give us the exclusive?"

"Yes." Stevens lit a cigarette for himself.

"You might try to sound a bit more enthusiastic."

"Just been a long day, boss, that's all."

"Sure you've got the stamina, Jim? I could lend you one of the newsroom crew . . . ?"

"Thanks but no thanks." Stevens heard his boss laughing. Ha bloody ha. "That's not the kind of back-up that worries me."

"You mean corroboration?"

"Lack of it, more like."

"Mmm." Thoughtful now. "Got a game plan?"

"You worked for a year or two in the States, didn't you?"

"While back."

"Still got friends there?"

"Might have one or two."

"I need to hook up with someone on a Seattle paper, see if I can talk to one of the cops who worked the Oakes case."

"One guy I knew now works news for CBS."

"That'd be a start."

"Soon as I get to the office, OK, Jim?"

"Thanks."

"And Jim? Don't worry too much about confirmation. First thing you need to get from our friend Oakes is a bloody good story. Whatever it takes."

Stevens put the phone down, lay back on his bed. Part of him wanted to chuck the job right now. But the other part was still hungry. It *wanted* those kids in the office to stare at him, wondering if they'd ever be as good, as sharp. It wanted Oakes's story. Afterwards, he could walk away if he liked: crowning glory and all that. He thought again of Rebus. Wondered what Oakes had to gain from sparring with him. From what Stevens knew, no one had ever got into the ring with Rebus and come away without at least a few cuts and bruises. And sometimes . . . sometimes there'd be traction and a hospital waiting.

But Oakes had looked keen. Oakes had looked ready, *making* Rebus come at him like that.

Jim Stevens was supposed to be Oakes's baby-sitter. But it seemed to him that Oakes had either an agenda or a death wish. Difficult to baby-sit either one.

"This is your last job, Jim," Stevens promised himself Decided a raid on the mini-bar would seal the contract.

13

The surveillance budget was so tight, they were reduced to singles. Four in the morning, Rebus couldn't sleep, so he drove down to the waterfront, stopping off at an all-night garage. Siobhan Clarke was in an unmarked Rover 200. She'd dressed for a mountain trek: trousers tucked into thick socks and climbing boots; thermal jacket and bobble hat. On the passenger seat: notebook and pen; three empty packets of lo-fat crisps; two flasks. Rebus climbed into the back and offered a microwaved pasty and beaker of coffee.

"Cheers," she said.

Rebus looked out at the hotel. "Any movement?"

She shook her head, chewed and swallowed. "I'm a bit worried though. There are service exits to the back of the building. No way I can cover those."

"He's probably jet-lagged anyway."

"Meaning awake all night, asleep all day?"

"I hadn't thought of that." Rebus leaned forward. "He hasn't been out *at all*?"

She shook her head. "All those years in jail, maybe he's turned agoraphobic."

"Maybe." Rebus knew she might have a point. He'd known ex-cons who just couldn't cope with the outside world—all that space and light. They ended up reoffending, only way they could get put away again.

"He ate dinner in the restaurant." She nodded towards the plate-glass windows of the hotel's dining room.

"Did he spot you?"

"Not sure. His room's on the second floor. That window at the far end."

Rebus looked. Twelve small square panes of glass. The

window was open an inch at the bottom. "How do you know?"

"I asked the manager."

Rebus nodded: orders from the Farmer—no need to be subtle. "How did the manager take it?"

"He seemed uncomfortable." She took a final bite of pasty.

"Don't want to make Oakes's stay too pleasant, do we?"

"No, sir," Clarke said.

Rebus opened his door. "Just going for a recce." He paused. "What do you do when you need to . . . ?"

She lifted one of the flasks, reached to the floor for a kitchen funnel.

"And what if . . . ?"

"Self-control, sir."

He nodded. "Don't get your flasks mixed up, will you?"

Outside, the air was fresh. Sounds of night traffic at the port, the occasional taxi cruising past the end of the road. Taxis: he had to ask them about Damon and the woman. He walked around the side of the hotel, wandered into the car park. The service exits were locked. Beside them were four rubbish skips, separated by a high wooden fence from the guests' cars. Jim Stevens's Astra was easy to spot. Rebus tore a page from his notebook, scribbled a couple of words, folded the sheet and fixed it beneath a wiper blade. Back at the service doors, Rebus checked they couldn't be opened from outside. He left satisfied that even if Oakes used them to get out of the hotel, he'd have to use the front entrance to get back in.

Always supposing he'd come back. Maybe he'd just scarper: wasn't that what they wanted? No, not exactly: they wanted to be *certain* he'd left Edinburgh. Oakes missing from his hotel wasn't quite the same thing. Rebus went back to Clarke's car, got out his mobile and made a call. Hotel reception answered.

"Good evening," Rebus said. "Could you put me through to Mr. Oakes's room, please?"

"One moment."

Rebus winked at Clarke. He held the mobile between them so she could listen. A buzzing noise repeated three or four times. Then the pick-up.

"Yeah? What is it?" Sounding authentically groggy.

"Tommy, is that you?" Mock-Glaswegian. "We're having a bit of a bevvy in my room. Thought you were coming up."

Silence for a moment. Then: "What room is it again?"

Rebus pondered an answer, cut the connection instead. "At least we know he's there."

"And awake now."

Rebus checked his watch. "Your shift ends at six."

"If Bill Pryde doesn't sleep in."

"I'll give him an alarm call for you." Rebus made to leave the car again.

"Look, sir." Clarke was nodding towards the hotel.

Rebus looked: second-floor window, right at the far end. No light on, but curtains open and a face at the window, peering out. Looking straight at them. Rebus gave Cary Oakes a wave as he made for his own car.

No need to be subtle.

At eight sharp he was in the office, typing up details of Damon Mee, preparing a blitz on charities, hostels and organisations for the homeless. At nine there was a message from the front desk. Someone to see him.

Janice.

"You must be psychic," Rebus told her. "I was just working on Damon. Any news?"

He was guiding her down Rankeillor Street. They'd find a café on Clerk Street. He didn't want to talk to her in the cop-shop. A bundle of motives: didn't want anyone to suspect he was working on a case that wasn't official L&B business; didn't want her seeing some of the stuff in St. Leonard's—photos of MisPers and suspects, cases dealt with without emotion or (often) enthusiasm; and maybe, just maybe, he didn't want to share her. Didn't want the part of her that belonged to his part intruding on his here and now, his workplace.

"No news," she said. "I thought I'd spend the day in Edinburgh, see if I couldn't . . . I don't know. I have to do *something*."

Rebus nodded. There were dark half-moons beneath her eyes. "Are you getting much sleep?" he asked.

"The doctor gave me some pills."

Rebus remembered the way her replies to questions could sometimes only *seem* to be answers.

"Do you take them?" She smiled, glanced at him. "Thought not," he said. It wasn't that Janice would lie to you, but you had to know how to phrase a question to make sure of getting a truthful response.

"We used to have these conversations all the time, didn't we?"

She was right, they did. Rebus wondering if she fancied any of his friends, trying to find ways of asking without seeming jealous. She telling him versions of her life before they'd started dating. Dialogues of the left-unsaid.

He guided her into the café. They took a corner table. The owner, recently arrived, had only unlocked the door because he recognised Rebus.

"I can't cook anything," he warned them.

"Coffee's fine for me," Rebus said. He looked to Janice, who nodded. Their eyes stayed on one another as the café owner walked away.

"Have you ever forgiven me?" she asked.

"For what?"

"I think you know."

He nodded. "But I want to hear you say it."

She smiled. "For knocking you out."

He looked around. "Keep your voice down, someone might hear."

She laughed, the way he'd meant her to. "You were always the joker, Johnny."

"Was I?" He tried to remember.

"Did you keep in touch with Mitch?"

He puffed out his cheeks. "Now there's a name from the past."

"The two of you were like this." She twisted two fingers together.

"I'm not sure that's legal these days."

She smiled, looked down at the tabletop. "Always the joker." There were spots of red high on her cheeks. Yes, he'd been able to make her blush back then too.

"What about you?" he asked.

"What about me?"

"You and Barney."

"Nobody calls him Barney these days." She sat back in her chair. "We were just friendly, stayed that way for a few years. One night he asked me out. Started seeing one another." She shrugged. "That's how it works sometimes. No Cupid's arrow, no fireworks. Just . . . nice." She looked up at him, smiled again. "As for the rest of the crew . . . Billy and Sarah are still around. They got married but split up, three kids. Tom's still around, got some industrial injury, hasn't been back to work in years. Cranny—you remember her?" Rebus nodded. "Some moved away . . . a few died."

"Died?"

"Car smashes, accidents. Wee Paula got cancer. Midge had a heart attack." She paused as their coffees arrived, topped with a froth of milk.

"I've got some biscuits . . . ?" the café owner suggested. They shook their heads.

Janice blew on the coffee, sipped. "Then there was Alec . . ."

"Never turned up?" Alec Chisholm, who'd gone to play football. Alec, who'd never reached the park.

"His mum's still alive, you know. She's in her eighties. Still wonders what happened to him."

Rebus said nothing. He could see what she was thinking: *maybe that's my future too*. He leaned across the table, squeezed her hand. It was warm, pliant.

"You can help me," he said.

She looked in her bag for a handkerchief. "How?"

Rebus took out the list he'd printed that morning. "Hostels and charities," he told her. She blew her nose and examined the list. "They all need contacting. I was going to do it myself, but we'd save time if you made a start."

"OK."

"Then there are the taxis. That means putting the word out, visiting each rank and letting them know what we need. Damon and the blonde, across the road from The Dome."

Janice was nodding. "I can do that," she said.

"I'll give you a list of where to find them."

The café owner was standing by the counter, smoking a breakfast cigarette and opening the morning's paper. Rebus caught a headline, knew he had to buy the paper for himself. Janice was checking in her purse.

"I'll get these," Rebus told her.

"I'll need coins for the phone," she said.

Rebus thought for a moment. "Why not use my flat as a base? It's not that much more comfortable than most phone boxes, but at least you can sit down, have a cup of coffee . . ." He held out a bunch of keys to her. She looked at him.

"Are you sure?"

"Sure I'm sure." He wrote his address on a page of his notebook, added his work and mobile phone numbers, tore the page out and handed it to her. She studied it.

"No secrets there you don't want anyone to see?"

He smiled. "I don't use the place much, to be honest. There's a couple of local shops if you need—"

"So where do you usually stay?"

He cleared his throat. "With a friend."

Her turn to smile. "That's nice."

Why had he said "friend" rather than "lover"? Rebus wondered if they sounded as awkward as he felt: kids again, language the clumsiest form of communication.

"I'll give you a lift," he said.

"Remember the list of taxi ranks," she told him. "And an A to Z if you've got one."

Rebus went to pay. The owner rang it up on the till. His paper was open at a court headline: previous day's testimony from the Shiellion case. KIDS' BOSS BRANDED MONSTER. There was a photograph of Harold Ince being led to a police van by the court guard Rebus had shared a smoke with. Ince looked tired, ordinary.

That was the trouble with monsters. They could be every bit as ordinary as anyone else.

Jim Stevens couldn't hide the relief on his face when he walked into the dining room. He made for one of the window tables. A couple of guests nodded and smiled at him as he passed them. He got the idea they'd been in the bar last night.

"Morning, Jim," Cary Oakes said, wiping egg yolk from the corners of his mouth. He gazed out of the window.

"Grey old day, just the way I remember." He picked up the last triangle of fried bread and started working on it. "Cops are still out there."

Jim Stevens looked out of the window. An unmarked car, but unmistakable. A man in the driver's seat, chewing on a roll.

"How long do you think they'll keep it up?" Oakes asked.

Stevens looked at him. "I tried phoning your room."

"When?"

"Fifteen, twenty minutes ago."

"I was down here, partner, soaking up the *ambience*."

Stevens looked around for a waiter.

"You help yourself to fruit juices and cereals," Oakes explained, nodding towards a self-serve area. "Then they take your order for the hot breakfast."

Stevens looked at Oakes's greasy plate. "After last night, I think I'll stick to orange juice and coffee."

Oakes laughed. "That's why I don't drink." Last night he'd been on pints of orange and lemonade: Stevens remembered now. "Besides," Oakes said, leaning over the table towards the reporter, "when I drink I do crazy things."

"Save it for the tape machine, Cary."

When the waiter came, Oakes asked if he could have another cooked breakfast. "Just the bits I missed out on last time." He studied the menu. "Uh, how about fried liver, some onions and maybe some fried haggis and black pudding." He patted his stomach, smiling at Stevens. "Just today, you understand. The fitness regime recommences tomorrow."

When the food arrived, Stevens, who'd been knocking back orange juice and trying to steel himself for toast, took one look at the plate and made his excuses. He drifted outside, lit a cigarette. There was a cold breeze blowing in from the docks. Just through the dock gates, he could see the Scot FM building. Turning his head, he saw the cop in the car watching him. He didn't recognise the face. Through the dining room window, Oakes was tucking in with exaggerated relish, teasing the detective. Smiling, Stevens walked around to the car park, examined the executive motors: Beamers, Rover 600s, an Audi. Noticed something on the windscreen of his own car. At first he took it for a piece of rubbish, gusted there. Then thought maybe it was a flyer for a carpet sale or antique show. But when he unfolded it, he knew who it was from. Two words:

DROP HIM.

Stevens tucked the note in his pocket, headed back to the hotel. Oakes had finished breakfast and was sitting on one of the sofas in reception, flicking through a newspaper: one of the broadsheets.

"I'm hurt," he said. "After that scrum at the airport . . ."

"Try the tabloids," Stevens said, sitting down opposite him. "Plenty of coverage there. I think my favourite is 'Killer Cary Comes Home.' "

"Well, isn't that nice?" Oakes tossed the paper aside. "So when do we get down to work?"

"Let's say fifteen minutes in your room?"

"Fine by me. Before that, though, I've another favour to ask."

"What?"

"Someone I want to find. His name's Archibald."

"Plenty of those around."

"That's his surname. First name, Alan."

"Alan Archibald? Should I know him?"

Oakes shook his head.

"Care to tell me who he is?"

"He was a policeman—maybe still is. Got to be getting on a bit, though."

"And?"

Oakes shrugged. "For now, that's *all* you need. If you're a good boy, I'll maybe tell you the story."

"For what we're paying you, we want *all* the stories."

"Just find him, Jim. You'll make me happy."

Stevens studied his charge, wondering just who was pulling the strings. He knew it should be him. But all the same . . .

"I can make a couple of calls," he conceded.

"That's my boy." Oakes got to his feet. "Fifteen minutes in my room. Bring all the papers with you. I like being the day's news."

And with that he set off towards the stairs.

14

It was Jamie's job to fetch milk, papers and breakfast rolls from the shop. He'd turned it into an art, skimming cash by lying about the prices. His mum complained, knew they could be found cheaper elsewhere, but "elsewhere" wasn't walking distance for Jamie. She didn't like him straying too far. That was fine: whenever he wanted to wander the city, he had Billy Boy to say he'd been round at his house.

Jamie thought he was pretty smart.

He stopped outside the shop for a cigarette. He didn't buy them there—it was against the law and the Paki owner wouldn't let him. Instead, he had a deal with an older kid at school, who supplied packets of twenty in exchange for scud mags. Jamie got the mags from under Cal's bed. There were so many of them. Cal never seemed to notice. Even in freezing weather, Jamie liked his smoke outside the shop. Early-rise kids on their way to school would stare at him. Friends would sometimes join him. He got noticed.

A neighbour once told his mum, and she'd tried whacking him, but he was super-fast and dodged beneath her arm, spinning out of the door, laughing at her curses. One time she'd really gone for him had been when the school had sent the letter home. He'd been skiving, whole weeks at a time. His mum had belted him purple and sent him crying to his room, face red with shame at his own tears.

He'd probably go to school some time today. Cal was good at forging letters. He'd been doing it so long, the school thought *his* signature was their mum's, and when she'd signed some note about going on a school trip, the headmaster had quizzed Jamie about its origins. He'd even picked up the phone to talk to Jamie's mum, which had made Jamie smile: they didn't have a telephone in the flat.

About two dozen ashtrays, most of them from holidays or nicked from pubs, but no telephone. Cal had a mobile, and that's what they used in emergencies—when Cal was in a mood to let them.

That was the problem with Cal. He could be great . . . and then he could lose the rag. Boom: like a bottle exploding against a wall. Or he'd get all quiet and lock himself in his room and refuse to write notes to the school. Jamie would go out and get him something, maybe nick it from a shop: peace offerings for some wrong he hadn't done. On good days, Cal would rub knuckles hard against Jamie's head, tell him he was the peacemaker: Jamie like the sound of that. Cal would say he was the United Nations, sustaining an uneasy truce. He got stuff like that from the papers: "United Nations"; "uneasy truce." Jamie asked him once: "If nations are supposed to be united, how come we want to split away?"

"How do you mean, pal?"

"Split from England."

Cal had folded the newspaper on his lap, flicked ash into an ashtray on the arm of his chair. "Because we don't like the English."

"How no?"

"Because they're *English*." An edge to Cal's voice, telling Jamie to back off.

"We've got cousins in England, haven't we? We don't hate them, do we, Cal?"

"Look . . ."

"And fighting the Germans, we fought with the English, didn't we?"

"Look, Jamie, we want to run our own country, OK? That's all it is. Scotland's a country, isn't it?" He'd waited for Jamie's nod. "Then who should be in charge of it? London or Edinburgh?"

"Edinburgh, Cal."

"Right then." Picking up the paper: discussion adjourned.

Jamie had a lot more questions, but never seemed to get answers. His mum was useless: "Don't talk to me about politics," she'd say. Or "Don't talk to me about religion." Or anything, really. As if she'd done all the hard thinking in her life, found satisfactory answers, and wasn't about to start over again for *his* benefit.

"That's why you've got teachers," she'd say.

Which was fair enough, but at school Jamie had a rep to maintain. He was *Cal Brady's brother*. He couldn't go asking the teachers questions. They'd begin to wonder about him. Cal had told him a long time ago: "With school, Jamie, it's definitely 'us' and 'them,' know what I mean? A battlefield, pal, take no prisoners, understood?"

And Jamie had nodded, understanding nothing.

As he stood at the shop, tapping the toe of one shoe against a rubbish bin, along came Billy Horman. Jamie straightened a bit.

"All right, Billy Boy?"

"No' bad. Got a fag?"

Jamie handed over one of his precious cigarettes.

"See the football last night?"

Jamie shook his head, sniffed. "Not bothered," he said.

"Hearts, ya beauties." The way Billy looked at him as he said this, seeking approval or something, Jamie knew Billy had heard it from someone else, maybe his mum's boyfriend, and wasn't sure about it.

"They're doing OK," Jamie conceded as Billy mimed a blazing shot at goal.

"You going home?" Billy asked.

Jamie tapped the paper and rolls, held under one of his arms.

"Wait a minute. I'll come with you." Billy marched into the shop, came out again with milk and a carton of marge. "Mum went spare this morning. Her new man got in from the pub and had about ten slices of toast." He tossed the marge and caught it. "Finished the tub."

Jamie didn't say anything. He was thinking about fathers, how it was funny neither Billy nor he had one. Jamie wondered where his was, which story about him to believe.

"Who was that you were with yesterday?" he asked as they began walking.

"Eh?"

"Bottom of St. Mary's Street. An uncle or somebody?"

"Aye, that's it. My Uncle Bill."

But Billy Boy was lying. His ears always went red when he lied . . .

Back at the flat, Jamie took the paper into Cal's bedroom.

"About fucking time, wee man." Cal lying in bed, portable telly on. The room smelled stale. Jamie sometimes tried to hold his breath. Cal had a mug of tea on the floor beside his ashtray.

"Switch the channel, will you?"

The TV was on a chest of drawers at the bottom of the bed. It didn't have a remote. Cal had just brought it home one night, said he won it in a bet at the pub. There was a little square beside the panel of buttons. It said "Remote Sensor." So Jamie knew there should be a remote with it. He had to jump over a pile of Cal's clothes on the floor to get to the TV. Pressed the button for Channel 4. You got some dolls on the breakfast show—Cal had taught him the word: dolls.

Jamie leapt back over the clothes and fled the room, letting out a huge exhalation in the hallway. Twenty-five seconds: not even near his record for breath-holding. His mum was buttering rolls at the kitchen table. She handed him one. He got himself a mug of milk and sat down. He'd told his mum that because of cutbacks, his school didn't start till half past nine. Either she'd believed him, or hadn't been up to arguing. She looked tired, his mum, looked like she needed a treat. But he knew looks could deceive: she could go from tired to mental in two seconds flat. He'd seen her do it with one of the old hoors from upstairs who'd come to complain about the noise. Pure mental. Same thing with the old guy who'd complained of the ball landing in his garden.

"Next time I'll put a garden fork through it, so help me."

"Do that," Jamie's mum had said, "and I'll take your fucking fork and stick it through your balls." Right up close to him, growing huge as he seemed to shrink.

Jamie had a lot of respect for his mum. Last time she'd clipped him, it had been because he'd tried calling her Van. Cal called her Van, but that was all right because he was grown up, same as she was. Jamie couldn't wait to grow up.

With a mug of tea in her hand, his mum went through her morning ritual: trying to remember where she'd put her cigarettes.

"Maybe Cal's got them," Jamie suggested.

"Finish what's in your mouth before you speak." She yelled towards Cal's room, got a yelled denial back. In the living room, she pulled cushions off the sofa and chair, kicked the pile of car and music magazines sitting on the floor. Found half a packet on top of the hi-fi. The top of the flip-pack was missing. Cal used them for his "special roll-ups." His mum pulled out a cigarette, but most of it was missing too. She sighed heavily, stuck it in her mouth anyway and lit it with the lighter she found inside the packet.

She didn't have any pockets, so put the cigarettes on the arm of her chair. She was wearing silver-grey shell-suit bottoms with a purple zip-up jogging top. The top was old, the lettering on its back—SPORTING NATION—cracked and peeling. Jamie wondered if Sporting Nation meant Scotland.

Roll and milk finished, he slid off his chair. He had plans for today: Princes Street maybe, or a bus out to The Gyle. On his own, or with anyone he could round up. Problem with The Gyle was, it was in the middle of nowhere. There was a games arcade on Lothian Road, he liked it there, but there were other regulars who were better than him at the games, and even if he didn't want to play against them, they'd stand and watch him on his machine, then tell him what mistakes he was making and say they could do better with their wrists in plaster.

Just as well, he knew he should tell them, *because the way you're going, your whole body's going to end up in plaster*. But he never did: most of them were bigger than him. And they didn't know Cal, so he was no use as a threat. Which was why Jamie didn't go in there so much any more . . .

Cal's bedroom door flew open and he stalked into the kitchen. He had his jeans on, but had forgotten to zip them up or buckle his belt. No shoes or socks, no T-shirt. He had nicks and bruises on his chest and arms. You could see the muscles moving beneath his skin. He flung the paper on to the table and slapped a hand down on it.

"Look at this," he hissed, face pink with anger. "Just take a look at this."

Jamie looked: double-page story. SEX OFFENDER WITH PLAYGROUND VIEW. There were photos. One showed a block of flats, an arrow pointing to one of the storeys. The other showed a patch of tarmac and a couple of kids playing.

"That's here," he said, amazed. He'd never seen Greenfield in the papers before, never seen photos of the place. His mum came over.

"What is it?" she asked.

"Fucking pervert living right under our noses," Cal spat. "Nobody told us." He stabbed the paper. "Says so right here. Nobody bothered to tell us."

Van studied the story. "There's no picture of him."

"No, but they as good as point at the bastard's door."

She remembered something. "Cops came round the other day. I thought they were looking for you."

"What did they want?"

"Just the one of them. Asked if I knew somebody called . . ." She squeezed shut her eyes. "Darren something-or-other."

"Darren Rough," Jamie said. Cal stared at him.

"You know him?"

Jamie didn't know what answer would please Cal. He shrugged. "Seen him around the place."

"How do you know his name?" Eyes burning into him.

"He . . . I don't know."

"He what?" Cal was facing him now, fists bunched. "Which flat's he in?" Jamie started to tell him, but Cal snatched the neck of his shirt. "Better still, show me."

But as they walked along the landing to Darren Rough's flat, they saw that others had the same idea. A group of seven or eight residents stood outside Rough's door. Most of them had the morning paper with them, rolled up and brandished like a weapon. Cal was disappointed they weren't the first.

"Is he no' in?"

"No' answering anyway."

Cal kicked at the door, saw from the looks around him

that they were impressed. Stood back and shouldered the door, kicked it again. Two locks: Yale and mortice. No way to see inside: letterbox was blocked up; a sheet pinned across the window. Everyone was talking about it.

"Wake up, ya bastardin' pervert!" Cal Brady shouted at the window. "Come and meet your fan club!" There were smiles around him.

"Maybe he works shifts," someone offered. Cal couldn't think of a smart remark to make back. He thumped on the window instead, then went back to kicking the door. A few more residents arrived, but more began to drift away. Soon there were just a couple of kids, plus Cal and Jamie.

"Jamie," Cal said, "go get me a spray can. Try under my bed."

Jamie already knew there were a couple of cans under there. "Blue or black?" he asked, before he realised what he'd done.

But Cal didn't notice. He was busy staring at the door. "Doesn't matter," he said. Jamie went off to fetch the can. His mum was outside, arms folded, talking with a couple of women from the landing. Jamie trotted past them.

"Well?" his mum said.

"Nobody's in."

She turned back to her friends. "Could be anywhere. Scum like that, there's no telling."

"What we need's a petition," one of the women said.

"Aye, get the council to rehouse him."

"Think they'll listen to us?" Van said. "Direct action, that's what we want. Our problem, we deal with it, never mind what anyone else says."

"People's Republic of Greenfield," another woman offered.

"I'm serious, Michele," Van said, "deadly serious." Behind her, Jamie disappeared into the flat.

15

"Mum and me, we seemed to move around a lot in the early days."

Cary Oakes was in a chair by his bedroom window, feet up on the table in front of him. Jim Stevens sat on a corner of the bed, holding the tape recorder at arm's length.

"Places? Dates?"

Oakes looked at him. "I don't remember the names of towns, people we stayed with. When you're a kid, that sort of thing doesn't matter, does it? I had my own life, my own little fantasy world. I'd be a soldier or a fighter pilot. Scotland would be full of aliens, and I'd be out to get them, a vigilante sort of scenario." He gazed out of the window. "Because we moved so much, I never really made any friends. Not close friends." He saw that Stevens was about to interrupt. "Again, I can't give any names. I remember coming to Edinburgh, though." He paused, stretched to rub his thumb across the toe of one shoe, removing a trace of dirt. "Yes, Edinburgh sticks in my mind. We stayed with family. My aunt and her husband. Don't remember which part of town they lived in. There was a park nearby. I went there a lot. Maybe we could get a picture of me there."

Stevens nodded. "If you can remember where it is."

Oakes smiled. "Any park would do, wouldn't it? We'd just pretend. That's what I did in that park. It was my universe. *Mine*. I could do whatever the hell I liked there. I was God."

"So what did you do?" Stevens was thinking: this is easy, fluid. Oakes was either a born storyteller or else . . . or else he'd been rehearsing. But something had jarred, something about family: *my aunt and her husband*. A strange way of putting it.

"What did I do? I played games, same as every other kid. I had an imagination, I'll tell you that. When you're a kid, nobody minds if you run around shooting up the world, know what I'm saying? In your head, you can kill whole populations. I'll bet there isn't one damned person on this planet hasn't thought about murdering someone at *some* time. I'll bet you have."

"I'll show you my collection of voodoo dolls."

Oakes smiled. "My mum, she did her best for me." He paused. "I'm sure of that."

"What happened to her?"

"She died, man." His eyes bored into the reporter's. "But then everybody dies."

"You played these games by yourself?"

Oakes shook his head. "The other kids got to know me. I joined a gang, rose through the ranks."

"See much action?"

Oakes shrugged. "There were a few fights. Mostly we just played football and glowered at strangers. Offed a few of the neighbourhood cats too."

"How?"

"Sprayed them with lighter fluid, torched them." Oakes's eyes fixed on Stevens. "Typical start to your basic serial killer. I read about it in jail. Loner who torches animals."

"But you weren't alone, you were with your gang."

Oakes smiled again. "But I was the one with the lighter, Jim. And that made all the difference."

When they took a break, Stevens returned to his own room. Two sachets of coffee into a cup of boiling water. He'd been wakened at four that morning by the telephone. His boss had worked a miracle, and Stevens found himself speaking to a Seattle journalist who'd followed the Oakes case all the way along. The journalist, Matt Lewin, confirmed that Oakes had attended regular Sunday services in the Walla Walla penitentiary.

"A lot of them do, doesn't mean they've seen the light."

Now Stevens lay back on the bed and sipped his coffee. He wanted to track down Oakes's teenage gang. It would be good background, another insight into Cary Oakes. If they ran the story, maybe someone from the gang would read it and come forward. Then Stevens could interview them for the book. He'd asked Matt Lewin if any American publishers would be interested.

"Not when he's not one of ours. We like home-grown product. Besides, Jim, serial killers went out of fashion a while back."

Stevens was hoping for a fashion revival. The book deal would be his gold watch, a little retirement gift to himself. He knew he should do some research, try to check the stories Oakes had been telling. But he felt so tired, and his boss had told him: get the story first, confirm it later. He finished his coffee and reached for a cigarette. Swung his legs off the bed.

Showtime.

Janice Mee took a break, ate at the restaurant at the top of John Lewis's. From one window, the view was of Calton Hill. They'd climbed it with Damon one day, back when he was seven or eight. She had photos of the trip in one of her albums: Calton Hill, the Castle, Museum of Childhood . . . There were dozens of albums. She kept them in the bottom of the wardrobe. She'd taken them out recently, brought the whole lot downstairs so she could go through them, reviving memories of holiday camps and days at the seaside, birthday parties and sports days. From one of the restaurant's other windows, she had a good view of the Fife coastline. She couldn't see as far inland as her home town. There were times in the course of her life when she'd contemplated a move: south to Edinburgh, north to Dundee. But there was something comfortable about the place where you were born, where your family and friends were. Her parents and grandparents had been born in Fife, the history of the place inextricably linked to her own. Her mother had been a little girl at the time of the General Strike, but remembered them putting up barricades around Lochgelly. Her father had clung to a lamp-post to watch Johnny Thomson's funeral. The way a family stretched back in time could be measured. But that sense of history misled you into thinking the future would be the same. As Janice was finding out, the thread of continuity could be snapped at any point along the way.

She ate the roll, filled with prawn mayonnaise, without any pleasure or sense of taste. She knew she'd drunk her coffee only because the cup was empty. One pale prawn sat on the rim of the plate, where it had fallen from the roll. She left it where it was and got up from the table.

Outside the St. James' Centre she crossed Princes Street and headed for Waverley Station. A line of taxi cabs snaked from the underground concourse back up on to Waverley Bridge. The drivers sat behind their wheels, some reading or eating or listening to their radios. Others staring into space or sharing news with fellow drivers. She started at the back of the queue and worked her way forwards. John Rebus had given her some names. One of them was Henry Wilson. The drivers all seemed to know him, called him "The Lumberjack." They put out a call to him. Meantime, she showed them her pictures of Damon and explained that he'd been picked up on George Street.

"Anyone with him, love?" one driver asked.

"A woman . . . short blonde hair."

The driver shook his head. "I've a good memory for blondes," he said, handing back the flyer.

The problem was, a couple of trains had just arrived—London and Glasgow. The taxis were moving faster than she could, heading down to where their passengers waited. She looked back up the slope. More taxis were joining the back of the queue. She couldn't tell who she'd talked to and who was new. Engines were starting, fumes getting into her lungs. Cars sounding their horns as they moved past her, heading down into the station, wondering what she was doing on the roadway when there was a pavement the other side. Day-trippers looked at her, too. They knew she'd never get a taxi here, knew the system: you queued at the rank.

Her mouth felt sour and gritty. The coffee had been strong: she could feel her heart pounding. And then another car sounded its horn.

"All right, all right," she said, passing down the line to the next taxi, which was already moving off. The car-horn sounded again: right behind her. She turned on it, glowering, saw it was another black cab, window open. Nobody

in the back, just the driver, leaning towards her. Short black
hair, long black beard, green tartan shirt.

"Lumberjack?" she said.

He nodded. "That's what they call me."

She smiled. "John Rebus gave me your name." Cars
were held up behind him. One flashed its lights.

"You better get in," he said. "Before they have my licence off me for obstruction."

Janice Mee got in.

The taxi went down into the station, and took the exit
ramp back up, then turned right and crossed the traffic,
settling at the back of the queue of cabs. Henry Wilson
pulled on the handbrake and turned in his seat.

"So what does the Inspector want this time?"

And Janice Mee told him.

It had to be serious: instead of summoning him, the Farmer
had come looking for Rebus, who was out in the car park
having a cigarette and thinking about Janice Playfair aged
fifteen . . .

"Is it the surveillance?" Rebus asked, thinking maybe
something had happened.

"No, it bloody well isn't." The Farmer stuck his hands
in his pockets: he meant business.

"What have I done this time?"

"The press have got hold of Darren Rough. One paper
printed the story this morning, the rest are busy catching
up. My secretary's fielded so many calls, she doesn't know
if she's in St. Leonard's or St. Pancras."

"How did they get the story?" Rebus asked, ditching his
cigarette.

The Farmer narrowed his eyes. "That's what Rough's
social worker wants to know. He's ready to make a formal
complaint."

Rebus rubbed at his nose. "He thinks I did it?"

"John, I know bloody well you did it."

"With respect, sir—"

"John, just shut up, will you? The reporter you spoke
to, first thing he did when you'd put the phone down was
hit 1471. He got the number you were calling from."

"And?"

"And it was The Maltings." Public house: almost directly across the street from St. Leonard's. "But better than that, our intrepid reporter asked the punter who answered about the person who'd last used the phone. Want me to read you the description?"

"Male, white, middle-aged?" Rebus guessed. "Could be a thousand blokes."

"Could be. Which hasn't stopped Rough's social worker thinking it's you."

Rebus looked out towards Salisbury Crags. "I'm glad somebody shopped him." He paused. "If that was what it was going to take."

"Take to do what? To run him out of town? To get a mob baying for his blood? John, I'd hate to see what you'd do to Ince and Marshall."

Ince and Marshall: the Shiellion accused.

"You wouldn't have to watch," Rebus said. He squared up to his boss. "What do you want me to do?"

"Steer clear of Rough, that's number one. Stay on the Oakes surveillance, at least that way you'll keep out of trouble for six hours at a stretch. And give Jane Barbour a bell." He handed Rebus a slip of paper with a phone number on it.

"Barbour? What does she want?"

"No idea. Probably something to do with Shiellion House."

Rebus stared at the phone number. "Probably," he said.

The Farmer left him to it, and instead of going back into the station, Rebus walked down the lane towards the main road, checked for traffic and walked briskly across. Stepped into The Maltings. It was quiet most daytimes. When he'd made the call, there'd only been one other drinker in the place. A minute after opening time, the same man was alone at the bar with a half-pint and a whisky in front of him.

"Alexander," Rebus said, "a word with you, please." He pulled the drinker by his arm towards the gents' toilets: didn't want the barmaid listening in.

"Christ, man, what is it?" The drinker's name was Alexander Jessup. He didn't like Alex or Alec or Sandy or Eck: it had to be Alexander. He'd run his own business at one time: a printer's. Did headed paper, account books, raffle tickets and the like. Sold it on and was quietly drinking the proceeds away. As a man about town, he heard things, but never gave Rebus much that proved useful. He did like to talk though; he'd talk to anyone who'd listen.

"Any reporters been after you?" Rebus asked.

Jessup looked at him with rheumy eyes, like those of an old dog. He shook his head. His face was a mess of puffiness and burst capillaries.

"You spoke to one on the phone," Rebus reminded him.

"Was he a reporter?" Jessup looked stung. "He never said."

"You gave him my description."

"I might've done." He thought about it, nodded, then held up a finger. "But no names, you know me, John. I never gave him your name."

Rebus kept his voice low. "If anyone comes looking, keep the description as vague as you can, understood? You never saw the guy on the phone before, he's not a regular." He waited for the message to sink in. Jessup gave him an enormous wink.

"Message received."

"And understood?"

"And understood," Jessup confirmed. "I didn't get you into trouble, did I?" Dying to know. "You know I'd never do something like that."

Rebus patted his shoulder. "I know, Alexander. Just remember who brings you your breakfast when they've put you in the cells for the night."

"Right enough, John." Jessup gave an "OK" sign with his hand. "Sorry if I got you into any bother."

Rebus pulled open the door. "Here, let me buy you one, eh?"

"Only if you'll take one back."

"It's tempting," Rebus said, as they headed for the bar. "I'd be lying if I said that it wasn't."

"Have you been drinking?" Janice Mee asked.

Rebus didn't reply straight away; he was too busy looking around his living room. Janice laughed.

"Sorry," she said. "Couldn't help myself."

The place had been tidied: newspapers and magazines now took up space on the bottom bookshelf. Books which had been scattered across the floor were on the second and third shelves up. Mugs and plates had vanished into the kitchen, takeaway wrappers and beer cans deposited in the bin. Even the ashtray had been cleaned. Rebus picked it up.

"I think that's the first time I've been able to make out what it says."

It was lifted from a pub, advertising some new beer which hadn't made the grade.

Janice smiled. "It's something I do when I'm nervous."

"You should be nervous round here more often."

She gave him a punch.

"Careful," he said, "last time you tried that, I was out cold for ten minutes."

"I bought teabags and milk while I was out," she told him, making for the kitchen. "Do you want a cup?"

"Please." He followed the trail of her perfume. He hadn't brought Patience here in over a year; had never entertained many women here. "So how did it go?"

"I liked The Lumberjack."

"But was he any help?"

She made herself busy with the kettle. "Oh, you know . . ."

"Did you get round all the cab ranks?"

"Your friend said I didn't need to. He'd do it for me."

"Which left you feeling useless again?"

She tried to smile. "I thought . . . I thought coming here I could . . ." She bowed her head, voice dropping to a whisper. "I'd have been better off staying at home."

"Janice." He turned her so she was facing him. "You're doing your best." Her height, her softness and slenderness. They stood as close together now as they had done when they'd danced at the school leaving party, their last night as a couple. Formal dances: waltzes and military two-steps and the Gay Gordons. She wanting each dance to last; he wanting to take her round the back of the school, to their secret place—the same secret place everyone else used.

"You're doing your best," he repeated.

"But it's not helping. Know what I found myself thinking today? I thought: I'll kill him for putting me through this." Bitter twist of a smile. "Then I thought: what if he's already dead?"

"He's not dead," Rebus said. "Trust me on this. He's not."

They took the tea through to the living room, sat at the dining table.

"What time are you headed back?" he asked.

"I thought six. There's a train around then."

"I'll drive you."

She shook her head. "Even a country girl like me knows what the traffic's like that time of day. I'd be quicker on the train."

Which was true. "I'll run you to the station then." What else had he to do before his shift started, other than try to doze for a while?

She placed her hands around the mug. "Why a policeman, Johnny?"

"Why?" He tried to form an answer she'd accept. "I'd been in the army, didn't like it, didn't know what I wanted to do."

"It's not exactly the kind of job you drift into."

"For some of us it is. See, I really got into it."

"And you're good at what you do?"

He shrugged. "I get results."

"Is that not the same thing?"

"Not exactly. Keeping your head down and your nose clean, being good at the office politics ... I fall down there." He shifted in his chair. "You always said you were going to be a teacher."

"I was a teacher ... for a while."

Rebus refrained from saying that his ex-wife had been a teacher too.

"Then you married Brian?" he asked instead.

"The two aren't connected." She looked down into her tea, seemed relieved when the phone rang. Rebus picked it up.

"Evening, Mr. Rebus."

"Henry," Rebus said for Janice's benefit, "got anything for us?"

"Might have. Two fares, picked up on George Street.

Driver remembered the blonde. Distinctive face, he said. Kind of hard. Cold eyes. He thought maybe she was a pro."

"Where did he take them?" Rebus looking at Janice, who had stood up, still clutching the mug.

"Down to Leith, dropped them by The Shore."

Leith: where the city's working girls plied their trade. The Shore: where Cary Oakes's hotel was.

"Did he see where they went?"

"The lad wasn't a big tipper. My mate got straight back on the road. Someone had tried flagging him down on Bernard Street. Not many places they could have been going. That time of night, the pubs would be on last orders if they weren't already shut. There are flats down there, though."

Rebus agreed. Flats . . . and the hotel.

"Unless they were going to that boat," Wilson said.

"What boat?"

"The one that's tied up down there." Yes: Rebus had seen it, looked like a semi-permanent mooring. "They use it for parties," Wilson was saying. "Not that I've ever been to one . . ."

He dropped Janice off at Waverley's concourse. They'd arranged to meet the next afternoon, go look at the boat.

"May be something or nothing," Rebus had felt obliged to warn her.

"I'll settle for that," she'd said.

As she made to leave the car, she hesitated, then leaned towards him and planted a kiss on his cheek.

"What, no tongues?" he said, smiling. She made to thump his arm, thought better of it. "Say hello to Brian from me."

"I will. If he's not out with his pals." Something in her tone made Rebus want to pursue the subject, but she was out of the car, closing the door. She waved, blew him a kiss, turned and walked towards her platform with the look of a woman who knows she's being watched. Rebus realised he had one hand on his door handle.

"Forget it," he told himself. Instead, he picked up his mobile, told Patience's machine that he was on night shift and was headed back to his own flat for a bit of kip.

But first, a pit-stop at the Oxford Bar: whisky with

plenty of water. Just the one: responsible car-driver. He caught up on the gossip, adding little to the conversation. George Klasser chastised him for a lapse of faith.

"You're becoming an irregular regular, John."

"I always was, Doc."

Further along the bar, a rugby argument was developing, drawing other drinkers in. Everyone had an opinion, everyone but Rebus himself. He stared at a print on the wall: portrait of Robert Burns. There was another on the far wall: Burns meeting a young Walter Scott. It looked like a fairly awkward affair, the artist working with benefit of hindsight. It was as if Burns knew the child before him was destined to outsell him, knew the runt would get a knighthood, build Abbotsford and cosy up to the King.

It was a great thing, hindsight.

He looked into his glass and saw the leavers' dance. Saw a gangly kid called Johnny leading his girlfriend out of the hall, out the school doors and down the steps. Making like it was a game, but tugging her hard by both hands. Both of them pretending it was all right, because that was part of the whole ritual. And back in the hall, Johnny's pal Mitch—best friends; always sticking up for one another—not realising he was being stalked by three boys who'd become his enemies. Boys who knew this might be their last chance for revenge. Revenge for what? They probably didn't know themselves. Maybe for some ugly feeling that life had already short-changed them; that people like Mitch were going to succeed where they'd taste only failure.

Three against one.

While Johnny Rebus played out another fate entirely.

Rebus finished his drink, drove home. Sank into his chair, a double malt in his fist. Listened to Tommy Smith, *The Sound of Love*. Pondered whether or not you really could *hear* love.

Fell asleep in the orange sodium glow of the streetlights.

As close to being at peace as he got.

It had taken them a while to find a church with an unlocked door.

"No one has any trust these days," Cary Oakes had said, "not even God."

They'd walked through Leith and up the Walk to Pilrig.
It was a Catholic church, nobody around but them. Cool
and dark inside. There were plenty of windows, but the
church was surrounded on three sides by tenement buildings. Time was, as Stevens recalled, you weren't allowed
to build anything higher than a church. Oakes was sitting
in a pew near the front, head bowed. He didn't look exactly
peaceful or contemplative: his neck and shoulders were
tensed, his breathing fast and shallow. Stevens wasn't comfortable. The door might not have been locked, but he felt
like a trespasser. A Catholic church, too: he didn't think
he'd been in one of those his whole life. Didn't look much
different from the Presbyterian model: no smell of incense.
Confession boxes, but he'd seen those before in films. One
of them, the curtain was open. He glanced in, trying not to
think that it looked like a Photo-Me booth. He tried to take
soundless steps; didn't want a priest appearing, having to
explain what they were doing there.

Oakes's request: "I'd like to go to church."

Stevens: "Can't it wait till Sunday?"

But Oakes's eyes had told him it was no joking matter.
So they'd headed off on foot, the surveillance car following
at a crawl, drawing attention to itself and to them.

"They want to play it that way," Oakes had said, "that's
fine by me."

Ten, fifteen minutes passed. Stevens wondered if maybe
Oakes had nodded off. He walked down the aisle, stopped
beside him. Oakes looked up.

"A couple more minutes, Jim." Oakes motioned with his
head. "Take a break, if you like."

Stevens didn't need telling twice. Stepped outside for a
cigarette. Cop car parked at the end of the street, driver
watching him. He'd just got one lit when the thought struck
him: you're a reporter on a story. You should be in there,
trying to find an angle, running phrases through your head.
Oakes in church: it could open one of the book chapters.
So he nipped the cigarette, slipped it back into the packet.
Pushed open the door and went inside.

There was no sign of Oakes in any of the pews. Sound
of running water. Stevens peered into the gloom, eyes adjusting slowly. A shape over by the confessional. Oakes

standing there, looking over his shoulder towards Stevens, body arched as he urinated through the curtain. Oakes grinned, winked. Finished his business and zipped himself up. He was walking back up the aisle, back to where Stevens stood, face failing to disguise his shock. Oakes pointed up towards the ceiling.

"Got to remind Him just who's boss, Jim." He moved past Stevens and out into daylight. Stevens stood there a moment longer. Pissing into the confessional: a message to God, or to the reporter himself? Stevens turned and left the church, wondering how the hell his world had come to this.

A young DS called Roy Frazer was the fourth member of the surveillance team. He'd arrived at St. Leonard's the previous month, a rare recruit from F Division, based in Livingston. Edinburgh city cops knew the Livingston operation as "F Troop." They'd had a few digs at Frazer, but he'd been able—or at least willing—to take them. The Farmer had chosen Frazer for the team. The Farmer thought Frazer was a bit special.

Rebus sat beside him in the Rover, listening to his report.

"Only real highlight," Frazer was saying, "that restaurant next to the pub back there, they took pity on me, brought me out a meal."

"You're kidding." Rebus looked back towards the pub in question. Just past closing time, and drinkers were taking their grudging leave.

"Carrot soup, then some chicken thing in puff pastry. Wasn't bad at all."

Rebus looked down at the carrier bag he'd brought with him: flask of strong coffee; two filled rolls (corned beef and beetroot); chocolate and crisps; some tapes and his Walkman; an evening paper and a couple of books.

"Brought it out on a tray, came back half an hour later with some coffee and mints."

"You want to be careful, son," Rebus cautioned. "No such thing as a free dinner. Once you start taking bribes . . ." He shook his head ruefully. "I mean, it might have been the done thing in Livingston, but you're not in the sticks now."

Frazer saw at last that he was joking, produced a grin which was two parts relief to one part humour. He was strong-looking, played rugby for the police team. Cropped black hair, square-jawed. When he'd arrived at St. Leonard's, he'd sported a thick moustache, but had shaved it off for some reason. The skin beneath still looked pink and delicate. Rebus knew he came from farming stock—somewhere between West Calder and the A70. His father still farmed there. Something he had in common with The Farmer, whose family had worked the land around Stonehaven. Another thing the two men shared: regular churchgoing. Rebus, too, went to churches, but seldom on a Sunday. He liked them empty except for his thoughts.

"Have you got the log?" Rebus asked. Frazer produced the A4-sized notebook. Bill Pryde had taken over from Siobhan Clarke at 6 a.m., recorded that Oakes and Stevens had stayed in the hotel until eleven. Up till then, they hadn't come downstairs—he'd checked with the front desk. Morning coffee for two had been ordered for Oakes's room. Pryde's interpretation: they were working. A cab had arrived at eleven, and both men had come out of the hotel. Stevens had handed a large envelope to the cabbie, who'd driven off again. Pryde's guess: tape of first interview, heading for the newspaper office.

With the taxi gone, Stevens and Oakes had walked into Leith Docks, Pryde following on foot. They looked like they were killing time, taking a breather. Then it was back to the hotel. Siobhan Clarke took over at noon: Rebus had persuaded her to change shifts with him. Not that it had been difficult: "I like my own bed at night," she'd admitted.

The afternoon had gone much as the morning: the two men ensconced in the hotel; taxi taking delivery of an envelope; the two men taking a break. Except this time they'd headed into town, stopping at a church in Pilrig. Rebus looked at Frazer.

"A church?"

Frazer just shrugged. After the church, they'd headed to the top of the Walk and John Lewis's, where they shopped for clothes for Oakes. New shoes, too. Stevens put everything on his plastic. Then they'd hit a couple of pubs: the Café Royal, Guildford Arms. Clarke had stayed outside: "Didn't know whether to go in or not. It's not as if they didn't know I was there."

Back to the hotel, Oakes giving her a wave as she pulled up outside.

Relieved by Frazer at 6 p.m. The two men, Stevens and Oakes, had walked to one of the new restaurants built facing the Scottish Office. One wall was all glass, affording them a view of Frazer as he kicked his heels outside. Apart from his own surprise dinner—not mentioned in the notebook—that was about it.

"Would I be right in thinking this is a complete waste of time?" Frazer stated when Rebus had finished reading.

"Depends on your parameters," Rebus said. He'd lifted the line from a training course at Tulliallan.

"Well, they're obviously here for the duration, aren't they?"

"We just want Oakes to know."

"Yes, but surely the time to let him know is when he's left to his own devices. Once he's found himself a place to live, and all the media stuff's finished."

Frazer had a point. Rebus conceded as much with a slow nod of his head. "Don't tell me," he said, "tell the Chief Super."

"That's just what I did." Rebus looked at him, waiting for more. "He turned up about nine o'clock, wanting to know how things were going."

"And you told him?"

Frazer nodded; Rebus laughed.

"What did he say?"

"He said to give it a few more days."

"You know they think Oakes might kill again?"

"Only person within range at the moment is that reporter. Anything happened to him, I'd be heartbroken."

Rebus burst out laughing again. "Know something, Roy? You're going to be all right."

"The power of prayer, sir."

Rebus had been in the car by himself for an hour, cold seeping inside his three pairs of socks, when he saw some-one push open the door of the hotel and step outside. The hotel bar was still open, wouldn't close till the last guest had had enough. Stevens wore his tie loose around his neck, top two shirt buttons open. He was blowing cigarette smoke up into the sky, shuffling his feet to keep his balance. Been there, done that, Rebus thought. Eventually, Stevens fo-cused on the police car, seemed to find it amusing. Chuck-led to himself, bending forward at the waist, shaking his head slowly. Came walking towards the car. Rebus got out, waited for him.

"So we meet at last, Moriarty," Stevens said. Rebus folded his arms, leaned against the car.

"How's the baby-sitting?"

Stevens puffed out his cheeks. "To tell you the truth, I'm having trouble getting a handle on him."

"How do you mean?"

"All that time behind bars—no pun intended—you'd think he might want to celebrate."

"I'm guessing he doesn't drink."

"Your guess is correct. Says drink contaminates his mind, makes him feel dangerous." A humourless laugh.

"How much longer?" Rebus could smell the whisky on Stevens' breath. Give him a minute or two, he'd place the brand.

"Couple more days. It's good stuff, wait till you read it."

"Know what the Yanks told us? They said he'll kill again."

"Really?"

"Has he said anything?"

Stevens nodded. "Gave me a list of his next victims. Nice tie-in with the story." Stevens grinned lopsidedly, saw the look on Rebus's face. "Sorry, sorry. Not in very good taste. I've got a publisher interested, did I tell you? Coming back to me tomorrow or the day after with an offer."

"How can you do it?" Rebus asked quietly.

Stevens got his balance back. "Do what?"

"Do what you do."

"Sounds like a Motown line." He sniffed, coughed. "It's an interesting story, Rebus. That's what he means to me: a story. What does he mean to you?" He awaited a response, didn't get one, wagged a finger. "That note you left me: 'Drop him.' Think I'd suddenly see the light, hand him over to somebody else, some other paper? No chance, pal. This isn't the Damascus Road."

"I'd noticed."

"And my boy's not the only ex-offender in the news, is he? I see someone outed a paedophile. Word is, it was a cop." He tutted, wagged his finger again. "Any comment to make, Inspector?"

"Go fuck yourself, Stevens."

"Ah, now there's another thing. Guy's been in the nick fourteen years, and here we are in Leith, Edinburgh's knocking-shop, and he's not interested. Can you credit that?"

"Maybe he's got other things on his mind."

"Wouldn't bother me if he preferred chickens, just so long as he gets me a book deal." He rubbed his hands together. "Look at us, eh? You out here, me in that big hotel. Makes you think."

"Go to bed, Stevens. You need all the beauty sleep you can get."

Stevens turned away, remembered something and turned back. "OK for a wee photo-shoot tomorrow night? Photographer's coming anyway, and I thought it'd make a nice sidebar: cop who'll never sleep while killer's at large."

Rebus said nothing, waited till the reporter had turned away again. "What did he want in the church?" The question stopped Stevens cold. Rebus repeated it. Stevens half-turned towards him, shook his head slowly, then walked back across the road. There was something tired in the walk now, something Rebus couldn't interpret. He reached into the car for his cigarettes, lit one. Closed the driver's door and walked fifty yards to the end of the road, then across the bridge to the other side of the basin, where a boat was moored. There was a sign telling patrons to respect the neighbours and keep the noise down late at night. But the boat wasn't being used tonight, no private party or celebration. Nearby, they were building more "New York loft-style apartments" for young professionals, part of Leith's revival. Rebus crossed back to the pub, but it was closed now. The bar staff would probably be inside, enjoying a drink as they replayed the evening's highlights. Rebus walked back to the car.

An hour later, a taxi pulled up outside the hotel. His first thought: another tape for the newspaper. But someone was in the taxi. They paid the driver, got out. Rebus checked his watch. Two fifteen. One of the guests who'd been out on the town. He took a nip from his quarter-bottle, slipped the headphones back on to his ears. String Driven Thing: "Another Night in This Old City."

That's all it ever was . . .

Forty minutes later, the man from the taxi exited the hotel. He waved back to the night porter. Window down, Rebus heard him say, "Good night." He stood outside, glanced at his watch, looked up and down the street. Looking for a taxi, Rebus thought. Who would be visiting a hotel this time of night? *Who* would he be visiting?

The man's gaze fell on the police car. Rebus wound the window down further, flicked ash on to the roadway. The man was making his way towards the car. Rebus opened his door, got out.

"Inspector Rebus?" The man held out his hand. Rebus gave him a once-over. Late fifties, well-dressed. Didn't look the type to pull a stunt, but you could never be sure. The man read his thoughts, smiled.

"I don't blame you. Middle of the night, stranger wants to make friends, already knows your name . . ."

Rebus narrowed his eyes. "We've met before, haven't we?"

"A while back. You've got a good memory. My name's Archibald. Alan Archibald."

Rebus nodded, finally shook Archibald's hand. "You had a posting at Great London Road."

"For a couple of months, yes. Before I retired, I was based at Fettes, pushing paper around a desk."

Alan Archibald: tall, cropped salt-and-pepper hair. A face full of strong features, a body resisting the ageing process.

"I heard you'd retired."

Archibald shrugged. "Twenty years in, I thought it was time." His look said: what about you? Rebus's mouth twitched.

"It's warmer in the car. I can't offer you a lift, but I could probably . . ."

"I know," Alan Archibald was saying. "Cary Oakes told me."

"He what?"

Archibald nodded towards the car. "I'll take you up on your offer, though. I'm not used to night shifts these days."

So they got into the car, Archibald tucking his black woollen overcoat around him. Rebus ran the engine, stuck the heating on, offered Archibald a cigarette.

"I don't, thanks all the same. But don't let me stop you."

"You'd need heavy artillery to stop me." Rebus said, lighting another for himself. "So what's the story with Oakes?"

Archibald touched his fingers to the dashboard. "He called me, told me where he was." He looked at Rebus. "He knows all about you."

Rebus shrugged. "That's the point."

"Yes, he knows that too. But he knew *you* were on the late shift."

"Not difficult. He can see me from his bedroom window." Rebus pointed towards it. "Or maybe his minder told him."

"The journalist? I didn't meet him."

"Probably in bed."

"Yes, I had to ring up to Oakes's bedroom. He wasn't sleeping, though, told me it's jet-lag."

"How did he get your number?"

"It's unlisted." Archibald paused. "I'm guessing the journalist pulled a few strings."

Rebus inhaled smoke, let it pour down his nostrils. "So what's the story?"

"My guess is, Oakes wants to play some game."

Rebus looked at his passenger. "What sort of game?"

"The sort that gets me out of bed at one in the morning. That's when he phoned, said we had to meet now or never at all."

"What about?"

"The murder."

Rebus frowned. "Murder singular?"

"Not one of the ones he committed in the States. This happened right here in Edinburgh. More specifically, out at Hillend."

Hillend: at the northern tip of the Pentland Hills—hence the name. Known locally for its artificial ski-slope. From the bypass, you could see the lights at night. Suddenly, Rebus remembered the case. An outcrop of rocks, a woman's body. Young woman: student at a teacher-training college. Rebus had helped with the initial search. The search had taken him from Hillend to Swanston Cottages, an extraordinary cluster of homes, seemingly untouched by modernity. All at once he'd wanted to buy a place there, but it had been too isolated for his wife—and outwith their means anyway.

"This was fifteen years ago?" Rebus said.

Archibald shook his head. He'd slipped his hands into his pockets, was staring at the windscreen. "Seventeen years," he told Rebus. "Seventeen years this month. Her name was Deirdre Campbell."

"Were you on the case?"

Archibald shook his head again. "Wasn't possible at the time." He took a deep breath. "Never found the killer."

"She was strangled?"

"Beaten about the head, then strangled."

Rebus remembered Oakes's *modus operandi*. Again, it was as if Archibald could read his mind.

"Similar," he said.

"Was Oakes here at the time?"

"It was just before he left for the States."

Rebus gave a low whistle. "He's owned up?"

Archibald shifted in his seat. "Not exactly. When he was arrested in the States, I followed his trial, noticed similarities. I went out there to interview him."

"And?"

"And he played his little games. Hints, smiles and half-truths and stories. He led me a merry little dance."

"I thought you weren't on the case?"

"I wasn't. Not officially."

"I don't get it."

Archibald examined his fingertips. "All these years he's been inside, we've played his games. Because I know I can wear him down. He doesn't know how persistent I can be."

"And now he phones you in the middle of the night?"

"And feeds me more stories." A half-smile. "But he doesn't seem to realise, the gameboard has changed. He's in Scotland now. *My* rules." A pause. "I've asked him to come out to Hillend with me."

Rebus stared at Archibald. "The man's a killer. Psych reports say he'll do it again."

"He kills the weak. I'm not weak."

Rebus wondered about that. "Maybe he's switched games," he said.

Archibald shook his head. He looked like a man obsessed. Jesus, Rebus could write the book on that one: cases which grabbed you and wouldn't let go; unsolveds which stayed with you all the long sleepless nights. You sifted through them time and again, examining the grains of sand, seeking anomalies . . .

"I still don't get it," Rebus said. "You weren't on the original case . . . how come you're . . ."

Then he remembered. It should have come to him sooner. The story had gone around at the time, had been passed between the searchers on the hillside.

"Oh shit," Rebus said. "She was your niece . . ."

17

It had been easy, finding an unoccupied room in the hotel. Simplicity itself to pick the door lock. So it was that Cary Oakes sat in darkness at the window, a window unwatched by Detective Inspector John Rebus. He had to smile: the watcher had become the watched, without realising it.

There was an *A-Z* on his lap. He'd told Stevens he needed it so he could reacquaint himself with his city. Earlier, Stevens had let slip that Rebus used to live in Arden Street, and maybe still did. Arden Street in Marchmont. Page 15, square 6G. Alan Archibald lived in Corstorphine, or had done when he'd written to Oakes in prison. All those letters, he'd never once let the prisoner know his phone number. It had taken Oakes less than a day to discover it. Strength in knowledge; always surprise your opponent— that's how games were played.

Oakes watched the two men talking in the car. He felt a certain pride, almost like running a dating agency. He'd brought the two of them together; he felt sure they'd get along. They sat there for an hour, even sharing a hot drink from a flask. Then a patrol car turned up—Rebus must have radioed for it. Wasn't that thoughtful: a free ride home for the retired detective. Archibald had aged well, maybe out of spite. Oakes knew *he* didn't look as fresh as the day he'd been incarcerated. Flesh sagged from his face, and there was a dead look to his eyes, despite the regular vitamins and exercise regime.

He slipped a hand into his pocket, felt a fold of bank-notes there. He'd been drinking at the bar, spinning a line to some business types, Stevens his quiet partner. Stevens had given up eventually, left them to it. Oakes had learned many trades during his time inside. Lock-picking was one;

pocket-picking another. He'd left the credit cards alone:
that was the sort of thing that could be traced, get him in
trouble. He let cash alone be his guide. He knew Stevens
wanted him to be dependent on the paper, knew that was
why Stevens was holding back payment. Well, for now he
needed Stevens, but that would change. And meantime, he
had work to do.

And the money would be his means.

He left the room and made his way down the stairs to
the first-floor landing. At the end was a window which
opened on to a line of lock-up garages. Eight-foot drop to
the roof of the nearest garage. He crouched on the window-
ledge, waited for the taxi to come. Heard its engine as it
rolled towards the hotel. He'd given the name and room
number of one of his drinking companions. He listened for
the moment when the taxi would pass Rebus's car, the moment when the detective would be least likely to hear anything, then dropped through the darkness on to the roof,
sliding down and on to solid tarmac. Not even pausing for
breath or to dust himself off, immediately jogging towards
the wall which would take him into the lane, the lane which
would take him away from the hotel.

With any luck, he'd pick up a taxi. There'd be one coming along in a minute, its driver disgruntled and seeking a
fare . . .

Four in the morning, Darren Rough reckoned it would be
safe. Everyone would be asleep. He counted himself lucky:
out late the night before this, picking up an early edition
of his paper on the way home, seeing his story twisted
there. He'd been in the flat, Radio Two playing quietly so
as not to disturb the neighbours: they had kids, kids needed
sleep, everyone knew that. Radio barely audible, tea and
toast, sitting by the gas fire.

Then coming upon those pages. Reading just the first
couple of paragraphs, enough to make him screw the paper
up, pace the floor, start hyperventilating. He breathed into
a paper bag until the attack passed. Felt weak, crawling
into the bathroom on hands and knees. Splashed water from
the toilet on to his face and neck. Hauled himself up on to
the pan, sat there for a while, head bowed under its massive

weight. When he got back the use of his legs, he uncrumpled the paper, spread it out on the floor. Read the story through.

So it starts again, he thought to himself.

Knew he had to get out before morning. Spent the rest of the night walking the streets, bones cold and aching with tiredness. A café first thing for breakfast. His social worker didn't get into the office till nine, said he'd talk to a solicitor, see what grounds they had for a complaint. Said everything would be fine.

"We just have to ride it out."

Easy words from a warm office; warm family probably waiting at home too. The car his social worker drove was an estate; kids' football boots in the back. Family man, doing his nine-to-five.

The rest of that day, Darren kept his distance from Greenfield. Walked as far as the Botanics, pretended to be interested in the plants. Kept warm in the hothouses: did about a dozen circuits. Back into town, Princes Street Gardens: he managed an hour's kip on a bench, until a policeman told him to move on. His plight was remarked on by a group of travellers. They offered him cigarettes and strong lager. He stayed with them for an hour, but didn't like them: too scruffy; not his kind of people at all.

Art galleries; churches: there was a lot that was free in Edinburgh. By evening, he reckoned he could write his own guidebook. Ate in a fast-food restaurant, taking as long as he could over the meal. Then a pub on Broughton Street. Waiting for a day to pass . . . it made you realise why people needed goals, needed work. He liked a structure to his day. Liked not to feel hunted.

After closing time, he'd met some more travellers, listened to more of their stories. Then had made his way carefully back towards Greenfield, turning away three times before finally confronting his own fear and overcoming it. Goal achieved.

He crept up the stairwell, expecting at every turn to find a waiting face, a knife-blade. Nothing. Just shadows. Along the landing, past closed doors, sleeping windows. His key sounded like a wood-saw as he slipped it into the lock. Then he noticed his hands were sticky. Stood back, noticed

for the first time that his door was smeared with mud . . .
No, not mud: excrement. He could smell it on the back of
his hand, his knuckles, fingers. And beneath the shit, something in black paint, some writing. He crouched, wiped his
hands on the concrete flooring, looked up at the message.

MONSTER YOU DIE.

The word DIE was underlined twice, just so he wouldn't
miss it.

This was the park.

It hadn't changed. They'd installed some swings and a
roundabout, but the roundabout was gone, leaving only a
metal stump. The swings were thick rubber tyres. Tarmac
underfoot, playing field off to the left. Trees had been
planted, but looked stunted. His aunt's house . . . you could
see a thin vertical slice of the park from the upstairs bathroom window, peering between two blocks of terraced
housing. The house was still there, in darkness, curtains
closed. He'd shared a bedroom with his mother at the back
of the house, with a view down on to a small neglected
garden, the hut which had become his refuge.

There hadn't been much refuge in the park. The local
gang hung out there, and Cary was never allowed to join.
He was an "incomer," an "outsider," the two terms sounding like opposites. He stayed on the periphery, clinging to
the park railings, until one of them, fed up of cursing him,
would come over to administer a kicking.

And he'd take it. Because it was better than nothing.

The one time he'd stalked a cat, squirting lighter fluid
on it, watching the tail catch fire . . . there'd been no one
there to see him. Police had questioned the gang, but no
one had bothered with Cary Oakes. No one had bothered
to ask "the runt."

He stood by the fence now. Half of it was missing. Middle of the night, no one was about. No cars passed. No one
to see him as his hands worked at the rusted railings, turning them in their sockets.

Then a sound: drunken laughter. Three of them, young,
wandering, not bothered who heard them, whose sleep they
might be disturbing. The teenage Cary had lain awake late
into the night, hearing above his mother's breathing the

sounds of revellers as they headed home, some singing songs about King Billy and the Sash.

Three of them, not worried about waking anyone because *they* ruled this place. They ran in the local gang. *They* were all that mattered.

They were on the other side of the road, but saw Oakes, saw him looking at them.

"What you staring at?"

No answer. They started a conversation among themselves, didn't seem to be stopping.

"One of them paedophiles."

"Always hang out in parks."

"Or maybe a poof like."

"This time of night, just standing there . . ."

Now they'd stopped. Turning back, crossing the road. Three of them.

Excellent odds.

"Hiy, pal, what you up to, eh?"

"Thinking about things," Oakes said quietly, one hand still working at the railing. The three youths looked at each other. They'd spent the night in town, pubbing and clubbing. Booze and some drugs maybe. A mix to up the aggression and confidence. While they were still considering what to do with this stranger, and which one of them should take the lead, Oakes hauled the steel rail up out of the fence and swung it. Caught the first one across the nose, which burst open like a flower in one of those speeded-up film jobs. Hands went to face as the young man screeched and dropped to his knees. As the rail finished one arc, Oakes swung it back again, pendulum-style, caught number two on the ear. Number three swung a kick, but the rail whacked against his shin, then swung upwards to smash into his mouth, breaking teeth. Oakes dropped the weapon. Broken Nose he felled with a kick to the throat. Eardrum he smashed with his fist. Shin and Teeth was limping away, but Oakes walked after him, tripped him, then sent a flurry of kicks to his head.

He stood up straight afterwards, got his breathing under control. Looked around at the houses he remembered so well. No one had moved from bed. No one had seen him in his moment of victory. He wiped the toes of his shoes against the prone figure's shirt, examined them to make sure they hadn't been scuffed in the fight. Walked over to Eardrum and pulled him up by the hair. Another squeal. Oakes put his lips close to the ear that wasn't bleeding.

"This is *my* place now, understood? Anyone fucks with me gets tenfold back."

"We didn't—"

Oakes pressed his thumb hard against the bleeding ear.

"None of you would ever listen." He was looking towards the gap in the terrace, where his aunt's house stood. He threw the youth's head hard against the ground. Patted it once, then turned to walk away.

At twenty past six, Rebus crept into Patience's flat on Oxford Terrace, armed with bread still warm from the oven, fresh milk and newspaper. He made himself a mug of tea and sat in the kitchen, reading the sports pages. At six forty-five he put the radio on, just as the central heating was kicking in. Made a fresh pot of tea, poured out a glass of orange juice for Patience. Sliced the bread and got a tray ready. Took it into the bedroom. Patience peered at him with one eye.

"What's this?"

"Breakfast in bed."

She sat up, arranged the pillows behind her. He laid the tray on her lap.

"Have I forgotten some anniversary?"

He pushed a strand of hair back from her eyes. "I just didn't want you oversleeping."

"Why not?"

"Because as soon as you get up, I'm into that bed and asleep."

He dodged the butter-knife as she swiped it at him. They were both laughing as he started to unbutton his shirt.

Jim Stevens went down to breakfast, expecting to find Cary Oakes halfway through another fry-up. But there was no sign of him. He asked at reception, but nobody had seen him. He called up to Oakes's room: no answer. He went up and banged on the door: ditto.

He was back in reception, ready to demand a duplicate

key, when Cary Oakes came walking in through the hotel door.

"Where the hell have you been?" Stevens asked, feeling almost dizzy with relief.

"No caffeine for you this morning, Jim," Oakes said. "Look at you, you've got the shakes already."

"I asked where you'd been."

"Got up early. Guess I'm still on US time. Walked down by the docks."

"Nobody here saw you leave."

Oakes looked over towards the reception desk, then back to Stevens. "Is there a problem? I'm here now, aren't I?" He opened his arms wide. "Isn't that what counts?" He placed a hand on Stevens' shoulder. "Come on, let's eat." Started leading them towards the dining room. "Have I got some great stuff for you this morning. Your editor's going to offer to blow you when he reads it . . ."

"Just another day at the office then," Stevens said, wiping sweat from his brow.

The businessman who owned the Clipper Night-Ship asked Rebus if he wanted to make him an offer.

"I'm serious. I'd be happy to make a loss, only no one wants to buy her."

He explained that the Clipper had brought him little but headaches. Licensing hassles, complaints from local residents, a council investigation, police visits . . .

"All that so punters can have a piss-up on a boat. I could run a pub with less grief and bigger takings."

"So why don't you?"

"I used to: the Apple Tree in Morningside. But at that time it seemed like every pub had to have a gimmick. God knows what it's all about with Irish pubs: whoever came up with the notion they're any better than Scottish ones? Then there's the other theme pubs—Sherlock Holmes or Jekyll and Hyde, or pubs for Australians and South Africans." He shook his head. "I took one look at the Clipper and thought I was on a winner. Maybe I am, only sometimes it seems like a lot of hard work and sweet FA to show for it."

They were seated in the offices of PJP: Preston-James Promotions. Rebus and Janice Mee were one side of the desk, Billy Preston the other side. Rebus didn't think Preston would appreciate being informed that his namesake used to play keyboards for the Beatles and the Stones.

Billy Preston was in his mid-thirties, immaculately turned out in a grey collarless suit with a metallic shine to it. You got the feeling nothing would stick to him, a regular Teflon Man. His head was shaved, but his long square chin sported a Frank Zappa beard. The offices of PJP took up two rooms on the first floor of a building halfway down Canongate. Below was a shop specializing in antiquarian maps.

"We'd move," Preston had told them, "find somewhere bigger, somewhere with parking, only my partner says to hold fire."

"Why?" Rebus had asked.

"The Parliament." Preston had pointed out of the window. "Two hundred yards that way. Property around here is rocketing. We'd be mugs to sell." He kept playing with his computer mouse, running it over its mat, clicking and double-clicking. It annoyed Rebus, who couldn't see the screen. "Now if they'd chosen Leith instead of Holyrood . . ." Preston rolled his eyes.

"The Clipper wouldn't be causing you this grief?" Rebus guessed.

"Bingo. We'd have bided our time, waited for the MPs and their staff, all on healthy salaries and looking to spend."

"The Clipper's like a private club?" Janice asked.

"Not exactly. She's for hire. If you guarantee me a minimum of forty punters on a week day, sixty at weekends, she's yours gratis, so long as they're drinking at the ship's bar. You pay for the disco, that's it."

"You say a minimum of forty. What's the maximum?"

"Public Safety regulations stipulate seventy-five."

"But forty guarantees you a profit?"

"Just barely," Preston said. "I've got staff, overheads, power . . ."

"So some nights you don't open?"

"It comes in waves, if you'll pardon the pun. We've had good times. Now we're in . . ."

"The doldrums?" Rebus offered.

Preston snorted, reached into a drawer for a ledger book. "So what date is it you're interested in?"

Janice told him. She had both hands cupped around a mug of coffee. It had been tepid and stewed on delivery. Rebus wondered at the qualifications of the tall blonde secretary in the outer office. Paperwork all over the floor, unopened mail . . . If Preston wasn't helpful, Rebus could foresee a phone call to the VAT inspectors.

But in fact he flicked quickly through the ledger. "Found this here when we moved in," he explained. "Thought I'd try to find a use for it." He looked up. "You know, a continuity kind of thing."

His finger found the date, ran along the line.

"Booking that night, private party. Fancy dress." He looked up at Janice. "Sure your son was headed for the Clipper?"

She shrugged. "It's possible."

"Whose party was it?" Rebus asked. He was already out of his chair. Preston, eyes on the ledger, didn't seem to notice Rebus coming around the side of the desk. Rebus's first impulse: look at the screen. A game of patience, sitting waiting for the player to start.

"Amanda Petrie," Preston said. "I was there that night. I remember it. There was a theme . . . pirates or something." He rubbed his chin. "No, it was *Treasure Island*. Some arsehole turned up dressed as a parrot. By the end of the night, he was as sick as one." He looked at Janice. "Can I see those photos again?"

She handed them over: Damon and the blonde from the security cameras; then Damon in a holiday snap.

"They weren't in fancy dress?" Preston asked.

Janice shook her head.

Preston's hands were busy with the ledger and the photos. Rebus, leaning over to examine the ledger, found that his elbow had nudged the mouse up the screen, to where it could close the game. Slight pressure on the mouse, and the screen changed. From a game of patience to the image of a woman on all fours. The photo had been taken from behind, the model turning her head to pout at the photographer. She was wearing white stockings and suspenders, nothing else. The pout was exaggerated. On the floor nearby, an empty champagne bottle. Rebus looked up to the windowsill, where an empty champagne bottle sat.

"But is she any good at shorthand?" Rebus said. Preston saw what he was looking at, switched the screen off. Rebus took the opportunity to lift the heavy ledger from the desk, walk back around to his chair with it.

"So you were there that night?" he asked.

Preston looked flustered. "Keeping an eye on things."

"And you didn't see either Damon or the blonde?"

"I don't remember seeing them."

Rebus glanced up. "Not quite the same thing, is it?"

"Look, Inspector, I'm trying to help . . ."

"Amanda Petrie," Rebus said. Then he saw her address, recognised it. He looked up at Preston again.

"The judge's daughter?"

Preston was nodding. "Ama Petrie."

"Ama Petrie," Rebus echoed. He turned to Janice, saw the question in her eyes. "Edinburgh's original wild child." Back to Preston: "I see you didn't charge her for the boat."

"Ama always brings a good crowd."

"She uses the Clipper a lot?"

"Maybe once a month, usually fancy dress of some kind."

"Does everyone play along?"

Preston saw what he was getting at. "Not all the time."

"So this night, there'd have been guests in normal clothes?"

"Some, yes."

"And they wouldn't have been quite as eye-catching as pirates and parrots?"

"Agreed."

"So it's possible . . . ?"

"It's possible," Preston said with a sigh. "Look, what do you want me to say? Want me to lie and say I saw them there?"

"No, sir."

"Best person to talk to is Ama herself."

"Yes," Rebus said thoughtfully. Thinking of Amanda Petrie, her reputation. Thinking too of her father, Lord Justice Petrie.

"She runs with a pretty fast bunch," Preston said.

Rebus nodded. "Pretty rich too."

"Oh yes."

"The kind of customers you could do with more of."

Preston glared at him. "I wouldn't lie for her. Besides, I'm not sure the old ticker could cope with more than one Ama. Takes an age to clean up after her—more expense for me. And I always seem to get the bulk of complaints after Ama's parties. God knows, they're loud enough when they arrive . . ."

"Anything out of the ordinary that night?"

Preston stared at Rebus. "Inspector, this was *Ama Petrie.* With her, there *is* no 'ordinary.' "

Rebus was copying her phone number from the ledger into his notebook. His eyes ran down other bookings, saw nothing to interest him.

"Well, thanks for your time, Mr. Preston." A final glance towards the computer. "We'll let you get back to your game."

Outside, Janice turned to him. "I get the feeling I missed something back there."

Rebus shrugged, shook his head. The car was parked on a sideroad. Drizzle was being blown into their faces as they walked.

"Ama Petrie," Rebus said, keeping his head bowed. "She doesn't fit my picture of Damon."

"The mystery blonde," Janice stated.

"Friend of hers, you reckon?"

"Let's ask Ms. Petrie."

Rebus tried the number from his cellphone: got an answering machine, and didn't leave a message. Janice looked at him.

"Sometimes it helps not to give too much advance warning," he explained.

"Gives people time to concoct a story?"

He nodded. "Something like that."

She was still looking at him. "You're good at this, aren't you?"

"I used to be." He thought of Alan Archibald: all those years on the force, all that persistence, pursuing Deirdre Campbell's killer . . . It might be a kind of madness, but you had to admire it. It was what Rebus liked about cops. Only thing was, most of them weren't like that at all . . .

"Back to Arden Street," he told Janice. There were calls she still had to make; his flat was still her base.

"What about you?" she asked.

"Things to do, people to see."

She took his hand, squeezed it. "Thanks, John." Then reached up to touch his face. "You look tired." Rebus removed her fingers from his cheek, held them to his mouth, kissed them. Reached down with his free hand to turn the ignition.

The first instalment of Cary Oakes's "Lifer Story" was perfunctory: a couple of paragraphs about his return to Scotland, a couple more about his incarceration, and then early biography. Rebus noted that place-names were kept to a minimum. Oakes's explanation: "I don't want anywhere getting a bad rep just because Cary Oakes once spent a wet winter there."

Thoughtful of him.

Several times, revelations were hinted at—teasers to keep the audience coming back for more—but on the whole it looked like whatever the paper had paid Oakes, they'd got themselves a pig in a poke. Rebus doubted Stevens' editor would be chuffed. There were photos; Oakes at the airport; Oakes on his release from the penitentiary; Oakes as a baby. A small photo too of "reporter James Stevens," alongside his byline. Rebus noted that the photographs took up more space than the actual story. Looked like the reporter would be struggling to get a book's worth.

He folded the paper and looked out of his car window. He was parked at the gateway to a Do-It-Yourself superstore, one of those thinly disguised warehouses which, cheaply and quickly built, seemed to surround the city. There were only four cars in the capacious car park. He didn't know this part of the city well: Brunstane. Just to the west was The Jewel, with its mandatory shopping centre; to the east stood Jewel and Esk College. The message Jane Barbour had left for him at the office had been perfunctory: time and place, telling him to meet her. Rebus lit another cigarette, wondering if she was ever coming. Then a car pulled up alongside him, sounded its horn, and proceeded into the car park. Rebus started his engine and followed.

DI Jane Barbour drove a cream-coloured Ford Mondeo. She was getting out as Rebus parked alongside her. She reached back into the car for an A4 envelope.

"Nice car," Rebus said.

"Thanks for coming."

Rebus closed the car door for her. "What's up? Run out of rawl-plugs?"

"Have you been here before?"

"Can't say that I have."

The wind blew her hair across her face. "Come on," she said, all businesslike, verging on the hostile.

He let himself be led round the side of the building. This was where staff parked their cars and bikes. There were two fire-exit doors, painted a green as drab as the grey of the corrugated walls. The back of the warehouse was a waste and delivery area. Skips spilled out flattened cardboard boxes. A dozen terracotta pots waited to be taken inside and displayed for sale. A low brick wall surrounded the area.

"Is this where you mug me?" Rebus asked, sticking his hands in his pockets.

"Why have you got it in for Darren Rough?"

"What's it to you?"

"Just tell me."

He tried for eye contact, but she wasn't playing. "Because of what he is, what he was doing at the zoo. Because he slandered a fellow officer. Because of . . ."

"Shiellion?" she guessed, her eyes meeting his at last.

"You couldn't touch Ince and Marshall, but suddenly there was *someone* you could replace them with."

"It wasn't like that."

Barbour reached into the envelope, lifted out a black and white photograph. It looked old, showed a three-storey Georgian house. A family posed in front of it, proud of their new motor car. The car was a 1920s model.

"They knocked it down six years ago," Barbour explained. "It was either that or wait for it to disintegrate of its own accord."

"Nice-looking house."

"The patriarch there," Barbour said, tapping the man with one foot on the car's running-board, "he went bankrupt. Mr. Callstone, he was called. Worked in jute or something. The family home had to be sold. Church of Scotland snapped it up. But part of the deal was, they had to retain the family's name. So it stayed Callstone House."

She waited for him to get the name. "Children's home," he said at last, watching her nod.

"Ramsay Marshall worked there, prior to his transfer to Shiellion. He already knew Harold Ince before the move." She handed him more photos.

Rebus looked through them. Callstone House as a children's home, run by the Church of Scotland. Kids grouped outside the same front door, kids photographed inside, seated at long tables, looking hungry. Dormitory beds. Some photos of stern-looking staff. Rebus's mind was working now. "Darren Rough spent some time at Callstone . . ."

"Yes, he did."

"During Ramsay Marshall's reign?"

She nodded again.

"You . . ." he said, suddenly getting it. "It was you that wanted Darren Rough back here."

"That's right."

"For the trial?"

She nodded. "Arranged a flat for him, wanted him amenable. Worked on him for weeks."

"He was abused?" Rebus frowned. "He's not on the list."

"The Procurator Fiscal didn't think he'd make a good witness."

Rebus nodded. "Criminal record. Couldn't risk cross-examination."

"That's right."

Rebus handed back the photographs. He knew where this was leading now. "So what happened to him?"

She busied herself putting the photos back in their envelope. "One night, Marshall went into the dorm. Darren wasn't asleep. Marshall said they were going on a drive. He took Darren to Shiellion."

"Proving that Marshall and Ince were already in cahoots?"

"That's how it looks. The two of them and a third man took turns."

"Christ." Rebus stared at the warehouse, imagining it as a children's home, a supposed refuge. He wondered what Mr. Callstone's ghost would be making of it. "Who was the third man?"

Barbour shrugged. "They had Darren in a blindfold."

"How come?"

"The thing is, John, I made certain promises to him."

"To a convicted paedophile," Rebus felt bound to add.

"Ever heard of environment working on character?"

"The abused becoming the abuser? You think that's a reasonable excuse?"

"I think it's a reason." She was calmer now. "Professor Calder in Glasgow, he has this test. It shows how likely it is someone will reoffend. Darren came out low-risk. All his time inside, he went to the meetings, kept the therapy going."

Rebus wrinkled his nose. "How come he's not registered?" He'd checked: forty-nine sex offenders registered with police in Edinburgh; Rough wasn't among them.

"That was part of the deal. He's terrified they'll get him."

" 'They'?"

"Ince and Marshall. I know they're locked up, but he still has nightmares about them." She waited for him to say something, but Rebus was thoughtful. "What's happening down at Greenfield," she pressed on, "it's not right. Is that your answer: hound them, chase them out? They'll end up *somewhere*, John. We need to deal with them, not hand them to the mob."

Rebus looked down at his shoes. As ever, they needed a clean. "Did Rough tell you?"

She shook her head. "When I saw the paper, I tried to find him. Then I spoke to his social worker. Andy Davies is pretty sure it was you."

"You believe him?"

She shrugged. They were walking back towards their cars. "So what do you want?" Rebus asked. "An apology?"

"I just want you to understand."

"Well, thanks for the therapy. I think I'm ready to be released back into the community."

"I'm glad you can make a joke of it," she said coldly.

He turned to her. "Rough comes back to Edinburgh, and Jim Margolies, the cop he accused of beating him up, decides to take a walk from Salisbury Crags. I think there might be a connection. *That's* why I'm interested in . . ." He saw her face change at Jim Margolies' name. "What?" he asked. She shook her head. Rebus narrowed his eyes. "You spoke to Jim, didn't you? Had the same conversation we've just had?"

She hesitated, then nodded. "I was bringing Darren back to Edinburgh. He was reluctant, wanted to know if DI Margolies was still around."

"So you met with Jim, explained it all?"

"I wanted to know there'd be no . . . conflict, I suppose."

"So Margolies knew Rough was coming back?" Rebus was thoughtful. A mobile phone sounded: hers. She lifted it from her pocket, listened for a moment.

"I'll head straight there," she said, terminating the call. Then to Rebus: "You'd better come too."

He looked at her. "What is it?"

She opened her car door. "Ugly scenes in Greenfield. Looks like Darren's finally gone home."

There was a mob on the landing outside Darren Rough's flat, and the only thing standing between them and it was PC Tom Jackson. Van Brady was at the front of the queue, brandishing a crowbar. Other women crowded behind her. A local TV crew jockeyed for position. A news photographer was snapping a cluster of kids holding up a banner. The banner was homemade: half a bedsheet and black spray-paint. The message read: SAVE US FROM THE BEAST.

"Lovely," Jane Barbour said.

People in the other blocks were watching from their windows, or had opened them to shout encouragement. Rebus saw that paint had been daubed on the door of the flat. Eggs and grease had been smeared on the window. The crowd was baying for blood, and more people seemed to be joining in all the time.

Rebus thought: *What in God's name have I done?*

Tom Jackson glanced in Rebus's direction. His face was red, lines of sweat trickling from both temples. Jane Barbour was pushing her way to the front.

"What's going on here?" she shouted.

"Just bring the bastard out here," Van Brady yelled back. "We'll bloody well lynch him!"

There were cries of agreement—"String him up!"; "Hanging's too good!" Barbour held up both hands, appealing for quiet. She saw that most of the protesters were wearing white sticky labels on their jackets and jumpers. Plain labels on which had been written three letters—GAP.

"What's that?" she asked.

"Greenfield Against Perverts," Van Brady told her.

Rebus saw a kid handing the labels out. Recognised him as Jamie Brady, Van's youngest.

"Since when was it your job to stick up for sick bastards like him?" one woman asked.

"Everybody's got certain rights," Barbour replied.

"Even sickos?"

"Darren Rough served his sentence," Barbour went on. "He's now on a rehab programme." She saw the film crew getting close, whispered something to Tom Jackson. He pushed his way to the camera, held a hand in front of it.

"We want answers," Van Brady was shouting. "Why was he put here? Who knew about it? Why weren't we told?"

"And we want him out!" a male voice called. A newcomer, the sea of bodies parting to let him through. A young man, chiselled face, bare-armed. He stood shoulder to shoulder with Van Brady, ignoring Barbour and directing his comments towards the film crew.

"This is our community here, not the police's." Applause and cheers. "If they can't deal with scum," jerking his thumb back towards Rough's front door, "no problem— we'll deal with it ourselves. We've always been tidy that way in Greenfield."

More cheers; nods of agreement.

One protestor: "You said it, Cal."

Cal Brady, standing next to his mum, who looked on with pride at her son's oratory. Cal Brady: Rebus's first sighting in the flesh.

Well, not exactly: first sighting with the knowledge of who he was. But Rebus had seen Cal Brady before. At Gaitano's nightclub, standing at the bar with the under-manager, Archie Frost. Frost with his pigtail and bad manners; his friend saying nothing, then making himself scarce . . .

"Could we talk about it?" Jane Barbour asked.

"What's there to talk about?" Van Brady asked, folding her arms.

"This whole situation."

Cal Brady ignored her, spoke to his mother. "Is he in there?"

"One of his neighbours heard sounds."

Cal Brady thumped on the window, then had to wipe grease off on his jeans.

"Look," Jane Barbour was saying, "if we could all—"

"Right you are," Cal Brady said. Then, swiping the crowbar from his mother, he swung it at the window, shattering the glass. Grabbed at the soiled sheet, pulling it down from where drawing-pins held it in place. He was halfway over the windowsill and into the room, crowbar still in his hand. Rebus grabbed him by the feet, pulled him back. Glass shards ripped the front from Brady's T-shirt.

"Hey, you!" Van Brady yelled, swinging a punch at Rebus. Cal Brady wriggled free, pulled himself up and got into Rebus's face.

"You want it, do you?" Brandishing the crowbar. Not recognising the policeman.

"I want you to calm down," Rebus said quietly. He turned to Van. "And you, behave yourself."

The crowd had formed around the window, keen for a view of the flat's interior. It looked much like any other: emulsioned walls, sofa, chair, bookcase. No TV, no hi-fi. Books piled on the sofa: photography texts; fiction titles. Newspapers on the floor, empty pot noodle containers, a pizza box. Cans and lemonade bottles on the bookcase. They all looked disappointed with this haul.

"He's polis," Van warned her son.

"Listen to your mother, Cal," Rebus said.

Cal Brady was lowering the crowbar as half a dozen uniforms came out of the stairwell.

First thing they did was disperse the crowd. Van Brady shouted that there'd be a GAP meeting in her flat. The TV crew looked ready to follow. The photographer lingered to take shots of Darren Rough's living room, until uniforms moved him on too. Barbour was on her mobile, calling for someone to come and board up the window.

"And pronto, before someone tips a can of petrol into the place."

Tom Jackson, mopping his brow, came over to where Rebus was standing.

"Christ almighty," he said. "I think I preferred it the way it was before."

When Rebus looked up, Jackson's eyes were on him.

"You're blaming me for this?" Rebus asked.

"Did I say that?" Jackson was still busy with his hand-kerchief. "I don't remember saying that." He turned and walked away.

Rebus looked in through the window. There was a musty smell from the room; hardly surprising, when it got neither fresh air nor sunlight. In for a penny, he thought to himself, lifting a foot on to the sill and pulling himself up.

Broken glass crunched underfoot. No sign of Darren Rough.

This is what you wanted, John. The voice in his head: not his own, but Jack Morton's. *This is what you wanted, and now you've got it . . .*

No, he thought, I didn't want *this*.

But Jack was right to a degree: here it was anyway.

A narrow archway from the living room led into the kitchenette. Rebus felt the electric kettle: a trace of warmth. Looked in the fridge: bread, marge, jam. No milk. In the swing-top bin: empty milk carton, baked bean tins.

Jane Barbour looked in at him. "Anything?"

"Nothing much."

"How about opening the door?"

"Sure." He opened the door to the hall, which was in darkness. Fumbled and found a light switch. Bare forty-watt bulb. He tried opening the door, but the mortice had been locked, no sign of a key anywhere. The letterbox was protected by a block of wood. Not that Rough would get much mail. He went back to the window, let Barbour know she'd have to climb in if she wanted the tour.

"No thanks," she said. "Once was enough." Rebus looked at her. "When I first brought him here."

Rebus nodded, went back into the hall. Just the two bed-rooms, plus bathroom and separate toilet. The first bedroom contained a sleeping bag on the floor. Bedtime reading: the Bible, Good News version. Empty crisp packets. Rebus picked them up. There was a used condom inside one. Cur-tain across the window: Rebus pulled it open, looked down on to a roadway. Second bedroom was empty, not even a lightbulb. Same view as bedroom one. The bathroom needed a clean. There was mould on the walls. The only

towel was a pitifully small and frayed affair, hospital
knock-off or similar. Rebus tried the toilet door. It was
locked. He pushed harder, definitely locked. He tapped on
the wood.

"Rough? You in there?" No way of locking the door
from the outside. "Police," Rebus called. "Look, we're
about to move out, and your front window's smashed. Minute we're gone, the barbarians will be back." Silence. "Fine
and dandy," Rebus said, turning away. "By the way, DI
Barbour's outside. Cheers, Darren."

Rebus was half out of the window when he heard the
noise behind him. Turned and saw Darren Rough standing
in the doorway, face gaunt, eyes flickering in terrified expectation. Looking both haunted and hunted. He held shivering hands up to his chest, like they'd protect him from a
crowbar's blows.

Rebus, immune to most things, felt a sudden stab of pity.
Jane Barbour was out on the walkway, talking to Tom Jackson. She saw Rebus's look, broke off the conversation.

"DI Barbour," he called. "One of yours, I believe."

Jim Stevens tried to put from his mind the sight of Cary
Oakes urinating in the church. Now that he had Oakes, he
needed the story, needed it to be *big*. His boss had complained about the first instalment, called it a "cocktease,"
hoped there was better to come. Stevens had given him his
word.

Oakes had a Bible beside his bed. Yet in the church . . .
Stevens didn't want to think about what it might mean.
There was something about Oakes . . . you looked into his
eyes sometimes and saw it, and if he caught you watching,
he was able to blink it away. But for seconds at a time, his
mind would be somewhere else, somewhere the reporter
didn't want to be.

Just do your job, he kept telling himself. A few more
days, plenty of time to score maximum brownie points with
his boss, show the other rags that he could still cut it, and
put together a proposal for whichever publisher made the
highest bid. He was already in negotiation with two London
houses, but four more had turned the idea down.

"Killers' life stories," one editor had said dismissively, "been there, done that."

To get a bidding war going, he needed more offers. Two interested parties barely qualified as a tiff.

And now this.

Oakes had said he was going to his room for half an hour after lunch. The morning session had been good; not brilliant, but all right. Enough nuggets for the next instalment. But Oakes had complained of a headache, said he wanted to soak in a bath. After half an hour, Stevens had tried his room: no one answering. Reception hadn't seen him. Stevens had thought about going out and asking the surveillance, but that would have been rash. He persuaded the manager that he was worried about his colleague's health. A skeleton key got them into the room. No one there, no one at all. Stevens had apologised to the manager, gone back to his own room. Where he now sat, nipping at his fingernails and wondering where his story had gone.

It had to be bravado.

Caught snivelling and shivering like that by the police . . . The only way for Darren Rough to scrape together any self-esteem was to turn down Barbour's offer of a move. She could offer a police cell until something better came up; could no longer guarantee his safety in Greenfield.

Rough had smiled as she said "no longer," both of them knowing she was playing with words.

"I'm staying," he'd said. "Got to stop running some time, might as well be here and now." And he'd chuckled. "Like some old Western, isn't it? Whatsisface, John Wayne." He made his fingers into a six-shooter, blasted the air. Then he looked around and sniffed, his face losing its animation.

"I don't think it's a good idea," Barbour said.

"I agree," Andy Davies said. It was the first time Rebus had met Darren Rough's social worker. He was tall and thin and bearded, red hair going bald at the dome. Laughter lines around his eyes; small pink mouth.

"There *is* something you could do for me," Rough said.

Davies leaning forward on the sofa, hands pressed between his knees. "What's that, Darren?"

"A dustpan and brush, so I can clear up all this shit."
Kicking at a fragment of glass.

A council workman had arrived to put boards across the
window. There was a dull loathing in his eyes. Someone
down below had pressed a GAP label on to his toolbox.
He used a cordless screwdriver, saw and hammer to fix the
sheets of board to the windowframe, blotting out the last
of the daylight.

When Rough went into the kitchenette, Rebus made to
follow. The social worker stood up.

"It's OK," Rebus told him, "I just want a word." The
two men fixed one another with a stare. Rebus motioned
for Davies to sit back down, but instead Davies walked to
the window. Rebus made his way to the kitchenette's archway. Rough was opening and closing cupboards, not really
sure what he was doing or why. He knew Rebus was there,
but wouldn't look at him.

"Got what you wanted," he muttered.

"What I want are some answers."

"Funny way to go about it."

Rebus slid his hands into his pockets. "How long have
you been back?"

"Three, four weeks."

"I don't suppose you've seen DI Margolies?"

"He's dead. I saw it in the paper."

"Yes, but before then."

Rough slammed shut one of the doors, turned on Rebus,
voice shaking. "Christ, what now? He topped himself,
didn't he?"

"Maybe."

Rough rubbed a hand over his forehead. "You think
I . . . ?"

Andy Davies had come over. "What the hell is it now?"

"He's trying to set me up," Rough blurted out.

"Look, Inspector, I don't know what you think—"

"That's right," Rebus snapped back, "you don't. So why
don't you just keep out of it?"

"I can't handle this," Rough bawled, on the verge of
tears.

Jane Barbour came in from the hall. Rebus read her
look: four parts accusation to one part disappointment. He

remembered what she'd told him about Rough. The man was sniffing now, rubbing the back of his hand beneath his nose. His knees looked like they were about to give way. The workman was nearly finished, leaving the room in twilight. Each screw that went home was like fixing the lid on a coffin.

"Did DI Margolies come to see you?" Rebus persisted.

Rough fixed him with a defiant look. "No."

Rebus stared him out. "I think you're lying."

"So slap me around a bit."

Rebus took a step towards him. The social worker was pleading with Barbour.

"DI Rebus," Barbour warned.

Rebus got right up into Rough's face. Rough had backed all the way into the kitchenette, nowhere else to go.

"Did he come to see you?"

Rough looked away, bit his lip.

"Did he?"

"Yes!" Darren Rough screamed. He bowed his head, pulled a hand through his hair. Incessant hammering of nails into wood. He pushed both palms against his ears. Rebus pulled them away, using as little force as possible. Kept his voice quiet when he spoke.

"What did he want?"

"Shiellion," Rough groaned. "It's always been Shiellion."

Rebus frowned. "DI Rebus . . ." Barbour's voice growing taut, breaking point almost reached.

"What about Shiellion?"

Rough looked to Jane Barbour, his words directed at her. "You told him what happened to me."

"And?" Rebus probed.

"He wanted to know why they'd blindfolded me . . . kept asking who else was there."

"Who else *was* there, Darren?"

Through gritted teeth: "I don't know."

"That what you told him?"

A slow nod. "Could have been anyone."

"Someone they didn't want you to see. Maybe you knew them."

Rough nodded. His voice was calmer. "I've often wondered. Maybe I'd have recognised . . . I don't know, a uniform or something. Priest's dog collar." He looked up. "Maybe even one of your lot."

But Rebus had stopped listening. "Priest?" he said. "Callstone and Shiellion were run by the Church of Scotland. They don't have priests."

But Rough nodded. "We had one."

Barbour, looking intrigued now, frowned. "You had a priest?"

"Visited for a while, then stopped coming. I liked him. Father Leary, his name was." A weak smile. "Told us to call him Conor."

When Rebus headed downstairs, Jane Barbour followed.

"What do you make of it?" she asked.

Rebus shrugged. "Why was Jim Margolies interested in Shiellion?"

Her turn to shrug.

"You told Jim that Rough was abused there?"

She nodded. "You think it has something to do with his suicide?"

"If it *was* suicide."

She blew air from her cheeks. "I'd better talk to the vigilantes," she told him. "Keep the lid on the pressure cooker."

"Tom Jackson's already had a word."

They turned, hearing footsteps behind them on the stairwell: Andy Davies.

"We should move him," Davies said. "It's not safe for him to stay here."

"He doesn't want to leave."

"We could insist."

"If that mob up there couldn't make him leave, what chance have *we* got?"

"You could arrest him."

Rebus burst out laughing. "A couple of days back—"

Davies turned on him. "I'm talking about *protecting* him, not harassment."

"We'll keep someone in the vicinity," Barbour said.

"Tom Jackson's got to go home some time," Rebus commented.

"I'll do guard duty myself if need be." She turned to Davies. "At the moment, I'm not sure what more we can be expected to do."

"And if he'd proved useful to you in court . . . ?"

"I'll ignore that remark, Mr. Davies." Said with ice in her voice, and eyes like weaponry.

"They'll kill him," the social worker said. "And I don't suppose you'll be shedding too many tears."

Barbour looked to Rebus, wondering if he would respond. All Rebus did was shake his head and light up a cigarette.

Rebus had known Father Conor Leary for years. For a time, he'd visited the priest regularly, sharing conversation and cans of Guinness. But when Rebus called Leary's number, another priest answered.

"Conor's in hospital," the young priest explained.

"Since when?"

"A few days ago. We think it was a heart attack. Fairly mild, I think he'll be fine."

So Rebus drove to the hospital. Last time he'd visited Leary, there'd been a fridge full of medicine. The priest had explained that they were for minor ailments.

"How long have you known?" Rebus asked, drawing a chair over to his friend's bedside. Conor Leary looked old and pale, his skin slack.

"No grapes, I notice," Leary said, his voice lacking its usual gruff power. He was sitting up in the bed, surrounded by flowers and get-well cards. On the wall above his head Christ on the cross gazed down.

"I only heard half an hour ago."

"Nice of you to drop by. Can't offer you a drink, I'm afraid."

Rebus smiled. "They say you'll be out in no time."

"Ah, but did they say whether I'd be leaving in a box?"

Rebus managed a smile. Inside, he saw a carpenter, hammering home nails.

"I've a favour to ask," he said. "If you're up to it."

"You want to turn Catholic?" Leary joked.

"Think the confessional could cope?"

"True enough. We'd need a relay team of priests for a

sinner like yourself." He rested his eyes. "So what is it then?"

"Sure you're up to it? I could come back . . ."

"Cut it out, John. You know you're going to ask me anyway."

Rebus leaned forward in his chair. His old friend had flecks of white at the corners of his mouth. "A name you might remember," he said. "Darren Rough."

Leary thought for a moment. "No," he said. "You'll need to give me a clue."

"Callstone House."

"Now that was a while back."

"You spent time there?"

Leary nodded. "One of those multi-faith things. God knows whose idea it was, but it wasn't mine. A minister would visit Catholic homes, and I got to spend time in Callstone." He paused. "Was Darren one of the kids?"

"He was."

"The name doesn't mean anything. I spoke with a lot of them."

"He remembers you. Says you told him to call you Conor."

"I'm sure he's right. Is he in trouble, this Darren?"

"You haven't heard?"

"This place tends to swaddle you. No newspapers, no news."

"He's a paedophile, released into the community. Only the community doesn't want him."

Conor Leary nodded, eyes still closed. "Did he abuse another child?"

"When he was twelve. The victim was six."

"I remember him now. Whey-faced, wouldn't say boo to a goose. The man who ran Callstone . . ."

"Ramsay Marshall."

"He's on trial, isn't he?"

"Yes."

"Did he . . . ? With Darren?"

"Afraid so."

"Ah, dear Lord. Probably going on under my very nose." He opened his eyes. "Maybe the boys . . . maybe they tried to tell me, and I couldn't hear what they were saying."

When the priest's eyes closed again, a tear escaped from one and trickled down his cheek.

Rebus felt bad, which hadn't been his intention in coming here. He squeezed his friend's hand. "We'll talk again, Conor. But you need to rest now."

"John, when do the likes of you and me ever rest?"

Rebus got up, looked down at the figure on the bed. *Priest's dog collar* . . . Maybe, but never Conor Leary. *Even one of your lot* . . . Someone in uniform. Rebus didn't want to think about it, but Jim Margolies had put some thought into it. And soon afterwards, he'd died.

"John," the priest was saying, "remember me in your prayers, eh?"

"Always, Conor."

Hadn't the heart to admit he'd stopped praying long ago.

Back at his flat, he made two mugs of coffee and took them through to the living room. Janice was on the phone to yet another charity, giving them details of Damon. Rebus sat at the dining table. It was a big room, twenty-two feet by fourteen. Bay window (still with the original shutters). High ceiling—maybe eleven feet—with cornicing. Rhona, his ex-wife, had loved the room, even with the original wallpaper from when they'd bought it (purple wavy lines which made Rebus feel seasick whenever he walked past). The wallpaper had gone, as had the brown carpet with matching paintwork.

He thought of Darren Rough's flat. He'd seen worse in his time, of course, but not much worse. Janice put down the receiver and scratched at her hair with a pen, before scribbling a note on a pad of paper. Having scored a line through the charity's phone number, she threw the pen on to the table.

"Coffee," Rebus told her. She took the mug with a smile of thanks.

"You look glum."

"My natural disposition," he said. "Mind if I use the phone?"

She shook her head, so he moved over to the chair, sat down and picked it up. A cordless model; he'd only had it a few months. He called Ama Petrie's number again. A flustered male voice told him to try one of the function rooms at the Marquess Hotel, told him what he'd find there.

"You got a message from Damon's bank manager," Janice told him, when the call was finished.

"Oh yes?"

"Head office approval. If there are any debits from Damon's account, he'll let you know."

"Nothing so far?"

"No."

"Night he vanished, he took out a hundred."

"How far does that go these days?"

"If he's sleeping rough, quite a way."

"We're talking as if he's a runaway."

"Until proved otherwise, that's what he is."

"But why would he . . . ?" She broke off, smiled. "Same old questions. You must be sick of hearing them."

"The only one who can explain is Damon himself. Doing your head in isn't going to help in the interim."

She looked at him. "Right as ever, Johnny."

He shrugged. "Pleased to be of service."

When Janice had finished her coffee, using the last mouthfuls to wash down two paracetamol tablets, he told her they were going out.

"Where?" she asked, looking around for her jacket.

"A beauty contest," Rebus told her. Then he winked. "Brought your swimsuit with you?"

"No."

"Doesn't matter, you wouldn't be eligible anyway: too old."

"Thanks very much."

"You'll see," he said, leading her to the door.

*   *   *

Cary Oakes had a newspaper cutting. It was old and fragile. These days, he didn't look at it much for fear that it would crumble between his fingers. But today was a special occasion, sort of, so in the café he withdrew it from his pocket and read it through. Faded words on grey paper. A report of his trial and verdict, clipped from one British tabloid. And words of hate: "He should have had the electric chair." A simple statement of belief.

But they hadn't given him "Old Sparky," and here he was, back in the same town as the person who'd wanted them to fry him. The anger rising in him again, his hands trembled a little as he folded the cutting along its well-creased lines, slipping it back into his pocket. One day very soon, he'd make someone eat those words. He'd sit there watching them chew, seeing fear and knowledge in their eyes.

And then he'd spark out *their* life.

Leaving the café, he headed uphill, wandering past bungalows, along quiet pavements. Until he reached his destination. Stared at the building.

He was in there. Oakes could almost taste and smell him. Maybe he was alone in his room, resting or asleep. Or reading the newspaper, catching up on the exploits of Cary Oakes.

"Soon," Oakes said quietly to himself, turning away, not wanting to seem conspicuous. "Soon," he repeated, beginning to walk back down the hill towards the town.

The hotel was a 1930s design, next to a roundabout on the western edge of Edinburgh.

"Looks like the Rex, doesn't it?" Janice said.

She had a point. The Rex had been one of Cardenden's three cinemas, perched on a prominent site on the town's main street. As a kid, it had looked to Rebus like one of those state buildings you saw in films about the Iron Curtain: forbidding, all straight lines and right angles. This hotel was an elongated version of the Rex, as though someone had gripped its sides and pulled. The spaces in the car park were taken, so Rebus did what others before him had done:

bumped the Saab up on to the grass verge so that its nose touched the flower beds.

There was a large noticeboard in the middle of the hotel lobby. It told them that Our Little Angels could be found in the Devonshire Suite. Through a double set of doors and along a corridor, hearing a smattering of applause. At the door to the Devonshire Suite was a large woman in a fuchsia two-piece. She sat behind a small table with half a dozen name-tags left lying on it. She asked them their names.

"We're not expected," Rebus told her, taking out his warrant card. Her eyes widened, and stayed that way as Rebus led Janice into the room.

There was a temporary stage at one end, rows of chairs arranged in front of it, pink and blue drapes hanging behind it. Burgeoning vases of flowers sat along the front of the stage and at the ends of each row of chairs. The room was about half-full. Around the walls sat bags and coats. Mothers and daughters were busy at work, primping and preening. Hair was brushed and teased, make-up perfected, a dress straightened or a ribbon retied. The daughters looked around the room, studying the competition nervously—or occasionally with a hint of contempt. None of them could have been older than eight or nine.

"It's like a dog show," Janice whispered to Rebus.

A man at a microphone was reading from a prompt-card, introducing the next contestant.

"Molly comes from Burntisland and attends the local primary school. Her hobbies are pony-trekking and dress-designing. She designed her own dress for today's competition." He looked up at his audience. "How about that, eh, folks? The next Dior. Please welcome Molly."

The mother patted her daughter on the shoulder, and with hesitant tread Molly made her way up the three wooden steps to the stage. The compère crouched down, microphone in hand. Fake tan and hair-weave—or maybe Rebus was just jealous. The judges were in the front row, trying to hide their voting papers from prying eyes.

"And how old are you, Molly?"

"Seven and three-quarters."

"Seven and three-quarters? You're sure it's not seven-eighths?" The compère was smiling, but Molly's face had turned panicky, unsure how to respond. "Not to worry, my darling," the compère went on. "So tell us about that lovely dress you're wearing."

Rebus looked around him. Make-up applied to faces not yet ready for it, so that the girls looked like clowns. Hair spun into grown-up shapes. Mothers fussing, looking fraught and expectant. The mothers wore make-up too, and bright clothes. Some of them had dyed hair. A few had probably been under the knife. Nobody was paying any attention to Rebus and Janice: there were plenty of couples in evidence. But this was a mother-and-daughter show, no doubt about that.

No sign of Ama Petrie, and he'd no idea what she'd be doing here anyway. The voice on the phone hadn't had time to explain. Then he saw two figures he recognised. Hannah Margolies, long blonde hair curling past her shoulders. At her father's funeral she'd worn white lace. Today she was in a pale-blue dress with white tights and glossy red shoes. There were blue bows in her hair, her mouth a glistening crimson button. Her mother, Katherine Margolies, was kneeling in front of her, giving a final pep-talk. Hannah kept her eyes on her mother's, nodding slightly from time to time. Katherine took her hands and squeezed them, then stood up.

Jim Margolies' widow had looked composed at the funeral; she looked more nervous now. She was still wearing black—skirt and jacket over a white silk blouse. She glanced towards the stage where Molly, aided by tape-recorded backing, was singing "Sailor," a song Rebus associated with Petula Clark. Janice, who had found a seat at the end of a row, turned to look up at Rebus with disbelieving eyes. When he looked back at Hannah, he saw Katherine Margolies studying him, as if trying to work out where she'd met him before. Molly was finishing her act, taking the applause with a curtsey. She fairly skipped off the stage, grinning to show wide-spaced teeth.

"Our next contestant," the compère was saying, "is Hannah, who lives right here in Edinburgh . . ."

When Hannah had taken the stage, Rebus wandered across to her mother.

"Hello, Mrs. Margolies."

She put a finger to her lips, her concentration focused on the stage. She pressed her hands together in something like prayer as she watched Hannah's performance, her mouth twisting when the compère asked what seemed to her a tricky question. Finally, the mother reached down into one of her bags and walked to the stage with a recorder, handing it to her daughter with a smile. Unaccompanied, Hannah played a tune which Rebus suspected was classical. He'd heard it on an advert somewhere, couldn't think what the advert was for. Looking towards Janice, Rebus saw that seated next to her were an elderly couple, beaming at the stage. They held hands. In the man's free hand was a walking stick. Rebus recognised them: Jim Margolies' parents.

Finally: applause, and Hannah came back to her mother, who kissed her hair.

"You were perfect," Katherine Margolies said. "Just perfect."

"I played a wrong note."

"I didn't hear it."

Hannah turned to Rebus. "Did you hear it?"

Rebus shook his head. "Sounded fine to me."

Hannah's face relaxed a little. She whispered something to her mother.

"Off you go then."

As Hannah made her way to her grandparents, Katherine Margolies got slowly to her feet, watching her leave.

"We haven't actually met, Mrs. Margolies," Rebus said, "but I was at Jim's funeral. I used to work with him. My name's John Rebus."

She nodded distractedly. "You must think I'm . . ." She sought the words. "I mean, so soon after Jim's accident. But I thought it might take Hannah's mind off things."

"Of course."

"She's been so upset."

"I'm sure." He noticed that she was now studying the judges, the members of the audience, as if looking for some clue as to Hannah's success. "You think Jim fell?" he asked.

She looked at him. "What?"

"People seem to think it was suicide."

"Let them think what they like," she snapped. Then she

turned to him. "You want me to tell Hannah her father took his own life?"

"Of course not . . ."

"He was out walking, got too close to the edge. It was dark . . . a gust of wind maybe."

"Is that what you believe?" She didn't reply. "Did Jim often go out walking at night?"

"What business is it of yours?"

He looked down at the carpet. "Frankly, none."

"Well then."

"It's just that I've been trying to make sense of it."

She looked at him again. "Why?"

"For my own satisfaction." He held her stare. She was beautiful. Black hair pulled back to show the geometry of her face. Thin arched eyebrows, good cheekbones. Hannah's eyes were blue, same as her father's, but Katherine Margolies' were hazel. "And because," Rebus went on, "I thought it might have something to do with Darren Rough."

"Who's he?"

"Didn't Jim mention him?"

She shook her head, sighed with impatience, and turned her gaze towards the judges again. One of them was having a conversation with the compère, who had switched his microphone off.

Rebus thought she was about to say something. When she didn't, he tried another question.

"He didn't take his car, did he?"

"What?"

"It was raining that night."

"When you go for a walk, do you take *your* car?"

"I wouldn't head up Salisbury Crags in a downpour, day or night."

"Well, Jim did, didn't he?"

"Yes, he did . . . and I still don't understand why."

"Well, Mr. Rebus, I've enough to worry about, so if you'll excuse me . . ." She looked over his shoulder and her face brightened.

"Amanda, darling!"

A young woman had breezed through the door, completely ignoring the woman at the desk. She now came forward with arms open, shopping bags swinging from both hands, and embraced Katherine Margolies.

"Sorry I'm late, Katy. Traffic was murder. Tell me I haven't missed her."

"Afraid so."

"Oh, fuck it!" Loud enough for heads to turn. From a distance of four feet, Rebus could smell the cigarettes and booze. The shopping bags: Jenners, Cruise, Body Shop. "How was she? I'll bet she was brilliant..." Looking around. "Where is she anyway?"

Hannah was coming towards them, leading her grandmother by the hand, her grandfather following. Her face lit up at the sight of her new visitor. Amanda crouched down and opened her arms again, and Hannah ran into them.

"Careful with her make-up, Ama," Katherine Margolies warned.

"You look like an angel," Amanda told Hannah. "Not that angels ever wore lipstick."

Katherine Margolies was looking at Rebus. "I'm sorry, I thought we'd finished chatting." A polite dismissal.

"We had," Rebus said. "But it's Miss Petrie I've come here to see."

Amanda Petrie stood up. She was wearing a clinging black mini-dress and black leather jacket with zips to spare. Black high heels and bare legs. She looked Rebus up and down.

"Who do I owe money to?" she asked. Her attention shifted to Dr. and Mrs. Margolies. "Hello, you two." She kissed and embraced both of them. "How are you bearing up?"

"Well, you know, dear," Mrs. Margolies said.

"Hannah was *splendid*," Dr. Margolies said. "We haven't been introduced." He held a hand towards Rebus.

"DI Rebus," Rebus said, watching the old man's face fall. And now Ama Petrie was studying him. He smiled. "I've been taken for worse things than a loan-shark's muscle," he told her. "Maybe we could have a drink at the bar...?" But Amanda Petrie wasn't that stupid. Rebus's thinking: a couple more drinks would loosen her up even more. Amanda, however, had insisted on a pot of tea and several glasses of orange juice. Rebus, Janice and Ama

Petrie: just the three of them, seated in the hotel lounge.
Ama tucking a strand of blonde hair behind one ear. Rebus
looking at her, knowing what Janice was thinking: could
she be the mystery blonde? He didn't think so; her build
was different, not so tall, narrower at the shoulders. He
couldn't see any resemblance to her father . . .

She played with one of the shoulders of her dress. Her
eyes kept scanning the lounge, looking for anyone more
interesting, more glamorous, anyone she should know.

"I want to be back for the judging," she reminded them.
"Hannah's bound to win."

"Why do you say that?"

"She's got breeding. It's not something you can paint
on to a face or run up with a sewing-machine."

"Ever done any sewing yourself?" Rebus asked.

She pulled her attention back to him. "Needlework and
home economics. My school wanted to make little women
of us." She lit a cigarette, tucked her legs under her. Since
she hadn't offered, Rebus made a show of taking out his
own pack, lighting one for himself and offering another to
Janice.

"Sorry," Ama Petrie said, offering them her pack. Rebus
waved his already lit cigarette at her. "How did you find
me?" she asked.

"Phoned your number."

"You probably spoke to Nick." She blew out smoke.
"He's my brother. Always ready to shop his sis to the filth."

Rebus let that one go. "How do you know Hannah?" he
asked.

"We're cousins or something. Twice removed, you
know how it is with families."

Rebus knew Jim Margolies had married someone with
"society connections." He hadn't known Katherine was related to Lord Justice Petrie.

"Not that I'd have anything to do with most of my family," Ama Petrie went on, "but Hannah's just adorable,
don't you think?" She asked the question of Janice, who
nodded.

"I'm not sure about these shows, though," Janice said.

Ama seemed to agree. "Yes, but Katy loves them, and
I think Hannah does too."

"All those mothers . . ." Janice mused. "Pushing their daughters."

"Yes, well . . ." Ama tapped her cigarette against the ashtray. "What is it you want, anyway?"

Rebus explained the situation. As he talked, Ama's attention moved to Janice. At one point, she leaned forward and took her hand, squeezing it.

"You poor dear."

An agony aunt's look on her face; someone who'd been touched by loss only at one remove.

"I did have a party that night," she agreed. "Not that I remember it too well. Bit too much to drink, too many people . . . as per. Word gets around, I do get the occasional gatecrasher. I don't mind, so long as they're interesting, but · the boat's owner goes on about overcrowding. He's always asking me if I know this or that person, did I invite them?" She drained her second glass of orange. "Christ knows why I bother."

"Why do you bother?"

A smirk. "Because it's fun, I suppose. And because while I'm doing it, I'm *somebody*." She thought about this, shrugged the thought aside as if it were the wrong jacket. "You're sure he was coming to *my* party?"

"It's the last time he was seen," Janice confirmed.

Rebus got out the photographs: Damon; Damon and the mystery blonde. As Ama studied them, he asked casually if she'd ever been to Gaitano's.

"Do people call it Guiser's?" He nodded confirmation. "Yes, once or twice. Lots of sweaty job-creation-schemers and dole-fiddlers. Off their faces on happy-hour cocktails, dropping E in the lavs." She smiled. "Not my scene, I'm afraid." She handed back the photos. "Sorry, don't mean a thing to me."

"Not even the woman?"

She wrinkled her nose. "Looks a bit tarty."

"It couldn't be someone you know?"

"Inspector." A throaty laugh. "That's hardly narrowing things down. I know *everybody*."

"But you don't know my son," Janice said grimly.

"No," Ama said, face making a show of contrition. "I'm

very much afraid I don't." She sprang to her feet. "I'd better get back. They'll have started the judging."

Rebus and Janice followed her, stood in the doorway as the prizes were handed out. Hannah was runner-up. As the winner was announced, and went forward to receive a sparkling tiara, everyone clapped and cheered. Everyone except Ama Petrie, who bounced on her toes, booing at the top of her voice as she gave an enthusiastic thumbs-down to the little girl with voluminous black hair, shimmering with glitter.

Katherine Margolies tried to stop Ama making a scene, but to Rebus's eyes she didn't try very hard . . .

"Where the hell have you been?"

Stevens found Cary Oakes in the bar, where he was drinking orange juice and talking to the staff.

"Walking, thinking." Oakes looked at him. "Want to make sure I don't forget anything."

Stevens picked up Oakes's glass. "Then don't forget this: that's *my* juice you're drinking, *my* money paying for it. We've lost a whole session."

"I'll make it up to you." Oakes blew Stevens a kiss, grinned and winked at the barman. Turned back to Stevens. "Look at you, man, all trembling and sweating. A cardiac arrest's having your name paged as we speak. You got to slow down, Jim. Go with the flow."

"My editor wants better copy."

"You could give him Kennedy's assassin, he'd say he wanted better copy. You and I know, Jim, the best stuff has to wait for the book, right? The book's what's going to make us rich."

"If I find a publisher."

"It'll happen, trust me. Now sit down here beside me and let me buy you one. Hell, I don't mind putting my hand in my pocket for a friend." He wrapped an arm around Stevens' shoulders. "You're with Cary now, Jim. You're part of my exclusive circle. Nothing bad's going to happen." Oakes made eye contact, held it. "You can depend on that," he said. "Cross my heart."

*   *   *

"Just drop me off at Haymarket," Janice said. They were back in the car, heading into town.

"You sure? I could drive you—"

She was shaking her head.

"Look, Janice, a trail like this . . . we're bound to run into dead ends. Maybe a lot of them. It's something you'll have to accept."

She shook her head. "I was thinking of all those kids . . . wondering what they'll be like when they grow up. If I'd had a daughter . . ." She shook her head again.

"It was pretty ghastly," Rebus agreed.

She looked at him. "Did you think so? I thought so too, at first. But then I kept looking . . . and they all looked so beautiful." She took out a handkerchief, dabbed at her eyes.

"I think I'd better drive you home," he said.

"No, I don't want that." She paused, put a hand on his arm. "I just mean . . . I don't want to put you . . . Oh Christ, I don't know what I want any more."

"You want Damon back."

"Yes, I want that."

"What else?"

She seemed to consider the question. But in the end she made no answer, just turned to him again and smiled, eyes shiny from crying.

"In a funny way, it's like you've never been away," she told him.

He nodded. "Just the thirty-odd years. What's that between friends?"

They shared the laughter; he touched the back of her hand with his fingers. Parked outside Haymarket station, they sat in silence for a while. Then she opened the door, got out. Smiled one last time and walked away.

Rebus sat for another minute or two, imagining himself running down to the platform, seeking her amongst the crowds . . . Like in a film. Real life was never like that. In films, there was nothing you couldn't do; in the real world . . . in the real world it always got messy.

He went back to Oxford Terrace. Patience wasn't home. They'd passed beyond the stage of leaving notes. He soaked in a bath for half an hour, drifting off to sleep, startling himself awake as his chin dipped beneath the water. He saw the headline: dog-tired cop in bathtime tragedy. One for Jim Stevens to relish.

He lay on the sofa, put some music on. Pete Hammill: "Two or Three Spectres." He knew they were there, his ghosts, settling around him, getting comfortable. More comfortable than he could ever be. Patience, Sammy, Janice . . . A point was coming, between Patience and him. A crisis point maybe, but then they'd been there before. But was there some point coming between Janice and him too? Something very different . . . ? He picked up a book, covered his eyes with it.

Slept.

Ama Petrie wasn't the only one who'd thought the mystery blonde looked "tarty" or a bit like a pro. On his way down to The Shore that evening, Rebus decided on a slight detour. A few of the working girls still plied their trade dockside. Most of the city's prostitutes worked in licensed premises masquerading as saunas, but a few still took risks by walking the streets. Sometimes it was because they were desperate or unemployable—which meant they had an obvious drug habit—while others just liked to do their own thing, despite the dangers. Over in Glasgow, there were fewer saunas and more girls on the street. Result: seven murders in as many years.

Rebus's thinking: street girls worked Leith; the blonde looked "tarty"; the taxi had brought her and Damon to Leith. It was another possibility. Say they hadn't been making for the Clipper. Say they'd been heading for her room.

Her room, or maybe a hotel . . .

There were only three women out this evening on Co-

burg Street, but he knew one of them. Stopped the car and
called her over. She got into the passenger seat, bringing
waves of perfume with her.

"Long time no see," she said. Her name was Fern. Punters assumed it was made up, but Rebus knew from her
records that she'd been born Fern Bogot. He knew too that
she worked the streets because she liked to be her own boss.
In saunas, the proprietor was always taking a cut. She had
her regulars; didn't often go with strangers. Mature gentlemen preferred. She found them less aggressive.

Her mane of red hair was a wig, though it looked natural
enough. Rebus put the car into gear and signalled to move
off. She took her punters to some waste ground in Granton.
If Rebus stuck around, he wasn't a punter, and that made
everyone uneasy. Looking in his rearview, he saw one of
the remaining women peering at the car, then turning to
scrawl something on a wall.

"What's she doing?" he asked.

Fern turned back. "Good old Lesley," she said. "She's
taking your registration. That way, if my body turns up,
there's something for the cops to go on. We call it our
insurance policy. Can't be too careful these days."

Rebus nodded agreement, drove them around the streets,
asking his questions. She studied the photographs in detail,
but was forced to shake her head.

"Nobody like that works down here."

"What about the lad?"

"Sorry." She handed the photos back. Rebus exchanged
them for one of Janice's flyers.

"Just in case," he said.

When he dropped her back at her patch, he got out of
the car and went to look at the wall. Sure enough, there
were rows of car registration numbers scrawled there, most
of them in various shadings of lipstick, some worn away
by the elements. His own was at the bottom of the last
column. He looked up the column, started to frown. At the
top was a number he thought he recognised. Where did he
know it from . . . ?

Suddenly it dawned on him: he'd seen it in a file at Leith
police station. Leith: where Jim Margolies had been stationed. It was mentioned in the file on Jim's suicide.

It was the registration number of his car.

"What is it?" Fern asked.

Rebus tapped the wall. "This one. Belongs to a guy called Jim. A cop."

She frowned in concentration, then shrugged. "Not one of mine," she said. "But it's orange lipstick."

"So?"

"Lesley has a code, her way of telling who's gone in which car."

"And who does orange lipstick mean?"

She was shaking her head. "Not a who so much as a what. Orange means whoever it was, he liked them young . . ."

Roy Frazer wasn't the only one waiting for Rebus down at The Shore. Sitting in the car alongside him was the Farmer.

"Checking up on us, sir?" said Rebus, getting into the back seat. As he got in, Frazer got out, closing the door after him.

"Where the hell have you been?" the Farmer said. "I've spent half the day trying to find you." He handed Rebus the day's surveillance notes. "First entry," he snapped.

Rebus looked. Bill Pryde recorded himself taking over from Rebus at 0600. His next entry: "Cary Oakes entered hotel at 0745."

"Which means," the Farmer said, "he left the hotel at some point, and one of you missed him."

"I saw his bedroom light go off," Rebus said.

"That's right, you did. It's in the log."

"Which means he sneaked out on my shift?" Rebus's fingernails dug into his palms.

"Or during the first hour of Bill Pryde's."

"Either's possible. We're only covering the front of the building. Plenty of access points at the rear."

The Farmer turned to face him. "Access isn't our problem, John. Our problem is that he seems to be able to leave whenever he likes."

"Yes, sir. But a single-officer surveillance . . ."

"Is no bloody use at all if we're not keeping tabs on him."

"I thought the point was to needle him, let him know we can make things difficult."

"And does it look to you like we're succeeding, Inspector?"

"No, sir," Rebus conceded. "Thing is, if he's got a way of getting out undetected, why not go back the same way?"

"Because the doors at the back can only be opened from within."

"That's one possibility, sir."

"And the other?"

"He's playing with us, having a little joke at our expense. He *wants* us to know what he's been doing."

"And what has he been doing, all the time he's been out roaming?"

Rebus shook his head. "I don't know, sir. Why don't we ask him?"

When Frazer and the Farmer had left, Rebus decided to follow his own advice. He found Cary Oakes in the bar: no sign of Jim Stevens. Oakes was sitting on a stool, chatting with the two barmen. There were a few other drinkers scattered round the tables, business types, discussing deals even in their cups.

Oakes waved for Rebus to join him, asked him what he was drinking.

"Whisky," Rebus said. "A malt."

"Take your pick, Mr. Stevens is paying." Oakes allowed himself a little chuckle, chin tucked into his neck. He looked like he'd had a few, but Rebus saw he was drinking cola. "What about something to chase it down?"

Rebus shook his head. "And I pay for my own," he said.

There was plenty of choice behind the bar. Rebus decided on something fiery: Laphroaig, with a splash of water to damp the flames. Cary Oakes tried signing for the drink, but Rebus was insistent.

"Your good health then," Oakes said, lifting his own glass.

"You like playing games, don't you?" Rebus asked.

"Not much else to do in jail. I taught myself chess."

"I don't mean board games."

"What then?" Oakes' eyes were heavy-lidded.

"Well, you're playing a game right now."

"Am I?"

"Bar-room raconteur. A couple too many, telling stories to anyone who'll listen." He nodded towards the barmen, who'd moved to the far end to wash glasses. "Just another piece of play-acting."

"You could go on TV with this stuff. No, I mean it. You're *so* shrewd. Guess you have to be in your profession."

"Is Jim Stevens falling for it?"

"For what?"

"The stories you're telling him. How much of the truth are you giving him?"

Oakes narrowed his eyes. "How much truth do you think he can take? If I went into details, think his newspaper would publish them?" He shook his head slowly. "People can only take so much truth, John." He leaned towards Rebus. "Want me to tell *you* about it, John? Want me to tell you how many I really did kill?"

"Tell me about Deirdre Campbell."

Oakes sat back, took a sip of his drink. "Alan Archibald thinks I killed her."

"And did you?" Rebus tried to keep the question casual. Lifted his glass to his lips.

"Does it matter?" Oakes smiled. "It matters to Alan, doesn't it? Why else would he have come running when I called?"

"He wants the truth—all of it."

"Maybe you're right. And what do you want, John? What brought *you* running in here? Shall I tell you?" He made himself comfortable on the stool. "The morning shift saw me coming back. I wasn't sure he was awake: arms folded, head over on one shoulder. I thought he'd nodded off." He tutted. "I'm not sure his heart's in it. The job, I mean, police work. He looks the type who's coasting to retirement."

Which just about summed up Bill Pryde; not that Rebus was about to admit it.

"I think you have problems with your job, too, but not in the same way."

"Taught yourself psychology along with the chess?"

"When there were no new books to read, I started reading people."

"You killed Deirdre Campbell, didn't you?"

Oakes put a finger to his lips. Then: "Did *you* kill Gordon Reeve?" Gordon Reeve: another ghost; a case from years back . . . Jim Stevens had been shooting his mouth off.

"Tell me," Rebus said, "do you trade with Stevens? You tell him a story, he has to tell you one?"

"I'm just interested in you."

"Then you'll know I killed Gordon Reeve."

"Did you mean to?"

"No."

"Are you sure about that? You stabbed a drug-dealer . . . he died."

"Self-defence."

"Yes, but did you want him dead?"

"Let's talk about you, Oakes. What made you pick Deirdre Campbell?"

Oakes gave another wry smile. Rebus wanted to rip his lips from his face. "See, John? See how easy it is to play the game? Stories, that's all they are. Way back in the past, things we'd like to think we can forget." He slipped off the stool. "I'm going to my room now. A nice hot bath, I think, then maybe one of the in-room movies. I might call down for a sandwich later. Would you like something sent out to the car?"

"I don't know, what's the menu like?"

"No menu, you just order what you like."

"Then I'll have your head on a plate, no garnish required."

Cary Oakes was laughing as he left the bar.

There was someone in the car.

Rebus started forward, saw they were in the passenger seat. As he got close, he saw it was Alan Archibald. Rebus opened the driver's side door and got in.

"Car wasn't locked," Archibald said.

"No."

"Didn't think you'd mind."

Rebus shrugged, lit a cigarette.

"Have you been talking to him?" Archibald needed no confirmation. "What did he say?"

"He's playing a game with you, Alan. That's all it is to him."

"He told you that?"

"He didn't need to. It's what he does. Stevens, you, me . . . we're how he gets his kicks."

"You're wrong there, John. I've seen how he gets his kicks." He leaned down to the floor, brought out a green folder. "Thought you might like something to read."

Alan Archibald's file on Cary Dennis Oakes.

Cary Oakes had travelled to the USA on a tourist visa. His biography prior to this time was sketchy: a father who'd died when he was young; a mother who'd had psychological problems. Cary had been born in Nairn, where his father had worked as a green-keeper at one of the local golf courses, and his mother as a maid at a hotel in the town. Rebus knew Nairn as a windswept coastal resort, the kind of destination that had lost out as cheap foreign holidays had prospered.

When Oakes's father had died following a stroke, the mother had experienced a breakdown. Her employers had let her go, and she'd headed south with her son, finally stopping in Edinburgh, where she had a half-sister. They'd never been particularly close, but there was no one else, no other family, so mother and son had been squeezed into a room in the house in Gilmerton. Soon afterwards, Cary had started running away. His school had notified his mother that his attendance was irregular at best. There were nights and weekends when he just didn't bother going home at all. His mother was beyond caring, and her half-sister preferred him out of the house anyway, since her husband had taken a furious dislike to the boy.

Where did the money come from for his trip to the States? Alan Archibald had done some digging, uncovering a series of muggings and break-ins in Edinburgh, unsolved, but tailing off at about the time Cary Oakes made his trip. The mystery of his niece's murder made for a file in itself. Archibald had interviewed Oakes's mother and half-sister (both now deceased) and the husband (still alive; living alone in sheltered accommodation in East Craigs). They hadn't remembered anything specific about the night of the murder, couldn't even be sure that Cary had been near the house that day or the next.

Deirdre Campbell had been out dancing in town, ending up at a club on the corner of Rose Street—not a hundred yards from where Gaitano's was now sited. She'd been picked by one particular man, had danced the last four or five dances with him. She'd introduced him to her friends. She had exams coming up, shouldn't have been there in the first place. The club was for over-twenty-ones only, and Deirdre had been underage. The owner had got into trouble afterwards. His defence: "If she hadn't come in here, they'd have let her in someplace else." Which was true: make-up, choice of clothes and hairstyle could add half a dozen years to a teenage girl. After the club, the group had headed out to Lothian Road, trying hard not to let the night die. A pizza restaurant, and then taxis. Deirdre had said she'd walk. She lived in Dalry, it would only take her twenty minutes.

Police questioned the young man who'd been with her, the one she'd danced with. He'd asked if he could see her home, but she'd shaken her head. He lived way out at Comiston, so had accepted a ride in one of the taxis. Deirdre had started walking home.

Only to end up murdered on a hillside. Clothing interfered with, but no sign of rape or assault. A blow to the head, then strangulation.

Three days later, Cary Oakes had been heading out of Scotland, taking with him a rucksack and sports holdall. None of his family knew what he was up to. First they'd heard was when he'd been arrested, over two months later.

They hadn't bothered contacting police, registering him as missing.

"He was old enough to make his mind up what he wanted to do," his uncle had told Alan Archibald. "We knew he'd taken some clothes and stuff, figured he'd just took off."

Archibald had used police reports and trial evidence to piece together Cary Oakes's American travels. From New York he'd taken a bus cross-country. At his trial, Oakes stated that he did this "because it's what all the pioneers did: headed west." He spent a week in Chicago, just criss-crossing the city on foot and by means of public transport. Then, hitching rides west, he stopped at Minneapolis, where he decided he needed more money and tried his hand at mugging. A couple of minor successes, and one major set-back: picked on a woman with Mace in her coat pocket and a lethal left hook. He left Minneapolis with a swollen left eye and the right bloodshot and stinging. He ate at truck stops along I-94, passing through Fargo and Billings, mak-ing it as far as Spokane before his need for dollars became desperate. He broke into a couple of houses, tried pawning his meagre findings. The brokers knew swag when they saw it, offered him a few dollars, then, when he bad-mouthed them, called his description in to the police.

He'd taken to sleeping rough, finding like-minded indi-viduals. Joined a little shoplifting gang. With his "funny accent," he'd keep the staff busy and interested while the others went about their work undetected. Already, he was boasting that he was on the run, that he'd "offed" someone back in Scotland. No details, the assertion taken for bra-vado. Everyone on the street hid behind a shield of lies and fantasies. They'd all tasted the good life; all fallen from a state of grace.

In Spokane, he'd murdered Dorothy Anne Wreiss, a forty-two-year-old divorcee who taught kindergarten three days a week. She lived in a sprawling suburban tract. It was thought Oakes had spotted her at the mall, followed her home or trawled the neighbourhood until he'd spotted her station wagon parked in the drive.

She was found in her kitchen, groceries still in their bags on the breakfast bar. Her two cats had curled up on her back and were sleeping. She'd been beaten with a rock, then strangled with a dishtowel. Her purse had been emp-tied, as had the jewellery box in her bedroom. Next day, Oakes had tried pawning her watch. At the trial, he'd say it had been gifted to him by one of his drifter friends, the one called Otis. But no one who'd known him had known anyone called Otis.

He ran towards Seattle, stayed there over a week. There was one unsolved they'd tried pinning on him: man found unconscious in the car park of the King Dome. He'd been beaten around the head, his car stolen. Died in hospital of his injuries. The car turned up in Ballard, as did Cary Oakes. By now, the police forces of several states were interested in the "Scottish drifter." A couple of serious assaults in Chicago; a known homosexual found dead in his car in the La Grange district of the city. A woman attacked and left for dead in a mall on the outskirts of Bloomington, Minneapolis. The death of a seventy-eight-year-old following a break-in at her home in Tacoma, Washington. Sometimes, police had physical descriptions of someone at or near the scene; sometimes all they had was an MO. No useful fingerprints, no positive IDs of Cary Oakes.

The final killing: another homosexual, Willis Chadaran, age sixty. The attack had taken place in the master bedroom of his home in Bellevue. A heavy statuette, which Chadaran had won for his editing work on a documentary film back in 1982, was the weapon. He'd been beaten senseless with it, then finished off with the belt from his red silk *yakuta*. Cary Oakes's fingerprints were found on the headboard. When arrested and presented with the fingerprint match-up, he admitted he'd been to Chadaran's home, but denied killing him. Detectives had asked how his prints had ended up on the headboard. Oakes said he'd sneaked into the room looking for stuff to steal, maybe he'd touched it then.

He was finally arrested at Pike Place Market. Traders had complained that he'd looked ready to swipe something. Police had asked for his ID. He'd offered his passport, with its invalid tourist visa, then made a run for it. They'd caught him, taken him in, and someone had connected him to various descriptions which had been coming in from all across the country.

At the trial, the prosecution's summing-up had been succinct.

"This is a man for whom brutal murder has become a way of life, a commonplace. If he needs something, wants something, covets something . . . he kills for it. He sees us all as potential victims. We're not fellow humans to him; he's ceased to think of us in those terms, the terms by which we co-ordinate and validate our society, terms without which we cannot call ourselves *civilised*. His soul has shrivelled to the size of a walnut, maybe not even that big. Cary Oakes, ladies and gentlemen of the jury, has stepped outside our society, our laws, our civilisation, and he must pay the price."

The price being two life sentences.

Rebus put down the file. "Lots of circumstantial evidence," he mused.

"It all adds up though. More than enough to make a case."

Rebus nodded agreement. "But I can see where he found his loopholes." He tapped the folder, thought of the summing-up.

"Wonder how big a soul usually is . . ." He turned to Archibald. "He plays games."

"I know that. The version Jim Stevens' paper is printing . . . Oakes is spinning them a line."

"He told me one of his victims was the same age as my daughter. Nobody in here fits with that."

Alan Archibald shrugged. "Your daughter's mid-twenties, Deirdre was eighteen." He paused. "Maybe there are others we don't know about."

Yes, thought Rebus, and maybe it had been just another lie. "So what are you going to do?" he asked.

"Keep at him."

"Play along with him?"

"I don't see it that way."

"I know you don't; that's what worries me."

"She wasn't *your* niece."

Rebus looked into Alan Archibald's eyes; saw courage and grit, the vital energies which had stayed with him all his working years, not about to be jettisoned now.

"How can I help?"

"What makes you think I want any help?"

"Because you came back tonight. Not to talk to him, but to see me."

Alan Archibald smiled. "I know a bit about you, John. I know we're not so very different."

"So how can I help?"

"Help me make him come to Hillend."

"What good do you think it would do?"

"He ran from the crime, John. Ran as far as he could

from the memory of it. Take him back there, back to his *first* killing . . . I think it would bring it all back: the terror, the uncertainty. I think he'd start to unravel."

"Is that what we want?" Rebus thinking: *He'll kill again . . .*

"It's what I want. I just need to know if I'll have your help."

Rebus rubbed his hands over the steering-wheel. "I'll need to think."

"Well, don't be too long about it. I get the feeling maybe you need this as much as I do."

Rebus looked at him.

"We can't always live by faith alone," Archibald went on. "Now and then, there has to be something more."

After a further hour of conversation, Archibald left, saying he'd find himself a taxi. He'd talked about his niece, his memories of her, the way her murder had affected the family.

"We disintegrated," he'd said. "So slowly, I don't think anybody noticed. I think we felt guilty whenever we met, like we were to blame. Because when we got together, there was only one possible subject, one thing on our minds, and we didn't want that."

He'd talked too about his work on the case: weeks spent in police archives; months spent piecing together Cary Oakes's history; trips to the US.

"It must all have cost a lot," Rebus had said.

"Worth every penny, John."

Rebus hadn't added that money wasn't his point. He knew all about obsession, knew how it could rob you of everything. He'd been given a jigsaw one year as a Christmas present, back when Sammy was just a kid. He'd cleared a table and started work on it, found he worked late into the night, even though he knew the picture he was making—knew because it was right there on the box. Only he tried not to look at it, wanting to complete the puzzle without any help.

And one piece was missing. He'd asked Rhona, questioned Sammy: had she taken it? Rhona told him maybe it wasn't in the box to start with, but he couldn't accept that. He'd stripped the sofa and chairs, pulled up the carpet, gone over the room inch by inch, then the rest of the flat—just in case Sammy *had* put it somewhere. Never found it. Even years later, he would find himself wondering if maybe it had slipped between the floorboards, or under the skirting-board . . .

Police work could affect you like that, if you let it. Unsolved cases; questions that niggled; people you *knew* were the culprits but couldn't incriminate . . . He'd had more than his fair share of those. But eventually he let them go, even if it meant drinking them into oblivion. Alan Archibald didn't look capable of putting Cary Oakes behind him. Rebus got the feeling that even if Oakes were proved innocent, Archibald would go on believing in his guilt. It was in the nature of obsession.

Alone with his thoughts, Rebus reached into his pocket for the quarter-bottle, drained it dry.

Proved innocent . . . He thought of Darren Rough, shaking with fear, holed up in his locked toilet. All because Social Work had put him in a flat above a kids' playground. And because John Rebus had placed on Rough's shoulders the sins of others—the sins of men who had themselves abused Rough.

Rebus rubbed at his eyes. It wasn't unusual for him to feel a weight of guilt. He carried Jack Morton's death with him. But something had changed. In the old days, he wouldn't have given much thought to Darren Rough. He'd have told himself Rough deserved what he got, for being what he so evidently was. But go back further . . . back to the cop he had once been, so long ago now, and he wouldn't have taken Rough's story to the tabloids. Maybe

Mairie Henderson was right: *something's gone bad inside you.*

He admired Alan Archibald's persistence, but wondered what would happen if he were proved *wrong*. Would he still pursue Cary Oakes? Would he take things further than mere pursuit . . . ? Rebus stared out at the night sky.

It's all pretty tricky down here, isn't it, Big Man?

He wondered what point the surveillance was serving. Oakes seemed to be turning it to his own advantage, coming and going as he pleased, letting them know he could do it. So that all their efforts seemed so much waste. He closed his eyes, listened to the occasional message on the police radio, his thoughts turning to Damon Mee. The boat looked like another dead end. Damon had walked out of the world, given his life the slip. Thoughts of Damon took him to Janice, and from there to his schooldays, when everything had just started to get complicated in his life.

Alec Chisholm had disappeared one day; never found.

Rebus had gone to the school leaving dance, with something he wanted to tell Mitch.

Then Janice had knocked him cold, a gang had descended on Mitch, and suddenly Rebus's whole life was decided . . .

A noise brought him out of his reverie. He thought it had come from the back of the hotel. He decided to investigate. The car park and service entrance in darkness, but he swept his torch around. Looked up at the hotel windows. You could tell the corridors: lights still burned in those windows. One of the windows was open, curtains flapping. Rebus moved his torch in a downward arc, its beam landing on the roof of a lock-up garage, one of a row of three. They were separated from the hotel property by a wall. Rebus pulled himself up and over it. A narrow alley, puddles and rubbish underfoot. No sign of life, but footprints in the mud. He followed the path. It led him around the back of a factory unit and tenement, then up on to the busy thoroughfare of Bernard Street, where late-night cars and taxis idled at traffic lights. Where drunks stumbled their way home. One man was doing an elaborate dance and providing his own musical accompaniment. The woman with him thought he was hilarious. Can: "Tango Whiskyman."

There was no sign of Cary Oakes, no sign at all, but Rebus got the feeling he was out there. He retraced his steps, stopped at a rubbish skip parked next to one of the service doors, took the empty bottle from his pocket and tossed it in.

Felt his head jerk forward as a blow hit him from behind. Searing pain, his eyes screwing shut. He raised a hand, half-turned. A second blow laid him out cold.

It was pitch black, and when he moved there was a dull steel echo.

And a smell.

He was lying on something soft. Voices above him, then blinding light.

"Dear oh dear."

Second voice, amused: "Sleeping it off, sir?"

Rebus shielded his eyes, peered up at sheer walls. Two heads bobbing over the rim. He pulled his knees up, slithered as he tried to stand. His hands were tingling. His head pulsed with pain.

He was . . . he knew where he was. In a rubbish skip, the one behind the hotel. Wet cardboard boxes beneath him, and Christ knew what else. Hands were helping him to his feet.

"Come on then, sir. Let's . . ." The voice died as the torch found his face again. Two uniforms, probably from Leith cop shop. And one of them had recognised him.

"DI Rebus?"

Rebus: dishevelled, whisky on his breath, being helped from a skip. Supposedly on surveillance. He knew how it must look.

"Christ, sir, what happened to you?"

"Get that torch out of my face, son." Their faces were shadows to him, no way to tell if he knew them. He asked the time, worked out that he'd been unconscious only ten or fifteen minutes.

"Call from a public box on Bernard Street," one of the uniforms was explaining. "Said there was a fight going on at the back of the hotel."

Rebus examined the back of his head: no blood on his palm. Hands still tingling. He rubbed at the fingers. They hurt when he worked them. Lifted them into the torchlight. One of the uniforms whistled.

The knuckles were grazed, bruised. A couple of the joints seemed to be swelling.

"Gave him a sore one, whoever he was," the uniform said.

Rebus studied the scrapes. Like he'd been punching concrete. "I didn't hit anyone," he said. The uniforms shared a glance.

"If you say so, sir."

"I suppose it's asking too much to tell you to keep this to yourselves."

"We won't breathe a word, sir."

An outright lie; it didn't do to beg favours from uniforms.

"Anything else we can do, sir?"

Rebus started to shake his head, felt a wave of nausea as the pain slammed in. Steadied himself with a hand on the skip.

"My car's round the corner," he said, voice brittle.

"You'll want a shower when you get home."

"Thank you, Sherlock."

"Only trying to help," the uniform muttered.

Rebus walked slowly around the building. The receptionist looked ready to call security until Rebus produced ID and asked her to buzz Oakes's room. There was no reply.

"Will there be anything else, sir?"

Rebus was looking in his wallet. His cards were there, but the cash had gone.

"Any idea where Mr. Oakes is?" he asked.

She shook her head. "I didn't see him leave."

Rebus thanked her and walked over to a sofa, fell down on to it. A little later, he asked for aspirin. When she brought them, she had to shake his shoulder to wake him up. He headed for Patience's: sod the surveillance. Oakes wasn't in his room. He was out on the streets. Rebus needed clean clothes, a shower, and more painkillers. As he stumbled through the door, Patience came into the hall, blinking her eyes sleepily. He held up both hands to pacify her.

"It's not what you think," he said.

She came forward, held his hands, looking at the swelling.

"Explain," she said. So Rebus did just that.

He lay in the bath, a cold compress on the back of his skull. Patience had rigged it up from a sandwich bag, some ice cubes, and a bandage. She was treating his hands with antiseptic cream, having cleaned them and established nothing was broken.

"This man Oakes," she said, "I'm still not sure why he'd do it."

Rebus adjusted the ice-pack. "To humiliate me. He made sure I'd be found by uniforms, out cold in a rubbish skip."

"Yes?" She dabbed on more ointment.

"Knuckles bruised like I'd been fighting. And whoever I'd fought had whipped me. Found like that at the back of the hotel, there's only one real candidate. By morning, it'll be round every station in the city."

"Why would he do that?"

"To show me he can. Why else?" He tried not to flinch as she rubbed cream into a cut.

"I don't know," she said. "Maybe to distract you."

He looked at her. "From what?"

She shrugged. "You're the detective here." She examined her handiwork. "I need to wrap your hands."

"So long as I can still drive."

"John . . ." Knowing he'd pay no attention.

"Patience, if I go round with hands looking like a mummy's, he's won this round."

"Not if you refuse to play."

He saw the depth of concern in her eyes, brushed her cheek with the back of his hand. Saw Janice doing the selfsame thing to him, and withdrew his hand guiltily.

"Hurts, does it?" Patience asked, misreading the gesture. He nodded, not trusting himself to speak.

Later, he sat on the sofa with a mug of weak tea. He'd washed down two more painkillers, prescription-strength. His soiled clothes had been bundled into a black bin-liner, ready for a trip to the cleaner's. Such a shame, he thought, that his soiled thoughts couldn't be steam-pressed so easily.

When his mobile phone sounded, he stared at it hard. It lay on the coffee table in front of him, alongside his keys and small change. Patience was standing in the doorway as he finally picked the phone up. There was a little smile on her lips, but no humour in her eyes. She'd known all along he would answer it.

Cal Brady came home from Guiser's feeling pretty good. The buzz lasted all of ten seconds. As he flopped on to his bed, he remembered about the pervert. His mum was in her bedroom with some bloke; walls were so thin they'd have been as well having it off in front of him. All the flats were like that, so that things you wanted done in secrecy you had to do quietly. He put his ear to one wall, then another: his mum and her bloke; a couple of television stations— Jamie was still awake, watching the box in the living room, and the portable was on in Van's room, a weak attempt to mask other sounds. He put his ear to the floor. He could still hear all of it, plus the people below's movements, coughs and conversations. He'd gone to the doctor a while back, asked if maybe he had ears that were more sensitive than the norm.

"I keep hearing things I don't want to."

When he'd explained that he lived in one of the high-rises in Greenfield, the doctor had suggested a personal stereo.

But it was the same on the street: he overheard snippets of conversation, stuff the talkers didn't think he could hear. Sometimes he thought it was getting worse, thought he could hear people's hearts beating, the quick flow of blood around their bodies. He thought he could hear their *thoughts*. Like at Guiser's, when girls looked at him and he smiled back. They were thinking: he might not look much, but he's with Archie Frost, so he must be important in some way. They'd think: if I dance with him, let him buy me a drink, I'll be closer to the *power*.

Which was why he seldom did anything, just stayed by the bar, affecting a cool poise and saying nothing. But listening, always listening.

Always hearing things . . . Things about Charmer, things about the clients—Ama Petrie, her brother and the rest. His own version of the *power*.

It had been quiet in the club tonight. If it hadn't been

for a busload from Tranent, the place would have been dead. They hadn't looked too impressed: nobody to dance with but themselves. Archie doubted they'd be back. Archie was already looking for other work: plenty more clubs in the city. Cal hadn't started looking though. Cal believed in loyalty.

"I know Charmer's trying to collect on some debts," Archie had said, "but the problem is, he's got debts of his own. Only a matter of time before people come calling . . ."

Cal had straightened his back, as if to say: fine by me.

He wanted to think things through, get them straight in his head, which was why he'd come into his bedroom rather than sitting up with Jamie. But even before he'd reached that sanctuary, his thoughts had turned to Darren Rough. The hall was half-full of placards. They sat against the wall, still smelling of fresh paint. Cardboard boxes had been cut up flat, messages written on their blank sides. DESTROY ALL MONSTERS; KEEP AWAY FROM OUR KIDS; LET'S PLAY HANG THE PERV.

Destroy all monsters, Cal was thinking, lying on his bed, smoking a cigarette. He got up abruptly, thumped on the far wall.

"Will you fucking well shut up, the pair of you!"

Silence, then muffled laughter. For a moment, Cal was ready to burst in on them, but he knew what his mum would do to him. And besides, last thing he wanted was to see her like that.

Destroy all monsters.

The doorbell. Who the fuck at this time of night . . . ? Cal went to see. Recognised the woman. She looked agitated, rubbing her hands like she was doing the washing-up.

"You haven't seen our Billy, have you?" She was Joanna Horman, Billy's mum. Billy was one of Jamie's pals. Cal called for him and Jamie came out of the living room.

"Have you seen Billy Boy?" Cal asked. Jamie shook his head. He had a packet of crisps in his hand. Cal turned back to Joanna Horman. Some of his friends reckoned she looked all right. Right now, though, she looked a mess.

"What's up?" he asked.

"He went out to play about seven, I haven't seen him

since. I thought maybe he'd gone to his gran's, but when I checked she hadn't clapped eyes on him."

"I'm just in. Hold on a minute." He went and banged on Van's door: as good an excuse as any to break things up in there. "Hiy, Maw, has Billy Horman been round here the night?"

Noises from within. Joanna Horman was leaning against the door, looking ready to fall down. Not a bad body, Cal decided. Bit squishy, but he didn't like them all skin and bones. His mother's bedroom door opened. Van was wearing her dress, arranging it over her. Nothing on underneath, he'd bet. She closed the door quickly behind her; no way to tell who else was in the room.

"Something the matter, Joanna?" Pushing past Cal, ignoring him altogether.

"It's wee Billy, Van. He's disappeared."

"Aw, Christ. Come into the living room."

"I just don't know what to do."

"Where have you looked?"

Cal followed the two women into the living room.

"Everywhere. I think maybe it's time I called the police."

Van snorted. "Oh aye, they'd be round here like a shot. Only thing those buggers are interested in is protecting perverts . . ." Her voice died away; for the first time, she looked at her son. They knew one another so well, no words were needed.

"Joanna, pet," Van said quietly, "you stay there. I'm going to round up the troops. If your Billy's anywhere on the estate, we'll find him, don't you worry."

Within half an hour, Van Brady had the search parties organized. People were going from door to door, asking questions, getting new volunteers. Jamie had been sent to bed, but wasn't asleep, and Joanna Horman was in the living room with a tumbler of rum and Coke. Cal had offered to keep an eye on her. She was on the sofa, and he was in the chair. He couldn't think of anything to say. Wasn't normally this tongue-tied. He found himself aroused by her grief, the way it softened her. But he felt ashamed to be so affected by her, and his brain was spinning the way it did when he'd drunk too much or taken some speed.

He got up, opened the door to Jamie's room.

"Get up, you, and keep an eye on Billy's mum. I've got to go out."

Then he opened the main door and stalked down the hallway. Down the stairwell and out into the night. There were some lock-ups across the way. He had the key to one of them. He was keeping some stuff there. Jerry Langham's lock-up it was, but Jerry was serving three-to-five in Saughton, another six months before he'd have even a whiff of roly-paroley. He kept his car in the lock-up. It was a 1970s Merc with rusty sills and a custard-yellow paint job, but Jerry loved it.

"I don't keep my missus under lock and key, but no way am I letting any bastard near my Merc."

This was by way of a warning: use the lock-up, keep an eye on the motor, but never think of touching it. Not that Cal had heeded the advice. He unlocked the car sometimes and sat in it, pretending to be driving. And he'd opened the boot once, too, so he knew what was inside.

He unlocked it now, lifted out the jerrycan and gave it a shake. He was sure there'd been more than that; it was barely half-full now. Evaporation or something. He supposed petrol could do that. On a stack of shelves he found some oily rags. Stuffed them into his pockets and he was ready.

Back to the block of flats, taking the steps two at a time. He had a purpose now, jerrycan making quiet sloshing sounds. Close your eyes, you could almost be at the seaside. Crept along to Darren Rough's flat. Fresh lengths of board across his window. The kids had already been busy with their aerosols. GAP had made the flat their first stop tonight: no answer, nobody home. Cal opened the mouth of the can, held it high so the petrol trickled out of it, running it the length of the boarded window, then across the door. Took a ball of rag from his pocket and doused it in petrol. Stuffed it into the narrow gap between board and wall. Then another and another. Chucked the empty can over the balcony, then cursed to himself: there'd be prints on it. And besides, Jerry might want it. He'd go retrieve it in a minute.

Took out his cigarette lighter, the one Jamie had given

him for Christmas. Jamie . . . he was doing this for Jamie
and his pals, for all the kids. Jamie was bright. Didn't like
school, but then who did? Didn't make him thick. He could
go places, do things with his life: a couple of times when
drunk, Cal had tried to tell him as much. He got the feeling
it hadn't come out right, had come out like he was envious.
Maybe he was, just a little. A kid like Jamie, the world was
his oyster. Cal looked at the lighter. Another thing about
his wee brother: he had shoplifting down to an art.

When Rebus got to Greenfield, half the estate was out
watching the fire, or what was left of it.

Rebus knew one of the firemen, guy called Eddie Dickson. Dickson nodded a greeting. He was in full uniform,
standing guard by his engine.

"If I move, they'll be in about it." Meaning the local
kids; meaning they'd strip it of anything they could find.
"We got bottled coming in."

"Who by?"

Dickson shrugged. "Came flying out of the dark. I get
the feeling we weren't wanted."

Uniforms from St. Leonard's were trying to get the spectators to go back to bed.

"Any casualties?"

Dickson shrugged again. "You mean from the bottles?"

Rebus stared at him. "I mean in there." Pointing towards
Darren Rough's flat.

"Place was empty when we got here."

"Door open?"

Dickson shook his head. "Had to kick in what was left
of it. Grudge thing, is it?"

"Don't you read the papers?"

"When do I get the time, John?"

"Paedophile."

Dickson nodded. "Remember it now. Frying's too good for them, eh?"

Rebus left him to his guard duty, headed for Cragside Court. The uniform in the lobby told him not to bother with the lifts.

"One's buggered, the other's a toilet."

Rebus would have taken the stairs anyway. Nothing left of the boards across Rough's window but a few charred scraps clinging to their screws. The door had been torched, too. DC Grant Hood was standing in the hallway of the flat. Rebus toed open the toilet door: nobody home.

"Your pal," Hood said. He was young, bright. Followed Glasgow Rangers with a passion, but nobody was perfect.

"Wasn't me," Rebus commented. "But thanks for the call."

Hood shrugged. "Thought you might be interested." He nodded towards Rebus's bandaged hands. "Had an accident yourself?"

Rebus ignored the question. "No chance *this* was an accident, I suppose?"

"Bits of rag hanging from the windowframe. Petrol spilt on the walkway . . ."

"No sign of the occupier?"

Hood shook his head. "Any ideas?"

"Look around, Grant. It's the Wild West out here. Any one of them's capable." Rebus had walked back through what remained of the door, was leaning over the balcony. "But if it was me, I'd be asking Van Brady and her eldest son."

Hood jotted the names down. "I don't suppose Mr. Rough will be coming back."

"No," Rebus said. Which had been the point all along. But now that they'd come to that point, Rebus wondered why he felt so lousy inside . . . Jane Barbour's words came back to him: low chance of reoffending . . . abused as a child himself . . . need to give him a chance.

Then he saw Cal Brady, down amongst the thinning crowd. He was fully clothed, looked like he hadn't yet been to bed. Rebus went back downstairs. Cal was handing out

GAP stickers to anyone who didn't have one. Women with coats thrown over their nighties were getting them. Cal placed each one on its recipient with exaggerated gentleness, causing some of the women—not exactly coy maidens—to blush.

"All right, Cal?" Rebus said. Cal looked round at him, peeled off a sticker and slapped it on Rebus's jacket.

"I hope you're with us, Inspector."

Rebus started removing the sticker. Cal put out a hand to stop him, and Rebus caught it, lifted it to his nose. Cal pulled away quickly, but not quickly enough.

"Soap and water's usually a good idea," Rebus told him.

"I haven't done anything."

"You stink of petrol."

"Not guilty, Your Honour."

"I'm not one to prejudge, Cal—"

"Not what I hear."

"But in your case I'll definitely make an exception." Thinking: who had Cal been talking to? Who'd been telling him about Rebus? "DC Hood's going to want to ask you some questions. Be nice to him."

"Fuck the lot of you."

"Think your dick's long enough?" Said with a smile.

Cal stared him out; then broke off and laughed. "You're a clown. Go home to your circus."

"What do you think *you* are, Cal? The ringmaster?" Rebus shook his head. "No, son, you'll do tricks for whoever's cracking the whip." Rebus turned away. "Whether it's your mum or Charmer Mackenzie."

"What do you mean?"

"You work for him, don't you?"

"What's it to do with you?"

Rebus just shrugged and went back to his car. He'd parked it right next to the fire engine: didn't want to find it up on bricks.

"Hey, John," Eddie Dickson said, "won't it be perfect?"

"What?"

"When they build the Parliament." He swept an arm before him. "Right next door to all this."

Rebus looked up, saw the dark form of Salisbury Crags. Once more he felt like he was in a canyon of some kind, sheer walls affording no escape. Your fingers would be raw and bleeding from trying.

Either that or stained with four-star.

Hood came running up as Rebus was flexing his hands. "I think we've got a problem."

"Be a miracle if we didn't."

"There's a kid missing. They weren't even going to tell us."

Rebus was thoughtful. "It's UDI," he said. Hood looked puzzled. "A Unilateral Declaration of Independence, son. So who spilt the beans?"

"I went to Van Brady's flat. Door was open, young woman in the lounge." He checked his notebook. "Name's Joanna Horman. Kid's name is Billy."

Rebus remembered his first visit to Greenfield, Van Brady leaning out of her window: *I saw you, Billy Horman!* He couldn't remember much about the kid, only that he'd been playing with Jamie Brady.

"Now we know why they torched the flat," Hood went on.

"A brilliant deduction, Grant. Maybe we better go talk to the lady in question."

"The kid's mum?"

Rebus shook his head. "Van Brady."

Having opened negotiations with Van Brady, her kitchen providing an unpromising table for such a high-powered summit, Rebus called for reinforcements. They'd organise more search parties, police and residents working together.

"This is your patch," Rebus had conceded, washing down more pills with a mug of cheap chicory coffee. "You know the place better than any of us: any hidey-holes, gang huts, anywhere he might stop the night. If his mum gives us a list of his school pals, we can contact their parents, see if he's maybe staying with one of them. There are things we can do best, and things you can do." He'd kept his voice level, and maintained eye-contact throughout. There were eight bodies in the kitchen, and more in the hallway and living room.

"What about the pervert?" Van Brady had asked.

"We'll find him, don't worry. But right now, I think we should concentrate on Billy, don't you?"

"What if he's the one who's *got* Billy?"

"Let's wait and see, eh? First thing is to get the search going again. We're not going to find anyone sitting here."

Meeting over, Rebus had sought out Grant Hood.

"This is yours, Grant," he said. "I shouldn't even be here."

Hood nodded. "Sorry I got you involved."

"Don't be. But keep yourself straight: wake up DI Barbour and let her know the score."

"What happens if they find him first?" Meaning Darren Rough rather than the kid.

"Then he's dead," Rebus said. "It's as simple as that."

He drove out of Greenfield, wondering at what point Darren Rough had vacated his flat. Wondering where the young man would go. Holyrood Park: once, centuries back, it had been sanctuary for convicts. As long as you didn't cross the boundary, you were on Crown Estate and couldn't be touched by the law. Debtors would flee there, live there for years, existing on charity, fish from the lochs and wild rabbits. When their debts were finally paid or written off, they'd cross the boundary, step back into society. The park had provided them with an illusion of freedom; in reality, they'd merely been in an open prison.

Holyrood Park: a road wound its way around the base of Salisbury Crags and Arthur's Seat. There were car parks near the lochs, popular with families and dog-owners during the day. At night, couples drove there for sex. The Royal Parks Police made irregular patrols. There had been talk of their disbanding, of the park falling within Lothian and Borders jurisdiction. It hadn't happened yet.

Rebus made three circuits of the park. Driving slowly, not really interested in the few parked cars he passed. Then, by St. Margaret's Loch, just as he was readying to exit at Royal Park Terrace, he thought he caught shadow play at the edge of his vision. Decided to stop the car. Maybe just the headache and the pills, tricking his vision. He kept the engine running, wound down the window and lit a cigarette. Foxes, maybe even badgers . . . he could have been mistaken. There were all kinds of shadows in the city.

But then a face appeared at the open window.

"Any chance of a ciggie?"

"No problem." Rebus averted his face as he searched his pockets.

"Eh . . . look, I'm not sure . . ." A clearing of the throat. "I mean, you're not looking for company, are you?"

"As a matter of fact, I am." Now Rebus looked up. "Get in, Darren."

Shock hit Darren Rough's face as he recognised Rebus. His face was blackened. He coughed again, doubling over.

"Smoke inhalation," Rebus observed. "You left it pretty late getting out."

Rough wiped his mouth. The sleeves of his green raincoat were singed where he'd held them in front of his face.

"I thought they'd be waiting for me outside. I kept listening for a fire engine."

"Somebody called one eventually."

He snorted. "Probably afraid it would spread to their flat."

"Nobody was waiting outside?"

Rough shook his head. No, Rebus thought, because they'd all been out searching for Billy Horman. Cal Brady had torched the flat alone and hadn't stuck around to be spotted.

It had started to rain; sudden gobbets which bounced off Rough's shoulders. He lifted his face to the sky, opened his scorched mouth to the drops.

"You better get in," Rebus told him.

He angled his head, stared at Rebus. "What am I charged with?"

"A kid's gone missing."

Rough lowered his eyes. Said something like "I see," but so quietly Rebus didn't catch it. "They think I . . . ?" He stopped. "Of course they think I did it. In their shoes, I'd think the same."

"But it wasn't you?"

Rough shook his head. "I don't do that any more. That's not me." He was getting soaked.

"Get in," Rebus repeated. Rough got into the passenger seat. "But you still think about it," Rebus said, watching for a response.

Rough stared at the windscreen, his eyes glinting. "I'd be a liar if I said I didn't."

"So what's changed?"

Rough turned to him. "Are you charging me?"

"No charge," Rebus said, putting the car into gear. "Tonight, you ride for free."

24

Rebus took Darren Rough to St. Leonard's.

"Don't worry," he said. "Call it protective custody. I just want to make your answers on the missing kid official."

They sat in an interview room with the recording machine running and a uniform on the door, drinking watery tea and with the rest of the station practically empty. All the spare bodies were down at Greenfield, looking for Billy Horman.

"So you don't know anything about a missing child?" Rebus asked. Because there was no one around to tell him not to, he'd lit himself a cigarette. Rough didn't want one, but then changed his mind.

"Cancer's probably the least of my problems right now," he surmised. Then he told Rebus that all he knew was what he'd heard from the detective himself.

"But the locals warned you off, and you stayed put. There must have been a reason."

"Nowhere else to go. I'm a marked man." Glancing up. "Thanks to you." Rebus stood up. Rough flinched, but all Rebus did was lean against the wall, so he was facing the video camera. Not that it mattered: the camera wasn't on.

"You're a marked man because of what you are, Mr. Rough."

"I'm a paedophile, Inspector. I suppose I'll always be one. But I have ceased to be a *practising* paedophile." A shrug. "Society's going to have to get used to it."

"I don't think your neighbours would agree."

Rough allowed himself a condemned man's smile. "I think you're right."

"What about friends?"

"Friends?"

"Others who share your interests." Rebus flicked ash on to the carpet; the cleaners would be in before morning. "Had any of them round to the flat?"

Rough was shaking his head.

"Sure about that, Mr. Rough?"

"Nobody knew I was there till the papers splashed me across a double-page spread."

"But afterwards . . . nobody from the old days got in touch?"

Rough didn't answer. He was staring into space, still thinking of newspapers. "Ince and Marshall . . . I see the stories about them. Where they are . . . in the cells . . . do they get to see the news?"

"Sometimes," Rebus admitted.

"So they'll know about me?"

Rebus nodded. "Don't worry about them. They're on remand in Saughton Prison." He paused. "You were going to testify against them."

"I wanted to." He stared into space again, his face tightening with memories. Rebus knew the story: the abused became abusers themselves. He'd always found it easy to discard. Not every victim turned abuser.

"That time they took you to Shiellion . . ." Rebus began.

"Marshall took me. Ince told him to." His voice was trembling. "Didn't pick on me specially or anything—could have been any one of us. Only I think I was the quietest, the least likely to do anything about it. Marshall was right under Ince's thumb at that time, loved the way Ince ordered him about. I saw a photo of Ince, he hasn't changed. Marshall's got a lot tougher-looking, like he's grown an extra skin."

"And the third man?"

"I told you, could have been anybody."

"But he was already there, waiting at Shiellion when you arrived."

"Yes."

"So probably a friend of Ince, rather than Marshall."

"They took it in turns." Rough's hands were holding the edge of the desk. "Afterwards, I tried telling people, but nobody would listen. It was: 'You mustn't say that'; 'Don't tell such stories.' Like it was all *my* fault. I'd touched up a neighbour's kid, so I deserved everything I got . . . Even worse, some of them thought I was lying, and I never lied . . . never." He closed his eyes, rested his forehead on his hands. He muttered something that might have been "Bastards." And then he started to cry.

Rebus knew he had choices. Phone Social Work and have them take Rough somewhere. Put him in a cell. Or drop him off somewhere . . . anywhere. But when he tried the Social Work emergency number, no one answered. They'd be out on a call. The recorded message told him to keep trying the number every ten minutes or so. It told him not to panic.

There were empty cells in the station, but Rebus knew word would get out, and when it came time to release Darren Rough, there'd be a crowd waiting. So he lit another cigarette and went back to the interview room.

"Right," he said, opening the door, "you're coming with me."

"Nice room," Darren Rough said. He looked around, examining the high cornicing. "Big," he added, nodding to himself. He was trying to be pleasant, make conversation. He was wondering what Rebus was going to do with him, here in Rebus's own flat.

Rebus handed over a mug of tea and told him to sit down. He offered Rough another cigarette, the offer refused this time. Rough was sitting on the sofa. Rebus wanted to tell him to move on to one of the dining chairs. It was as if Rough could contaminate everything he touched.

"Your social worker better find you something in the morning," Rebus said. "Something far from Edinburgh."

Rough looked at him. His eyes were dark-ringed, his hair needing a wash. The green raincoat was draped over the back of the sofa. He wore a check suit-jacket with jeans and baseball boots, white nylon shirt. He looked like he'd won a ninety-second dash through an Oxfam shop.

"Keep moving, eh?"

"A moving target's harder to hit," Rebus told him.

Rough smiled tiredly. "I see you've been hitting a target yourself."

Rebus flexed his fingers again, trying to stop them seizing up.

Rough sipped his tea. "He did beat me up, you know."

"Who?"

"Your friend."

"Jim Margolies?"

Rough nodded. "All of a sudden he got this look in his eyes. Next thing the fists were flying." He shook his head. "When he killed himself, I read the obituaries. They all said he was a 'fine officer,' a 'loving father.' Attended church regularly." A half-smile. "When he laid into me, he must have been demonstrating muscular Christianity."

"Careful what you say."

"Yes, he was your friend, you worked with him. But I wonder if you *knew* him."

He didn't say as much, but Rebus was beginning to wonder the same thing. Orange lipstick, meaning he liked them young. He'd asked Fern how young. Nothing illegal, she'd told him.

"Why do you think he died?" Rebus asked.

"How should I know?"

"When the two of you talked . . . how did he seem?"

Rough was thoughtful. "Not angry with me or anything. Just wanting to know about Shiellion. How often I'd been . . . you know. And who by." He glanced towards Rebus. "Some people get a kick that way, listening to stories."

"You think that's why he was asking?"

"Why are *you* asking all these questions, Inspector? Outing me to the papers, then coming to the rescue. I think maybe that's how *you* get your kicks, fucking with people's heads."

Rebus thought of Cary Oakes and his games. "I think you had something to do with Jim Margolies' death," he said. "Whether you know it or not."

They sat in silence after that, until Rough asked if there was anything he could eat. Rebus went through to the kitchen, stared at one of the cupboard doors, wanting to punch it. But his knuckles wouldn't thank him for that. He looked at them. He knew what Oakes had done, rubbed them hard over the floor of the car park, maybe bunched them into fists and driven them into the steel skip. Twisted little bastard that he was. And Patience wondered if it was all a blind, some way of diverting Rebus from some other scheme. His head seemed full of diversions. How could he trust what Rough was telling him? He didn't see Rough as a schemer; too weak. But Jim Margolies . . . had *he* been playing some game?

And had it killed him?

Rebus opened the cupboard door, called out that he could do beans on toast. Rough said that would be fine. There was no marge for the toast, but Rebus reckoned the tomato sauce would soften it up. He emptied the beans into a pot, stuck the bread under the grill, and went to sort out the sleeping accommodation.

Not his own room; definitely not his own room. He opened the door to what had been the guest room, and—long before that—Sammy's room. Her single bed was still there; posters on the walls; teenage girls' annuals on a bookshelf. One of the last people to use the room had been Jack Morton. No way was Darren Rough sleeping there.

Rebus opened the wardrobe, found an old blanket and pillow, took them through to the living room.

"You can have the sofa," he said.

"Fine. Whatever." Rough was standing at the window. Rebus crossed over to him. A couple of kids lived across the street, but their shutters were closed, no peep-show available.

"It's so quiet here," Rough said. "In Greenfield, there always seems to be a row going on. Either that or a party, and most of the parties turn into a row."

"But you're a good neighbour, eh?" Rebus said. "Quiet, keep yourself to yourself?"

"I try to."

"What about when the kids are noisy: don't you want to do something about them?"

Rough closed his eyes, pressed his forehead to the glass. "I won't make any excuses," he whispered.

"And no apologies either?"

Another smile, eyes still shut. "I can apologise until the cows come home. It doesn't change anything. It doesn't change how I feel." He opened his eyes, turned to Rebus. "But you don't want to hear about that, do you?"

Rebus stared at him. "The toast's burning," he said, turning away.

At five o'clock, with Rough hidden under the blanket on the sofa, Rebus telephoned Bill Pryde.

"Sorry to wake you, Bill."

"The alarm was about to go off anyway. What's up?"

"The surveillance car."

"What about it?"

"It's not at The Shore." He explained where it was.

"Christ, John, what about Oakes?"

"He comes and goes as he likes, Bill. The only thing we were doing there was keeping him amused."

"You better tell that to the Farmer."

"I will."

"Meantime, you want me to pick up the car from your flat?"

"I've filled in the log, explained everything."

"What about the keys?"

"Under the front seat, same place the log is. I've left it unlocked."

"And now you're about to get your head down?"

"Something like that." He stared at Darren Rough, watching the rise and fall of the blanket. He looked about as dangerous as pastry dough. Rebus cut the connection, tried the station. There was still no sign of Billy Horman. They'd looked everywhere. The search was being called off until daylight. Rebus called the hotel, asked for Cary Oakes's room: still no answer. He put down the phone, went into his bedroom. Lay on his bed—a mattress on the floor. He'd thought about going back to Patience's, but didn't like the thought of Rough being here by himself. He might explore, find Sammy's room. Pull open drawers, touch things. As soon as feasible, Rebus wanted him out.

You brought him here, a voice in his head seemed to say. *You brought him to this*. Sticks and crowbars and angry

voices. The residents of Greenfield roused to a mob. Cal
Brady with his petrol and denials. He worked for Charmer
Mackenzie, worked the door at Guiser's. Damon Mee had
left there, got into a taxi with a blonde. Last seen in the
vicinity of the Clipper, the night of one of Ama Petrie's
parties. Her father was presiding over Shiellion, where Darren Rough should have given evidence, where Rebus had
been steamrollered by Richard Cordover. Lord Justice Petrie . . . who was related to Katherine Margolies.

Ama, Hannah, Katherine . . . Sammy, Patience, Janice
. . . The never-ending dance of relationships and criss-
crossings which took up so much space in his head. The
party that never stopped, the invitations guilt-edged.

Life and death in Edinburgh. And space still left over
for a few ghosts, their numbers increasing.

If I'd stuck around Fife, he thought, *not joined the army
. . . what would I be thinking now? Who would I be?*

The voice in his head again—was it Jack Morton's? *It
was never going to happen. This is where you were always
headed.* He looked around the room for whisky, but he was
all cleaned out. Closed his eyes instead. Still that dull pain
at the back of his skull. *Please, Lord, let my sleep be
dreamless.*

His first prayer in a while.

Cary Oakes had been in Arden Street for Rebus's return,
had seen him get out of his car with another man, lead the
man into his tenement. He wondered who this stranger was,
wondered where Rebus had met him. He'd been standing
across the road, hidden in the shadow of a tenement doorway. He had a plastic bag with him, a paperback book
inside to give it weight. If anyone saw him, he had his story
ready: working shifts, waiting for his lift to turn up. They
were late, he'd say.

Only no one saw him. No one entered or left the building. But he saw the lights come on in Rebus's living room.
Saw the stranger approach the window, put his head to it.
Saw Rebus over the man's shoulder, staring down. Oakes
stood his ground, felt he hadn't been spotted. The beauty
was, even if Rebus *did* see him, well, that was all right too.
Then Rebus had come out of the tenement, gone to his car

to fetch something: a book of some kind. Way he was moving, acting, Oakes hadn't done too much damage. Rebus took the book upstairs with him, then came back down half an hour later, put it back in the car. When he'd gone back up again, Oakes crossed to where the car was parked, tried the driver's door. It wasn't locked. He got in, felt on the floor for where Rebus had put the book. Found it. And the car keys. Smiled to himself. He turned the ignition, powered up the police radio: easy listening while he perused the surveillance notes. Rebus hadn't put in anything about Alan Archibald. That was interesting.

Fifty minutes later, when the tenement door rattled open, he slid down in his seat, rose up again to watch the stranger walk away from the building. He looked dirty and dishevelled. Some secret little vice of Rebus's? Oakes didn't think so. But it intrigued him all the same. He waited till the man had rounded the corner, then started the engine and began to follow . . .

At six o'clock, Rebus was wakened by the front buzzer. He went to the door, pushed the intercom.

"Who is it?"

"It's me." Bill Pryde, not sounding happy.

"What's the matter?"

"This car I'm supposed to pick up. Just where exactly have you hidden it?"

"Hang on."

Rebus walked into the living room, glanced at the sofa. Saw the blanket had been folded neatly; no sign of Darren Rough. Peered out of the window. A space where the car had been. He cursed under his breath. Put his shoes on and headed downstairs.

"I think someone took it," he told Bill Pryde.

"This isn't my fuck-up, John." Pryde: ticking off the days till retirement.

"I know," Rebus said, unwilling to add that he might know who'd taken it: Darren Rough.

Pryde pointed at his hands. "Word's out you lost the punch-up. How does Oakes look?"

"That's not what happened," Rebus said.

"You were found KO'd in a skip, way I heard it."

Rebus stared at him. "You want to walk to work, Bill?"

   Pryde shook his head. "I want to be ringside for the main bout: you telling the Farmer how you came to lose the car."

   Rebus stared up and down the road again. "Better slip a horseshoe into my glove for that one," he said, turning back into the tenement.

Rebus drove them to St. Leonard's in his Saab and reported the theft, cheering up the day shift who'd just come on. At quarter to nine, he was in the Farmer's office, explaining the whole thing yet again, including the scrapes on his hands. The Farmer busied himself at his coffee machine all the time Rebus was making his report. It was an espresso-maker with a spout for steamed milk. He hadn't offered Rebus a cup. When Rebus stopped talking, the Farmer poured the foamy milk into his mug, switched off the machine, and sat behind his desk. Holding the mug in both hands, he looked at Rebus.

   "I always thought surveillance was a fairly simple procedure. Once more, you've managed to prove me wrong."

   "It wasn't going anywhere, sir."

   "Unlike the missing car."

   Rebus looked down at the floor.

   "So let me see where we stand," the Farmer continued, taking another sip. "I tell you to lay off Darren Rough. You go out looking for him. I tell you to keep an eye on a man whom experts say may murder someone. You end up unconscious in a rubbish skip." The Farmer's voice was rising. "You find Darren Rough and take him to your flat. He then leaves, taking one of our cars with him, along with the surveillance log. Does that just about cover it?" His face was growing red with anger.

   "Clear and concise, sir."

"*Don't you dare be amused!*" The Farmer slapped a hand down on the desk.

"I'm anything but, sir." Rebus gritted his teeth. "But I thought I was doing the right thing at the time."

"No, Inspector. As usual, what you were doing was following your own agenda, and to hell with the rest of us. Isn't that nearer the mark?"

"With respect, sir——"

"Don't give me that. You've no respect for me, no respect for the job we're supposed to be doing here!"

"Maybe you're right, sir," Rebus said quietly, his head beginning to throb again.

The Farmer looked at him, leaned back in his chair and took another mouthful of coffee. "So what are we going to do about that?"

"I don't know, sir. I mean, you're right: I've been having doubts about the job for months. Ever since Jack Morton . . ."

"Maybe even before then?" Sounding calmer now.

"Maybe, sir. More than once, I've thought about chucking it." He looked at his boss. "Make your life a bit easier."

"But you haven't chucked it."

"No, sir."

"Must be a reason."

"Maybe a bit of me still believes, sir. And funnily enough, that part's been growing."

"Oh?"

Alan Archibald; Darren Rough: he hadn't mentioned Archibald to the Farmer, hadn't seen the point.

"I was wrong about Rough, I admit that. Well . . . I'm not sure I was wrong, to tell you the truth. But I know now why he's in Edinburgh. I know a bit more about his background."

"What are you saying?" The Farmer narrowed his eyes. "You *understand* him, is that it?" A smile with an edge of cruelty to it. "Compassion? *You*, John? I didn't know dinosaurs could evolve."

"Either that or the species dies," Rebus said, pressing his hands to his knees. How could he explain it, explain what he was learning: that the past shapes the present, that free will is a fantasy, that a force we could call Fate or

God controls the paths we take? Janice throwing a punch . . . young Darren Rough in a car on the way to Shiellion . . . Alan Archibald and his niece. All seemed connected in some strange and intricate way.

"You'll want a full report," Rebus said, straightening in his chair.

The Farmer nodded. "I was about to pull the surveillance anyway." He put down his mug. "Do you think Cary Oakes is dangerous?"

"Definitely. But I think he's changed."

"Changed how?"

"His spree in the States, it wasn't planned. There was a lack of deliberation, and it always seemed to be part of some other strategy."

"Explain."

"He killed because he needed things: money, a car, whatever. But towards the end, I think he was really getting a taste for it. Then he got caught. He's been all these years in jail, remembering that buzz."

"So now he might kill for no other reason than the buzz?"

"I'm not sure. I think he has some sort of plan, something that involves Edinburgh." And Alan Archibald, he might have added. "I think he's getting all sorts of tingly feelings just planning it."

"Maybe he'll put it off indefinitely."

Rebus smiled. "I don't think so. This is foreplay to him."

The Farmer seemed embarrassed by the image, relieved when his phone sounded. He picked up the receiver, listened.

"Good," he said at last. "I'll let him know."

He put down the receiver, looked up at Rebus. "The car's turned up."

"Great."

"Handily parked, too."

Rebus asked what the Farmer meant. The answer gave him the shock of his life.

A couple of uniforms were already on the scene when Rebus, the Farmer and Bill Pryde arrived at The Shore. The Rover was sitting in its usual spot, opposite the hotel.

"I don't believe it," Rebus said for the fifth or sixth time.

"This isn't some joke of yours?" Bill Pryde asked.

The Farmer looked inside. "Where's the log?"

"It was under the seat, sir."

The Farmer reached in, pulled out the log and a set of car keys.

"Did you say anything to Rough about the surveillance?" he asked. Rebus shook his head. "So can we assume Rough did *not* take the car?" Rebus shrugged.

"Looks like it was someone who knew what we were up to," Bill Pryde admitted.

"Or simply read about it in the log," Rebus said. "Anyone finding the keys would have found the log."

"True," Pryde conceded.

"Which might put Rough back in the frame," the Farmer said. "Thing is, it also means whoever stole the car read the surveillance notes."

"Red faces all round, sir," Pryde said.

"More than that if Fettes get to hear about it."

"Who's going to tell them?"

The Farmer had flipped through the notes, coming to Rebus's final section—or what should have been the final section. He opened the book wide, held it out so Rebus and Pryde could see it.

"What's this?"

Rebus looked. Written in big capitals, red felt pen. Someone had added a postscript to Rebus's thoughts on the case:

NAUGHTY, NAUGHTY. WHERE'S MR. ARCHIBALD????

The Farmer was staring at him.

"Who's Mr. Archibald?"

Pryde was shrugging. "Search me."

But the Farmer had eyes only for John Rebus.

"Who's Mr. Archibald?" he repeated, red rising to his cheeks. Rebus said nothing, crossed the street and looked in through the large windows of the restaurant. They were serving late breakfasts, tables half-hidden behind potted plants and hanging baskets. But there, at a window table and enjoying the show, sat Cary Oakes. He waved a fork at Rebus, sat beaming a grin as he lifted a glass of orange juice and toasted him. Rebus made for the hotel door, pushed it open, strode inside. Cooking smells were wafting from the restaurant. A waiter asked if he wanted a table for one. Rebus ignored him, walked straight up to the table where Cary Oakes was seated.

"Care to join me, Inspector?"

"Not even if you were coming apart at the seams." Rebus pushed his knuckles into Oakes's face. "Remember these?"

"Looks nasty," Oakes said. "I'd get a doctor to look at them. Lucky you already know one."

"You know where I live," Rebus hissed. "Jim Stevens told you."

"Did he?" Oakes started cutting up a sausage. Rebus noticed that he sliced it lengthwise first, as though dissecting it.

"You took the car."

"Bit early for riddles." Oakes lifted a morsel of meat to his lips. Rebus flung out a hand, sent fork and sausage flying. Then he hoisted Cary Oakes to his feet.

"What the fuck are you up to?"

"Shouldn't that be my line?" Oakes said, grinning. There was a sudden explosion of light. Rebus half-turned his head. Jim Stevens was behind him. Next to him stood a photographer.

"Now," Stevens was saying, "if we could have the two of you shaking hands in the next one." He winked at Rebus. "Told you I wanted some pictures."

Rebus dropped Oakes, flew towards the journalist.

"Inspector!"

The Farmer's voice. He was in the restaurant doorway, face like fury. "A word with you outside, if you don't mind." A voice not to be disobeyed. Rebus stared hard at Jim Stevens, letting him know this wasn't the end of anything. Then he walked out of the dining room and into reception. The Farmer was after him.

"I'm still waiting for an answer. Who is Mr. Archibald?"

"A man with a mission," Rebus told him. In his mind, he could still see the grin on Oakes's face. "Problem is, he's not the only one."

*   *   *

Rebus spent till lunchtime "in conference" with the Farmer. Just before midday, Archibald himself joined them, the Farmer having dispatched a squad car to Corstorphine to pick him up. The two men knew one another of old.

"Thought you'd have had the gold watch by now," Archibald said, shaking the Farmer's hand. But the Farmer was not to be mollified.

"Sit down, Alan. For a retired copper, you haven't half been busy."

Archibald glanced at Rebus, who was staring at the window-blind.

"I'm going to nail him, that's all."

"Oh, that's all, is it?" The Farmer looked mock-astonished. "John tells me you've seen the files on Cary Oakes. In fact, you've got more gen on him than we have. So you should know who you're dealing with."

"I know *what* I'm dealing with."

The Farmer's gaze went from Archibald to Rebus and back again. "It's bad enough I'm lumbered with this one," he said, nodding towards Rebus. "Last thing I need is yet another headcase out there trying to take the law into his own hands. You think Oakes killed your niece, show me the evidence."

"Come on, man . . ."

"Show me the evidence!"

"I would if I could."

"Would you, Alan?" The Farmer paused. "Or would you want to keep it personal, right to the bitter end?" He turned to Rebus. "What about you, John? Were you going to lend a hand burying the body?"

"If I'd wanted him dead," Archibald said, "he'd be in the ground by now."

"But what if he confesses, Alan? Just you and him, no third party." The Farmer shook his head. "Wouldn't be enough to go to court with, so what would you do?"

"It'd be enough," Archibald said quietly.

"For what?"

"For me. For Deirdre's memory."

The Farmer waited, turned to Rebus. "Do you buy that? You think Alan here would listen to Oakes's confession and then just walk away?"

"I don't know him well enough to comment." Rebus still seemed mesmerised by the window-blind.

"Two peas in a pod," the Farmer said. Rebus glanced at Archibald, who was looking at him. There was a knock at the door. The Farmer barked an order to enter. It was Siobhan Clarke.

"Come to intercede?" the Farmer asked.

"No, sir." She seemed unwilling to come in; stood with only her head showing round the door.

"Well?"

"Suspicious death, sir. Up on Salisbury Crags."

"How suspicious?"

"First reports say very."

The Farmer pinched the bridge of his nose. "This is one of those weeks that seem to last a fortnight."

"Thing is, sir, from the description, I'd say we have an ID."

He looked at her, hearing something in her tone. "Someone we know?"

Clarke was looking towards Rebus. "I'd say so, sir."

"This isn't a parlour game, DC Clarke."

She cleared her throat. "I think it might be Darren Rough."

26

"Start any time you're ready."

Jim Stevens' room was beginning to look messy and lived-in, just the way he liked. But they weren't in Stevens' room, they were in Oakes's, and it looked like its occupant hadn't spent any time there at all. There were two chairs at a small circular table by the window. The complimentary book of matches still sat folded open in its ashtray. Two magazines of interest to visitors to Edinburgh sat beside it, and lying on top of them was the guests' comment card, yet to be filled in, or even perused.

Most people, Stevens guessed, even people who'd spent a third of their life enjoying the facilities of a foreign country's prison service, would do what he'd done in his own room: explore it, try out and touch everything, flick through every piece of literature.

But not Cary Oakes, who now cleared his throat.

"Aren't you curious about what Rebus wanted?"

Stevens looked at him. "I just want this finished."

"Lost the old vigour and vim, eh, Jim?"

"You have that effect on people."

"Tracked down any of my old teenage gang?" Oakes laughed at the look on Stevens' face. "Thought not. Probably scattered to the four winds by now."

"Last time we broke off," Stevens said coldly, checking the spools were turning, "you were crossing America."

Oakes nodded. "I got to a place called, believe it or not, Opportunity, a ratty little truck-stop on the Washington-Idaho border. That's where I met the trucker, Fat Boy. I never learned his real name; I think even the ID he carried was fake."

"What name was on the ID?"

Oakes ignored the question. "Fat Boy had these notions about a government conspiracy, told me he kept his home booby-trapped whenever he was working long-distance. He said truckers got a real good view of the world—by which he meant the USA; that's as far as his world stretched—a real good view from behind the wheel of a truck. He knew a trucker would make a damned good President.

"So that was Fat Boy. My introduction to him. Opportunity, Washington. Lots of names like that in the States. Lots of Fat Boys, too. We got talking about murder. The radio was on, and every other station had news flashes about unlawful killing. He said the word 'unlawful' was a misnomer. There was 'wrong' killing and 'right' killing, and which was which was down to the individual, not the lawmakers."

"And what kind did you do?"

Oakes didn't like his flow being interrupted. "I'm talking about Fat Boy, not me."

"How long did you travel with him?" Stevens was trying to keep the chronology right.

"Three, four days. We headed south to make a delivery, then back up on to I-90."

"What was he carrying?"

"Electrical goods. He worked for General Electric. Meant he travelled all over. He said that was good, considering his hobby. His hobby was killing people." Oakes looked to Stevens. "It was supposed to unnerve me, him saying something like that while we're travelling fifty-five on an interstate. Maybe if it had, that would have been it: he'd have tried skinning me. But I just looked at him, told him that was interesting." A laugh. "Mild understatement, right? Someone tells you they're a serial killer and you say, 'Mm, that's interesting.' "

"But you believed him?"

"After a while, yes. And I thought: all this stuff he's telling me, no way is he letting me go. Every time we stopped, I thought he was about to whack me."

"You were ready for him?" Stevens was staring at Oakes, trying to gauge how much of the story was true. Did it relate in some way to the relationship between Oakes and the reporter himself?

"You know the strange part? I just let myself relax into it. Like, if he was going to kill me, OK, that's what was going to happen. It was as if I didn't care; I could have died right then, and it would have been poetic justice or something."

"Did he kill anyone while you were on the road?"

"No."

"But he convinced you he wasn't lying?"

"You think he was lying, Jim?"

"When they arrested you, did you tell the police about him?"

"Why the hell would I do that?"

"Might have scored you some points."

"Truth is, I never thought about it."

"But he made you think about killing?"

"He knew what he was talking about. I mean, you can always tell when someone's making it up, can't you?" Oakes beamed a smile. " 'Can the world really be like this?'

I remember asking myself that as I listened to him. And the answer came back: yes, of course. Why should it be any different?"

"You're saying Fat Boy made you feel all right about killing?"

"Am I?"

"Then what are you saying?"

"Just telling you my story, Jim. It's up to you how you read it."

"What about in jail, Cary? All that time to yourself, thoughts that you're thinking . . . ?"

"Jim, you get no time to yourself. There's always noise, disruption, routine. You sit there trying to think, they send you for psychiatric evaluation." Oakes took a final sip of orange juice. "But I see what you're getting at." He examined his empty glass. "How's the background check going, by the way? Spoken to anyone at Walla Walla?" Turned the empty glass in his hand. "Take away the juice and the ice, you're left with a lethal weapon." He pretended to smash the glass against the edge of the table, and then laughed a laugh which sent a shiver right along Jim Stevens' arms.

Climbing back up Salisbury Crags, Rebus kept his hands in his pockets and his thoughts to himself. He knew what the Farmer was thinking. This morning, Darren Rough had been in Rebus's flat. As far as they knew, Rebus was the last person to have seen him alive.

And Rebus had been his tormentor, his nemesis. The Farmer wouldn't make anything of it, but others might: Jane Barbour; Rough's social worker.

Radical Road was a stony footpath which led around the Crags. You could start near the student residences at Pollock Halls and end up at Holyrood. Along the way, you had the city skyline for company, stretching from the south and west to the city centre and beyond. All spires and crenellations. Manfred Mann: "Cubist Town." With Greenfield almost directly below.

"You picked him up here, didn't you?" the Farmer asked as they walked.

Rebus shook his head. "St. Margaret's Loch." Which lay

around a long curve in the rock and down an impossibly
steep bank. "Tell you what, though," he added. "Jim Margolies jumped from up there." And he pointed with his
finger, way up to where the rock-face ended in something
akin to a clifftop. People took their dogs for walks across
the plateau, not straying too close to the edge. Edinburgh
was prone to sudden, malevolent gusts, any one of which
could have you over the side.

The Farmer was breathing hard. "You still see a connection between Rough and Jim Margolies?"

"Now more than ever, sir."

The body lay a little further along the path, cordoned
off by warning tape. A few walkers, wrapped up against
the weather, had gathered at the cordon, stretching their
necks for a view. A white plastic contraption like a wind-
break had been placed around the body, so that only those
who needed to see it would. A woman with a black springer
spaniel was being interviewed: she'd been the one to find
the body. Out walking the dog, a daily ritual which both
had looked forward to. From now on, she'd find another
route, a long way from Salisbury Crags.

"Hard to believe they're putting our Parliament there,"
the Farmer commented, looking down towards Holyrood
Road. "A real old backwater. Traffic's going to be a nightmare."

"And it's on our patch."

"Not my problem, thank God." The Farmer sniffed. "I'll
have that gold watch on one hand and a golfing glove on
the other."

They passed through the cordon. The scene-of-crime
team was at work, securing the *locus* and ensuring what
they liked to call its "purity." This meant Rebus and the
Farmer had to don coveralls and overshoes, so they'd leave
no trace elements at the scene.

"The wind up here will probably have scattered them to
the four corners anyway," Rebus said. But it was a half-
hearted grouch: he knew the worth of scene-of-crime work,
knew that science and forensics were his friends. A police
doctor had declared the victim deceased. Dr. Curt was the
usual pathologist, but he was in Miami to give a paper at
some convention. His superior, Professor Gates, had

stepped in, and was examining the body *in situ*. He was a large man with thick brown hair slicked back from his forehead. He carried a hand-held tape recorder, talking into it as he moved around. He was forced to jostle for space: a photographer and video cameraman both wanted shots of the corpse.

DS George Silvers came over. He nodded a greeting to his Chief Superintendent, but took it further, so that it turned into something more akin to a ceremonial bow. That was typical of Silvers, whose station nickname was "Hi-Ho." He was in his late thirties, always smartly dressed and coiffed, always on the eye for promotion without the necessary concomitant of hard work. His black hair and deep-set eyes gave him the look of football pundit Alan Hansen.

"We think we've got the murder weapon, sir. A rock with some blood and hair on it." He pointed up the path. "Forty yards or so that way."

"Who found it?"

"A dog, sir." One eye twitching. "Licked most of the blood off before we could get to it."

Professor Gates looked up from his work. "So if the lab gets a match," he said, "and tells you the victim had a lovely shiny coat, you'll know what the problem is."

He laughed, and Rebus laughed with him. It was like that at the *locus*, everyone pretending nothing was out of the ordinary, erecting barriers to separate them from the glaring fact that *everything* was out of the ordinary.

"I'm told you might manage an informal ID," Gates said. Rebus nodded, took a deep breath and stepped forward. The body was lying where it had fallen, the back of the skull smashed open and caked with blood. The face rested against the jagged path, one leg bent at the knee, the other straight. One arm was trapped beneath the body, the other stretching so the fingers could claw at the cold earth. Rebus could tell from the clothes, but crouched down to study what could be seen of the face. Gates lifted it a little to help. Light had died behind the eyes; the three-day growth of beard would need to be shaved by the undertaker. Rebus nodded.

"Darren Rough," he said, his voice growing thick.

*　　*　　*

Having taken a break from recording, Jim Stevens sat naked on the edge of his bed, discarded clothes strewn around him, two empty miniatures of whisky on his bedside cabinet. The empty glass was clutched in one hand, and he stared at it and through it, focusing on things the world couldn't see . . .

Part Two
FOUND

I invite you to examine more closely your duty and the obligations of your earthly service because that is something which all of us are only dimly aware of, and we scarcely . . .

27

One of Rough's shoes had come off at some point, about halfway between the spot where his body had fallen and where the rock had been found. One early theory: someone had thumped him hard. He'd stumbled, staggered on, trying to get away from his attacker. His shoe had come off and been discarded. Finally, he'd fallen to the ground, where he'd died from the earlier blows. A barking dog approaching had alerted the attacker to the need to flee.

Another theory: after being hit, Rough had died instantly. His attacker had then dragged him along the path, the shoe coming free. Maybe intending to set things up so it looked like Rough had jumped or fallen from the Crags. But the dog-walker had come along, scaring off the killer.

"What was he doing up there anyway?" someone back at the station asked.

"I think he liked it there," Rebus said. He was now officially the St. Leonard's expert on Darren Rough. "It was like a sanctuary, somewhere he felt safe. And he could look down on Greenfield from there, see what was happening."

"So someone followed him? Sneaked up on him?"

"Or persuaded him to go there."

"Why?"

"To make it look like suicide. Maybe they read about Jim Margolies in the paper."

"It's a thought . . ."

There were plenty of thoughts, plenty of theories. One thought was: good riddance to the bastard. A week ago, it would have been Rebus's view, too.

The murder room was being prepared, computers moved from other parts of the building into the room set aside for such work. The Farmer had put Chief Inspector Gill Templer in charge. Rebus had been her lover for a time, so long ago now it might have been in some past life. Her hair was a dark-streaked feather-cut. Her eyes were emerald green. She moved confidently across the room, checking preparations.

"Good luck," Rebus told her.

"I want you on the team," she said.

Rebus thought he could understand. She was circling the wagons, and it was better to have him in the ring shooting out, than outside shooting in.

"And I want a report on my desk: everything you can tell me about you and the deceased."

Rebus nodded, got to work on one of the computers. *Everything you can tell me*: Rebus liked her wording, it gave him an escape clause—not everything he *knew* necessarily, but all he felt able to divulge. He looked across to where Siobhan Clarke was compiling a wall-mounted duty roster. She saw him and made a T sign with her hands. He nodded, and five minutes later she was back with two scalding beakers.

"Here you go."

"Thanks," he said. She was looking over his shoulder at the screen.

"Nothing but the truth?" she asked.

"What do you think?"

She blew on her cup. "Any idea who'd want him dead?"

"I can't think of many who didn't. We've got half the population of Greenfield to start with." Especially Cal Brady, with his previous convictions; and not forgetting his mother . . .

"Chasing him out and killing him aren't quite in the same league."

"No, but something like that can escalate. Maybe Billy Horman was all it took."

She rested against the corner of the desk. "Hit with a rock . . . doesn't sound premeditated, does it?"

Hit with a rock . . . Deirdre, Alan Archibald's niece, had been killed in a similar way: smashed over the head with a rock and then strangled. Clarke could read his mind.

"Cary Oakes?"

"Have we got a time of death yet?" Rebus asked, reaching for a telephone.

"Not that I know of. Body was found at eleven thirty."

"And we're guessing the killer heard someone coming and ran for it." Rebus had pressed the digits and was waiting. Connected. "Hello, could you put me through to James Stevens, please?"

Clarke looked at him. He put his hand over the mouthpiece. "I want to know what happened after breakfast." He listened again, took his hand away. "Could you try Cary Oakes's room for me?" Shook his head to let Clarke know Stevens wasn't in his own room. This time the call was answered.

"Oakes, is that you? It's Rebus here, put Stevens on." He waited a moment. "One question: what happened after breakfast?" Listened again. "Was he out of your sight? You've been there all morning?" Listened. "No, it's all right. You'll find out soon enough."

Replaced the receiver.

"They've been working all morning."

"No chance it was Oakes then." She looked at the computer screen. "What would be his motive anyway?"

"Christ knows. But he was at my flat. He took the patrol car. Maybe he saw Rough leave, worked out he was connected to me."

"Can you prove that?"

"No."

"Then all he has to do is deny it."

Rebus exhaled noisily. "It's all games with him."

Gill Templer was staring at them from across the room.

"I'd better get back to work," Clarke said, taking her tea with her. Rebus finished his report, printed it out, handed it personally to Gill Templer.

"When's the post-mortem?"

She checked her watch. "I was just about to head over there."

"Need a driver?"

She studied him. "Has your driving improved?"

"I'll let you be the judge, ma'am."

*   *   *

The city mortuary wasn't in business. Health and Safety; changes needed to be made. Meantime, they were using the Western General Hospital. Because they couldn't find any relatives or friends, Andy Davies had been called to verify Rebus's identification. The social worker was waiting when Rebus and Gill Templer arrived. He made the ID, said nothing to Rebus but shot him a cold look before leaving.

"Bad blood?" Templer asked.

"Better than none at all, Gill."

Professor Gates was already at work by the time they'd got their gowns and masks on. For the official ID, Rough's corpse had worn a shroud. Now, lying on the stainless-steel bench, it wore nothing at all. Prominent ribs, Rebus noted. He was thinking of the meal he'd made for Rough. Grudgingly made. Beans on toast. Probably the man's last meal ever. And eventually, Gates would reveal it to the world again. Rebus half-turned his face.

"Seasick, Inspector?" Gates asked.

"I'll be fine so long as we keep out of the bilges."

Gates chuckled. "But below decks is the most interesting part." He was measuring, muttering his findings to his assistant, a young man with a face the colour of a cancer bed.

"And how are you, Gill?" he asked at last.

"Overworked."

Gates glanced up. "Fine lassie like you should be at home, bringing up strong healthy bairns."

"Thanks for the vote of confidence."

Gates chuckled again. "Don't tell me you lack suitors?"

She chose to ignore the remark.

"What about you, John?" Gates persisted. "Love life satisfactory? Maybe I should play Cupid, put the two of you together. What do you say to that now, eh?"

Rebus and Templer shared a look.

"Professions like ours," Gates drawled on, "aren't the same as being a lawyer or a novelist, are they? Not much of an ice-breaker at parties." He nodded towards his assistant. "Bear that in mind, Jerry. No nookie unless you lie about what you do." Gates's final chuckle turned into a choking bark, a bronchial cough which almost doubled him over. He wiped his eyes afterwards.

"Time to stop smoking," Templer warned him.

"I can't do that. It would spoil the bet."

"What bet?"

"Dr. Curt and myself: who'll live the longer on twenty a day."

"That's . . ." Templer had been about to say "sick," but then she saw that the body had been opened up almost without her noticing, and she realized why Gates kept the conversation going: it was to take everyone's mind off the task at hand. And for a few moments, it had worked.

"I'll tell you one thing straight off," the pathologist said. "His clothes were damp, and to me that means rain. I've checked: we had a short shower early this morning and nothing since."

"Could he have got wet lying on the path?"

"He was lying on his front. The back of his clothing was damp. So he was out in that shower, whether alive or dead I can't say. But his hair was wet, too. Now, if you're caught in a sudden downpour, wouldn't you usually pull your jacket up over your head?"

"Depends on your state of mind," Rebus said.

Gates shrugged. "I'm only surmising. But one thing I'm sure of." He ran a finger along the body, tracing patches of pale bluish markings. "*Livor mortis*. It was present at the scene. I arrived forty-five minutes after the body was discovered."

"But lividity starts . . . ?"

"Well, it starts from the moment the heart stops pumping, but it becomes visible somewhere between half an hour and an hour after death. This was well-established by the time I arrived."

"What about rigor mortis?"

"Eyelids had stiffened, as had the jaw. I'll take a potassium sample from the eye, to get a better idea of timing, but right now I'd guess the body had been lying there for three hours, maybe more."

Rebus took a step forward. If Gates was right—and he invariably was—the dog-walker had not disturbed the killer. The killer had been long gone by the time the spaniel and its owner had arrived, and Darren Rough had died around seven or eight in the morning. At five he'd been asleep on Rebus's couch; by six he'd gone . . .

"Did he die where we found him?" Rebus asked, wanting to be sure.

"Judging by the patterns of lividity, I'd say it's a racing certainty." The pathologist paused. "Of course, I've lost a few pounds on horses in my time."

"We need a more specific time of death."

"I know you do, Inspector. You *always* do. I'll do what tests the budget will stretch to."

"And ASAP."

Gates nodded. He was about ready to begin removing the inner organs. Jerry was fussing with the necessary tools.

Rebus was thinking: three, maybe four hours.

Thinking: Cary Oakes was back in the running.

They took him in for questioning, Rebus keeping out of the way, listening to the tapes afterwards. Stevens' paper had provided their client with a solicitor from one of the city's top firms, despite Templer's insistence that all they had were a few questions, easily cleared up. But Oakes was saying nothing. Templer was good, and she had Pryde with her: their routine was well-honed, but Rebus got the feeling Oakes had seen all the moves before. He'd been examined and cross-examined and called to the stand again, he'd been through all that in an American courtroom. He just sat there and said he knew nothing about the patrol car, nothing about where Rebus lived, and nothing about any dead paedophile. His final comment:

"What's all the fuss about a kiddie-fucker?"

Pryde, listening to the tape, folded his arms at that and puckered his lips, most of him agreeing with the sentiment. When Pryde asked if Rebus was heading outside for a smoke, Rebus, inwardly gasping for one, shook his head.

Later, he went out into the car park alone, pacing as he sucked hungrily on first one Silk Cut and then a second. Ten a day, he was keeping to ten a day. And if he went as high as twelve today, that meant only eight tomorrow. Eight was fine, he could handle that. It gave him a margin for today, a margin he reckoned he'd need.

Only thing was, he was already in arrears for the week; for the whole month, truth be told.

Tom Jackson came out, lit one of his own. They didn't speak for the first couple of minutes. Jackson scuffed his shoes on the tarmac and broke the silence.

"I hear you took him in."

Rebus blew smoke from his nose. "That's right."

"Rescue act, let him stay the night."

"So?"

"So not everyone would have been so charitable."

"I'm not sure it was charity."

"What then?"

What then? It was a good question.

"Thing is," Jackson went on, "a few days back, you were all for stringing him up."

"Don't exaggerate."

"You set that pack of wild dogs on him."

"You mean the papers or his neighbours?"

"Both."

"Careful, Tom. You're their community officer. That's your flock you're talking about."

"I'm talking about *you*: what happened?"

"He only slept on my couch, Tom. It's not like I gave him a gam or anything." Rebus flicked his third cigarette on to the ground, stubbed it out. Only half-smoked, so he'd count two and a half; round it down to two.

"We still haven't turned up the kid."

"How's his mother doing?"

Jackson knew the question's subtext, answered accordingly. "Nobody seems to think she's a suspect."

"What's her history?"

"Billy's her only kid. Had him at nineteen."

"Is the father around?"

"Did the usual vanishing act before the baby was born. Ran off to Ulster to join the paramilitaries."

"He'll be running for office now then."

Jackson snorted. "She's had half a dozen blokes since; been living with the latest for the past few weeks."

"The three of them in the flat together?"

Jackson nodded. "He's being interviewed. We're digging into his history."

"A fiver says he's got form."

"What? Living in Greenfield?" Jackson smiled. "Keep your money in your pocket." He paused. "You really don't think this connects to our deceased friend?"

"It might do, Tom. But just maybe not in the way we think."

"What do you mean?"

"Be seeing you," Rebus said, moving away.

Thinking of an old Gravy Train song: "Won't Talk About It."

He told Patience he wouldn't be seeing her. There must have been something in his tone of voice.

"Out on the ran-dan?" she said.

"You know me too well." He put the receiver down before she could say anything else. He started at The Maltings, headed up Causewayside to Swany's, then took a taxi to the Ox. His car was back at St. Leonard's: no problem, he could walk into work next morning. Salty Dougary, one of the Young Street regulars, had just been in hospital: a coronary; they'd operated, angioplasty or something like that. He was telling the bar all about it. For some reason Rebus couldn't fathom, the operation had apparently started at Dougary's groin.

"Way to a man's heart," Rebus commented, sinking another whisky. He was diluting them with water, but not overly so. He felt fine, as in not drunk; mellow, kind of. But he knew if he walked out of the bar, he'd start to feel the alcohol. A good excuse to stay put, like that character in *Apocalypse Now*: "Never get out of the boat." It was only when you left the boat that you got into trouble. The same thing, in Rebus's experience, was true of pubs, which was why he was still in the Ox at half past midnight. The back room had been taken over by musicians, a dozen or more of them; guitars mostly, twelve-bar blues. One guy

with a beard was playing the harmonica like he was in front
of a Madison Garden crowd. Janis Joplin: "Buried Alive in
the Blues."

Rebus was talking with George Klasser, a doctor at the
Infirmary. Klasser usually left early—sevenish or a little
after. When he stayed late, it was a sign things were fraught
at home. He'd started the evening advising Salty Dougary
to regulate his alcohol intake.

"The pot calling the kettle black," had been Dougary's
riposte. Dougary looking like he'd just been on holiday
rather than in surgery: face tanned, ciggies cut down from
forty a day to ten. Klasser with dark shadows under his
eyes, a slight trembling to the hand when he picked up his
glass. Rebus had had an uncle who'd smoked a pack of
cigarettes every day of his life and lived to be eighty. His
own father had died younger, having given up cigarettes
two decades previously.

You never could tell.

There were only four of them in the front bar, five including Harry. Dougary, who'd drunk in every pub in the
city, reckoned Harry was Edinburgh's rudest barman,
which was quite a feat, considering the competition.

"I wish youse lot would bugger off home," Harry said,
not for the first time that evening.

"Night's young yet, Harry," Dougary said.

"How come they let you out of intensive care?"

Dougary winked. "Intensive care's what I come in here
for." He toasted them with his glass and raised it to his lips.
Twenty minutes before, Rebus had told Klasser about Darren Rough. Now Klasser turned to him, eyes heavy-lidded.

"There was a famous murder case. Turn of the century,
I think it was. German couple came here on their honey-
moon, only it turned out he wanted her money rather than
love. He planned to kill her, make it look like suicide. So
they went for a walk up on Arthur's Seat, and he pushed
her off the Crags."

"But he didn't get away with it?"

"Obviously not, or there'd be no story to tell."

"So how was he caught?"

Klasser stared into his glass. "I can't recall."

Dougary laughed. "Don't let him start telling any jokes, he always forgets the punchline."

"I'll punch *you* in a minute, Salty."

"Get in the queue," Harry commented.

Some nights it was like that in the Oxford Bar. When the guitar-players packed up, Rebus put his coat on. There was a stiff breeze outside, and it had been raining again, the streets black and shiny as a beetle's back. He'd meant to phone Janice, but what would he have said? There was no news of Damon. He walked along Princes Street, deciding he liked the city best like this: all the visitors tucked up in bed. Outside the Balmoral Hotel, a line of Jags and Rovers sat, their chauffeurs waiting for some function to finish. A young couple walked past, sharing a bottle of cheap cider. The male wore a jacket with a badge on it. The badge said Stockholm Film Festival. Rebus had never heard of it. Maybe it was the name of a band: you couldn't be sure these days.

He walked up the Bridges, stopped at some railings so he could look down on to the Cowgate. There were clubs still open down there, teenagers spilling on to the road. The police had names for the Cowgate when it got like this: Little Saigon; the blood bank; hell on earth. Even the patrol cars went in twos. Whoops and yells: a couple of girls in short dresses. One lad was down on his knees in the road, begging to be noticed.

Pretty Things: "Cries from the Midnight Circus."

In Edinburgh, sometimes it could be midnight in the middle of the day . . .

He didn't know where he was going, what he was doing. If he was going home, he was doing so only by degrees. When a taxi came, he flagged it down. On sudden impulse, he named his destination.

"The Shore."

29

The idea was . . .

The idea was to stand in the freezing cold outside the hotel, call up to Oakes's room on the mobile. Get him downstairs . . . no crack to the back of the head this time. Face to face. But it was the drink, that was all. Rebus knew he wouldn't do it; knew Oakes wouldn't fall for it anyway. Looking across from The Shore, he saw there were lights from the Clipper, and a minder on the door. So Rebus crossed the bridge, introduced himself. The minder was wiping sweat from his face. From within, Rebus could hear raised voices, laughter.

"Party?" he asked.

"Don't tell me there've been complaints," the minder growled. His accent was Liverpudlian. From his size, Rebus would bet his family had worked dockside. "That's all I need right now."

"What's up?"

"Buggers don't want to leave, do they?"

"Have you tried asking nicely?"

The man snorted.

"Nobody here to help you?"

"When we turned the music off, looked like they weren't going to stick around. DJ packed up and sodded off home. So did Mr. Frost—my boss. Told me all I had to do was switch off the lights and lock up after me."

"You're new to this game."

The bouncer smiled. "Does it show?"

"I take it you've got a mobile about your person. Why not call Mr. Frost?"

"Don't have his home number."

Rebus rubbed his chin. "Is that as in Archie Frost?"

"That's him."

Rebus was thoughtful for a moment. "Want me to talk to them?" He nodded towards the boat. "See if I can get them to pack up?"

The minder stared at him. He was well-educated in the relationship that should exist between his profession and Rebus's: a favour done now might mean a favour asked later. He turned towards a noise. One of the revellers had come up on deck and was preparing to urinate off the side. He sighed.

"Why not?" he said.

And Rebus was in.

One guy had pegged out on the deck, champagne bottle held to his chest. His bow tie was hanging from his neck; his watch was a gold Rolex. The guest using the Albert Basin as his own private loo rocked to and fro on his heels. He was humming the chorus of some pop song. Seeing Rebus, he beamed a smile. Rebus ignored him, headed down the steps into the main body of the boat. It was set up for a party: chairs and tables around a long narrow dancefloor. Bar at one end, makeshift stage at the other. There was a lighting rig, a mirror-ball over the dancefloor. Shutters had been brought down across the bar and fixed with a padlock, which another drunk was trying to pick with a plastic toothpick. A couple of the tables had been knocked over, along with a dozen or so chairs. There were forgotten items of clothing strewn across the floor, along with crisps, peanuts, empty bottles, and bits of sandwich and squashed quiche. The main action was centred on two tables which had been pushed together. Fourteen or fifteen people sat here. Women sat on men's laps, kissing deeply. A few couples were indulging in muted conversations. One or two individuals were fast asleep. A hard core of five—three men, two women—were telling slurred stories, de-tailing the party highlights, mostly involving drink, vomit and snogging.

"Hello again," Rebus said to Ama Petrie. "This your do, is it?"

She had her head on the shoulder of the young man next to her. Her mascara was smeared, making her look tired. Her short dress was a meshing of black gauzy layers. Her bare feet were in the lap of the man on the other side of her. He was playing with her toes.

"Oh, Christ," this man said, eyes drooping, "they've sent in the heavy brigade. Look, my good man, we've paid for this evening—cash, and upfront. So kindly bugger off and—"

"Oscar, you arse, he's a policeman," Ama Petrie said. Then, to Rebus: "Nice to see you again." It was an automatic greeting, something she couldn't help but say, even though her eyes told a different story. Her eyes told Rebus she wasn't in the least pleased to see him.

"Well," Oscar said, smiling to the assembly, "in that case, it's a fair cop, guv, but society's to blame. I never had a chance." He slipped into the role effortlessly, drawing smiles and laughter from his audience. Rebus looked at the faces around him: the faces of Edinburgh's rich young things. They'd have their own flats in the New Town, gifts from indulgent parents. They had their parties and their nights out. Maybe by day they shopped or lunched or attended a couple of lectures at the university. Maybe they drove their sports cars out to the country. Their lives were predestined: a job in the family business, or something "arranged"—a position they could cope with, something requiring inbred charm and minimal effort. Everything would fall into their laps, because that's the way the world was.

"Shame he's not in uniform, eh, Nicky?"

"What have we done, Officer?" another of the men asked.

"Well, you've overstayed your welcome," Rebus said. "But that doesn't really concern me. Might I ask whose party this is?" He was looking at Ama.

"Mine, actually," the man with the toothpick said, turning away from the bar. He pushed his thick fair hair back from his forehead. A thin face, soft-featured. "I'm Nicol Petrie, Ama's brother." Rebus guessed this was "Nicky": *Shame he's not in uniform, eh, Nicky?*

He was in his early twenties, fashionably unshaven so his face shone a spiky gold. "Look," he said, "I'll move this lot off the boat, promise." And to his friends: "We'll go back to my place. Plenty of drink there."

"I want to go to a casino," one woman complained. "You *said* we'd go."

"Darling, he only said that so you'd give him a blow job."

Hoots of laughter, pointed fingers. Ama had her eyes closed but was chuckling, her feet grinding against her companion's groin.

Everyone seemed to have forgotten Rebus. The conversations were starting up again. He reached into his pocket, handed two photographs to Nicol Petrie.

"His name's Damon Mee. He left a nightclub with the blonde woman. We think they were on their way to a party on this boat, hosted by your sister."

"Yes," Nicol Petrie said, "Ama told me." He studied the photos, shook his head. "Sorry." Handed them back.

"You were at the party in question?" Petrie nodded. "All of you?"

They looked to Ama, who told them which party it had been. A couple hadn't been present—previous commitments. Rebus handed the photos out anyway. Nobody paid much attention to them; they kept talking to each other as they passed them round.

"I could just go some smoked salmon."

"Alison's bash next Friday: are you going?"

"Hair extensions, they change your whole face instantly . . ."

"Thought about putting a consortium together, buy a racehorse . . ."

Ama Petrie didn't even glance at the pictures, just passed them along.

"Sorry," the last of the group said, handing them back to Rebus before continuing a conversation. Nicol Petrie looked apologetic.

"I promise we'll leave soon, assemble some taxis."

"Right, sir."

"And I'm sorry we couldn't be more help."

"Not to worry."

"I ran away from home once . . ."

"Nick, you were only *twelve*," Ama Petrie drawled.

"All the same, I know how much it hurt our mother and father."

Ama disagreed. "They hardly noticed you were gone." She looked up at him. "It was me who called the police."

"What happened?" Rebus asked.

"I'd been staying at a friend's house," Nicol Petrie explained. "When his parents heard I was supposed to be missing, they drove me home." He shrugged. A couple of his friends laughed.

"Right," he said, raising his voice slightly. "Back to my place. The night is still young, and so are we!"

There were cheers at this. Rebus got the feeling Nicol had roused the troops like this before.

"Where's Alfie?" Ama asked.

"Taking a leak," she was told.

Rebus made for the stairs. "Thanks anyway," he said to her brother. Nicol Petrie shot out a hand, which Rebus shook.

Shame he's not in uniform . . . What the hell had that meant? Some private joke? Rebus climbed back up into fresh air. The man who'd been relieving himself—Alfie—was sitting on the floor of the boat, legs splayed. He'd forgotten to button his flies.

"Leaving so soon?" he asked.

"Everyone's going back to Nicky's," Rebus said, like he was one of the gang.

"Good old Nicky," Alfie said.

"You're Alfie, aren't you?"

The young man looked up, trying to place Rebus. "Sorry," he said, "can't seem to . . ."

"John," Rebus said.

"Of course, John." Nodding briskly. "Never forget a face. You're in the finance sector?"

"Securities."

"Never forget a face." Alfie started to get up. Rebus helped him. He still had his photos in one hand.

"Here," he said. "Take a look." Didn't say any more than that, just handed them over.

"Photographer must have been pissed," Alfie said.

"Not very good, are they?"

"Bloody awful. I've got a friend who's a photographer. Let me give you his number." Reaching into his jacket.

"You'll know his face, though," Rebus said, tapping the holiday snap of Damon.

Alfie squinted at the photo, brought it close to his nose, moved it to pick up the available light.

"I pride myself," he said, "on never forgetting a face. But in this chap's case, I'll make an exception." Smiled crookedly at his own little joke. "Now the lady, on the other hand . . ."

"Alfie!" Ama Petrie was standing at the top of the stairs, arms folded against the chill. "Come on, we're getting ready to go."

"Super idea, Ama." Alfie blinked so slowly, Rebus thought he'd nodded off.

"About the blonde . . ." Rebus persisted.

Ama had come up to them, was tugging on Alfie's sleeve. Alfie patted Rebus's arm. "See you at Nicky's, old boy."

"Come on, Alfie." Ama pecked his cheek, led him to the stairs. A quick backward glance towards Rebus. Looking . . . angry? Relieved? A mix of the two? When they disappeared from view, Rebus walked off the boat.

"They're on their way," he told the minder.

"Cheers."

"That's one you owe me," Rebus said, waiting till the minder had nodded. "To square things, I want you to tell me what Archie Frost has to do with Billy Preston."

"He just works for them, same as I do."

"But he runs Gaitano's for Charmer Mackenzie."

The minder was nodding. "That's right."

"No conflict of interests?"

"Should there be?"

Rebus narrowed his eyes. "Mackenzie owns this boat?"

The minder licked his lips. "Part-owns. Mr. Preston has the other half."

Charmer Mackenzie had a half-share in the Clipper. And he owned Gaitano's. Damon had been at Gaitano's, and was last seen near the Clipper. Rebus was beginning to wonder . . .

"That's us quits," the minder said, as the party-goers did a conga towards the gangway.

*   *   *

He went back to his flat but couldn't sleep. The blanket Darren Rough had slept under was still folded on the sofa. He couldn't bring himself to move it. Instead, he sat in his chair, waiting for the ghosts to come. Maybe Darren would be with them, or maybe he'd have other souls to haunt.

But no ghosts came. Rebus dozed, came awake with a start. Decided he'd be better off out of doors. He cut through The Meadows, past the Infirmary. It was due to move out of town, south to Little France. There was talk the old Infirmary site would be turned into upmarket flats, or maybe a hotel. Prime city-centre-site, but who'd want a flat where a hospital ward had been?

He paused at the statue of Greyfriars Bobby. When you thought of it, Bobby was just a dog with nowhere better to go, nothing better to be doing. Rebus reached out and patted the statue's head.

"Stay," he said, heading down George IV Bridge. A couple of taxis slowed beside him, touting for custom, but he waved them on, took the Playfair Steps down to the National Gallery and Royal Academy. He passed a couple of people sleeping rough, watched the Castle beginning to assume shape again against the sky as night segued into morning. He thought of his grandfathers, whose names were buried somewhere in the Castle's Books of Remembrance. He couldn't even recall what regiments they'd served in. Both had died in the 1914–18 campaign, long before Rebus's parents had even met.

Princes Street had the usual haphazard look to it. The pavements seemed plenty wide when there was no one else about. He nipped up the side of Burger King and into the Penny Black, which opened for business at five. There were a couple of drinkers already in. Rebus ordered a whisky, added plenty of water.

"Man, you're drowning it," one drinker commented.

Rebus just smiled; didn't tell the man that water was his lifeline. An early edition of the *Scotsman* sat on the bar. Rebus flicked through it. A report of the previous day's doings in the Shiellion trial, plus the "suspicious death" of Darren Rough and the disappearance of Billy Horman. There was an anonymous quote from a member of GAP, to the effect that they blamed Rough for the boy's disappearance.

"And we're just glad and relieved that one piece of vermin has departed this earth. May all the others do the same."

Van Brady in preaching mode. There was talk of a residents' committee, of new arrivals in Greenfield being vetted by their neighbours. There was going to be discussion of neighbourhood patrols, spot checks, and even some kind of barrier to stop "undesirables" from entering Greenfield and "defacing" it.

Rebus knew Scotland was gearing up for self-rule, but this was taking it to extremes.

"We've got a computer in the community centre," the spokesperson said, "and now we want hooked up to the Internet so we can ask the Guardian Angels for advice. We're hoping a lottery grant will get us the software. This community deserves no less."

If there was going to be a private police force in Greenfield, Rebus wondered who'd be best placed to operate it. The name Cal Brady came readily to mind . . .

He finished his drink and decided to have breakfast down in Leith, where there was a café open at six with huge portions and little fuss. He walked the length of Leith Walk, found the café and settled down. With the paper already read, he'd nothing to do but chew on a half-slice of fried bread and stare out of the window. When a taxi stopped at the lights outside the café, Rebus caught a glimpse of the passenger. He tried for a better look, but the taxi was already on the move, taking Cary Oakes back to his hotel. He got the licence number, jotted it on the back of his hand. A mouthful of scalding tea helped him wash down the bread, then he asked to use the owner's phone. Called a cab company and asked about the reg.

"You kidding? Know how many cabs we've got?"

"Do your best, eh?" He gave them his mobile number, then tried the other companies in the city. They all seemed to think he was asking a lot, but by the time he got to St. Leonard's, he had a result. The cabbie was actually back at base, his shift over. Rebus spoke to him.

"You took a fare down to Leith, I'm guessing The Shore. About an hour ago."

"Yeah, last pick-up I had."

"Where exactly did you pick him up?"

"Out Corstorphine way, just before the Maybury round-about. What's he done?"

Corstorphine: where Alan Archibald lived. Rebus thanked the driver and terminated the call. He went to the toilets for a wash and shave, swallowed two paracetamol with some coffee. The murder room was empty, no one yet at work. He examined the photos on the wall. Archibald's niece had been murdered on a hillside; Darren Rough had been murdered on a hillside. Was it a connection? He thought of Cary Oakes, roaming freely through the city. Picked up one of the phones and called Patience.

"Moming," she said sleepily.

"This is your alarm call."

He could hear her stretch her back, sitting up in bed. "What time is it?"

He told her. "I couldn't get back for breakfast, thought I'd phone instead."

"Where are you?"

"St. Leonard's."

"Did you sleep at Arden Street?"

"I managed a nap."

"I don't know how you do it." She was probably pushing hair out of her eyes. "I need eight hours minimum."

"They say it's the sign of a clear conscience."

"What does that say about you?" She knew he wasn't going to answer that, asked instead if she'd see him for dinner.

"Sure," he told her. "Unless you don't, of course."

"Of course," she said. Then: "How's the head?"

"Fine."

"You liar. Try one day off the booze, John, just for me. One day, and tell me you don't feel better in the morning."

"I know I'll feel better in the morning. Problem is, as soon as I have a drink, I forget."

"Bye, John."

"Bye, Patience."

Patience: more than living up to her name . . .

30

Rebus and Gill Templer, in Interview Room B with Cal Brady. Interview Room B: same room Rebus had taken Darren Rough. Same room he'd first met Harold Ince during the Shiellion inquiry. They were talking to Cal Brady again because Templer had a few things to clear up.

"You started that fire," she said.

"Did I?" Brady looked around, wide-eyed. "Maybe we better get a solicitor in here then."

"Don't try to be funny, Mr. Brady."

"Only jokers I see around here are you lot."

"Billy Horman is reported missing, next thing you're out torching Darren Rough's flat. If I was of a mind, I might think *you* had something to gain from that." She paused, shifting the paperwork in front of her. "Or something to hide."

"Such as?" Brady sat back in his chair, arms folded.

"That's what I'm wondering."

Brady snorted, looked to where Rebus was standing. "Lost your voice or what?"

Rebus didn't rise to it. Gill Templer was quite capable of dealing with the likes of Cal Brady.

"Everyone else went out looking for Billy," she continued, "but you held back. Why's that, Mr. Brady?"

Brady shifted in his seat. "Kept an eye on Billy Boy's mum."

Templer made a show of checking her notes. "Joanna Horman?" She waited for Brady to nod agreement. "That's women's work, isn't it, Calumn? Holding the mother's hand, offering sympathy and a rum and Coke. Thought you were more of an Action Man."

"Someone had to do it."

"But why *you*, that's what I'm getting at? Maybe you fancied her. Maybe the two of you know one another . . . ?" She paused. "Or could it be that you already knew there was no point looking for Billy Horman . . . ?"

Brady thumped the desk. "Don't you start on this!" Quick to ignite. "Everybody knows what happened to Billy Boy. He got snatched by Rough or one of his cronies."

"Then where is he?"

"How the hell should I know?"

"And who killed Darren Rough?"

"If it had been me, he'd've been missing some bits."

"What if I tell you he was?" Templer playing a little game.

Brady looked surprised. "Was he? Nobody said . . ."

Templer looked at her notes. Then: "DI Rebus, I believe you have a few more questions for Mr. Brady."

Rebus having cleared things with her first, explaining his interest. He moved towards the desk, rested his knuckles on it.

"How do you come to know Archie Frost?"

"Archie?" Brady looked at Templer. "What's this got to do with anything?"

"Another inquiry, Mr. Brady. Unconnected to the other two, except, perhaps, by you."

"I don't get it."

"You want that solicitor now?"

He thought about it, shrugged his shoulders. "I do some work for him."

"For Mr. Frost?"

"That's right. I work on the door some nights."

"You're a bouncer?"

"I keep an eye out for trouble."

Rebus produced the photographs again. They had curled and creased at the edges, and were smeared with finger-prints.

"Do you remember me asking about these people?"

Brady looked at the photos, nodded. "I wasn't on the door that night."

"And which night is that?" Brady looked up from the photos. Rebus was smiling. "I don't recall giving Mr. Frost any particular night."

"If I'd been working that night I'd have spotted him. I had a run-in with him once before. No way he would have got past the door with me there."

Rebus narrowed his eyes. "What sort of run-in?"

Brady shrugged. "Nothing much. He was just a bit pissed, making too much noise. I told him to calm down and he didn't, so a couple of us escorted him off the premises."

Brady liked this last phrase; smiled at it. A nice official ring to it: "escorted," "premises."

"You ever do any door work at the Clipper?"

Brady shook his head.

"But you work for its owner."

"Mr. Mackenzie has a share of the boat, that's all."

"But he provides the bouncers too."

"I tried it once, didn't like it."

"Why not?"

"All these stuck-up tarts and Hooray Henries, thinking they could walk all over you because they had a bit of cash."

"I know what you mean." Brady looked at him. "No, really. I've seen them for myself." Rebus was still thinking about Brady's run-in with Damon Mee. He'd thought it was Damon's first visit to Gaitano's; no one had told him any different. "Thing is, Cal. Damon's a missing person, and I'm a bit like Gulliver in one of Lilliput's toilets."

"Eh?"

"I've not got much to go on." Gill Templer groaned at the joke, while Rebus counted off on his fingers. "I've got Damon going missing, last seen with a blonde being dropped by taxi outside the Clipper. The boat's part-owned by Charmer Mackenzie, who also owns Guiser's, which is where Damon and the blonde seemed to meet. See, there's a connection there. Right now, it's the only thing I've got, which is why I'm going to keep working away at it until I've got some answers." He paused. "Only you don't have any of the answers, do you?"

Brady stared at him. Rebus turned to Templer.

"No further questions, m'lud."

"All right, Mr. Brady," she said. "You can go now."

Brady walked to the door, opened it, turned his head back towards Rebus.

"Gulliver," he said. "Is he the one in the cartoon with the little people?"

"That's him," Rebus acknowledged.

Brady nodded thoughtfully. "I still don't get it," he said, closing the door after him.

At lunchtime, Rebus sat in his car and slept for half an hour, before heading back to the office with a beaker of tomato soup and a cheese and Branston sandwich.

"We've got something," Roy Frazer informed him. "Sighting of a white saloon car, exiting Holyrood Park at the Dalkeith Road end. Someone from maintenance at the Commonwealth Pool noticed it. Early morning, no traffic about. This car was doing a fair lick, went through a red light. He's a cyclist, pays attention to that sort of thing."

"And a model citizen too, I'll bet. Never sneaks through a red on his bike when nobody's watching." Rebus thought for a moment. "Any surveillance cameras that might have caught it?"

"I'll check."

"Clear it with DCI Templer first. She's in charge."

"Yes, sir." Frazer bounded off in search of her. He reminded Rebus of a pet spaniel, always ready for attention and praise. White saloon car . . . Something was niggling Rebus. He put in a call to Bobby Hogan at Leith police station.

"If I say the words 'white saloon car' to you, what would you say to me?"

"I'd say my brother's got one, a Ford Orion."

"I'm thinking of Jim Margolies."

"Something in the notes?"

"Yes. I'm sure there was a white saloon."

"Can I call you back?"

"Soon as poss." He put down the receiver, scribbled circles within circles on his pad, then sent lines radiating out from the centre. He couldn't decide if it looked more like a spider's web or a dartboard, came to the answer: neither. The telescopic sight from a warplane maybe? Or a section through a tree-trunk? All possibilities, but really all it was in the end was a meaningless squiggle. And when he ran over it a few times with the pen, it became clotted past interpretation.

His phone rang and he picked up.

"Is it important?" Bobby Hogan asked.

"I don't know. Might connect to something else."

"Want to tell me what?"

"You go first."

He seemed to be considering the offer, then began to recite from the case-notes. "Light-coloured saloon car, possibly white or cream. Seen parked on Queen's Drive."

"Where on Queen's Drive?" Queen's Drive being the roadway that wound around Holyrood Park.

"You know The Hawse?"

"Not by name."

"It's at the foot of the Crags, near where the path starts. This car was parked there, lights on, apparently nobody in it. Someone came forward when they heard about the suicide. But the timing was wrong. They spotted it at around ten thirty that night. It was gone by the time a patrol went past at midnight. Margolies didn't head up there until later."

"According to his widow."

"Well, she should know, shouldn't she? So are you going to tell me what this is all about?"

"Another sighting of a white saloon, the morning Darren Rough was killed. Seen haring out of Holyrood Park."

"What's that got to do with Jim's suicide?"

"Probably nothing," Rebus said, thinking of the doodle again. "Maybe I'm just seeing things." He saw the Farmer standing in the doorway, beckoning. "Thanks anyway," he said.

"Any other fantasies you get, they've got special phone numbers these days."

Rebus put down the receiver, started towards the door.

"My office," the Farmer said, moving away before Rebus could reach him. There was a mug of coffee already sitting on the Farmer's desk. He poured Rebus one, handed it over.

"What have I done this time?" Rebus asked.

The Farmer motioned for him to sit. "It's Darren Rough's social worker. He's made an official complaint."

"About me?"

"He reckons you 'outed' his client, and brought this whole thing on. He's asking questions about how closely you tie in to Rough's death."

Rebus rubbed his eyes, managed a tired smile. "He's welcome to his opinions."

"No danger he can back them up with hard proof?"

"Not a chance in hell, sir."

"It's still not going to look good. You were the last person Rough had any contact with."

"Only if you discount the killer. Have forensics turned up anything?"

"Only that the killer probably got some of Rough's blood on him."

"What if I put forward a proposal?"

The Farmer picked up a pen, studied it. "What sort of proposal?"

"That we bring in Cary Oakes again. I'm positive he nicked my car, which puts him in Arden Street around the time Darren Rough was leaving. What was he doing there in the first place? Staking the place out? In which case, he'd been there a while, maybe saw us going in, took Rough for a friend of mine . . ."

The Farmer was shaking his head. "We can't bring in Oakes, not without something solid."

"How about a mallet?"

It was the Farmer's turn to smile. "Stevens' paper has lawyers, John. And you've said yourself, Oakes is a pro. He'll sit there keeping schtum till they spring him. At which point, the daily rags have got themselves another story about police harassment."

"I thought we were *trying* to harass him?"

The Farmer dropped the pen on the floor, stooped to pick it up. "We've been through all this."

"I know."

"So now we're going in circles. Bottom line, a complaint from Social Work has to be followed up."

"And meantime, I can't work the investigation."

"It would look bloody odd under the circumstances. What other work have you got?"

"Officially, not a lot."

"I heard you had a MisPer."

"I was working it in my own time."

"So spend a bit more time on it. But—and this is off the record, mind—keep close to Gill and the team. You seem to know more about Rough and Greenfield than most."

"In other words, you need me, but can't afford to be seen with me?"

"You always had a way with words, John. Off you go now. POETS day, you know, weekend coming up. Go and enjoy yourself."

31

Janice Mee turned up at Arden Street for want of anything more constructive to do. She had all this time to herself, and over in Fife she felt she was accomplishing nothing. If she sat at home, the patterns on the wallpaper started swirling, and the clock's tick seemed amplified beyond all enduring. But if she went out, there were questions to be answered by neighbours and passers-by—"Is he no' back yet?," "Where do you think he'd have went?"—and comments to be fielded—usually to do with having patience or keeping fingers crossed. Besides, she had a feeling whenever she stepped off the train at Waverley that Damon was nearby. It was true people had a sixth sense: you could feel when someone was creeping up behind you. And every time she stepped on to the platform, stopping there while the workers and shoppers made to pass her, hurried lives they had to be getting on with . . . when she stopped there, it was as if her world stopped turning, and everything became still and peaceful. In those moments, with the city hushed and the blood singing in her heart, she could almost hear him, smell him—everything but reach out and touch

his arm. She saw herself pulling him to her, scolding him
as she poured kisses on his face, and him all grown-up and
trying to resist, but pleased, too, to be wanted like this and
loved like this, loved the way no one in the universe would
ever love him.

Since he'd gone missing, she'd been sleeping in his
room. At first, she'd reasoned to Brian that Damon might
sneak back in the night for his things. This way, she'd be
there to confront him, to snare him. But then Brian had said
he'd move into the room too, and she'd pointed out there
was just the single bed, and he'd countered that he'd sleep
on the floor. On and on the discussion had gone, until she'd
lost it and blurted out that she'd rather be on her own.

The first time she'd spoken the words.

"Frankly, Brian, I'd much rather be on my own . . ."

His face had lost all rigidity, had folded in on itself, and
she'd felt sick in her stomach. But she'd been right to say
the words, wrong to keep them inside the past months and
years.

"It's Johnny, isn't it?" Brian, face averted, had plucked
up the courage to ask.

And in a way it was, though not quite the way Brian
meant. It was that Johnny had shown her another road she
might have taken, and in doing so had opened up the possibility of all the other roads left untravelled, all the places
she'd never been. Places like Emotion and High and Ela-
tion. Places like Myself and Free and Aware. She knew
she'd never say these things to anyone; they sounded too
much like stuff from the magazines. But that didn't stop
her feeling they were true. Born and bred in the town, lived
most of her days there: did she really want to die there?
Did she want it that thirty-odd years of her life could be
summarised in five minutes to a friend she hadn't seen since
secondary school?

She wanted more.

She wanted out.

Of course, she knew what people would say: you're just
emotional, dear. It's bound to be upsetting, something like
this. And it was. Oh, Jesus sweet Christ almighty, it was.
Yet she felt more powerless and aimless than ever. She'd
told her story to all the charities, she'd done her bit talking

to the taxi drivers, but what was left? She knew there must be something she hadn't tried, but couldn't think what. All she knew was, this was where she had to be.

Now that she had a feel for the city, she enjoyed the walk to Marchmont. The steep climb up Cockburn Street, full of "alternative" shops—some of them had even taken her flyers. Then up the High Street to George IV Bridge, and down past libraries and bookshops to Greyfriars Bobby. Past the university and the milling students, carrying books with them or pushing their bicycles. Then The Meadows, flat and green and with Marchmont rising in the distance. She liked the shops near Johnny's flat; liked the tenement itself and all the streets around it. The roofs seemed to her like castle turrets. Johnny said the area was full of students. She'd always imagined students living in poorer places.

She opened the main door and climbed to Johnny's landing. There was mail behind his door. She picked it up, took it through to the living room. It looked like bills and junk; no real letters. No photos in his living room; gaps in the wall-units which she would have filled with ornaments. Books tidied away into piles: before she moved them, they'd been lying everywhere. There was a time Brian wouldn't have stood for it if she'd moved his stuff around; these days, he probably wouldn't even notice. Johnny had noticed when she'd tidied up, but she wasn't sure he'd been pleased, even though he'd said "Thanks."

She took mugs, plate and ashtray through to the kitchen. Took a blanket from the sofa and put it on the bed in the spare room. When everything was to her satisfaction, she wondered what to do next. Clean the windows? With what? Make herself a cup of something? Listen to some music . . . when had she last sat down and listened to music? When had she last had time? She looked through Johnny's collection. Pulled out an album—one of the first by the Rolling Stones. It looked the same copy he'd had when they'd been going out together. On the back she found an ink doodle: JLJ—Janice Loves Johnny. She'd put it there one night, wondering if he'd notice. He always liked to study his LP sleeves. And when he had noticed, he hadn't been too thrilled, had tried taking a rubber to it. You could still see the smudge . . .

Summers in the café, long evenings with the Coke machine and the jukebox. Then a bag of chips, salt and vinegar. Maybe a film some nights, or just a stroll in the park. The youth club was run by the local church. Johnny hadn't liked that; hadn't been churchy. Yet here was a copy of the Bible, sitting alone on the mantelpiece. And other books that looked religious: *The Confessions of St. Augustine; The Cloud of Unknowing*. She liked the sound of that last one. Lots of books, yet he didn't seem much of a reader, and the books looked brand new, most of them.

His bedroom . . . she'd sneaked a peek in there. Not the most inviting of rooms: mattress on the floor, clothes in piles in a corner, waiting to be decanted into the chest of drawers. Odd socks: what was it with men and odd socks? The whole flat had an unloved feel to it, despite some redecoration in the living room. His chair, positioned next to the bay window, phone on the floor next to it—the whole flat seemed to revolve around that one space. Kitchen cupboards: bottles of whisky and brandy and vodka and gin. More vodka in the freezer; beer in the fridge, along with cheese, marge, and an unpromising quarter of corned beef. Jars of beetroot and raspberry jam on the worktop, breadbin with two stale rolls and the heel of a loaf.

They said you could tell a lot about a man from his home. She got the feeling Johnny was lonely, but how could that be when he had the doctor, Patience whatsername?

The doorbell. She wondered who it could be. Went and opened the door, not even bothering with the spy-hole. A man standing there, smiling.

"Hiya," he said. "Is John in?"

"No, I'm afraid not."

The smile disappeared; the man checked his watch. "I hope he's not going to stand me up again."

"Well, in his job . . ."

"Oh, that's true enough. You'll know all about it, I suppose."

She felt herself blushing under his gaze. "I'm not his girlfriend or anything."

"No? And here I was thinking he'd struck lucky, the old devil."

"No, I'm just a friend."

"Just good friends, eh?" He tapped his nose. "You can trust me, I won't tell Patience."

Her blush spread. "We were at school, Johnny and me. Met up again recently." She was babbling, and knew it, but somehow couldn't stop herself.

"That's nice: old friends getting together. Plenty to catch up on, eh?"

"Plenty."

"I know the feeling. I was out of touch with John for years too."

"Really?"

"Working in the States."

"How interesting. Were you there long . . . ?" She caught herself. "Sorry, I can't keep you standing out there, can I?"

"I was beginning to wonder."

She opened the door wider, took a step back. "You better come in. My name's Janice, by the way."

"You'll laugh when I tell you my name. All I can say is, nobody consulted *me*."

"Why, what's your name?" Laughing now as he stepped past her into the hall.

"Cary," he told her. "After the actor. Only I've never managed to be quite so suave."

He was winking at her as she closed the door.

The flat was empty when Rebus got home, but he sensed someone had been there: things moved, things tidied. Janice again. He looked for a note, but she hadn't left one. He took a beer from the fridge, then turned on the hi-fi. The Stones: "Goat's Head Soup." On the album cover, David Bailey had photographed them with their made-up faces covered by some diaphanous material, making Jagger look more feminine than ever. Rebus turned the volume down and called Alan Archibald's number. Nobody home but the answering machine. Archibald's voice sounded clipped and distant.

"It's John Rebus here. A simple message: ca' canny. A taxi driver picked Oakes up near your home. I can't think of any other reason he'd have been in the neighbourhood. He's also been in my street. I don't know what his thinking

is, maybe he just wants to rattle us. Anyway, consider yourself forewarned."

He put down the phone. Forewarned is forearmed, he
thought, wondering how Alan Archibald would arm himself.

He turned up the volume, sat by the window and stared
out at the opposite tenement. The kids were home from
school, playing at their living room table. Some card game,
it looked like. Happy Families maybe. Rebus had never
been much good at that. When he turned from the window,
he saw a shape in the doorway.

"Christ," he said, putting a hand to his chest, "don't do
that to me."

"Sorry," Janice said, smiling. She raised a carton of milk
for him to see. "You were running out."

"Thanks." He followed her through to the kitchen,
watched her put the milk in the fridge.

"Did you forget your appointment?" she asked.

"Appointment?" Rebus was thinking: doctor? Dentist?

"You stood your friend up. He was round here an hour
ago. I went with him for a coffee." She tutted at Rebus's
fecklessness.

"You've lost me," he said.

"Cary," she told him. "The two of you were going out
for a drink."

Rebus felt his spine turn cold. "He came here?"

"Looking for you, yes."

"And you went out with him?"

She'd been wiping the worktop, but turned towards him,
saw the look on his face.

"What is it?" she asked.

He looked towards the cupboards, made a show of opening one to check for something. He couldn't tell her. She'd
have a fit. He closed the cupboard door.

"Have a nice chat, the two of you?"

"He told me about his job in the States."

"Which one? I think he had a couple."

"Did he?" She frowned. "Well, the only one he told me
about was being a prison guard."

"Oh, right." Rebus nodded. "I suppose you told him
about us?"

She gave him a sly glance. There were spots of red on her cheeks.

"What's to tell?"

"I mean, told him about yourself, how we know one another . . . ?"

"Oh, yes, all that."

"And Fife?"

"He seemed really interested in Cardenden. I told him off, thought he was taking the mickey."

"No, Cary's always interested in people."

"That's exactly what he said." She paused. "Sure you're all right?"

"Fine. It's just . . . work-related problems." Namely, Cary Oakes, who had now pulled Janice into his game. And Rebus, himself in the middle of the board, had yet to be told the rules.

"Want some coffee or something?"

Rebus shook his head. "We're going somewhere." *We?* If Cary Oakes had gone to Fife, it was safer for Janice to stay in Edinburgh. But stay where? Rebus's flat was proving no sanctuary. She was safer with Rebus, and Rebus had somewhere he needed to be.

"Where?"

"Back to Fife. I've a few more questions for Damon's friends." And terrain to scout, seeking signs of contamination by Oakes.

She stared at him. "Have you . . . are you on to something?"

"Hard to tell."

"Try me."

He was shaking his head. "I don't want to raise your hopes. It might turn out to be nothing." He started to move out of the kitchen. "Give me a minute to do some packing."

"Packing?"

"Weekend's coming, Janice. Thought I might stay over till tomorrow. Is there still a hotel in town?"

She hesitated for a moment. "You can stay with us."

"A hotel will be fine."

But she shook her head. "You'll understand, I couldn't let you have Damon's room, but there's always the couch."

Rebus pretended to be torn. "OK then," he said at last.

Thinking: I want to be there overnight; I want to be close
to her. Not for any obvious reasons—reasons he might have
put to himself a day or two ago—but because he wanted
to know if Cary Oakes would travel to Cardenden, stake
out her home. Whatever Oakes was planning, it was moving apace. If he was going to move on Janice, Rebus reckoned it would be at the weekend.

If anything happened, Rebus needed to be there.

"I'll just throw some stuff in a bag," he said, heading
for his bedroom.

Rebus took Janice to Sammy's first of all. He just wanted
to check on her. She was doing pull-ups with the help of
her parallel bars, hoisting herself to standing, locking her
knees, then easing herself back into the wheelchair. The
front door was unlocked: she kept it that way when Ned
wasn't home. Rebus had been worried, until she'd explained her reasoning.

"I had to weigh up the chances, Dad: me needing help,
versus someone breaking in. If I'm lying paralysed on my
back, I want any Good Samaritans to be able to get in."

She wore a grey sleeveless T-shirt, its back turned a
darker grey by sweat. There was a towel around her shoulders, and her hair was matted to her forehead.

"God knows if this is helping my legs," she said, "but
I'm getting a shot-putter's biceps."

"And not an anabolic steroid in sight," he said, leaning
down to kiss her. "This is Janice, old school-pal of mine."

"Hello, Janice," Sammy said. When she looked back at
her father, he felt embarrassed, and wasn't sure why.

"Her son's disappeared," he explained. "I'm trying to
help."

Sammy wiped her face with the towel.

"I'm sorry," she said. Janice smiled and shrugged.

"Janice still lives in Cardenden," Rebus went on. "We're headed back there, in case you were thinking of phoning me tonight."

"Right," Sammy said, her face still busy in the towel. Now that he was here, he knew he'd made some kind of mistake, knew Sammy was jumping to all the wrong conclusions, and couldn't think of a way out without embarrassing Janice.

"So I'll see you some time," he said.

"I'm not going anywhere." She had finished with the towel; was studying the bars, the extent of her current universe.

"We'll have to go through there some day. I can show you my old hunting-ground."

She nodded. "We can take Patience, too. I'm sure she wouldn't want to be left out."

"Have a nice weekend, Sammy," he said, making for the door.

She neglected to tell him to do the same.

"I'll just phone Patience," he said, easing his mobile out of his pocket. They were back in the car, heading for the A90. Patience sometimes went out with friends on a Friday night; it was a regular thing—drinks and a meal, maybe a play or concert. Three other women doctors: two of them divorced, one still apparently happily married. She answered on the fourth ring.

"It's me," he said.

"What have I told you about using that thing when you're driving?"

"I'm stalled at lights," he lied, giving Janice a conspirator's wink. She looked uncomfortable.

"Got plans?"

"I have to go to Fife, couple of interviews I want to get out of the way. I'll probably stay the night. Are you going out?"

"In about twenty minutes."

"Say hello to the gang from me."

"John . . . when are we going to see one another?"

"Soon."

"This weekend?"

"Almost certainly."

"I'm going over to Sammy's tomorrow."

"Right," he said. Sammy would tell Patience about Janice. Patience would know Janice had been in the car when he'd called her. "I'm staying the night with some friends: Janice and Brian."

"The ones you were at school with?"

"That's right. I didn't realise I'd mentioned them."

"You hadn't. Thing is, as far as I'm aware you haven't *made* any friends since school."

"Bye, Patience," he said, easing into the outside lane and putting his foot down.

Dr. Patience Aitken had a taxi ordered. When it arrived, the driver pushed open her gate, headed down the steep and winding set of stone steps which led to her garden flat. He rang the doorbell and waited, scuffing his feet on the flagstones. He liked the New Town's garden flats, the way they were below street level at the front, but had gardens at the back. And they had these little courtyards at the front, with cellars built into the facing wall. Not that you'd use the cellars for much; too damp. Certainly not for keeping wine in. He'd taken the wife to the Loire the previous summer, learned all about the wines. He had three mixed cases now, stored in the cupboard beneath his stairs. Far from ideal conditions: a modern two-storey semi out at Fairmilehead. Too dry, too warm. What he needed was a flat like this one—he'd bet there'd be cupboards inside just right for laying down wine, cool and dryish with thick stone walls.

He noticed that the doctor had tried for a sort of garden feel in the courtyard: hanging baskets, terracotta pots. Nothing down here would get too much light, that was the thing. First thing he'd done with his front garden when he'd moved in: put flagstones over most of it, leaving just a square of earth in the middle, couple of roses planted in there. Minimum maintenance.

The door opened and the doctor stepped out, pulling a shawl around her shoulders. Perfume wafted out with her: nothing too overbearing.

"Sorry I've kept you," she said, pulling the door closed and making for the steps.

"I'd double-lock it if I were you," he suggested.

"What?"

"Yales," he explained, shaking his head. "A kid could be inside in ten seconds flat."

She thought about it, shrugged her shoulders. "What's life without a bit of a risk?"

"As long as you're insured," he said, studying her ankles as he climbed the steps after her.

Jim Stevens lay on his bed, one hand covering his eyes, the other holding the telephone receiver to his ear. He was listening to Matt Lewin, who had just told him how good the weather was in Seattle. Stevens had faxed him portions of Cary Oakes's "confession," and Lewin was giving his views.

"Well, Jim, bits of it seem to tally all right. The truck driver story is new, and frankly, I don't think it's worth chasing."

"You think he made it up?"

"Not my problem, thank God. I tell you, Jim, no disrespect, but I wouldn't trust anything that bastard told me, and I sure as hell wouldn't give him the satisfaction of seeing it in print."

Which seemed to be Stevens' boss's view, too. The projected eight-parter had been cut to just five.

"I'm sure as hell glad he's your problem now and not ours," Lewin went on.

"Thanks."

"He giving you any trouble?"

Stevens didn't see the point in telling Lewin that Oakes was proving more awkward by the day. He'd slipped away from the hotel again that afternoon, stayed out the best part of three hours and wouldn't say where he'd been.

"It's nearly over anyway," Stevens said, rubbing his hand over his brow.

"Good riddance, that's my advice."

"Yes." But Stevens couldn't help but worry. He worried about what Oakes would do with himself afterwards, once he was out on the street. No way was Stevens' paper going to come up with ten K, not for the scraps Oakes had given them. Stevens still had to break that news to Oakes.

He worried for himself too. He was part of Oakes's sphere now, and was just hoping Oakes would let him go.

He got the feeling, God help him, that it might not be all that easy . . .

Cary Oakes watched the taxi leave. Dr. P, he presumed. Getting on a bit, but then the state Rebus was in, he doubted he'd be complaining. Basement apartment too: perfect for what he had in mind. He came out from behind the parked car and looked up and down the street. The place was dead. Half of Edinburgh seemed dead to him: you could wander around for ages and not go noticed, never mind raise suspicion.

Jim Stevens had been in a foul mood, watching the Cary Oakes story relegated as the editor decided to run a special on vigilanteism. Stevens blamed the paedophile murder.

"Bloody Rebus again," he'd muttered, and Oakes had asked him to explain.

Stevens' theory: Rebus had outed Darren Rough, raised the mob against him. And now one of them had taken it too far. Everything Oakes learned about the detective made Rebus seem more interesting, more complicated.

"What sort of code does he live by, do you think?" he'd asked.

Stevens had snorted. "Could be Morse or Highway for all I know."

"Some people make up their own rules," Oakes had mused.

"You mean like the serial killer?"

"Hmmm?"

"The one who picked you up in his truck."

"Oh, him . . . Well, yes, of course."

And Stevens had looked at him. And Cary Oakes had stared back.

He crossed the road now. No houses across the street from where he'd be working, just a wrought-iron fence, a bank of grass behind it. No neighbours to spot him as he went about his business.

He expected no interruptions at all.

*   *   *

The batteries were fading anyway, Rebus rationalised, and he didn't have the recharger with him. So he switched off his mobile.

"The weekend starts here," he said, as they crossed the Forth Road Bridge into Fife.

Later: "Roads have changed," as they came off the dual carriageway outside Kirkcaldy. But the old Kirkcaldy-Cardenden road seemed much the same, same twists and turns, potholes and bumps.

"Remember we walked to Kirkcaldy once to go to the pictures?" Janice said.

Rebus smiled. "I'd forgotten that. Why didn't we just take the bus?"

"I think we didn't have enough money."

He frowned. "Was it just us?"

"Mitch and his girlfriend too. Can't remember who he was dating at the time."

"He went through them, all right."

"Maybe *they* got fed up of *him*."

"Maybe." They sat in silence for a minute. "What was the film?"

"Which film?"

"The one we walked six miles to see."

"I don't recall watching much of it."

They glanced at one another, burst out laughing.

Brian Mee heard the car, came out to meet them.

"This is a surprise," he said, shaking Rebus's hand.

"I need to talk to Damon's pals," Rebus explained.

Janice touched her husband's arm. "He said he wanted to go to the hotel."

"Rubbish, you can stay with us. Damon's room's . . ."

"I thought maybe the sofa," Janice interjected.

Brian recovered well. "Oh aye, it's not that old. Comfy too. I should know: I nod off on it most nights myself."

"That's settled then," Janice said. She had a man on either arm as she walked up the front path.

They ordered Chinese from the takeaway, opened a couple of bottles of wine. Old stories, rekindled memories. Half-remembered names; the exploits of those who'd grown old in the town; changes to the fabric of the place.

Rebus had phoned Damon's friends, the ones who'd been with him at Gaitano's, but neither of them was in. He'd left messages, saying he had to see them in the morning.

"We could go out for a drink," he told his hosts. His eyes were on Janice as he spoke. "Be the first time we had a drink together in the Goth without being underage."

"The Goth's shut, John," Brian said.

"Since when?"

"They're turning it into a centre for the unemployed."

"Isn't that what it always was?"

They smiled at that. The Goth closed: his dad's watering-hole; the first place John Rebus had ever bought a round.

"Railway Tavern's still going," Brian added. "We'll be there tomorrow night for the karaoke."

"You'll stay for that, won't you?" Janice asked.

"I'm kind of allergic to karaokes, actually." Rebus was again in the "seat by the fire," the one he'd been made to sit in on his first visit. The TV was playing, sound turned down. It was like a magnet, their eyes sliding towards it throughout the conversation. Janice cleared away the dishes—they'd eaten with the plates on their laps. He helped her take the things through to the kitchen, saw it was too small for three people to eat in. There was a dining table in front of the living room window, but set with ornaments, its leaves folded. Used for special occasions only. With the leaves opened, it would all but fill the room. They ate all their meals on their laps, in front of the TV. He imagined the three of them—mother, father, son—staring at the screen, using it to excuse the lengthening gaps in conversation.

After coffee, Janice said she was going up to bed. Brian said he'd be up in a while. She brought down blankets and a pillow for Rebus, told him where the bathroom was. Told him where the light-switch was in the hall. Told him there was plenty of hot water if he wanted a bath.

"See you in the morning."

Brian reached for the remote, switched off the TV, then caught himself.

"There wasn't something you wanted to . . . ?"

Rebus shook his head. "I'm not a big fan."

"And what would you say to a wee whisky?"

"More my cup of tea altogether," Rebus acknowledged with a smile.

They sipped the whisky in silence. It wasn't a malt: maybe Teacher's or Grant's. Brian had added a dollop of water to his, but Rebus hadn't bothered.

"Where do you think he is?" Brian asked at last, swirling the drink around the rim of his glass. "Just between us, like."

As if Janice couldn't take it; as if he were stronger than her.

"I don't know, Brian. I wish I did."

"They normally go to London, though."

"Yes."

"And most of them do OK for themselves?"

Rebus nodded, not wanting any of this, wishing of a sudden that he was back in his flat with his own whisky, his music and books. But Brian had a need to talk.

"I blame us, you know."

"I'd guess most parents do."

"I think he picked up on the atmosphere, and it drove him away." He sat on the edge of the sofa, hands squeezing his glass. He was looking at the floor as he spoke. "I got the feeling Janice was just waiting for Damon to go. You know, get a place of his own. That's what she was waiting for."

"And then what?"

Brian glanced up at him. "Then she'd have no reason to stay. Every time she goes to Edinburgh, I think that's it: she won't be back."

"But she always comes back."

He nodded. "But it's different now. She comes back in case Damon's here. Nothing to do with me." He coughed, cleared his throat, drained the whisky. "Want a refill?" Rebus shook his head. "No, suppose not. Time for kip, eh?" Brian got to his feet, managed a smile. "Schooldays, eh, Johnny?"

"Schooldays, Brian," Rebus agreed. He watched something brighten behind Brian Mee's eyes, then die again.

Rebus brushed his teeth in the kitchen—didn't want to intrude upstairs, not with Brian readying for bed. He laid the blankets out on the sofa. Sat there with the lights out, then got up and went to the window. Peered through the curtains. Outside, the street-lamps cast a faint orange glow. The street itself was empty. He crept into the hall, opened the front door quietly, leaving it on the latch. Five minutes outside told him Cary Oakes wasn't in the vicinity. He headed back indoors, needed the toilet. The kitchen sink seemed inappropriate, so he listened at the foot of the stairs then headed up. He knew the bathroom door, went in and did his business. One bedroom door was closed, the other slightly open. The open door had a football scarf pinned to it, and half a dozen used concert tickets from a few years before. Rebus pushed his head around the door: saw the outlines of posters, a wardrobe and chest of drawers. Saw the window with the curtains drawn. Saw the single bed, and Janice sleeping in it, her breathing regular.

Crept downstairs again feeling like a housebreaker.

Next morning after breakfast, he had a meeting with Damon's friends.

They came round to the house, while Janice and Brian were out shopping. Joey Haldane was tall and skinny with closely cropped bleached hair and dark bushy eyebrows. He wore all denim—jeans, shirt, jacket—with black Dr. Marten shoes. Rebus noticed that his mouth hung open most of the time, as though he had trouble breathing through his nose.

Pete Mathieson was as tall as Joey but a lot broader, the kind of son a farmer would be proud of (and probably exploit). He wore red jogging pants and a blue sweatshirt, Nike trainers with the soles almost rubbed away. They sat on the sofa. Rebus's sheets and pillow had disappeared upstairs before breakfast, while he'd been soaking in the bath.

"Thanks for coming," Rebus began. Instead of one of the overstuffed armchairs, he was seated on a straight-backed dining chair, planted in the middle of the room. Below him, the boys sank into the sofa. He'd turned his chair so he could straddle it, leaning his arms on its back.

"I know we've talked before, Joey, but I've got a couple of back-up questions. So-called because when I think someone's not playing straight with me, it tends to get my back up."

Joey wet his lips with his tongue, Pete twitched a shoulder, angled his head and tried to look bored.

"See," Rebus went on, "I was told the three of you had gone just that once to Edinburgh for your night out. But now I think I know differently. I think you'd been there before. I think maybe it was a regular thing, which makes me wonder why you'd lie. What is it you're trying to hide? Remember, this is a missing person investigation. No way you're not going to be found out."

"We haven't done nothing." This from Joey, his voice a hoarse local accent, the sound of carpentry work.

"Know what a double negative is, Joey?"

"Should I?" Holding Rebus's stare for the briefest of moments.

"If you say you haven't done nothing, it means you've done *something*."

"I've told you, we haven't done nothing."

"You haven't lied about that night? You hadn't been to Edinburgh for a night out before . . . ?"

"We'd been before," Pete Mathieson said.

"Hello there, Pete," Rebus said. "Thought you'd lost the power of speech for a minute there."

"Pete," Joey spat, "for fuck's—"

Mathieson gave his friend a look, but when he spoke it was for Rebus's benefit.

"We'd been before."

"To Guiser's?"

"And other places—pubs, clubs."

"How often?"

"Four, five nights."

"Without telling your girlfriends?"

"They thought we were down Kirkcaldy, same as always."

"Why not tell them?"

"That would have spoiled it," Joey said, folding his arms. Rebus thought he knew what he meant. It was only an adventure if it was furtive. Men liked to have their little secrets and tell their little lies. They liked a sense of the illicit. All the same, he got the feeling it went further. It was the way Joey was leaning back in the sofa, crossing one ankle over the other. He was thinking of something, something about the nights out, and the thought was making him feel good . . .

"Was it just you that was cheating, Joey, or was it all of you?"

Joey's face grew darker. He turned to his friend.

"I never said nothing!" Pete blurted out.

"He didn't need to, Joey," Rebus said. "It's written on your face."

Joey wriggled in his seat, less comfortable by the second. Eventually he sat forward, arms on knees. "If Alice finds out she'll kill me."

So much for the thrill of the illicit.

"Your secret's safe with me, Joey. I just need to know what happened that night."

Joey glanced towards Pete, as though giving him permission to do the talking.

"Joey met a girl," Pete began. "Three weeks before. So every time we went across, he hooked up with her."

"You weren't in Guiser's?"

Joey shook his head. "Went back to her flat for an hour."

"The plan was," Pete explained, "we'd all meet up later at Guiser's."

"You weren't there either?"

Pete shook his head. "We were in a pub beforehand, I got chatting to this lassie. I think Damon was a bit bored."

"More likely jealous," Joey added.

"So he headed off to Guiser's on his own?" Rebus asked.

"By the time I got there," Pete said, "there was no sign of him."

"So he wasn't at the bar for a round of drinks? You

made that up so nobody would know you were busy elsewhere?" He was looking at Joey.

"That's about it," Pete answered. "Didn't think it made
any difference."

Rebus was thoughtful. "What about Damon? Did he ever
hook up with anyone?"

"Never seemed to get lucky."

"It wasn't because he was thinking of Helen?"

Joey shook his head. "He was just useless with birds."

And he'd gone off to Guiser's on his own . . . thinking
what? Thinking about how of the three, he was the only
one who couldn't pick up a girl for the night. Thinking he
was "useless." Yet somehow he'd ended up sharing a taxi
with the mystery blonde . . .

"Does it matter?" Pete asked.

"It might. I'll have to think about it." It mattered because
Damon had been there alone. It mattered because now Rebus had no idea what had happened to him between leaving
Pete in the pub and standing at the bar in Guiser's waiting
to be served, with a blonde at his shoulder. They might
have met en route. Something might have happened. And
Rebus couldn't know. Just when the picture should have
been becoming clearer, it had been torn apart.

When Janice and Brian started bringing bags in from the
car, Rebus dismissed Pete and Joey. Something else they'd
said: Damon wouldn't have minded finding a girl for the
night. What did that say about his relationship with Helen?

"All right, John?" Janice said, smiling.

"Fine," he replied.

After lunch, Brian invited him to the pub. It was a regular
thing—Saturday afternoon, football commentary on the radio or TV. A few drinks with the lads. But Rebus declined.
He had the excuse that Janice had offered to take a walk
around the town with him. Rebus didn't want to be out
drinking with Brian, a time when bonds could be made or
tightened, secrets could dribble out "in confidence." Now
that he'd seen Janice sleeping in a separate room. Rebus
felt he knew things he shouldn't.

Of course, she might be sleeping there because of Damon, because she missed him. But Rebus didn't think that was it.

So Brian went off to the pub, and Janice and Rebus went walking. Rain was falling, but lightly. She wore a red duffel coat with a hood. She offered Rebus an umbrella, but he declined, explaining that ever since he'd seen someone almost get their eye taken out with one on Princes Street, he'd regarded them as offensive weapons.

"Where we're walking won't be quite so crowded," she told him.

And it was true. The streets were empty. Locals went to Kirkcaldy or Edinburgh for their shopping. When Rebus had been young his family hadn't owned a car. The shops on the main street had catered for all their needs. The needs these days seemed to be videos and takeaway food. The Goth was indeed closed, its windows boarded up, reminding Rebus of Darren Rough's flat. The flats on Craigside Road had been demolished, new houses replacing them. Some of them were owned by the local housing association, the others were private.

"Nobody owned their own house when we were growing up," Janice stated. Then she laughed. "I must sound about seventy-eight."

"The good old days," Rebus agreed. "Places do change, though."

"Yes."

"And people are allowed to change too."

She looked at him, but didn't ask what he meant. Maybe she already knew.

They climbed up to The Craigs, a high ridge of wilderness above Auchterderran, and walked along it until they could see the old school.

"Not that it's used as a school any more," Janice explained. "Kids these days go to Lochgelly. Remember the school badge?"

"I remember it." Auchterderran Secondary School: ASS. Kids from other schools used to bray at them, poking fun.

"Why do you keep looking round?" she asked. "Think someone's following us?"

"No."

"Brian's not like that, if that's what you're thinking."

"No, no, nothing—"

"Sometimes I wish he was." She strode ahead of him. He took his time catching up.

They walked back into town past the Auld Hoose pub. Cardenden as it now was had at one time been four distinct parishes known as the ABCD—Auchterderran, Bowhill, Cardenden and Dundonald. When they'd been going out together, Rebus had lived in Bowhill, Janice in Dundonald. He would take this route walking her home, going the longest way round they could think of. Crossing the River Ore at the old humpbacked bridge—now long replaced by a tarmac road. Sometimes, in summer, say, cutting through the park, crossing the river further up at one of the wide-diameter pipes. Those pipes had provided a test for the local kids. Rebus had known boys freeze halfway across, until their parents had to be fetched. He'd known one boy pee in his trousers with fear, but keep on moving his feet inch by inch along the pipe, while the river surged below him. Others took the crossing at a canter, hands in their pockets, needing no help with balancing.

Rebus had been one of the cautious ones.

The same pipe ran the length of the park before disappearing into the undergrowth beyond. You could follow it all the way to the bing—the hill-sized mound of dross and coal-shavings which the local colliery had deposited. Fires started on the bing could smoulder for months, wisps of smoke rising from the surface as from a volcano. In time, trees and grass had grown on the slopes, so that more than ever the bing came to resemble a natural hill. But if you climbed to the top, there was a plateau, an alien landscape, wired off for safety's sake. It was like a small loch, its surface oily, thick-looking, and black. Nobody knew what it was, but they respected it—kept their distance and threw stones, watching them sink slowly from view as they were sucked beneath the surface.

Boys and girls went into the wild areas behind the park and found secret places, flattened areas of fields which they could call their own. And that had been Janice and Johnny, too, once upon a time . . .

The Kinks: "Young and Innocent Days."

Now, the place had changed. The bing had gone, the

whole area landscaped. The colliery had been demolished. Cardenden had grown up around coal, hurried streets constructed in the twenties and thirties to house the incoming miners. These streets hadn't even been given names, just numbers. Rebus's family had moved into 13th Street. Relocation had taken the family to a pre-fab in Cardenden, and from there to a terraced house in a cul-de-sac in Bowhill. But by the time Rebus had been at secondary school, the coal was proving difficult to mine: fractured strata, so that a face might yield low tonnage. The colliery had become uneconomic. The daily siren signalling the change of shifts had been silenced. Schoolfriends of Rebus, boys whose fathers and grandfathers had been miners, were left wondering what to do.

And Rebus too had been asking himself questions. But with Mitch's help he'd come to a decision. They'd both join the army. It had seemed so simple back then . . .

"Is Mickey still around?" Janice asked.

"Lives in Kirkcaldy."

"He was a pest, your wee brother. Remember him charging into the bedroom? Or opening the bowley-hole all of a sudden so he could catch us?"

Rebus laughed. *Bowley-hole*: a word he hadn't heard in years. The serving-hatch between kitchen and living room. He could see Mickey now. He'd be up on the worktop in the kitchen, trying to spy on Rebus and Janice while they were alone in the living room.

Rebus looked around again. He didn't think Cary Oakes was in town. A place this size, where everyone knew everyone, it was hard to hide. He'd already had a couple of people come up and say hello, like they'd seen him just the other day, rather than a dozen or more years ago. And Janice had been stopped by half a dozen people—neighbours or the plain curious—and asked about Damon. It was hard to escape him: every wall, lamp-post and window seemed to have his picture stuck to it.

"I was here a few years back," he told Janice. "Hutchy's betting shop."

"You were after Tommy Greenwood?"

He nodded. "And I bumped into Cranny." Their old nickname for Heather Cranston.

"She's still around. So's her son."

Rebus sought the name. "Shug?"

"That's it," Janice said. They were back on the pavement outside the cemetery. "If you're lucky, you might see Heather tonight."

"Oh?"

"She often comes to the karaoke."

Rebus asked Janice if they could turn back. "I want to see the cemetery," he explained. And backtracking, he might have added, as he'd learned in the army, was a good way to find if you were being followed. So they headed back through Bowhill, and up the cemetery brae. He was thinking of all the stories buried in the graveyard: mining tragedies; a girl found drowned in the Ore; a holiday car crash which had wiped out a family. Then there was Johnny Thomson, Celtic goalkeeper, fatally injured during an Old Firm derby, only in his twenties when he died.

Rebus's mother had been cremated, but his father had insisted on a "proper burial." His headstone was over by the end wall. Loving husband to . . . and father of . . . And at the bottom, the words *Not Dead, But at Rest in the Arms of the Lord*. But as they approached, Rebus saw that something was wrong.

"Oh, John," Janice gasped.

White paint had been poured down the headstone, covering most of the lettering.

"Bloody kids," Janice said.

Rebus saw tracks of paint on the grass, but no sign of the empty tin.

"This wasn't kids," he said. Too much of a coincidence.

"Who then?"

He touched his finger to the headstone: the paint was still viscous. Oakes *had* been in town. Janice was squeezing his arm.

"I'm so sorry."

"It's only a bit of stone," he said quietly. "It can be fixed."

They drank tea in the living room. Rebus had tried Oakes' hotel—Stevens' room, the bar, no one was there.

"We've had phone calls," Janice told him.

"Cranks?" he guessed.

She nodded. "Telling us Damon's dead, or we killed him. Thing is, the callers . . . their voices sound local."

"Probably are local then."

She offered him a cigarette. "It's pretty sick, isn't it?"

Rebus, looking around, nodded his agreement.

They were still sitting in the living room when Brian came back from the pub.

"I'll just take a shower," he said.

Janice explained that he always did this. "Clothes in the washing basket, and a good wash. I think it's the cigarette smoke."

"He doesn't like it?"

"Hates it," she said. "Maybe that's why I started." The front door was opened again. It was Janice's mum. "I'll fetch a cup," Janice said, getting to her feet.

Mrs. Playfair nodded a greeting towards Rebus and sat down opposite him.

"You haven't found him yet?"

"Not for want of trying, Mrs. Playfair."

"Ach, I'm sure you're doing your best, son. He's our only grandchild, you know."

Rebus nodded.

"A good laddie, wouldn't harm a fly. I can't believe he'd get into trouble."

"What makes you think he's in trouble?"

"He wouldn't do this to us otherwise." She was studying him. "So what happened to you, son?"

"How do you mean?" Wondering if she'd read his thoughts.

"I don't know . . . the way your life's gone. Are you happy enough?"

"I never really think about it."

"Why not?"

He shrugged his shoulders. "I like looking into people's lives. That's what detective work is."

"The army didn't work out?"

"No," he said simply.

"Sometimes things don't work out," she said, as Janice came back into the room. She watched her daughter pour the tea. "A lot of marriages break up round here."

"Do you think Damon and Helen would have made a go of it?"

She took a long time thinking about it, accepted the cup from Janice. "They're young, who knows?"

"What odds would you give them?"

"You're talking to Damon's gran, John," Janice said. "No girl in the world's good enough for Damon, eh, Mum?" She smiled to let him know she was half-joking. Then, to her mother again: "Johnny's had a shock." Describing the vandalised grave. Brian came in rubbing his hair. He'd changed his clothes. Janice repeated the story for him.

"Wee bastards," Brian said. "It's happened before. They push the stones over, break them."

"I'll fetch you a mug," Janice said, making to get up again.

"I'm fine," Brian said, waving her back. He looked towards Rebus. "Probably don't feel like eating out then? Only we were going to treat you."

After a moment's thought, Rebus said, "I'd like to get out. But I should be paying."

"You can pay next time," Brian said.

"Judging on past history," Rebus said, "that'll be roughly thirty years from now."

Rebus drank nothing but mineral water with his curry. Brian was on the beers, and Janice managed two large glasses of white wine. Mr. and Mrs. Playfair had been invited, but had declined.

"We'll let you young things get on with it," Mrs. Playfair had said.

From time to time, when Janice wasn't looking, Brian would glance in her direction. Rebus thought he was worried: worried his wife was going to leave him, and wondering what he was doing wrong. His life was falling apart, and he was on the lookout for clues as to why.

Rebus considered himself something of an expert on break-ups. He knew sometimes a perspective could shift, one partner could start wanting things that seemed outwith their reach as long as they stayed married. It hadn't been that way with his own marriage. There, it had been down to the fact that he never should have married in the first place. When work had begun to consume him, there hadn't been much left to sustain Rhona.

"Penny for them," Janice said at one point, tearing apart a nan bread.

"I'm wondering about getting the headstone clean."

Brian said he knew a man who could do it: worked for the council, took graffiti off walls.

"I'll send you the money," Rebus told him. Brian nodded.

After the meal, he drove them back to Cardenden. The karaoke night was held in a back room at the Railway Tavern. The equipment sat on a stage, but the singers stayed on the dancefloor, eyes on the TV monitor with its syrupy videos and the words appearing along the bottom of the screen. Sheets came round, printed with all the songs. You wrote your choice on a slip of paper and handed it to the compère. A skinhead got up and did "My Way." A middle-aged woman had a go at "You to Me Are Everything." Janice said she always took "Baker Street." Brian switched between "Satisfaction" and "Space Oddity," depending on his mood.

"So most people sing the same song every week?" Rebus asked.

"That guy getting up just now," she said, nodding towards the corner of the room, where people were shifting their seats to allow someone out, "he always chooses REM."

"So he's probably pretty good at it by now?"

"Not bad," she agreed. The song was "Losing My Religion."

Drinkers were wandering through from the front bar, standing in the doorway to watch. There was a small bar specially for the karaoke: a hatch, manned by a teenager who kept testing the acne on his cheeks. People seemed to have their regular tables. Rebus, Janice and Brian were seated near one of the loudspeakers. Brian's mum was there, alongside Mr. and Mrs. Playfair. An elderly man came over to talk to them. Brian leaned towards Rebus.

"That's Alec Chisholm's dad," he said.

"I wouldn't have known him," Rebus admitted.

"They don't like talking to him. He's always on about how long Alec's been gone."

It was true that the Playfairs and Mrs. Mee sat stony-faced as they listened to Chisholm. Rebus got up to get a round in. He felt numb, remembering the scene which had greeted him in the cemetery, Oakes letting him know he was one step ahead, making it *personal*. Rebus saw it as another part of the test, knew Oakes was trying to break him. Rebus was more determined than ever not to let that happen.

Janice's mum was drinking Bacardi Breezes, watermelon flavour. Rebus doubted she'd ever seen a watermelon in her life. He saw Helen Cousins standing in the doorway with a couple of friends, went up to say hello.

"Any news?" she asked.

He shook his head, and she just shrugged, like she'd already given up on Damon. So much for the big romance. She was holding a bottle of Hooch, lemon flavour. All these sugary drinks, perfect for Scotland: a sweet tooth and a kick. Through in the saloon, he'd noticed they kept the bottles of mixers—lemonade and Irn Bru—on the bar, to be used freely by the punters. Not many pubs did that any more. Another thing: cheap beer. A lesson in economics: where you had a depressed area, you had to make your beer affordable. He'd spotted Heather Cranston through in the bar, seated on a stool, eyes drooping as some man talked into her ear and rested his hand on the back of her neck.

Helen handed her bottle to one of her friends, said she was off to the loo. Rebus hung around. The two girls were staring at him, wondering who he was.

"She must be taking it hard," he said.

"What?" the one chewing gum asked, face creasing into puzzlement.

"Damon disappearing."

The girl shrugged.

"More embarrassed than anything," her friend commented. "Doesn't do much for your morale, does it, your boyfriend doing a runner?"

"I suppose not," Rebus said. "I'm John, by the way."

"Corinne," the gum-chewer said. She had long black hair

crimped with curling-tongs. Her pal was called Jacky and was tiny with dyed platinum hair.

"So what do you think of Damon?" he asked. He meant about Damon disappearing, but they didn't take it that way.

"Ach, he's all right," Jacky said.

"Just all right?"

"Well, you know," Corinne said. "Damon's heart's in the right place, but he's a bit thick. A bit slow, like."

Rebus nodded, as if this were his impression too. But the way Damon's family had spoken of him, he'd been more of a genius in waiting. Rebus realised suddenly just how superficial his own portrait of Damon was. So far, he'd heard only one side of the story.

"Helen likes him, though?" he asked.

"I suppose so."

"They're engaged."

"It happens, doesn't it?" Jacky said. "I've got girlfriends who got engaged just so they could throw a party." She looked at her pal for support, then leaned towards Rebus to utter a confidentiality. "They used to have some mega arguments."

"What about?"

"Jealousy, I suppose." She waited till Corinne had nodded confirmation. "She'd see him notice someone, or he'd say she'd been letting some guy chat her up. Just the usual." She looked at him. "You think he's gone off with someone?" Rebus saw behind her eyeliner to a sharp intelligence.

"It's possible," he said.

But Corinne was shaking her head. "He wouldn't have had the guts."

Looking along the corridor, Rebus saw that Helen hadn't made it to the toilets. She was chatting to some guy, her back to the wall, hands behind her. Rebus asked Corinne and Jacky what they were drinking. Two Bacardi-Cokes. He added them to the shopping list.

When he got back to his table, Janice was taking the floor. She sang "Baker Street" with real emotion, eyes closed, knowing the words by heart. Brian watched her, his face giving away little. He probably didn't realise he spent the whole song tearing a beer-mat into tinier and tinier pieces, piling them on to the table before sweeping them on to the floor as the number finished.

Rebus stepped outside, took deep gulps of the crisp night air. He was sticking to whisky, heavily watered. There were shouts in the distance, football chants. UVF spray-painted on the side wall of the pub. A man was urinating there. Afterwards, he reeled towards Rebus, asked if he could borrow a cigarette. Rebus gave him one, lit it.

"Cheers, Jimmy," the drunk said. Then he studied Rebus's face. "I knew your father," he said, walking away before Rebus could quiz him further.

Rebus stood there. This wasn't where he belonged, he knew that now. The past was a place you could visit, but it didn't do to linger there. He'd drunk too much to drive, but first thing . . . first thing he would head back. Cary Oakes wasn't here. He'd visited only long enough to leave a message. Rebus felt sorry for Janice and Brian, the way things had gone for them. But right now they were the least important of his many problems. He'd allowed his perspective to skew, and Oakes had made far too much capital from that.

Back indoors, no one tried to press the microphone on him. By now they all knew who he was, knew about the act of desecration. Stories passed quickly through a town the size of Cardenden. What else was history made up of?

It was still dark when he awoke. He dressed, folded the blankets, left a note on the dining table. Then headed out to his car, drove through the quiet streets and quieter countryside, hitting dual carriageway and giving the Saab's engine a proper work-out as he sped south towards Edinburgh.

He found a space round the corner from Oxford Terrace and walked back to Patience's flat. It was still too dark to see the door; he ran his fingers over it, found the lock and keyed it open. The hall was in darkness too. He walked on tiptoe, headed for the kitchen, poured water into the kettle. When he turned round, Patience was standing in the doorway.

"Where the hell have you been?" she said, tiredness failing to dampen her irritation.

"Fife."

"You didn't call."

"I told you I was going."

"I tried your mobile."

He switched the kettle on. "I had it turned off." He saw pain suddenly crease her face. Took her by the arms. "What is it, Patience?"

She shook her head. There were tears in her eyes. She sniffed them back, took him by the hand into the hallway, where she switched on the light. He saw marks on the floor, a trail of them leading to the front door.

"What happened?" he asked.

"Paint," she said. "It was dark, I didn't see I was treading it in. I've tried cleaning it off."

A white snail's trail of footprints . . . Rebus thought of the white tracks leading to his father's grave. He stared at her, then went to the front door and opened it. Behind him, she reached for the light-switch, illuminating the patio. Rebus saw the paint. Words daubed in foot-long letters on the paving-stones. He angled his head to read them.

YOUR COP LOVER KILLED DARREN.

The whole message underlined.

"Christ," he gasped.

"Is that all you can say?" Her voice trembled. "I've been trying to get you all weekend!"

"I was . . . When did it happen?" He was walking around the message.

"Friday night. I came home late, went to bed. About three, I woke up with a headache. Went to get some water, put the hall light on . . ." She was pulling back her hair with her hands, her face stretching, tightening. "I saw the paint, came out here, and . . ."

"I'm sorry, Patience."

"What does it mean?"

"I'm not sure." Oakes again. All the time Rebus had been in Fife, Oakes had been right here, making his next move. He didn't just know about Janice, he knew about Patience too. And had told Rebus as much, telling him it was lucky he knew a doctor.

He'd telegraphed the move, and Rebus hadn't read it.

"You're lying," Patience said. "You know damned well. It's *him*, isn't it?"

Rebus tried putting his arms round her, but she shrugged him off.

"I called St. Leonard's," she said. "They sent someone round. Two kids in uniform. Then next morning, Siobhan turned up." She smiled. "She took me out for breakfast. I think she knew I hadn't been to sleep. It made me realise how vulnerable this place is. Garden at the back: anyone could scale the wall, get in through the conservatory. Or break down the front door: who's going to notice?" She looked at him. "Who am I going to call?"

He made again to put his arms around her. This time she allowed it, but he could feel resistance.

"I'm sorry," he repeated. "If I'd known ... if there'd been any way ..." Friday night he'd switched off his mobile. Now he asked himself why. To conserve the battery? It was what he'd told himself back then, but maybe he'd been trying to block Fife off from everything else in his life; so busy thinking about Janice, he'd ignored Oakes's more obvious move. He kissed Patience's hair. Skewed perspectives, not thinking straight. Oakes was winning every fucking round. The bond Rebus felt with Janice was undeniable, but was all about failed chances. In the here and now, Patience was his lover. Patience was the one he was holding and kissing.

"It'll be all right," he told her. "Everything's going to be OK."

She pulled away from him, wiped her eyes with the sleeve of her gown. "Something funny's happened to your voice. You've gone all Fife."

He smiled. "I'll make us some tea. You go back to bed. If you need me, you know where I'll be."

"And where's that?"

"Ben the scullery, hen."

"It's got to be Oakes," he said.

He'd called Siobhan to thank her. Patience had told him
to ask her to lunch. So now, with the sun overhead, they
were seated at the table in the conservatory. The Sunday
papers lay unread in a pile in the corner. They ate Scotch
broth, cooked ham and salad. A couple of bottles of wine
had taken a pasting.

"Know what she did last night?" Patience had said—
meaning Siobhan; talking to Rebus. "Phoned to check I was
all right. Said if I wasn't, I could sleep round at her place."
A lazy half-drunken smile, and she got up to make the
coffee. It was then that Rebus voiced his suspicions to Siobhan.

"Evidence?" she replied, before finishing her wine: just
the two glasses—she was driving.

"Gut feeling. He's been watching my flat. He knows I
was the last person to see Rough alive. He took Janice out,
and now it's Patience's turn."

"What has he got against you?"

"I don't know. Maybe it could have been any one of us;
just so happens I got the short straw."

"From what you say, he's more calculating than that."

"Yes." Rebus pushed a cherry tomato around the bed of
lettuce on his plate. "Patience said something a while back.
She said it all could be some kind of tactic to keep us from
seeing what he's really up to."

"And what might that be?"

Rebus sighed. "I wish to God I knew." He studied the
salad again. "Remember when you could only get one kind
of lettuce? One kind of tomato?"

"I'm too young."

Rebus nodded thoughtfully. "Do you think she'll be
OK?" Meaning Patience.

"She'll be fine."

"I should have been here."

"She said you were in Fife. What were you doing
there?"

"Living in the past," he said, finally stabbing the tomato with his fork.

He spent the rest of the day with Patience. They took a walk in the Botanic Gardens, then dropped in on Sammy. Patience hadn't gone to see her on Saturday—had phoned to say something had come up, not elaborating. She had a lie prepared for their visit, briefed Rebus so he'd back her up. Another walk: this time with Sammy in the wheelchair. Rebus still felt awkward, going out with her in public. She teased him about it.

"Ashamed to be seen with a cripple?"

"Don't talk like that."

"What is it then?"

But he had no answer for her. What was it? He didn't know himself. Maybe it was other people, the way they stared. He wanted to say: she's going to get better, she won't be in this thing forever. He wanted to explain how it had happened and how well she'd taken it. He wanted to tell them she was *normal*.

With Sammy in a wheelchair . . . it was like she was a toddler again, and he felt himself watching for bumps and dips in the pavement, for awkward kerbs and safe crossing-places. He was insistent they wait for the green man, even when there was no traffic in sight.

"Dad," she would say, "what are the odds of me getting hit again?"

"Don't forget, the bookies had us odds-on for Culloden."

And she would laugh.

Her boyfriend Ned was with them, but Sammy insisted on pushing herself, leaning back to do wheelies and show her mastery of the vehicle. Ned laughed with her, walked alongside with hands in pockets. Patience slipped her hand into Rebus's.

A Sunday outing: that's what it was.

And afterwards, back at the flat there were cream cakes and mugs of Darjeeling, football highlights on the TV with the sound turned down. Sammy talking to Patience about her latest exercise regime. Ned talking to Rebus. Rebus not listening, his eyes half-turned to the window, wondering if Cary Oakes was out there . . .

That evening, he told Patience he had to go home. "Couple of things I need. I'll be back later." He kissed her. "You all right here, or do you want to come with me?"

"I'll stay," she said.

So Rebus got into his car and drove. Not to Arden Street but down to Leith. He walked into the hotel and asked to speak to Cary Oakes. Reception tried his room: no answer.

"Maybe he's in the bar," the woman said.

But Cary Oakes was not in the bar—Jim Stevens was.

"Let me get you a drink," he said. Rebus shook his head, noticed Stevens was on large G and Ts.

"Where's your boy?"

Stevens just shrugged.

"I thought you'd want to keep tabs on him," Rebus said, trying to control his anger.

"I do, believe me. But he's a slippery little bugger."

"How much more can you milk out of him?"

Stevens smiled, shaking his head. "Something strange and wonderful has happened. You know me, Rebus, I'm what they call a seasoned hack, meaning I'm tough and I'm relentless and I don't take shit."

"And?"

"And I think he's been giving me shit." Stevens shrugged. "It's not bad stuff, don't get me wrong. But where's the corroboration?"

"Since when has that stopped you?"

Stevens bowed his head, acknowledging the point. "For my own satisfaction," he added, "I'd like to know. And along the way, dear old Cary seems to have managed to weasel almost as many stories out of me as I've had from him."

"Oh, you've always been known for your reticence."

"I don't mind telling stories . . . bit of repartee at the bar. But Oakes . . . I don't know. It's not the stories themselves that interest him so much as what they say about the people involved." He picked up his drink. There were three empty glasses beside it. He'd decanted all the lemon slices into the most recent arrival. "That probably makes no sense. I don't care: I'm off duty."

"So are you finished with him?"

Stevens smacked his lips. "I'd say we're getting there. The question is: is *he* finished with *me*?"

Rebus took out a cigarette and lit it, offered one to the reporter. "He's been tailing me, people I know."

"What for?"

"Maybe he wants another story for you." Rebus moved closer. "Listen, off the record, just two old bastards talking . . ."

Stevens blinked away some of the alcohol. "Yes?"

"Has he said *anything* about Deirdre Campbell?" Stevens couldn't place the name. "Alan Archibald's niece."

"Oh, right." An exaggerated nod, face dipping towards the gin glass, then a frown of concentration. "He did say something about clear-up rates. Said that's what happened when they pinned you for something: they tried to tidy away a few unsolveds by sweeping them into your case-file."

Rebus had eased himself on to a stool. "He didn't mention specifics?"

"You think there's something I've missed?"

Rebus was thoughtful. "You've said it yourself: you think he's using you."

"By putting clues in his story that I'm not going to get? Give me a bit of credit."

"He likes *games*," Rebus hissed. "That's all we are to him."

"Not me, pal. I'm his sugar daddy."

"Sugar daddies get cheated on."

"John . . ." Stevens sat up straight, took a reviving lungful of air. "This story's put me back on the map. *I* got to him first. Me, washed-up old Jim Stevens, gold-watch contestant. Even if he buggered off tonight, I'd have the best part of a book's-worth." He nodded to himself, eyes on the glass he was picking up. Rebus found himself not believing the reporter. "See, when I make a toast these days," Stevens went on, raising his glass, "it's only ever to Number One. As far as I'm concerned, pal, the rest of you can go straight to hell, no Just Visiting and no Free Parking." He drank, drained the glass dry.

He was ordering another as Rebus made for the door.

35

When Rebus left Patience's next morning, she was out on
the patio, discussing with two workmen how best to clean
the paint off the flagstones. As he walked into St. Leonard's
and made for the CID suite, he could feel that something
had happened. There was activity around him and the air
felt charged. Siobhan Clarke was first with the news.

"Joanna Horman's lover." She handed Rebus a report.
"He's dirty."

Rebus glanced down the sheet. The lover's name was
Ray Heggie. He'd done time for housebreaking and as-
sorted acts of drunken violence. He was ten years older than
Joanna. He'd been living with her for six weeks.

"Roy Frazer's got him in the interview room."

"How come?" Rebus handed back the report.

"A previous girlfriend of Heggie's. She read about the
kid going missing, phoned to tell us he'd abused her little
girl. That was why they broke up."

"She didn't think to tell us before?"

Clarke shrugged. "She's told us now."

Rebus twitched his nose. "How old's the girl?"

"Eleven. Someone from Sex Offences is talking to her
at home." She looked at him. "You're not buying it, are
you?"

"*Caveat senator*, Siobhan. I'll decide after the test
drive." He winked, moved away. An old girlfriend with a
grudge, probably all it was. Saw a chance to make mischief
. . . All the same, if Heggie was an abuser, maybe he'd
known Darren Rough. Rebus knocked on the interview
room door.

"Detective Inspector Rebus enters the room," Frazer
said, for the benefit of the recording tape. He was following

procedure: audio- *and* video-taping. "Hi-Ho" Silvers sat beside him at one side of the table, arms folded, looking unimpressed by everything he'd heard. That was Silvers's role: say nothing, but make the suspect uncomfortable. Across the table sat a man in his forties, black curly hair with a pronounced bald spot. He hadn't shaved for a couple of days. His eyes were dark-ringed. He wore a black T-shirt, and ran his hands over thickly haired arms.

"Join the party," was his comment to Rebus. The room was so small, Rebus stood by the wall, folding his own arms and preparing to listen.

"The locals organised a search party," Frazer went on, "you weren't part of it. How come?"

"I wasn't there."

"Where were you?"

"Glasgow. I went out drinking with a mate, stayed the night at his place. Ask him, he'll tell you."

"I'm sure he will. Mates are good that way, aren't they?"

"It's the truth."

Frazer scribbled a note to himself. "You went out drinking, that means there'll be witnesses." He looked up from his notebook. "So name me some."

"Give me a break. Look, the pubs were all dead, so we got a carry-out and went back to his flat. Sat watching some videos."

"Anything good?"

"Top-shelf stuff." Heggie winked. Frazer just glared back.

"Porn?"

"That's what I said."

"Straight?"

"I'm not a poof." Heggie stopped rubbing his arms.

"I meant, was there any lezzie action?"

"Might have been."

"Bondage? Animals? Kids?"

Heggie saw where this was leading. "I'm not into any of that, I've told you."

"Your ex says different."

"That slut'd say anything. Wait till I see her . . ."

"Anything happens to her, Mr. Heggie, if she so much as catches a cold, I'll have you back in here. Understood?"

"I didn't mean anything. It's just a saying, isn't it? But she's been slagging me off, telling people I've got AIDS, you name it. Vindictive, she is. Any chance of a cuppa?"

Frazer made a show of checking his watch. "We'll take a break in five minutes." Rebus had to stifle a smile, knowing they'd only break when Frazer was good and ready. "You've got a record of violence, Mr. Heggie. My thinking is: you lost patience with the kid, didn't mean to hurt him. But a valve blew, and next thing you knew he was dead."

"No."

"So you had to hide him somewhere."

"No. I keep telling you—"

"Where is he then? How come he goes missing and you turn out to have a record of hurting kids?"

"All you've got is Belinda's word for it!" Belinda: the ex. "I'm telling you, get a doctor to look at Fliss." Fliss: the ex's daughter. "And even if it turns out someone's been poking her, no way it was me. No fucking way. Ask her." He scratched at his hair with one hand.

"We're doing that, Mr. Heggie."

"And if she says I did anything, her mum's put her up to it." He was growing more agitated. "I don't believe this, really I don't." He shook his head. "You lot told Joanna. Now what's she going to think?"

"Why do you always shack up with single mothers?"

Heggie raised his eyes to the ceiling. "Tell me this is a bad dream."

Frazer, who'd been resting his arms on the table, now sat back, glanced towards Rebus. It was the signal Rebus had been waiting for. It meant Frazer was finished for the moment.

"Did you know Darren Rough, Mr. Heggie?" Rebus asked.

"He's the one that got topped?" He waited for Rebus to nod confirmation. "Never knew him."

"Never spoke to him?"

"We weren't in the same block."

"You knew where he lived then?"

"It's been all over the papers. Perverted little bastard, whoever did it deserves a medal."

"Why do you say he was 'little'? He was, by the way.

Not tall, at any rate. But it wasn't in the papers."

"It's just . . . it's something you say, isn't it?"

"It's certainly something *you* say. Makes me think you'd seen him."

"Maybe I had. It's not that big a scheme."

"No, it's not," Rebus said quietly. "Everyone knows everyone else."

"Until the council move in bastards they can't put anywhere else."

Rebus nodded. "So you might have seen Darren Rough around?"

"What difference does it make?"

"It's just that he liked young kids too. Paedophiles seem to be good at recognising one another."

"I'm not a paedophile!" Losing it. His voice was trembling as he got to his feet. "I'd kill every last one of them."

"Did you start with Darren?"

"What?"

"Get rid of him, you'd be a hero."

A burst of nervous laughter. "So now I didn't just do in Billy, I topped the pervert as well?"

"Is that what you're telling us?" Rebus asked.

"I haven't killed anyone!"

"How did you get on with Billy, by the way? Must've been awkward, having him around, you wanting Joanna all to yourself."

"He's a nice kid."

"Sit down, Mr. Heggie," Frazer commanded.

Eventually Heggie sat down, but then leapt up again, his finger pointing at Rebus. "He's trying to set me up!"

Rebus shook his head, gave a wry smile. He pushed off from the wall.

"I'm just after the truth," he said, making to leave the room.

"Inspector Rebus leaving the interview room," he could hear Frazer saying behind him.

Later, Frazer stopped off at Rebus's desk. "You don't really make him for Darren Rough, do you?"

Rebus shrugged. "Do you make him for the kid?"

"Maybe if Sex Offences come up with something. From

what I hear, her mum's sticking to her like glue, answering for her, putting words in her mouth."

"Doesn't mean she's lying."

"No." Frazer was thoughtful. "Heggie doesn't give a shit about Billy Horman. All he's worried about is that Joanna will boot him out." He shook his head slowly. "People like him, you never get through to them, do you?"

"No."

"And you can't get them to change." He looked at Rebus. "That's what you think too, isn't it?"

"Welcome to my world, Roy," Rebus said, reaching for the telephone.

He had to keep working; had to stop letting thoughts of Cary Oakes consume him. So Rebus phoned Phyllida Hawes at Gayfield station.

"Has your MisPer turned up?" she asked.

"Not a bloody sign of him."

"Well, that can be good news too, can't it? Means he's probably still alive."

"Or the body's been well-hidden."

"I do like an optimist."

Another time, Rebus might have kept the banter going. "You know Gaitano's?" he said instead, getting to the point.

"Yes." Sounding curious, wondering what he was after.

"As owned by Charmer Mackenzie?"

"The same."

"What have you got on him?"

Silence for a moment. "Is he connected to your MisPer?"

"I'm not sure." Rebus told her about the boat.

"Yes, I knew about that," she said. "But it's strictly a money thing. I mean, Mackenzie has a share, but he doesn't interfere with the business. You've met Billy Preston?" Rebus admitted he had. "Charmer leaves him to get on with it."

"Not quite. The under manager at Gaitano's, young guy called Archie Frost, he keeps an eye on the Clipper. Plus provides muscle for the door."

"Is that so?" Rebus could hear her scribbling a note to herself.

"Does he have any other interests?" he asked.

"You might want to take this conversation to NCIS."

NCIS: the National Criminal Intelligence Service. Rebus leaned forward in his chair. "They have something on Mackenzie?"

"They have a file, yes."

"So he's got dirt under his fingernails: what is it exactly?"

"Farmyard mud for all I know. Go talk to NCIS."

"I will." Rebus put the phone down, logged on at one of the computer terminals and entered Mackenzie's details. At the bottom of the screen there was a reference number and an officer's name. Rebus called NCIS and asked to speak to the name: Detective Sergeant Paul Carnett.

"That's a misprint," the switchboard told him. "It's not Paul, it's Pauline." She put him through anyway, where a male voice told Rebus DS Carnett would be in a meeting for another hour, maybe an hour and a half. Rebus checked his watch.

"Has she anything after that?"

"Not that I can see."

"Then I'd like to make a reservation: table for two, the name's DI Rebus."

36

The Scottish office of NCIS was based at Osprey House in Paisley, not far off the M8. Last time Rebus had been this way had been to drop his ex-wife off at Glasgow Airport. She'd come up from London to see Sammy, and all the Edinburgh flights had been full. He couldn't remember what they'd talked about on the drive.

Osprey House was supposed to be the future of high-profile policing in Scotland, housing as it did the Scottish

Crime Squad and Customs and Excise as well as NCIS and the Scottish Criminal Intelligence Office. Its remit was intelligence-gathering. Having started with just the two officers, NCIS now had a staff of ten. There had been bad feeling when the office had opened, due to the fact that the Scottish NCIS team reported not to a Scottish chief constable but to the London-based director of the whole UK operation, who in turn reported to the Scottish Secretary. NCIS dealt with counterfeiting, money-laundering, organised drug and vehicle crime, and, if Rebus remembered correctly, paedophile gangs. Rebus had heard the officers at NCIS called "anoraks" and "computer nerds," but not by anyone who'd actually met them.

"It's fairly irregular," Pauline Carnett said, as Rebus explained why he was there.

They were seated in an open-plan office, around them the incessant humming of computer fans and quiet telephone conversations. The occasional flurry of keyboard strokes. Young men in shirtsleeves and ties; two women, both dressed for business. Pauline's desk was at the opposite end of the room from the other woman officer. Rebus wondered if there was any significance in this.

Pauline Carnett was in her mid-thirties with short blonde hair brushed out from a centre parting. Tall and broad-shouldered, she had offered a handshake firmer than most Masons Rebus knew. She had a gap between her two front teeth and seemed overly conscious of the fact, which made Rebus want to make her smile.

Like all the others, her desk was L-shaped, with one surface given over to a computer, the other to paperwork. The office shared a printer. It was churning out work, a young man standing beside it, looking bored.

"So this is the heart of the machine," had been Rebus's comment on entering the room.

Carnett put her cup down on a mouse pad stained with dozens of coffee rings. Rebus set his own cup on the worktop.

"Irregular," she said again, as if he might be persuaded to leave. Instead, he just shrugged. "Information is usually requested by telephone or fax."

"I've always preferred the personal touch," Rebus said.

He handed her a scrap of paper on which he'd jotted the reference number concerning Charmer Mackenzie. She slid her chair closer to the desk and hammered on the keys, as if meaning to do violence to the keyboard. Then she slid the mouse around the pad, expertly avoiding the coffee cup, and double-clicked.

Charmer Mackenzie's file came up. Rebus saw straight away that there was a lot of stuff there. He moved his own chair closer to hers.

"Initially," she said, "it looks like we got on to him because Crime Squad had him hosting private parties for someone called Thomas Telford."

"I know Telford," Rebus said. "I helped put him away."

"Good for you. Telford used Mackenzie's club for meetings, and also rented a boat part-owned by Mackenzie. The boat was used for parties. Crime Squad kept tabs on it because you never knew who might turn up. Didn't get much joy, though: operation suspended." She hit the return key, bringing up another page. "Ah, here we go," she said, leaning in towards the screen. "Money-lending."

"Mackenzie?"

She nodded. Rebus read over her shoulder. NCIS suspected Mackenzie of running a little business on the side, fronting money for criminal schemes—guaranteed payback, one way or another—but also loaning cash sums to people who either couldn't get the money elsewhere or had reasons not to go walking into a bank or building society.

"How accurate is this?" Rebus asked.

"It wouldn't be here if it wasn't one hundred per cent."

"All the same . . ."

"All the same, there's obviously not enough to go on, or we'd have had him in court." She pointed to an icon at the foot of the screen. "Case-notes went to the Procurator Fiscal, who decided there wasn't enough for a prosecution."

"So is the case ongoing?"

She shook her head. "We have patience, we can wait. We'll see what else filters down to us, decide when the time's right to try again." She glanced at him. "Robert the Bruce and all that."

Rebus was still studying the screen. "Have you got names?"

"You mean people who've borrowed from him?"

"Yes."

"Hang on." She hit more keys, studied the information as it came up on the screen. "Hard copies," she mumbled at last. Then she got up from her seat and told him to follow her. They went to a storeroom filled with filing cabinets.

"So much for the paperless office," Rebus said.

"I'm with you on that." She found the cabinet she was looking for, pulled out the top drawer and started riffling through the file-holders, found the one she was looking for and pulled it out.

Inside the green file were about three dozen sheets of paper. Two of the sheets listed "suspected" users of Charmer Mackenzie's loan scheme.

"No statements," Rebus said, sifting the sheets.

"Case probably didn't get that far."

"I thought it was your case."

She shrugged. "We get sent a lot of stuff from Crime Squad Customs, wherever. It goes into the computer and into a drawer—that's my job."

"You're a filing clerk?" Rebus suggested. Her eyes narrowed aggressively. "Sorry," he said. "Trying to make a joke." He went back to the file. "So how did you come by these names?"

"Probably one or two people talked."

"But didn't make reliable witnesses?"

She nodded. "People who need to go to a loan shark, we're not talking public-minded citizens here."

Rebus recognized a couple of names: known housebreakers. Maybe looking to finance some bigger scheme.

"Others on the list," Carnett was saying, "could be they got thumped by Mackenzie or his men, and Crime Squad got wind of it."

"And nobody would talk?" Rebus guessed. She nodded again. He'd come across this before; they both had. It was fine to have seven bells knocked out of you, but a black mark to talk to the filth about it. You'd get "GRASS" sprayed on your front door. People would cross the road to avoid you. Rebus started jotting down names and addresses, sure none of it was going to be any use. But he'd come all this way, after all.

"I can make copies," Carnett suggested.

Rebus nodded. "I'm a bit of a dinosaur, need to have the gist in my wee book." He tapped one entry. No name, just a series of numbers. "Is this what we're supposed to call Prince now?"

She smiled, covered it quickly with her hand. "Looks like another reference," she said. "I'll check it back at my desk."

So they went back there, and while Rebus finished his cold coffee, he watched her work.

"Interesting," she said at last, leaning back in her chair. "It's our way of keeping certain names quiet. Computers aren't always safe from prowlers."

"Hackers."

She looked at him. "Not quite a dinosaur," she commented. "Wait here a minute."

She was actually gone three minutes, long enough for her screen-saver to activate. When she returned, she had a single sheet of paper with her, which she handed to Rebus.

"We use numbers as codes when a name is judged too hot: that means someone we don't want everyone knowing about. Any idea who he is?"

Rebus was looking at the name on the sheet. There was nothing else printed there.

"Yes," he said at last. "He's a judge's son."

"That would explain it then," Pauline Carnett said, lifting her cup.

The name on the sheet was Nicol Petrie.

When they delved a little deeper, they found a Crime Squad report detailing a mugging attack. Nicol Petrie had been found unconscious in one of the shadowy back lanes off Rose Street—about a hundred yards from Gaitano's nightclub. Petrie had been taken by ambulance to hospital, a uniformed officer waiting to talk to him. But when he'd regained consciousness, he had had nothing to say.

"I can't remember," had been his refrain. He couldn't even say if anything had been stolen from him. But a couple of eye-witnesses gave descriptions of two men leaving the lane. They were laughing, lighting cigarettes. One of them even complained that he'd scraped his knuckles. Police got as far as holding an ID parade for the witnesses, but by then they'd long since sobered up and wanted nothing to do with it, refused to identify anyone.

Two bouncers from Gaitano's had been in the parade: one of them was named as Calumn Brady.

Rebus went through the witness statements. The descriptions of the attackers were vague. He could just about see one of them—the shorter of the two—as Cal Brady. But it didn't matter. Nicol Petrie wasn't about to say anything, and the witnesses had either been warned off, paid off, or had just come to their senses.

Crime Squad put it down to a "warning" from Mackenzie, and let it go at that. Speculation: that's all it was. But Rebus was willing to go along with it. All the same . . . something refused to click into place.

"Nicol's dad's a judge, plenty of money. Why didn't he just borrow from him?"

Pauline Carnett didn't have an answer for that.

Later, he asked if he could speak to someone from the paedophile unit. He was introduced to a woman officer called DS Whyte. He asked her about Darren Rough. She brought the details up on her screen.

"What about him?" she said.

"Known associates."

She hammered keys, shook her head. "He was a loner. NKA."

NKA: No Known Associates. Rebus scratched his chin. "How about Ray Heggie."

She hit more keys. "No record," she said at last. "Is he someone I should know about?"

Rebus shrugged.

"In that case . . ." she said, adding the name to her screen. Rebus's name went there too. "Just so I know where I first heard of him."

Rebus nodded. "Have you been following Shiellion?"

"I hear the jury's out. Looking good for guilty."

"Not if Richie Cordover has anything to do with it."

"He's good, but I've come across Lord Justice Petrie

before, and if there's one thing he can't stand, it's a paedophile. The way Petrie summed up, Ince and Marshall are fucked."

"Not before time," Rebus added, getting up to go.

Back in Edinburgh, he was wanted at Fettes—by the ACC, no less.

The Assistant Chief Constable (Crime) was known to be scrupulous, fair, and to have no record of suffering fools gladly. He had a nice fat file on Rebus which told him the officer was "difficult but useful." Rebus had made a career out of making enemies. The ACC, whose name was Colin Carswell, liked to think of himself as not among them.

There was an identifying plaque on the door, and the room number below it: 278. The room itself was large, with institutional carpet and curtains, and a bowl of flowers on the windowsill. There was little other decoration. Carswell, tall and thin with a good head of salt-and-pepper hair and moustache to match, rose from his chair just long enough to shake Rebus's hand. Typically, he didn't sit behind his desk for interviews, but conducted them in two chairs by the window. The chairs were swivel designs and sat on castors, so that unwary officers could find themselves spinning a hundred and eighty degrees or sliding backwards towards Carswell's desk. After an interview like that, most agreed they'd have settled for the old-fashioned kind.

Which, the ACC might have told them, was the whole point of the exercise.

The dark eyes spoke of lost sleep. Despite his advancing years, the ACC had recently become a father for the fourth time. As his other kids were all grown-up, the conclusion reached by every station in the city was that the new addition was an accident, which would make it practically the only thing in the ACC's life that he'd not been able to orchestrate or control.

"How are you, John?" he asked.

"Not bad, sir. How's the wee one?"

"Fit as a fiddle. Look, John . . ." Carswell never wasted time on preliminaries. "I've been asked to look into this murder case."

"Darren Rough?"

"That's the one."

"Social Work, was it, sir?" Rebus settled his hands on the arm rests.

"Fellow called Andrew Davies. Made a sort of complaint."

"Sort of?"

"Couched fairly ambiguously."

"He's probably got a point, sir."

The ACC held his breath for a second. "Am I hearing you right?"

"I chased Rough through the zoo without probable cause, giving our poisoner the chance to strike again. Then when I found out Rough was living upstairs from a play-ground, I put word out on the street."

Carswell put his hands together, as if in prayer. Knowing Rebus's reputation, a confession was the last thing he'd been expecting. "You outed him?"

"Yes, sir. I wanted him off my patch. At the time . . ." Rebus paused. "I didn't work through the consequences. Later on, I helped him get away from Greenfield—at least, that was the plan. Only he left my flat and got himself murdered. Right at the end, though . . . I think I did try to make amends."

"I see. You want me to take this to Social Work?"

"That's up to you, sir."

"Then what *do* you want?"

Rebus looked at him. It was bright outside: another ploy of the ACC's—he tended to use the chair trick when it was sunny. All Rebus could see of his superior was a haze of light.

"For a while, I thought I wanted out, sir. Maybe that was in my mind when I went after Rough: if I went after him hard, I might end up kicked off the force, but still feel all right about it."

"But that didn't happen."

"It hasn't happened yet, sir, no."

Carswell was thoughtful. "How do you feel now?"

Rebus squinted into the light. "I'm not sure. Tired, mostly." He managed a smile.

"A long time back, John—I know you all like to think I've spent my whole life behind a desk—but a long time back there was this man got himself into a fight down in Leith. Clean-cut type, suit and everything. Wife and kids at home. And he'd walked into a pub by the dockside, looked for the biggest, meanest-looking bugger he could find, and started having a go at him. I was young back then, they sent me to interview him in hospital. Turned out he'd been trying to commit suicide, hadn't had the guts. So he'd gone looking for someone to do the job for him. Sounds a bit like what you were up to with Darren Rough: assisted career suicide."

Rebus smiled again, but he was thinking: *Suicide again . . . like with Jim Margolies. Assisted career suicide . . .*

"I don't think I'm going to give this to our friends in Social Work," the ACC said finally. "I think I'm going to sit on it for a while. Maybe there's room for some sort of apology . . . that'll be up to you."

"Thank you, sir."

"And John," rising to his feet, taking Rebus's hand again, "I appreciate you not trying to spin me some yarn."

"Yes, sir." Rebus was on his feet, too. "And maybe, with respect, sir, there's a way you could show your appreciation . . ."

Nicol Petrie lived in a West End flat, sprawling over the top two floors of a Georgian pile. There was a shared entrance hall with occasional tables and rugs. The tables had vases and things on them. It was a far cry from the tenement stairwells Rebus was used to.

And there was a lift, its mirrored interior highly polished, the wooden surrounds gleaming. Beside the buttons for each floor were printed labels listing the occupants.

There were two Petries: N and A. Rebus guessed that A stood for Amanda.

The lift brought Rebus out on to a landing, glass cupola above. Pot plants surrounded him. And more carpeting. Nicol Petrie opened the door and gave a little nod, leading Rebus inside.

Rebus had been expecting antiquity, but was disappointed. The flat's walls were painted an almost luminous white and were devoid of paintings or posters. The floors had been stripped and varnished. It was like stepping into an Ikea catalogue. An internal stairway led up to the top floor, but Nicol led Rebus past it and into the living room, fully thirty-five feet long and twelve high, and with double sash windows giving uninterrupted views across Dean Valley and the Water of Leith. The Fife coastline was visible in the distance. Walking into the room, taking it all in, Rebus missed the doll on the floor and ended up giving it a kick, sending it flying towards its owner.

"Jessica!" the little girl squealed, moving on hands and knees to pick up her property and nurse it to her bosom. Then she slid back across the floor to where a toys' tea-party was in progress. Rebus apologized, but Hannah Margolies wasn't listening.

"Hello again," Hannah's mother said. She was seated on a white sofa. "Sorry about that. Hannah's toys get everywhere." She sounded tired. Rebus noted that she still wore black, albeit a short black dress with black tights. Mourning as fashion statement.

"Sorry," he said to Nicol Petrie, "I didn't know you had company."

"You know one another?" Petrie bowed his head at the stupidity of the question. "Through Jim, of course. Sorry."

It seemed to Rebus that all anyone had done so far was make apologies. Katherine Margolies got to her feet in a sudden elegant movement.

"Come on, Han-Han. Time to go."

Hannah didn't argue or complain, just rose to her feet and joined her mother.

"Nicky," Katherine said, kissing both his cheeks, "thanks as ever for listening."

Nicol Petrie embraced her, then crouched down for a

kiss from Hannah. Katherine Margolies lifted Hannah's coat from the back of the sofa.

"Goodbye, Inspector."

"Bye, Mrs. Margolies. Bye, Hannah."

Hannah gave him a look. "You think I should have won, don't you?"

Katherine stroked her daughter's hair. "Everyone knows you were robbed, sweetheart."

Hannah was still staring at Rebus. "Someone stole my father," she said.

Nicol Petrie made a fuss of her as he showed mother and daughter to the door. When he returned to the room, Rebus was standing at one of the windows, looking down into the street immediately below. Petrie began tidying the toys into a cardboard box.

"Sorry again if I disturbed you, sir," Rebus said, not managing much enthusiasm for the lie.

"That's all right. Katy often pops in unannounced. Especially since . . . well, you know."

"Do you make a good listener, Mr. Petrie?"

"No more than most, I don't suppose. Usually it's because I can't think of anything helpful to say, so all I do is fill the gaps with questions."

"You'd make a good detective then."

Petrie laughed. "I rather doubt that, Inspector." He opened one of the doors leading off the living room. It led to a walk-in cupboard. There were shelves inside, and he placed the box of toys on one of them. Everything tidied away. Rebus would bet the box always went back on the same shelf, always the same spot. He'd known people like that, people who managed their lives by compartments. Siobhan Clarke was just the same: if you wanted to annoy her, you only had to move something of hers from one desk-drawer to its neighbour.

Below him, Katherine Margolies and her daughter emerged from the building. Their car had remote locking. It was a Mercedes saloon, new-looking. The number plate was the same one he'd seen lipsticked on the wall in Leith.

It was a white Mercedes.

White . . .

"Has it hit her hard?" he asked, still watching from the window.

"Devastated, I should think."

"And the little one?"

"I'm not sure Han-Han's taken it in yet. Like she said, she thinks he's been stolen from her."

"She's right in a way."

"I suppose so." Petrie came to the window, watched with Rebus as the car drove off. "Nobody could fail to be shocked by something like that."

"Why do you think he did it?"

Petrie looked at him. "I haven't the faintest idea."

"His widow hasn't said anything?"

"That's between her and me."

"Sorry," Rebus said. "It's just curiosity. I mean, someone like Jim Margolies . . . it makes you ask questions of yourself, doesn't it?"

"I think I know what you mean." Petrie turned back into the room. "If you've got it all and you're still unhappy, what's the point of everything?" He slumped into a chair. "Maybe it's a Scottish thing."

Rebus took a seat on the sofa. "What is?"

"We're just not supposed to have it all, are we? We're supposed to fail gloriously. Anything we succeed at, we keep low-profile. It's our failures we're allowed to trumpet."

Rebus smiled. "Might be something in that."

"It runs right through our history."

"And ends at the national football team."

It was Petrie's turn to smile. "I've been very rude: can I offer you something to drink?"

"What are you having?"

"I thought maybe a glass of wine. I'd opened a bottle for Katy, thinking she'd come by taxi. Parking around here is hellish." He left the room, Rebus following. The kitchen was long and narrow and spotless. The hob looked like it had never been used. Petrie went to the fridge, lifted out a bottle of Sancerre.

"Lovely flat," Rebus said, as Petrie reached into a cupboard for two glasses.

"Thank you. I like it."

"What do you work at, Mr. Petrie?"

Petrie glanced at him. "I'm a student, second year into my PhD."

"Was your first degree at Edinburgh?"

"No, St. Andrews." Pouring now.

"Not many students with flats as grand as this—or am I behind the times?"

"It's not mine."

"Your father's?" Rebus guessed.

"That's right." Pouring the second glass; looking a little less serene now.

"He must like you."

"He loves his children, Inspector. I'd assume most parents do."

Rebus thought of himself and Sammy. "Not always a two-way thing, though, is it?"

"I don't know what you mean."

Rebus shrugged, accepted the glass. "Cheers." He took a sip. Petrie was at the end of the narrow kitchen: no way out of there except past Rebus. And Rebus wasn't moving. "Funny thing is, if I'd a father who loved me, who'd spent a fortune on a flat for me, any time I got into trouble I'd probably turn to him to bail me out."

"Look, what's—"

"Say, if I needed money. I wouldn't go to a loan shark." Rebus paused, took another sip. "How about you, Mr. Petrie?"

"Christ, is that what this is about? Those two thugs giving me a kicking?"

"Maybe it wasn't about money. Maybe they just didn't like your looks." Nicol Petrie: face unblemished, thin dark eyebrows, high cheekbones. A face so perfect you might just want to damage it.

"I don't know what they wanted."

Rebus smiled. "Yes you do. That handy amnesia of yours, you let it slip. You shouldn't have known there were two of them."

"The police said as much at the time."

"Two men employed by Charmer Mackenzie. We call them 'frighteners,' and believe me, I'd have been frightened too. He's a hard bastard, Cal Brady, isn't he?"

"Who?"

"Cal Brady. You must have come across him."

Petrie shook his head. "I don't think so."

"How much was it you owed? I'm assuming you've paid it off by now. And why didn't you tap your dad for a loan in the first place? See, I'm curious, Mr. Petrie, and when I start asking questions, I tend not to give up till I've found answers."

Petrie put his glass down on the worktop. He wasn't looking at Rebus when he spoke. "This is strictly between us? No way I'm taking this any further."

"Fair enough," Rebus said.

Petrie folded his arms around himself, looking skinnier than ever. "I did borrow money from Mackenzie. We knew, those of us who frequented the Clipper, knew he'd lend money. And I found myself needing some. My father can be generous when it suits him, Inspector, but I'd managed to fritter away a good deal of his money. I didn't want him knowing. So I went to Mackenzie instead."

"Surely you could have arranged an overdraft?"

"I dare say I could." Petrie looked away. "But there was something . . . the idea of dealing with Mackenzie was so much more appealing."

"How so?"

"The danger, the whiff of the illicit." He turned back towards Rebus. "You know Edinburgh society loves that sort of thing. Deacon Brodie didn't need to break into people's houses, but that didn't stop him. Strait-laced old town, how else are we going to get our thrills?"

Rebus stared at him. "Know something, Nicky? I almost believe you. Almost, but not quite." He raised a hand towards Petrie, who flinched. But all Rebus did was place a fingertip against the young man's temple. It came away with a bead of perspiration clinging to it. The droplet fell, splashed onto the worktop.

"Better wipe that up," Rebus said, turning away. "You wouldn't want anything marking that stainless surface of yours, would you?"

38

There was still no sign of Billy Horman.

His mother Joanna had cried at the press conference, ensuring TV coverage. Ray Heggie, Joanna's lover, had sat beside her, saying nothing. When the crying started, he'd tried to comfort her, but she'd pushed him away. Rebus knew he'd drift away eventually, as long as he was innocent.

GAP was as active as ever. They were holding a vigil outside the High Court while the jury retired to reach a verdict in the Shiellion case. They'd lit candles and tied placards to the railings. The placards detailed child-killers and paedophiles and their victims. The police were instructed not to move the protesters on. Meantime, there were fresh news reports of paedophiles being released from prison. GAP sent members to the relevant towns. It had become a movement now, Van Brady its unlikely figurehead. She hosted her own news conferences, blown-up photos of Billy Horman and Darren Rough on the wall behind her.

"The world," she'd said at one meeting, "should be a green field without limits, where our children can play free from harm, and where parents can leave their children without fear. That is the purpose and intention of the Green Field Project."

Rebus wondered who was writing her speeches for her. GFP was a departure for GAP, a funding application to set up patrolled play areas with security cameras and the like. To Rebus, it sounded less like the world as green field, more like the world as prison camp. They were applying to the Lottery and the EEC for cash. Other housing schemes had made successful bids in the past, and were lending a hand to Greenfield. They wanted something like two million quid. Rebus shuddered to think of Van and Cal Brady in charge of such a fund.

But then it wasn't his problem, was it?

His immediate problem, as he knew when he picked up the ringing phone, was Cary Oakes.

The voice on the line belonged to Alan Archibald. "He's agreed."

"Agreed to what?"

"To go out to Hillend with me. To walk across the hills."

"He's admitted it?"

"As good as." Archibald's voice shook with excitement.

"But has he said anything *specific*?"

"Once we get out there, John, I know he'll tell me, one way or the other."

"You're going to torture him, are you?"

"I don't mean it like that. I mean once he's there, the scene of the crime, I think he'll crack."

"I wouldn't be so sure. What if it's a trap?"

"John, we've been through this."

"I know." Rebus paused. "And you're still going."

The voice quiet now, calm. "I've got to, whatever happens."

"Yes," Rebus said. Of course Archibald would go. It was his destiny. "Well, count me in."

"I'll ask him—"

"No, Alan, you'll *tell* him. It's both of us or no go."

"What if he—"

"He won't. Trust me on this. I think he'll want me out there too."

The tape was still running, but Cary Oakes hadn't spoken for a couple of minutes. Jim Stevens was used to it, used to long pauses as Oakes gathered his thoughts. He let another sixty seconds spool on before asking: "Anything else, Cary?"

Oakes looked surprised. "Should there be?"

"That's it then?" Still Stevens left the tape running. Oakes only nodded, and reached his hands behind his head, job done. Stevens checked his watch, spoke the time into the machine, then squeezed the Stop button. He slipped the recorder into the breast pocket of his pale mauve shirt. It was pale because it had been through about three hundred washes in the five years since Stevens had bought it. He knew the other reporters thought he'd filled out in the past half-decade. The shirt could have proved them wrong, but would also have proved how seldom he bought new clothes.

"Satisfied?" Oakes said, getting to his feet, stretching as if after a long day at the coal-face.

"Not really. Journalists never are."

"Why's that?"

"Because no matter how much we're told, we *know* we're not getting everything."

Oakes held his hands out. "I've given you blood, Jim. I feel like you've taken a transfusion from me." That unnerving grin again; so lacking in humour. Stevens wrote date and time on a sticker, peeled it off and placed it down one edge of the cassette case. He made this tape number eleven. Eleven hours of Cary Oakes. It wasn't enough for a book, but it might get him the contract, and the rest of the book could be padded: trial reports, interviews, photographs.

Only thing was, he didn't think he was going to find a publisher. He wasn't even going to try.

"What are you thinking, big man?" Oakes asked. He'd taken to calling Stevens "big man." Stevens wasn't naive enough to take it as a compliment; at best it was weighted with irony.

"I'm . . . not really thinking at all." Stevens shrugged. "Just that it's over, that's all."

"So now it's pay-off time for old Cary."

"You'll get your cheque."

"What good's a cheque? I said cash."

Stevens shook his head. "A cheque, has to be or our accounts department would have a breakdown. You can use it to open a bank account."

"And sit around how long waiting for it to clear?" Oakes had been pacing the room. Now he came to Stevens' chair and leaned down over him, staring him out. Stevens blinked first, which seemed victory enough for Oakes. He propelled himself back upright and angled his head to the ceiling, letting out a whoop of laughter. Then he leaned down again long enough to pat one of Stevens' resilient cheeks.

"It's OK, Jim, really it is. I never really needed the money anyway. What I needed was for you to think you had me by the balls."

"I never ever thought that, Oakes."

"No more first names, huh? Did I upset you or something?"

Stevens shook the tape box. "How much of this is crap?"

Oakes grinned again. "How much do you think, partner?"

"I don't know. That's why I'm asking." He saw Oakes glance towards the clock by the bed. "Going somewhere?"

"My work here's finished. Nothing to keep me."

"Where are you going?" Stevens didn't know why, but while Oakes had been laughing, he'd switched the recorder back on. Situated as it was in his shirt pocket, he didn't know how much it would pick up. He could hear its small motor working, feel it grinding against his chest.

"Why should you care?"

"I'm a reporter. You're still a story."

"You haven't seen the best of it, Jimmy baby."

Stevens ran a dry tongue over his lips.

"Do I scare you, Jim?"

"Sometimes," Stevens admitted.

"You're bigger than me, heavier anyway. You could take me, couldn't you?"

"It's not always down to size."

"True, true. Sometimes it's down to just how rip-roaring crazy and ferocious your opponent is. Is there a touch of madness in me, Jimbo?"

Stevens nodded slowly. "And ferocity too," he added.

"You better believe it." Oakes was examining himself in the wall-mirror, running a hand over his cropped head. "And it's a hungry madness, Jim. It wants me to eat people up." A sly sideways look. "Not you, though, don't worry on that score."

"What score should I worry on?"

"You'll find out soon enough." He studied himself in

the mirror again. "I have a date with my past, Jim. A date with destiny, as you and your fellow hacks might put it. With someone who never listened to me." He was nodding to himself. "Just one last thing, Jim." Turning towards the journalist. "I knew when I came out I'd be telling my story. I've had a long time to get it straight."

" 'Straight' rather than true?"

"You're smarter than you look, Jimbo." Oakes laughed.

Stevens' heart beat a little faster. It was what he'd suspected for some days, but that didn't make it any easier to hear.

"Some of it must have been accurate," he managed to utter.

"Scots are a nation of storytellers, Jim, isn't that right?" He patted Stevens' cheek again, then headed for the door.

"It was all shit, Jim. Remember that till the day you die."

After the door had closed on Oakes, Stevens put his head in his hands and sat there for a few moments, relieved it was all over, whatever the outcome. When his phone rang, he remembered the recorder in his pocket. Removed it and switched it off, rewound and hit Play.

Oakes's voice had grown small and tinny, but no less devilish. *It was all shit, Jim.* He turned off the tape and went to answer the phone. Cleared his throat first, sat down on the edge of the bed.

"Hello?" he said into the receiver.

"Jim, is that you? Peter Barclay here."

Barclay worked for a rival tabloid. "What do you want, Peter?"

"Caught you at a bad time?" Barclay chuckled. He always spoke with a cigarette in his mouth. It made him sound like a bad ventriloquist.

"You might say that."

"I do say that. Your boy's been telling tales out of school."

"What?" Stevens stopped rubbing the back of his neck.

"He's sent a letter to all your lovely competitors, saying his 'autobiography' is complete bollocks. Any comment to make, Jim? On the record, naturally."

Stevens slammed the receiver back into its cradle, then

swiped the apparatus off the bedside table and on to the floor.

"Number disconnected," he said, giving it a kick for good measure.

There was mist on the Pentland Hills, leaching colour from the landscape and threatening to cut Hillend and Swanston off from the city just north of them.

"I don't like it," Rebus said as they parked.

"Afraid we'll get lost?" Cary Oakes smiled. "Wouldn't that be a blow to humanity?"

He was sitting in the passenger seat, Alan Archibald in the back. Rebus hadn't wanted Oakes in the back; had wanted him where he could see him. Before setting off, he'd insisted on patting Oakes down. Oakes had asked if Rebus would reciprocate.

"I'm not the killer here," Rebus had said.

"I'll take that as a no." Oakes had turned to Archibald. "I thought it would just be the two of us. More intimate that way." Nodding towards Rebus. "No need for outsiders, Mr. Archibald."

"You're going nowhere without me," Rebus had said.

And here they were. Archibald seemed nervous. Getting out of the car, he dropped his Ordnance Survey map. Oakes picked it up for him.

"Maybe we should leave a little trail of breadcrumbs," he suggested.

"Let's just get on with it," Archibald answered, nerves lending his voice an edge of irritation.

Rebus was looking around. No other cars in the vicinity; no hill-walkers; no sounds of dogs being exercised.

"Creepy, isn't it?" Oakes said. He was donning a cheap green kagoul.

Rebus's jacket had an integral hood. He rolled it out but didn't put it over his head. He knew it would work like a pair of blinkers, and didn't want to be deprived of his peripheral vision. Archibald had a flat tweed cap with him, and was wearing hiking boots. Cap and boots looked brand new: they'd been waiting on this day for a while.

"Drinkie, anyone?" Oakes said, taking out a hip flask. Rebus stared at him. "You going to be scowling like that all day?" Oakes laughed. "Got something you want to get off your mind, maybe?"

"Plenty." Rebus's fists were clenched.

"Not here, John," Archibald pleaded. "Not now."

Eyes on Rebus, Oakes held out the flask to Archibald, who shook his head. Oakes tipped the flask to his own mouth, showing them the liquid trickling in. He swallowed noisily.

"See," he said, "it's not poisoned." He made the offer again, and this time Archibald took a sip. "I had them fill it at the hotel bar." He took the flask back from Archibald. "And yourself, Inspector?"

Rebus took the flask, sniffed its contents. Christ, it did smell good, but he handed it back untouched.

"Balvenie," he said. "If I'm not mistaken."

Oakes laughed again; Archibald forced a smile.

"I thought you didn't drink," Rebus said.

"I don't, but this is in the nature of a special occasion, wouldn't you say?"

Then Archibald started unfolding the map, and it became business, Oakes studying the area intently, aware of Rebus immediately behind him, and finally saying: "I'm not sure this is going to be much use." He looked around. "I think I'm going to have to follow my nose." He glanced at Archibald. "Sorry about that."

"Just take me to where she was killed," the older man said.

"Maybe you should lead the way," Oakes said. "After all, I've never been here before." And he gave a wink.

They started walking.

Eventually Rebus said: "Another game, Oakes?"

Oakes stopped walking, caught his breath. "You know how the song goes, Inspector: we can't go on together, if you're going to have a suspicious mind. Far as I'm concerned, we're just out for a breath of country air. Besides, I'm curious to see where the body was found."

"You know damned well where the body was found!" Alan Archibald snapped.

Oakes turned his lips into a pout. Rebus wanted to see blood there, wanted teeth dislodged and a gushing nose. Instead, his fingernails bit more deeply into his palms.

"Did you kill her?" he asked.

"Kill her when?"

Rebus felt his voice rising. "Did you kill her?"

Oakes wagged a finger. "I might not have been back that long, but don't think I don't know how it's played. There are two of you. Anything I admit, you've got corroboration."

"This is between ourselves," Alan Archibald said. "It's gone beyond anything I'd take to the police."

Oakes smiled. "How long have you been chasing ghosts? If I say I killed her, will you rest easy in your bed?" Archibald didn't answer. "How about you, Inspector: any ghosts keeping *you* awake at night?"

As if he knew. Rebus tried not to show anything, but Oakes was nodding, smiling to himself. "A career littered with bodies, man," Oakes went on, "and *I'm* the one they lock up." He paused. "Tell me something," folding his arms, eyes on Archibald now, "how did the killer get her up here? Long way to bring a victim."

"She was terrified."

"What if she wasn't? What if she was willing? She'd been out drinking, right? Feeling a bit horny . . ."

"Shut up, Oakes."

"I thought you *wanted* me to talk?" He opened his arms wide. "I might just be speculating here, but say he picked her up, drove her up here. Say it's exactly what she wanted. I mean, this is a complete stranger she's in the car with, but tonight she's in the mood for *danger*. She feels reckless. Who knows, maybe she even *wants* it to happen."

Archibald turned on him, waving his fist. "Don't talk about her like that."

"I'm just—"

"You abducted her. Knocked her cold and dragged her up here."

"Any signs of a struggle, Al? Huh? Did the post-mortem show she'd been dragged anywhere?"

Archibald looked at him. "You know it didn't."

More laughter. "No, Al, I don't know jack-shit. I'm just guessing, that's all. Same as you are."

Oakes started walking again. The wind was rising, a fine rain blowing into their faces, threatening to drench them. Rebus looked back. Already the car was lost to view.

"It's OK," Archibald assured him. "I'm marking our route as we go." He had the map folded, tapped a pen against one of the contour lines.

Rebus took the map from him, wanting to be sure. He'd done map-reading in the army. It looked like Archibald knew what he was doing. Rebus nodded and handed the map back. But the look in Archibald's eyes, that mix of fear and expectation . . . Rebus patted his shoulder.

"Come on, slowcoaches," Oakes said, waiting till they caught up.

"You took it too far," Rebus told him.

"Huh?"

"Your little joke with the skip, I didn't mind that so much. But the cemetery, the patio . . . no way you're getting away with those."

"You're forgetting your old flame." Oakes turned towards him. There wasn't more than a foot or two between them. "I talked to her, remember? How come she's not on your little hit-list? She told me the two of you might be hooking up again." He tutted. "Don't tell me you're going to let her down? Does she know?"

Rebus caught Oakes a glancing blow. Fist barely connected with cheek, Oakes arching back on the balls of his feet. Fast, he was hellish fast. Didn't change his stance, so confident, so sure of his opponent. Archibald's arms wrapped themselves around Rebus, but Rebus shrugged them off.

"I'm fine," he said, voice lacking emotion.

"Want some more?" Oakes threw open his arms. "I'm

right here, man." There was a graze on his cheek, but he paid it no notice.

Rebus *knew* he couldn't afford to lose it; had to stay calm. But Oakes had crawled all the way under his skin. Laughing at him now, putting a theatrical hand to his face. "Ouch! That *stings*." Laughing all the time. Then walking away, and now it was Archibald's turn to pat Rebus's shoulder.

"I'm OK," Rebus told him, making after Oakes.

A little later, Oakes stopped. Visibility was down to a hundred yards, maybe less. "Where's Swanston Village from here?" he asked. He seemed to have forgotten all about Rebus. Archibald checked the map, pointed with his finger. He was pointing into swirling smoke, pointing into nothingness.

"It's like bloody *Brigadoon*," Rebus said, lighting a cigarette. Oakes took a bar of chocolate from his pocket, offered it around:

"You know," he said, "I'm amazed you're trusting me. Not you, Mr. Archibald, you've got no choice. But the Inspector here." Oakes fixed Rebus with his dark, peering eyes. "You're a hard man to figure."

"And you're full of shite."

"Please, John . . ." Archibald had a hand on Rebus's shoulder. Despite his clothing, he looked cold and tired and suddenly so very old. Rebus realised what this meant to him: an answer, one way or another. Either Oakes had killed his niece—in which case there could be proper grieving—or someone else had, in which case he'd wasted these years with his pet theory, and her killer was still out there somewhere . . .

"OK, Alan," Rebus said. The three of them out here: an old man, a nutter with shorn head and piercing eyes, and John bloody Rebus. Oakes enjoying every moment, Archibald looking as brittle as the chocolate bar.

And Rebus? Trying hard not to add another body to the hill's death toll.

Oakes offered Archibald his flask, and Archibald took a grateful drink. Rebus declined, and Oakes screwed the top back on.

"Not having one yourself?" Rebus asked.

Oakes ignored him, offered him chocolate instead. Rebus again refused.

"So where exactly are we going?" Oakes asked.

"It's not far now," Archibald told him.

Oakes saw Rebus studying him. "Got any questions for me yourself, John? Any unsolveds you want to pin on me?"

"Anything in particular you want me to ask?"

"Nicely put, sir. I see someone killed Darren Rough."

"You were outside my flat that night."

"Was I?"

"You took the car." Rebus paused. "You saw Rough leave."

"Man, I was busy that night, wasn't I?" Rebus stared him out. Oakes came close, leaned in towards him as if to speak confidentially. Rebus moved away. "I'm not going to bite," Oakes said.

"Say what you were going to say."

Oakes put on a wounded look. "I don't know if I want to now." Then he grinned. "But I will anyway. I saw him leave your place, even followed him for a while. I wondered who he was, only found out later when I saw his picture in the paper."

"What happened?"

"You tell me. I lost him." Oakes shrugged. "He cut across The Meadows. No way to follow in a car." He gave another wink.

"This is all just another part of your little—"

"Don't say it!" Alan Archibald screeched. "Don't say it's a game! It's not a game, not to me!" He was shaking.

Rebus pointed to Oakes, but spoke to Archibald. "This is what he wants. You thought by bringing him up here you'd have the upper hand. Don't you think he knew that, played on it? Look at him, Alan, he's laughing at you. He's laughing at all of us!"

"I'm not laughing." And it was true: Oakes was stony-faced, his eyes on Archibald. He walked up to him, touched his arm. "Sorry," he said. "Come on, you're right—we've got work to do."

He started walking again. Archibald made to apologise to Rebus, but Rebus waved it aside. Oakes was moving off at a brisk pace, as if determined to finish things. That look on his face . . . Rebus couldn't read it. There had been something there, a gloss of sympathy. But beneath it he thought he detected something more feral, itself mixed with something like the curiosity of the scientist when faced with some unexpected result.

Visibility was decreasing as they climbed.

"You've been playing a little game with *me*, haven't you, Al?"

"What do you mean?"

"Come on, Al, the route you've brought us, we've already been past the spot where she was killed. I bet you've got it all planned so we'll end up circling it. You want me rattled, don't you, Al? It's not going to happen."

"How do you know where she was killed?" Rebus asked.

"I got all the newspapers. Plus Al kept sending me stuff, didn't you, Al?"

"You said you never read any of it," Archibald said, trying to catch his breath.

"So I lied. Thing is, I'm getting a picture in my head . . . They had sex further up the slope. Then she panicked, ran back down. That's when he hit her. But where they had sex . . . he left something behind."

"What?"

"Hidden."

"What?"

"Alan, he's—"

Archibald turned on Rebus. "Shut up!" he hissed.

"I'm seeing three hillocks," Oakes called back. "If there's a line of hillocks anywhere nearby, I'd be interested to see them."

"Hillocks . . . ?" Archibald broke into a trot, trying to reach Oakes. He had the map in front of his face, seeking the corresponding contours. "Maybe just to the west."

Rebus hadn't seen him mark anything on the map with his pen, not for a while.

"How's our position, Alan?"

But Archibald wasn't listening, not to Rebus.

"Maybe three-quarters of the way up the slope," Oakes was saying. "A line of three . . . maybe four . . . but three distinct outcrops, similar heights."

"Hang on a second," Archibald said. His finger

scratched over the map. He folded it smaller, brought it closer to his face, blinked so as to focus better. "Yes, just to the west. That way, about a hundred yards."

He started to climb. Oakes was already on his way, Rebus bringing up the rear. He looked behind him: couldn't see a damned thing. It was a landscape out of time. Kilted warriors might have emerged from that mist and he wouldn't have been surprised. He rounded some bracken and kept moving, his joints aching, a slight burning in his chest. Archibald was moving faster, moving with the zeal of the possessed.

Rebus wanted to tell him: *you've* got a map, what's to say Oakes didn't buy one too? What's to say he didn't study it, looking for certain features? He might even have been here already on a recce—he'd given his minders the slip plenty of times.

"Hang on!" he called, quickening his pace.

"John!" Archibald called back, his form ghostlike up ahead. "You try that way, we'll take the other two!" Meaning Rebus was to explore the easternmost outcrop.

"Will I need to dig?" he called out. Receiving laughter in reply: Oakes's laughter. The more unsettling for the fact he could barely be seen.

"Will we?" he heard Archibald asking Oakes.

"Oh, I don't think so," Oakes answered. "We'll just leave the bodies where they fall."

Rebus was still wondering if he'd misheard when he heard the dull sound of an impact, and a distant groan.

"Oakes!" he roared, upping his pace. He could make out the shadowy silhouette: Oakes standing over the fallen Archibald, a rock in his hand, raised to strike again.

"Oakes!" he repeated.

"I hear you!" Oakes yelled back, bringing the rock down on to Archibald's head.

By now Rebus was almost upon him. Oakes tossed the rock on to the ground and was licking his lips as Rebus reached him. "You'll never know the satisfaction," he said. "A flea's been biting me for years, and now I've squashed it." He slipped a hand into his waistband and brought out a folding knife.

"Amazing what the human body can hide," Oakes said,

grinning now. "A rock was good enough for the old man, but I thought maybe you deserved something with a bit more bite." He lunged. Rebus jumped back, lost his footing and was skidding back down the slope. Above him, he saw Oakes in pursuit, bounding like a mountain goat.

"I'm going to enjoy this!" Oakes called. "You'll never know how much!"

Rebus kept himself rolling until bracken stopped him. He clambered to his feet, picking up a stone and hurling it. His aim was wild. Oakes dodged it easily, only ten yards away now and slowing his descent.

"Ever skinned a rabbit?" Oakes said, breathing heavily, sweat glistening on his skull.

"You're just where I want you," Rebus hissed.

Oakes gave a look of mock surprise. "And where's that?"

"Committing an offence. Now I get to arrest you, and it's clean."

"You get to *arrest* me?" Spluttering laughter. He was so close, his saliva hit Rebus's face. "Man, you've got balls." Moving the knife. "Enjoy them while you can."

"All these games," Rebus was saying. "There's something else, isn't there? Something you don't want us to know. Keeping us all busy so we don't go looking."

"No shit?"

"What is it?"

But Oakes was shaking his head, working the knife. Rebus turned and ran. Oakes was after him, whooping, bounding through bracken. Rebus looking around, seeing nothing but hillside and a killer with a knife. He stumbled, came to a stop and turned to face Oakes.

"Gotcha," Oakes called out.

Rebus, almost out of breath, just nodded.

"Know what you are, man?" Oakes asked. "You're my spot of R&R, that's all."

Rebus, walking backwards, started tugging his shirt out of his waistband. Oakes looked puzzled, until Rebus pulled the shirt up, revealing a tiny mike taped to his chest. Oakes looked at him, Rebus holding the stare. Then looked around, seeking shapes.

Voices approaching at speed.

"Thanks for all that shouting," Rebus said. "Better than a trail of breadcrumbs any day."

With a roar, Oakes took a final lunge at him. Rebus sidestepped it, and Oakes was past him and running. Downhill to start with, then changing his mind and making an arc, climbing now, further into the hills. The first uniforms appeared out of the mist. Rebus pointed after Oakes.

"Get him!" he called. Then he started climbing too, making his way back to where Alan Archibald lay, still conscious but with blood pouring from his wounds. Rebus crouched beside him as more uniforms ran past.

"Radio down for help!" Rebus called out to them. One of the uniforms turned back to him.

"Don't need to, sir. You've already done it."

Rebus looked at the mike on his chest and realised this was true.

"Where did the cavalry come from?" Archibald asked, his voice faint.

"I got them from the ACC," Rebus told him. "He promised me a chopper too, but it would have needed X-ray eyes."

Archibald managed a smile. "Do you think . . . ?"

"I'm sorry, Alan," Rebus said. "It was all crap, that's what I think. He just wanted a couple more scalps."

Archibald touched shaking fingers to his head. "He nearly got one," he said, closing his eyes to rest.

Alan Archibald went to hospital, and Rebus went in search of Jim Stevens. He'd already checked out of the hotel, and wasn't at the newspaper office. Eventually, Rebus tracked him down to The Hebrides, a furtive little bar behind Waverley station. Stevens was sitting alone in a corner with only a full ashtray and glass of whisky for company.

Rebus got himself a whisky and water, gulped it down, ordered another and went to join him.

"Come to gloat?" Stevens asked.

"About what?"

"That wee shite set me up." He told Rebus what had happened.

"Then I'm an angel straight from heaven," Rebus said.

Stevens blinked. "How do you make that out?"

"I bring glad tidings. Or more accurately, a news story, and I'd say you're ahead of the pack."

Rebus had never seen a man sober up so quickly. Stevens pulled a notebook from his pocket and folded it open. His pen ready, he looked up at Rebus.

"It'll have to be a trade," Rebus told him.

"I need this," Stevens said.

Rebus nodded, told him the story. "And I'd have been next if he got his way."

"Jesus Christ." Stevens exhaled, took a gulp of whisky. "There are probably dozens of questions I should be asking you, but right now I can't think of any." He took out a mobile phone. "Mind if I call this in?"

Rebus shook his head. "Then we talk," he said.

While Stevens read from his notes, turning them into sentences and paragraphs, Rebus listened, nodding confirmation when it was demanded of him. Stevens listened while the story was read back to him. He made a few changes, then finished the call.

"I owe you," he said, putting the phone on the table. "What'll it be?"

"Another whisky," Rebus said, "and the answers to some questions."

Half an hour later he had a pair of headphones on and was listening to the tape of Oakes's last interview.

" 'A date with my past,' " he recited, slipping the headphones off his ears. " 'A date with destiny.' "

"That's Archibald, isn't it? Archibald's been hassling him for years."

Rebus thought back to Alan Archibald . . . the way he'd looked as they'd lifted him into the ambulance. He'd looked spent and stunned, as if his dearest possession had been torn from him. Easy to steal away a dream, a hope . . . Cary Oakes had done that.

And had gotten away.

"They didn't catch him then?" Stevens asked, not for the first time.

"He ran into the hills, could be anywhere."

"It's a hell of an area to search," Stevens conceded. "What made you take reinforcements?"

Rebus shrugged.

"You know, John, once upon a time you wouldn't have thought you needed them."

"I know, Jim. Things change."

Stevens nodded. "I suppose they do."

Rebus rewound the tape, listened to the last half again. "*A date with destiny, as you and your fellow hacks might put it. With someone who never listened to me . . .*" This time, he was frowning when he finished.

"You know," he said, "I'm not sure he means Archibald and me. He called us his spot of R&R."

Stevens had drained his glass. "What else could it be?"

Rebus shook his head slowly. "There was some reason for him coming back here."

"Yes, me and my chequebook."

"Something more than that. More than the chance to play games with Alan Archibald . . ."

"What?"

"I don't know." He looked at Stevens. "You could find out."

"Me?"

"You know the city inside out. It has to be something from his past, something from before he went to America."

"I'm not an archaeologist."

"No? Think of all the years you've spent digging dirt. And Alan Archibald has a lot of stuff on Oakes, better than anything the bastard gave you."

Stevens snorted, then smiled. "Maybe . . ." he said to himself. "It would be a way of getting back at him."

Rebus was nodding. "He's given you a tissue of lies, you bounce back with a whole boxful of truth."

"The truth about Cary Oakes," Stevens said, measuring it up for a headline. "I'll do it," he said at last.

"And anything you find, you share with me." Rebus reached for Stevens' notepad. "I'll give you my mobile number."

"Jim Stevens and John Rebus, working together." Stevens grinned.

"I won't tell if you don't."

40

There were messages for Rebus. Janice had called three times; Damon's bank manager once. Rebus spoke to the bank manager first.

"We have a transaction," the man said.

"What, when and where?" Rebus reached for paper and pen.

"Edinburgh. A cash machine on George Street. Withdrawal of one hundred pounds."

"Today?"

"Yesterday afternoon at one forty precisely. It's good news, isn't it?"

"I hope so."

"I mean, it proves he's still alive."

"It proves someone's used his card. Not quite the same thing."

"I see." The manager sounded a little dispirited. "I suppose you have to be cautious."

Rebus had a thought. "This cash machine, it wouldn't be under surveillance, would it?"

"I can check for you."

"If you wouldn't mind." Rebus wound up the call and phoned Janice.

"What's up?" he asked.

"Nothing." She paused. "It's just you ran off so early that morning. I wondered if it was something we'd . . ."

"Nothing to do with you, Janice."

"No?"

"I just needed to get back here."

"Oh." Another pause. "Well, I was just worried."

"About me?"

"That you were disappearing from my life again."

"Would I do that?"

"I don't know, John: would you?"

"Janice, I know things are a bit rocky between you and Brian . . ."

"Yes?"

He smiled, eyes closed. "That's it really. I'm not exactly an expert on marriage guidance."

"I'm not in the market for one."

"Look," he said, rubbing his eyes, "there's a bit of news about Damon."

A longer pause. "Were you planning on telling me?"

"I just did tell you."

"Only so you could change the subject."

Rebus felt like he was in the boxing-ring, cornered on the ropes. "It's just that his bank account's been used."

"He's taken out?"

"Someone's used his card."

Her voice was rising, filling with hope. "But nobody else knows his number. It has to be him."

"There are ways of using cards . . ."

"John, don't you *dare* take this away from me!"

"I just don't want you getting hurt." He saw Alan Archibald again, saw that look of final inescapable defeat.

"When was this?" Janice said; she was barely listening to him now.

"Yesterday afternoon. I got word about ten minutes ago. It was a bank on George Street."

"He's still in Edinburgh." A statement of belief.

"Janice . . ."

"I can feel it, John. He's there, I know he's there. What time's the next train?"

"I doubt he's still hanging around George Street. The withdrawal was a hundred pounds. Might have been travelling money."

"I'm coming anyway."

"I can't stop you."

"That's right, you can't." She put down the telephone. Seconds later, it rang again. Damon's bank manager.

"Yes," he said, "there's a camera."

"Trained on the machine?"

"Yes. I've already asked: the tape's waiting for you. Talk to a Miss Georgeson."

As Rebus finished the call, George Silvers brought him a cup of coffee. "Thought you'd have gone home," he said: Hi-Ho's way of showing he cared.

"Thanks, George. No sign of him yet?"

Silvers shook his head. Rebus stared at the paperwork on his desk. There were cases to write up, he could barely recall them. Names swimming in front of him. All of them demanding an ending.

"We'll catch him," Silvers said. "Don't you worry about that."

"You've always been a comfort to me, George," Rebus said. He handed back the cup. "And one of these days you'll remember that I don't take sugar."

He went to talk to Miss Georgeson. She was plump and fiftyish and reminded Rebus of a school dinner-lady he'd once dated. She had the videotape ready for him.

"Would you like to view it here?" she asked.

Rebus shook his head. "I'll take it back to the station, if you've no objection."

"Well, really I should make you a copy . . ."

"I don't intend losing it, Miss Georgeson. And I *will* bring it back."

He left the bank with the tape held tightly in one hand. Checked his watch, then headed down to Waverley. He sat on one of the benches on the concourse, drinking a milky coffee—or *caffe latte* as the vendor had called it—and keeping an eye open. He had the tape in his raincoat pocket; no way he was leaving it in the car. He flicked through the evening paper. Nothing about Cary Oakes—it would be an exclusive in Stevens' paper first thing in the morning, and Stevens would have answered his detractors with one mighty two-fingered salute.

A date with destiny . . .

What the hell did that mean? Was Oakes laying yet another false trail? Rebus would put nothing past him. He'd sold Stevens, Archibald, and himself dummies like he was vintage George Best and they were Sunday league.

Finally he saw her. Late-afternoon trains into Edinburgh

weren't busy; the traffic was all the other way. She was walking against the crowds as she came off the platform. He got into step beside her before she'd noticed him.

"Needing a taxi?" he said.

She looked surprised, then bemused. "John," she said. "What brings you here?"

For answer, he took the video out and held it in front of her. "A peace offering," he said, leading her back to his car.

They sat in the CID suite. It too was quiet. Most people had gone home for the day. Those who were left were trying to finish reports or catch up with themselves. No one was in the mood to dawdle. The video monitor sat in one corner. Rebus pulled two chairs over. He'd fetched them coffee. Janice was looking excited and fearful at the same time. Again, he was reminded of Alan Archibald on the hillside.

"Look, Janice," he warned her, "if it's not him . . ."

She shrugged. "If it's not him, it's not him. I won't blame you." She flashed him a momentary smile. He started the tape. Miss Georgeson had explained that the camera was motion-sensitive, and would only begin recording when someone approached the machine. Back at the bank, Rebus had taken a look at the cash machine. The camera was above it, shooting from behind one of the bank's glass windows. When the first face came on the tape, Rebus and Janice were looking at it from above. The time-counter said 08.10. Rebus used the remote to fast forward.

"We're looking for one forty," he explained. Janice was sitting on the edge of her chair, the coffee cup held in both hands.

This, Rebus thought, was the way it had started: with security footage, grainy pictures. Towards the middle of the day, more people were using the machine. There was a lot of tape to get through. Lunchtime queues built up, but by one thirty it was a little quieter.

The time-counter said 13.40.

"Oh, dear Lord, there he is," Janice said. She'd placed her cup on the floor, clapped her hands to her face.

Rebus looked. The face was angled down, looking at the

machine's keypad. Then it turned away, as if staring down the street. Fingers were tapped impatiently against the screen of the cash machine. The card was retrieved, a hand went to the slot to extract the notes. Didn't linger; didn't wait for a receipt. The next customer was already moving forward.

"Are you sure?" he asked.

A tear was falling from Janice's cheek. "Positive," she said, nodding.

Rebus found it hard to tell. All he had were photos of Damon and the footage from Gaitano's; he'd never met him. The hair looked similar . . . maybe the nose too, the shape of the chin. But it wasn't as though they were unusual. The person on view now, they looked much like the customer who'd just left. But Janice was blowing her nose. She was satisfied.

"It's him, I'd swear to it." She saw uncertainty on his face. "I wouldn't say it was if it wasn't."

"Of course not."

"It's not just the face or hair or clothes . . . it's the way he stood, the way he held himself. And those little twitches of impatience." She used a corner of the hankie to wipe her eyes. "It was him, John. It was him."

"OK," Rebus said. He rewound the tape, played the minutes leading up to 13.40. He was studying the background to see if he could spot Damon making for the machine. He wanted to know if he'd been alone. But he entered the picture suddenly, and from the side. That look again, towards where he'd just come from. Was there a slight nod of the head . . . some signal to another person just out of shot . . . ? Rebus rewound and watched again.

"What are you looking for?" Janice asked.

"Anyone who might have been with him."

But there was nothing. So he let the tape play on, and was rewarded a minute or two later by legs moving across the top of the picture, just behind the person at the machine. Two pairs, one male, one female. Rebus pressed freeze-frame, but couldn't get the picture to stay absolutely still and focused. So instead, he rewound and played it again, following the feet with his finger.

"Recognise the trousers, the shoes?"

But Janice shook her head. "They're just a blur."

And so they were.

"Could be anybody," she added.

And so it could.

She got to her feet. "I'm going to George Street." He made to say something but she cut him off. "I know he won't be there, but there are shops, pubs—I can show them his picture at least."

Rebus nodded. She gripped his forearm.

"He's still here, John. That's *something*."

As she left, she held the door open to someone just coming in: Siobhan Clarke.

"Any sign of him?" Rebus asked.

Siobhan slumped into a chair. "Billy Horman?"

Rebus shook his head. "Cary Oakes."

She stretched her neck. He heard the snap. "Another day down," he told her.

She nodded. "I'm not working Oakes. I'm on Billy Boy."

"No progress?"

She shook her head. "We need another dozen officers. Maybe a couple of dozen."

"I can see the budget stretching to that."

"Maybe if we got rid of a few of the bean-counters."

"Careful, Siobhan. That's anarchist talk."

She smiled. "How are you? I hear Oakes was ready to kill the pair of you."

"The tremors have stopped," he told her. "Buy you a drink?"

"Not tonight. I've a date with a hot bath and a takeaway. What about you?"

"Straight home, same as yourself."

"Well . . ." She stood up as though the effort was costing her. "See you tomorrow."

"Night, Siobhan."

She waved fingers over her shoulder as she left.

Rebus was almost as good as his word—just the one stop-off to make beforehand. He climbed the stairwell of Cragside Court. Darkness was falling, but there were still children out playing, albeit supervised by a member of

GAP. They'd had T-shirts printed up with a logo on the front, getting more organised by the day. The woman in the T-shirt had studied Rebus, knowing she'd seen him somewhere before, but not recognising him as a resident.

He stood looking out over Greenfield. On one side, Holyrood Park; on the other, the Old Town, and the site of the new Parliament. He wondered if the estate would be allowed to survive. He knew that if the council wanted it run down, they would work by stealth. Repairs would not be carried out, or would be botched. Flats would be found to be uninhabitable, tenants rehoused, windows and doors blocked and padlocked. Things would slowly deteriorate, causing residents to rethink their options. More of them would move out. The state of the high-rises would become a "cause for concern." There'd be a media outcry about conditions. The council would move in with offers of help—meaning relocation: cheaper than shoring up the estate. And eventually it would be deserted, a demolition site from which new buildings could rise. Expensive *pieds-à-terre* for parliamentarians, perhaps. Or offices and select shops. It was a prime site, no doubt about it.

As for Salisbury Crags . . . he didn't doubt there'd be people who would build on it too, given the chance. But that chance would be a long time coming. All the centuries of change, and the park was much as it ever had been. It made no judgements on the work around it, but merely sat there, above it all. And the people who tramped over it were minor irritations, dead by the age of seventy if not before. They made no impression on it, not when measured in millennia.

Rebus was outside Darren Rough's flat now. Darren had come home to give evidence against two evil men. As recompense, he'd been harried, cursed and eventually killed. Rebus didn't feel proud that he'd been the first player. He hoped Darren might one day forgive him. He almost said as much to the ghostly shape at the end of the walkway, but when it came towards him, he saw it was flesh and blood, very much alive.

It was Cal Brady, his face an angry scowl.

"What do you want?"

"Just taking a look."

"I thought you were another pervert."

Rebus nodded towards the mobile phone in Brady's hand. "Did the playground guard tell you?" He nodded to himself. "Nice little operation you've got here, Cal. Anything in it for you?"

"It's my public duty," Brady said, puffing out his chest.

Rebus took a step closer, hands in coat pockets. "Cal, the day people like you are deciding what's right and what's wrong, we're all in Queer Street."

"You calling me a poof?" Cal Brady yelled, but Rebus was already past him and heading for the stairs.

41

"Tell me about Janice," Patience said.

They were seated in the living room, a bottle of red wine open on the carpet between them. Patience was lying along the sofa. There was a paperback novel folded open on her chest. She had placed it there some time ago; had been staring into space, listening to the music on the hi-fi. Nick Drake, "Pink Moon." Rebus was in the armchair, legs hanging over its side. He had kicked off his shoes and socks, was catching up with the football news in that day's paper.

"What?"

"Janice, I'd like to know about her."

"We were at school together." Rebus stopped reading. "She's married with just the one son. She used to work as a teacher. I was at school with her husband, too. His name's Brian."

"You went out with her?"

"At school, yes."

"Sleep together?"

Rebus looked at her. "Didn't quite get that far."

She nodded to herself. "Are you curious about what it would have been like?"

He shrugged.

"I think I would be," she went on. Her glass was empty, and she leaned over to refill it. The book slid on to the floor, but she paid it no heed. Rebus was still on his first helping of the Rioja. The bottle was nearly empty.

"Anyone would think you were the one with the drink problem," he said, making sure he was smiling as he spoke.

She was getting comfortable again. A splash of wine fell on to the back of her hand, and she put her mouth to it.

"No, I just like a little bit too much now and again. So, have you thought about sleeping with her?"

"Christ, Patience . . ."

"I'm interested, that's all. Sammy says Janice had a look about her."

"What sort of look?"

Patience frowned, as if trying to recall the exact words. "Hungry. Hungry and a little desperate, I think. How's the marriage?"

"Rocky," Rebus admitted.

"And you going to Fife . . . did that help?"

"I didn't sleep with her."

Patience wagged a finger. "Don't go defending yourself before an accusation's made. You're a detective, you know how it looks."

He glared at her. "Am I a suspect?"

"No, John, you're a man. That's all." She took another sip of wine.

"I wouldn't hurt you, Patience."

She smiled, stretched out a hand as if to squeeze his, but he was too far away. "I know that, sweetheart. But the thing is, you wouldn't even be thinking of me at the time, so the idea of hurting me or not hurting me wouldn't enter into it."

"You're so sure."

"John, I get it every single day. Wives coming into the surgery, wanting anti-depressants. Wanting *anything* that'll help them get through the bloody awful marriages they've found themselves in. They tell me things. It all spills out. Some of them turn to drink or drugs, some slash their wrists. It's bizarre how seldom they just walk out. And the ones who do walk out are usually the ones married to the violent cases." She looked at him. "Do you know what *they* do?"

"End up going back?" he guessed.

She focused on him. "How do you know?"

"I get them too, Patience. The domestics, the neighbours who complain of screams and punches. The same wives *you* get, only further down the road. They won't press charges. They get put into a hostel. And later, they walk back to the only life they really know."

She blinked away a tear. "Why does it have to be like that, John?"

"I wish I knew."

"What's in it for us?"

He smiled. "A paycheque."

She had stopped looking at him. Picked her book off the floor, put down her wine glass. "The man who painted that message . . . What was he trying to do?"

"I'm not sure. Maybe he wanted me to know he'd been here."

She had found her page, stared at the words without moving her eyes. "Where is he now?"

"Lost on the hills and freezing to death."

"You really think so?"

"No," he admitted. "Someone like Oakes . . . that would be too easy."

"Will he come after you?"

"I'm not at the top of his list." No, because Alan Archibald was still alive. X-rays had shown a skull fracture; Archibald would be in hospital a little longer. There was a police guard on his bed.

"Will he come here?" Patience asked.

The CD had finished; there was silence in the room. "I don't know."

"If he tries painting my flagstones again, I'll give him a bloody good kicking."

Rebus looked at her, then began laughing.

"What's so funny?" she said.

Rebus was shaking his head. "Nothing really. I'm just glad you're on my side, that's all."

She raised the wine glass to her lips again. "What makes you so sure of that, Inspector?"

Rebus raised his own glass to her, pleased that until Patience had mentioned her, he hadn't thought once that evening of Janice Mee. He hit "Replay" on the CD remote. "This guy sounds like he needs help," Patience said.

"He did," Rebus told her. "He OD'd." She looked at him and he shrugged. "Just another casualty," he said.

Later, he headed outside for a cigarette. The message was still there on the patio: YOUR COP LOVER KILLED DARREN. The workmen would start cleaning it off tomorrow. Oakes said he'd followed Darren but lost him. Well, someone had found him. Rebus wasn't going to take the blame for that. Cigarette lit, he climbed the steps. There was a marked patrol car parked directly outside, a message to Cary Oakes should he think about paying a visit. Rebus had a word with the two officers inside, finished his cigarette and headed back indoors.

"Fancy a run?" Siobhan Clarke offered.

"I trust you mean 'run' as in 'drive'?"

"Don't worry, I don't have you down as the jogging type."

"Perceptive as ever. Where are you going?"

It was morning in St. Leonard's. The weather up on the Pentlands had cleared, and Rebus had made sure the helicopter would be out scanning the area for signs of Cary Oakes. Villages and farms in the foothills had been warned to be on the look out.

"Don't try to corner him," the message had gone. "Just let us know if you see him."

So far, no one had called in.

Rebus felt like dead weight. He'd made breakfast for Patience—orange juice and two sachets of Resolve—and had been complimented on both his diagnosis and his bedside manner. She'd said she'd make the surgery OK.

"I just hope no one expects me to do my Agony Aunt bit today."

And now Rebus was in the CID suite with his coffee and a Mars Bar.

"Breakfast of coronaries," he said, noting Siobhan's distaste.

"We've had a sighting of Billy Boy. It'll probably turn out to be a waste of time . . ."

"And you'd rather waste it with me?" Rebus smiled. "Isn't that thoughtful?"

"Never mind," she said, turning away.

"Whoa, hold on. What side of the bed did you fall out of?"

"I didn't quite reach bed last night," she snapped. Then she melted a little. "It's a long story."

"Just right for a car-ride then," he said. "Come on, you've got me hooked."

The story was, her upstairs neighbours' washing-machine had sprung a leak. They'd been out, and hadn't noticed. And she'd only found out when she'd gone into her bedroom.

"Their washing-machine's above your bedroom?" Rebus asked.

"That's another bone of contention. Anyway, I noticed this stain on the ceiling, and when I touched the bed it was soaked through. So I ended up on the couch in a smelly old sleeping-bag."

"Poor you." Rebus was thinking of all the times he'd slept in his chair—but that had been voluntary. He looked in the wing mirror as they crawled westwards out of town. "Tell me something: why are we going to Grangemouth? Couldn't the locals handle it?"

"I'm reluctant to delegate."

Rebus smiled: she'd stolen one of his lines. "What you mean is, you don't trust anyone to do the job thoroughly."

"Something like that," she said, glancing at him. "I had a good teacher."

"Siobhan, it's been quite some time since I could teach you anything."

"Thanks."

"But that's because you've stopped listening."

"We are not amused." She craned her neck. "What is with this traffic?"

The vehicles ahead were barely moving.

"It's part of the new council initiative. Make things bloody awful for drivers, and they'll stop coming into town and making everything look untidy."

"They want a conservation village."

Rebus nodded. "And just the half a million villagers."

Eventually they got moving. Grangemouth lay out to the west along the Forth estuary. Rebus hadn't been to the town in years. As they approached, Rebus's first impression was that they'd wandered on to the set of *Blade Runner*. A vast petrochemical complex dominated the skyline, throwing up jagged chimneys and weird configurations of pipes. The complex looked like some encroaching alien life-form, about to throw its many mechanical arms around the town and squeeze the life out of it.

In fact, the contrary was true: the complex and all that went with it had brought employment to Grangemouth. The streets they eventually drove through were dark and narrow, with architecture from much earlier in the century.

"Two worlds collide," Rebus muttered, taking it all in.

"I feel they've spoiled their chances in the conservation village stakes."

"I'm sure the townsfolk are grieving." He was peering at the street names. "Here we go." They parked outside a row of cottage-type houses, all of which had added bedrooms and windows to their roof-space.

"Number eleven," Siobhan said. "Woman's name is Wilkie."

Mrs. Wilkie had been waiting for them. She seemed the type of neighbour every street has: interested to the point of nosiness. Her kind could be a distinct asset, but Rebus would bet some of her neighbours didn't see it that way.

Her living room was a tiny box, overheated and with

pride of place given to a large and ornate doll's-house. When Siobhan, out of politeness, showed interest in it, Mrs. Wilkie delivered a ten-minute speech concerning its history. Rebus could swear she didn't once draw breath, giving neither of her prisoners the chance to jump in and take the conversation elsewhere.

"Well, isn't that lovely?" Siobhan said, glancing towards Rebus. The look on his face had her sucking in her cheeks to stop from laughing. "Now, about this boy you saw, Mrs. Wilkie . . . ?"

They all sat down, and Mrs. Wilkie told her story. She'd seen the laddie's picture in the paper, and as she was coming back from the shops around two, caught him playing football in the street.

"Kicking the ball against the wall of Montefiore's Garage. There's this low stone wall around the . . ." She made motions with her hands. "What do you call it?"

"Forecourt?" Siobhan suggested.

"That's the word." She smiled at Siobhan. "I'll bet you're a dab hand at crosswords, brain like that."

"Did you say anything to the boy, Mrs. Wilkie?"

"It's Miss Wilkie actually. I never married."

"Really?" Rebus managed to put on a surprised look. Siobhan coughed into her hand, then handed some snaps of Billy Horman over to Miss Wilkie.

"Well, these certainly look like him," the old woman said, sorting through the photos. She lifted one out. "Except for this, that is."

Siobhan took the proffered photo, stuck it back in her folder.

Rebus knew she'd sneaked in a picture of a different kid to assess how alert her witness actually was. Miss Wilkie had passed.

"To answer your question," Miss Wilkie said, "no, I didn't say anything. I came back here and took another look at the paper. Then I phoned the number it said to call. Spoke to a very nice young man at the police station."

"This was yesterday?"

"That's right, and I haven't seen the laddie today."

"And you just saw him the once?"

Miss Wilkie nodded. "Playing all by himself. He looked

so lonely." She had handed back the photos, and got up to look out of her window. "You notice strangers on a street like this."

"I'm sure not much gets past you," Rebus said.

"All these cars nowadays . . . I'm surprised you found a space."

Rebus and Siobhan looked at one another, thanked Miss Wilkie for her time, and left.

Outside, they looked to left and right. There was a garage on the corner at the far end of the street. They walked towards it.

"What did she mean about the cars?" Siobhan asked.

"My guess is, there's always someone parked outside her window. Makes it harder for her to see everything that's going on."

"I'm impressed."

"Not that I speak from experience, you understand."

But back in the cottage, Rebus had felt a sudden depression. He, too, was a watcher. All the nights he sat in his flat, lights off, watching from the window . . . As he got older, would he turn into a Miss Wilkie: the street's nosy neighbour?

Montefiore's Garage consisted of a single line of petrol pumps, a shop, and a double work-bay. A man in blue overalls was in one of the work-bays, his head just visible as he stood in the pit, a blue Volkswagen Polo above him. There was another, older man behind the counter in the shop. Rebus and Siobhan stopped on the pavement.

"Might as well ask if they saw him," Siobhan said.

"Suppose so," Rebus replied, with little enthusiasm.

"I told you it was a wild shot."

"Could be a neighbourhood kid. New family moved in, hasn't had time to make friends."

"It was two o'clock she saw him. He should have been at school."

"True," Rebus said. "She seemed so certain, didn't she?"

"Some people do. They want to be helpful, even if it means making up a story."

Rebus tutted. "You didn't learn cynicism like that from me." He looked around at the bumper-to-bumper parking. "I wonder . . ."

"What?"

"He was kicking the ball off the forecourt wall."

"Yes."

"Not much of a game if all these cars were here. Pavement's not wide enough."

Siobhan looked at the wall, the pavement. "Maybe the cars weren't here."

"According to Miss Wilkie, that would be unusual."

"I can't see what you're getting at."

Rebus pointed to the forecourt. "What if he was in there? Plenty of space so long as no cars are using the pumps."

"They'd chase him off." She looked at him. "Wouldn't they?"

"Let's go ask them."

They went to the shop first, identified themselves to the man behind the counter.

"I'm not the owner," he said. "I'm his brother."

"Were you here yesterday?"

"Been here the past ten days. Eddie and Flo are on their hols."

"Somewhere nice?" Siobhan asked, making out they were just having a normal conversation.

"Jamaica."

"Do you remember a young boy?" Rebus asked. Siobhan held up one of the photographs. "Playing kickabout in the forecourt?"

The owner's brother nodded. "Gordon's nephew."

Rebus tried to keep his voice level. "Gordon who?"

The man laughed. "Gordon Howe, actually." He spelt the name for them, and they laughed along with him.

"Bet he gets jokes about that," Siobhan said, wiping an imaginary tear from her eye. "Any idea where we could find Mr. Howe?"

"Jock will know."

Siobhan nodded. "And who's Jock?"

"Sorry," the man said. "Jock's the other mechanic."

"Under the Polo?" Rebus asked. The man nodded.

"So Mr. Howe works for the garage?"

"Yes, he's a mechanic. He's got the day off today. Well, we're not busy, and with him looking after young Billy . . ." He waved the picture of Billy Horman.

"Billy?" Siobhan said.

Sixty seconds later they were out on the forecourt again and Siobhan was using Rebus's mobile. She got through to St. Leonard's and asked if Billy Horman had an uncle called Gordon Howe. Listening to the answer, she shook her head to let Rebus know what she was hearing. They walked towards the work-bay.

"Could we have a word?" Rebus called. They had their IDs ready as the mechanic called Jock crawled out from under the Polo and started wiping his hands on an impossibly oil-blackened rag.

"What have I done?" He had ginger hair, curling to the nape of his neck, and a long earring dangling from one ear. The backs of his hands were tattooed, and Rebus noticed he was missing the pinkie on his left hand.

"Where can we find Gordon Howe?" Siobhan asked.

"Lives on Adamson Street. What's the matter?"

"Will he be there just now, do you think?"

"How should I know?"

"He's got the day off," Rebus said, taking a step closer. "Maybe he told you how he planned to spend it?"

"Taking Billy out." The mechanic's eyes flicked from one detective to the other.

"Billy being . . . ?"

"His sister's kid. She's been poorly, one-parent family and that. Billy either went into care for the duration or Gordy looked after him. Is it Billy? Has he been up to something?"

"Do you think he's the type?"

"Not at all." The mechanic smiled. "Very quiet kid, actually. Didn't want to talk about his mum . . ."

"Didn't want to talk about his mum," Siobhan repeated, as they walked up the path to the house in Adamson Street. It was a sixties-built semi in an estate on the edge of town. Council-owned for the most part. You could tell the homes that had been purchased by their tenants: replacement windows and better doors. But they all had the same grey harled walls.

"Uncle Gordon's orders, no doubt."

They rang the bell and waited. Rebus thought he detected movement at an upstairs window. Took a step back to look, but couldn't see anything.

"Try again," he said, opening the letterbox while Siobhan pushed the doorbell. There was a door at the end of the corridor, half-open. He saw shadows beyond it, snapped the letterbox shut.

"Round the back," he said, heading for the side of the house. As they entered the back garden, a man was disappearing over a high bark fence.

"Mr. Howe!" Rebus shouted.

By way of response, the man called out, "Run for it!" to the boy who was with him. Rebus let Siobhan climb the fence. He headed back round to the front, ran down the road, wondering where the two would appear.

Suddenly they were ahead of him. Howe was limping, clawing at one leg. The boy was off like a shot, Howe spurring him on. But when the boy looked back, saw the distance widening between himself and Howe, his pace slowed.

"No! Keep running, Billy! Keep running!"

But the boy wasn't listening to Howe. He came to a dead stop, waited for the man to catch up. Siobhan came into view, a rip in the knee of her trousers. Howe saw he was going nowhere and put up his hands.

"All right," he said, "all right."

He looked despairingly at Billy, who was walking back towards him.

"Billy, will you never listen?"

As Gordon Howe dropped to his knees, Billy slid his arms around his neck, man and boy embracing.

"I'll tell them," Billy was wailing. "I'll tell them it's all right."

Rebus looked down at them, saw the tattoos on Gordon Howe's bare arms: No Surrender; UDA; the Red Hand of Ulster. He recalled Tom Jackson's story: *ran off to Ulster to join the paramilitaries* . . .

"You'll be Billy's dad then," Rebus guessed. "Welcome back to Scotland."

43

On the way back into Edinburgh, Rebus sat in the back with Howe, while Billy sat in the front with Siobhan.

"You read about Greenfield in the paper?" Rebus guessed. Gordon Howe nodded. "What's your real name?"

"Eddie Mearn."

"How long have you been back from Northern Ireland?" Siobhan asked.

"Three months." He reached out a hand to ruffle his son's hair. "I wanted Billy back."

"Did his mother know?"

"That cow? It was our secret, wasn't it, Billy?"

"Aye, Dad," Billy said.

Mearn turned to Rebus. "I used to visit him on the quiet. If his mum had found out, she'd've put a stop to it. But we kept it hush-hush."

"Then you read about Darren Rough?" Rebus added.

Mearn nodded. "Looked too good to be true. I knew if I snatched Billy, they'd just assume that wanker had him— at least for a while. Give us a chance to get settled. We were getting on fine, weren't we, Billy?"

"Grand," his son agreed.

"Your mum's been at her wits' end, Billy," Siobhan said.

"I hate Ray," Billy said, tucking his chin into his neck. Ray Heggie: Joanna Horman's lover. "He hits her."

"Why do you think I wanted Billy out of there?" Mearn said. "It's not right for a kid to have to deal with. It's not right." He bent forward to kiss the top of his son's head. "We were all fixed up, though, weren't we, Billy Boy? We'd've managed."

Billy turned in his seat, tried to hug his father, the seat-belt restricting him. Looking in the rearview, Siobhan fixed her eyes on Rebus's. Both knew what would happen: Billy would go back to Greenfield; Mearn would probably be charged. Neither officer felt especially great about it.

As they headed into central Edinburgh, Rebus asked Siobhan to make a detour along George Street. There was no sign of Janice . . .

"You know something?" Rebus asked Mearn.

They were in an interview room at St. Leonard's. Mearn had a cup of tea in front of him. A doctor had looked at his leg: just a sprain.

"What?"

"You said you knew they'd all blame Billy's disappearance on Darren Rough, and that would give you some time to get settled."

"That's right."

"But I can think of a better way, a plan that would mean they'd *give up* looking for Billy."

Mearn looked interested. "What's that then?"

"If Rough was dead," Rebus said quietly. "I mean, we'd look for Billy for a while, even if all we expected to find was a body hidden somewhere. But we'd call a halt eventually."

"I thought of that."

Rebus sat down. "You did?"

Mearn was nodding. "You know, after I read about him being topped. I thought it was the answer to our prayers."

Rebus was nodding. "And that's why you did it?"

Mearn frowned. "Did what?"

"Killed Darren Rough."

The two men stared at one another. Then a look of horror spread across Mearn's face. "N-n-no," he stammered. "No way, no way . . ." His hands gripped the edge of the table. "Not me, I didn't do it."

"No?" Rebus looked surprised. "But you've got the perfect motive."

"Christ, I was starting a *new* life. How could I contemplate *that* if I'd topped someone?"

"Lots of people do it, Eddie. I see them in here several

times a year. I'd've thought it would be easy for someone
with paramilitary training."

Mearn laughed. "Where did you get that idea?"

"It's what they're saying on the estate. When Joanna got
pregnant with Billy, you ran off to join the terrorists."

Mearn calmed down, looked around. "I think I want a
solicitor," he said quietly.

"One's on its way," Rebus explained.

"What about Billy?"

"They've phoned his mum. She's on her way too. Probably smartening herself up for the press conference."

Mearn squeezed his eyes shut. "Shit," he whispered.
Then: "Sorry, Billy." He was blinking back tears as he
looked towards Rebus. "What gave us away?"

A nosy old lady and a line of parked cars, Rebus could
have told him. But he hadn't the heart.

There were cameras and microphones outside St. Leonard's; so many that the journalists were spilling on to the
road. Cars and vans were sounding their horns, making it
hard to hear Joanna Horman speaking of her emotional re-
union with her son. No sign of Ray Heggie: Rebus wondered if she'd given him the push. And not much sign of
emotion from young Billy Boy. His mother kept hugging
him to her, almost smothering him as the cameramen bayed
for another shot. She pockmarked his face with lipstick
kisses. As she made to answer another question, Rebus noticed Billy trying to wipe his face clean.

There were civilians mixed in with the reporters:
passers-by and the curious. A woman in a GAP T-shirt was
trying to hand out leaflets: Van Brady. Across the road, a
kid sat balanced on his bike, one hand touching a lamp-
post for support. Rebus recognised him: Van's youngest.
No leaflets; no T-shirt—Rebus wondered about that. Was
the boy less easily swayed than those around him?

"And I'd like to thank the police for all their hard work,"
Joanna Horman was saying. You're welcome, Rebus
thought to himself, pushing through the scrum and crossing
the road. "But most of all, I'd like to thank everyone at
GAP for their support."

A loud roar of agreement went up from Van Brady . . .

"It's Jamie, isn't it?"

The boy on the bike nodded. "And you're the cop who came looking for Darren."

Darren: first name only. Rebus took out a cigarette, offered one to Jamie, who shook his head. Rebus lit up, exhaled.

"I suppose you saw Darren around a bit?"

"He's dead."

"But before then. Before the story got out."

Jamie nodded, eyes guarded.

"Did he ever try anything?"

Now Jamie shook his head. "He just said hello, that's all."

"Did he hang around the playground?"

"Not that I saw." He was staring at the scene across the road.

"Looks like Billy's the centre of attention, eh?" Rebus got the feeling Jamie was jealous, but trying not to let it show.

"Yeah."

"I bet you're glad he's back."

Jamie looked at him. "Cal's moved in with his mum."

Rebus took another draw on his cigarette. "She's booted Ray out then?" Jamie nodded again.

"And moved your brother in?" Rebus looked impressed. "That's fast work."

Jamie just grunted. Rebus saw an opening.

"You don't sound too chuffed: are you going to miss him?"

Jamie shrugged. "Not bothered." But he was. His brother had moved out; his mother was busy with GAP; and now Billy Boy Horman was getting all the attention.

"You ever see Darren with anyone? I don't mean kids, I mean visitors."

"Not really."

Rebus angled his face so Jamie had little choice but to look at him. "You don't sound too sure."

"Someone came looking for him."

"When?"

"When all the stuff about GAP started."

"Friend of Darren's?"

Another shrug. "He didn't say."

"Well, what did he say, Jamie?"

"Said he was looking for the guy from the newspaper. He had the paper with him." The paper: the story outing Darren Rough.

"Were those his exact words: 'the guy from the newspaper'?"

Jamie smiled. "I think he said 'chap.' "

"Chap?"

Jamie put on a posh voice. " 'The chap who was in the newspaper.' "

"Not a local then?"

Now Jamie let out a stuttering laugh.

"What did he look like?"

"Old, quite tall. He had a moustache. His hair was grey, but the moustache was black."

"You'd make a good detective, Jamie."

Jamie wrinkled his nose in distaste. His mother had spotted the conversation, was making to cross the road towards them.

"Jamie!" she called, trying to weave between traffic.

"What did you tell him, Jamie?"

"I pointed to Darren's flat. Told him I knew Darren wasn't in."

"What did the man do?"

"Gave me a fiver." He looked around, almost furtively. "I followed him back to his car."

Rebus smiled. "You really would make a detective."

Another shrug. "It was a big white car. I think it was a Merc."

Rebus backed off as Van Brady reached them.

"What's he been saying, Jamie?" she asked, staring daggers at Rebus. But Jamie looked at her defiantly.

"Nothing," he said.

She looked at Rebus, who just shrugged. When she turned back to her son, Rebus winked at him. Jamie gave the flicker of a smile. For a few moments, *he'd* been the centre of someone's attention.

"I was just asking about Cal," Rebus told Van Brady. "I've heard he's moving in with Joanna."

She turned on him. "What's it to you?"

He nodded towards the leaflet in her hand. "Got one of those for me?"

"If you did your job right," she sneered, "we wouldn't need GAP."

"What makes you think we need it anyway?" Rebus asked her, turning to walk away.

Rebus got on the computer, and decided to cover his bets by talking to the area's Merc dealerships. He already knew one person who drove a white Merc: the widow Margolies. Rebus tapped his pen against his desk, started calling. He got lucky with the first number he tried.

"Oh, yes, Dr. Margolies is a regular customer. He's been buying nothing but Mercedes for donkey's years."

"Sorry, I'm talking about a Mrs. Margolies."

"Yes, his daughter-in-law. Dr. Margolies bought that car, too."

Dr. Joseph Margolies . . . "He bought one for his son and daughter-in-law?"

"That's right. Last year, was it?"

"And for himself?"

"He likes to part-ex: keeps the model a year or two, then trades for something brand new. That way you don't get the same scale of depreciation."

"So what's he driving just now?"

The sales manager turned cautious. "Why don't you ask him yourself?"

"Maybe I'll do that," Rebus said. "And I'll be sure to tell him you could have saved me the trouble."

Rebus listened to the receiver making a sighing sound. Then: "Hang on a sec." He heard fingers on a keyboard. A pause, then: "An E200, purchased six months ago. Happy?"

"As a kid on Christmas morning." Rebus scribbled the details down. "And the colour?"

Another sigh. "White, Inspector. Dr. Margolies always buys white."

As Rebus put down the phone, Siobhan Clarke came over. She rested against the corner of his desk.

"Looks like someone got lazy," she said.

"How do you mean?"

"Eddie Mearn. As far as the inquiry was concerned, he

was still in Northern Ireland. Someone made a phone call to Lisburn, and took it as gospel when he was told Mearn was still around."

"Who made the call?"

"Roy Frazer, I'm sorry to say." ·

"It's the only way he'll learn."

"Sure, like you've learned from past mistakes."

He smiled. "That's why I never make the same one twice."

She folded her arms. "You think Mearn had this planned all along?"

Rebus nodded slowly. "I'd say it's likely. Moved back from Lisburn, maybe it's true he didn't tell anyone there he was leaving. Sets up a new identity for himself in Grangemouth—striking distance of Edinburgh. Why lie about who he was? Only reason I can think of is, he was going to snatch Billy. New life for both of them."

"Would that have been so bad?" Siobhan asked.

"No worse than where Billy is now," Rebus admitted. He looked at her. "Careful there, Siobhan. You're in danger of thinking the law's an ass. That's only one step away from making up your own rules."

"The way you've done." It was statement rather than question.

"The way I've done," Rebus was forced to agree. "And look where it's got me."

"Where's that?"

He tapped his sheet of notes. "Seeing white cars every-where."

44

A white car had been spotted the night Jim Margolies had
flown from Salisbury Crags. Fair enough, Jim himself
owned a white car, but according to his wife the car had
stayed in the garage. He'd walked all the way to the Crags.
How likely was that? Rebus didn't know.

Another white car had been spotted in Holyrood Park
around the time Darren Rough was bludgeoned to death.

And prior to this, someone in a white car had been looking for Darren.

Rebus told the story to Siobhan, and she pulled over a
chair so they could work through some theories.

"You're thinking they're all the same car?" she asked.

"All I know is, they're in the park when two apparently
unconnected deaths occur."

She scratched her head. "I'm not seeing anything. Any
other owners of white Mercs?"

"You mean, have any serial killers bought or hired one
lately?" She smiled at this. "I'm checking," Rebus went on.
"So far, the only name I have is Margolies." He was thinking: Jane Barbour drove a cream-coloured car, a Ford Mondeo . . .

"But there are more white Mercs than that out there?"

Rebus nodded. "But Jamie's description of the man
sounds awfully like Jim's father."

"You saw him at the funeral?"

Rebus nodded. And at a children's beauty show, he
might have added. "He's a retired doctor."

"Racked with grief at his son's suicide, he decides to
become a vigilante?"

"Ridding the world of corruption to protest at the iniq-
uity of life."

Her smile broadened. "You don't see it, do you?"

"No, I don't." He tossed his pen on to the desk. "To tell you the truth, I'm not seeing anything at all. Which must make it time for a break."

"Coffee?" she suggested.

"I was thinking of something stronger." He saw the look on her face. "But coffee will do in the meantime."

He went out to the car park for a cigarette, but ended up jumping into the Saab and heading down The Pleasance, across the High Street and past Waverley station. He drove west along George Street, then made an illegal turn to head back east along it. Janice was sitting on the kerb, head in her hands. People were looking at her, but no one stopped to ask if they could help. Rebus pulled up alongside and got her into the car.

"I know he's here," she kept repeating. "I know it."

"Janice, this isn't doing either of you any good."

Her eyes were bloodshot, looking sore from all the crying. "What would you know about it? Have you ever lost a child?"

"I nearly lost Sammy."

"But you didn't!" She turned away from him. "You've never been any good, John. Christ, you couldn't even help Mitch, and he was supposed to be your best friend. They nearly blinded him!"

She had plenty left to say, plenty of poison. He let her talk, resting his hands lightly on the steering-wheel. At one point, she tried to get out, but he pulled her back into the car.

"Come on," he said. "Give me more. I'm listening to you."

"No!" she spat. "Know why? Because so help me, I think you're enjoying it!" This time when she opened the door, he didn't try to stop her. She took a left at the corner, heading down into the New Town. Rebus turned the car again, took a right into Castle Street and a left into Young Street. Stopped outside the Oxford Bar and walked in. Doc Klasser was standing in his usual spot. The afternoon drinkers were in: most of them would clear out by five or six, when the place filled with office workers. Harry the barman saw Rebus and lifted a pint glass. Rebus shook his head.

"A nip, Harry," he said. "Better make it a large one."

He sat in the back room. Nobody there but the writer, the one with the big bag of books. He seemed to use the place as an office. A couple of times Rebus had asked him what books he should be reading. He'd bought the suggestions, but hadn't read them. Today, neither man seemed in need of company. Rebus sat with his drink and his thoughts. He was thinking back over thirty years, back to the last school party. His own version of the story . . .

Mitch and Johnny had a plan. They'd join the army, see some action. Mitch had sent away for the literature, then had dropped into the Army Careers Office in Kirkcaldy. The following week, he'd taken Johnny with him. The recruiting sergeant told them jokes and stories from his time "in the field." He told them they'd breeze through basic training. He had a moustache and a paunch and told them there'd be "shagging and boozing galore": "two good-looking lads like you, it'll be dripping out of your ears."

Johnny Rebus hadn't been sure what that meant exactly, but Mitch had rubbed his hands together and chuckled with the Sarge.

So that was that. All Johnny had to do was tell his dad and Janice.

His dad, it turned out, wasn't keen. He'd done some time in the Far East in World War II. He had some photographs and a black silk scarf with the Taj Mahal sewn into it. He had a scar on his knee that wasn't really a bullet wound, even though he said it was.

"You don't want that," Johnny's dad said. "You want a proper job." They kicked it back and forth between them. His dad's final shot at goal: "What will Janice say?"

Janice didn't say anything; Rebus kept putting off telling her. And then one day she learned from her mum, who'd been talking to Johnny's dad, learned Johnny was thinking of leaving.

"It's not like I'm going for good," he argued. "I'll have plenty of home visits."

She folded her arms, the way her mother did when she had right on her side. "And am I supposed to just wait for you?"

"Please yourself," Johnny said, kicking a stone.

"That's the plan," she said, walking off.

Later, they made it up. He went to her house, went up to her bedroom with her: it was the only place they could talk. Her mum brought up juice and biscuits; gave them ten minutes then came up again to check they didn't need anything. Johnny said he was sorry.

"Does that mean you've changed your mind?" Janice asked.

He shrugged. He wasn't sure. Who did he want to let down: Janice or Mitch?

By the night of the dance, he'd made his mind up. Mitch could go alone. Johnny would stay behind, get a job of some kind and marry Janice. It wouldn't be a bad life. Plenty before him had done the same thing. He would tell Janice, tell her at the dance. And Mitch too, of course.

But first they had a drink. Mitch had got some bottles and an opener. They sneaked into the churchyard next to the school, drank a couple each, lay there in the grass, the headstones rising all around them. And it felt good, felt comfortable. Johnny swallowed back his confession. It could wait; he couldn't spoil this moment. It was like their whole lives had been sorted out, and everything was going to be fine. Mitch talked about the countries they'd visit, the things they'd see and do.

"And they'll all be gutted, just you wait." Meaning everyone who stayed in Bowhill, all their friends who were going off to college or down the pit or into the dockyard. "We'll see the whole fucking world, Johnny. And all they'll ever see is this place." And Mitch stretched his arms out until his fingertips brushed the rough surfaces of two headstones. "All they'll ever have to look forward to is this . . ."

They were untouchable as they marched into the playground. A teacher and the deputy head were on the door, collecting tickets.

"I smell beer," the deputy head said, catching them off guard. Then he winked. "You might have saved one for me."

Johnny and Mitch were laughing, all grown-up now, as they walked into the assembly hall. There was music playing, people up dancing. Soft drinks and sandwiches on trel-

lis tables in the dining hall. Chairs around the perimeter of
the assembly hall; huddles of conversation, eyes darting
everywhere. It felt—just for a moment—as if everyone was
looking at the new arrivals . . . looking at them, *envying*
them. Mitch slapped Johnny's arm, headed towards his girlfriend Myra. Johnny knew he'd tell him at the end of the
dance.

He looked for Janice, couldn't see her. He had to tell
her . . . had to find the words. Then someone told him there
was whisky in the toilets, and he decided to stop there first.
Two cubicles, side by side. Three boys in each, passing the
bottle back and forth over the partition. Keeping silent so
they wouldn't be caught. The stuff tasted like fire. Its fumes
came rolling down Johnny's nostrils. He felt drunk; elated;
unstoppable.

Back in the hall, it was ladies' choice. A girl called Mary
McCutcheon asked him up. They danced well together. But
the reel made Johnny light-headed. He had to sit down. He
hadn't noticed some recent arrivals—three boys from his
year; boys who had over time become Mitch's implacable
enemies. The leader of the three, Alan Protheroe, had gone
one-on-one with Mitch. Mitch had pulverised him, eventually. Johnny didn't see them eyeing up Mitch. Didn't
think that the last dance of schooldays might be a time for
settling scores, for ending things as well as beginning them.

Because now Janice was in the hall. Seated next to him.
And they were kissing, even when Miss Dysart stood in
front of them clearing her throat in warning. When Janice
drew away eventually, Johnny stood up, pulling her to her
feet.

"I've something to tell you," he said. "But not here.
Come on."

And had led her outside, round the back of the old building to where the bike-sheds—now largely unused—still
stood. Smokers' Corner, they called it. But it was a place
for lovers too, for quick snogs at lunchtime. Johnny sat
Janice down on a bench.

"Aren't you going to tell me how lovely I look?"

He drank her in. She did look lovely. Light from the
school windows made her skin seem to glow. Her eyes
were dark invitations, her dress rustled with layers waiting

to be unpeeled. He kissed her again. She tried to break away, asked him what it was he wanted to tell her. But now he knew that could wait. He was light-headed and full of dreams and desire. He touched her neck where it was bare at the shoulders. He ran his hand down her back, slipping it beneath the material. Her mum had made the dress; he knew it had taken hours. When he pressed harder, he felt the stitching in the zip give way. Janice gave a gasp and pushed him away.

"Johnny . . ." Craning her neck to try to assess the damage. "You silly bugger, see what you've done."

His hands on her legs, sliding the dress up past the knee. "Janice."

She was standing now. He stood, too, pressing in on her for another kiss. She turned her face away. He seemed all limbs, sliding up her legs, slithering around her neck and down her back . . . She knew he tasted of beer and whisky. Knew she didn't like it. When she felt his hand trying to prise her legs apart, she pushed him away again, and he stumbled. Regaining balance, he wasn't so much smiling as leering as he moved in on her again.

And she swung back her hand, made a fist of it, and hit him a solid blow, almost dislocating her wrist in the process. She rubbed her knuckles, mouthing silent words of pain. He was flat out on the ground; knocked cold. She sat down again on the bench and waited for him to get up. Then heard what sounded like a commotion, and felt she'd much rather investigate than stay out here . . .

It was a fight. Slaughter might have been nearer the mark. The gang of three had somehow got Mitch on his own. They were at the edge of the playing-field, The Craigs silhouetted behind them. The sky was dark blue, bruise-coloured. Maybe Mitch had felt that tonight of all nights, he could take all three. Maybe they'd offered him a re-match, promising one-on-one. But it was three against one, and Mitch was on his hands and knees as the kicks rained in on his face and ribs. Janice was running forward, but a small, wiry figure beat her to it, legs and arms working like a windmill, head smashing into an unprotected nose, teeth bared with determination. She was amazed to identify the figure as Barney Mee, everyone's joker. What he lacked in elegance and precision, he more than made up for in sheer bloody-mindedness. He was like a machine. It only lasted a minute, maybe less, and at the end he was exhausted, but three figures were slouching off into the encroaching darkness as Barney slumped to the ground and lay on his back, staring up at the moon and the stars.

Mitch had pulled himself into a sitting position, one hand on his chest, the other covering an eye. Both hands were smeared with his own blood. His lip was split, and his nose was dripping red. When he spat, half a tooth was attached to the string of thick saliva. Janice stood above Barney Mee. He didn't seem so small, lying stretched out like that. He seemed . . . compact, but heroic. He opened his eyes and saw her, gave her one of his toothy grins.

"Lie down here," he told her. "There's something you should see."

"What?"

"You won't see it standing up. You've got to lie down."

She didn't believe him, but she lay down anyway. What did it matter if her dress got mucky: it was already split at the back. Her face was inches from his.

"What am I supposed to be looking at?" she asked.

"Up there," he said, pointing.

And she looked. The sky wasn't black, that was the first strange thing. It was dark, certainly, but streaked with seams of white stars and clouds. And the moon seemed huge and orange rather than yellow.

"Isn't it amazing?" Barney Mee said. "Every time I look at it, I can't help saying that."

She turned to him. "*You're* amazing," she said.

He smiled at the compliment. "What are you going to do?"

"You mean when I leave?" She shrugged. "Don't know. Look for a job, I suppose."

"You should go to college."

She looked at him more closely. "Why?"

"You'd make a good teacher."

She laughed out loud, but only for a second. "What makes you say that?"

"I watch you in class. You'd be good, I know you

would. Kids would listen to you." He was looking at her now. "I know I would," he said.

Mitch cleared some blood from the back of his throat. "Where's Johnny?" he asked.

Janice shrugged. Mitch eased his hand away from his eye. "I'm fucking blind," he said. "And it hurts." He bent over and began to cry. "It hurts inside my head."

Janice and Barney got up, helped him to his feet. They got one of the teachers to drive him to hospital. By the time Johnny Rebus came round, the show was over. He didn't even notice Janice dancing with Barney Mee. He just wanted a lift to the hospital.

"There's something I need to tell him."

Eventually Mitch's parents came, and gave Johnny a lift to Kirkcaldy.

"What in God's name happened?" Mitch's mum asked.

"I don't know. I wasn't there."

She turned to look at him. "Weren't there?" He shook his head, ashamed. "Then how did you get that bruise . . . ?"

His cheekbone, all the way down to his chin: a long purple trail. And he couldn't tell anyone how he'd come by it.

They had a long wait at the hospital. X-rays were mentioned. Cracked ribs.

"When I find whoever did this . . ." Mitch's dad said, balling his fists.

And then later, the bad news: a retina had been dislodged, maybe even worse. Mitch would lose the sight in one eye.

And by the time Johnny was allowed in to see him—with warnings not to stay too long, not to wear him out—Mitch had heard the news and was in tears.

"Christ, Johnny. Blind in one eye, how about that?"

There was a gauze patch over the eye in question.

"Long John fucking Silver and no mistake." One of the patients on the ward coughed at the swear-word. "And you can fuck off too!" Mitch yelled at him.

"Jesus, Mitch," Johnny whispered. Mitch grabbed his wrist, squeezed it hard.

"It's you now. For both of us."

Johnny licked his lips. "How do you mean?"

"They won't take me, not blind in one eye. I'm sorry, pal. You know I am."

Johnny was shaking, trying to think his way out. "Right," he said, nodding. It was all he could say, and he kept repeating it.

"You'll come back and see us, though, eh?" Mitch was saying. "Tell me all about it. That's what I'd like . . . as if I was there with you."

"Right, right."

"You're going to have to live it for me, Johnny."

"Sure, right."

A smile from Mitch. "Thanks, pal."

"Least I can do," said Johnny.

So he'd joined up. Janice hadn't seemed to mind. Mitch had waved him off at the station. And that was that. He sent Mitch and Janice letters; received none in return. By the time of his first leave, Mitch was nowhere to be found, and Janice was on holiday with her parents. Later, he found out Mitch had run off somewhere, no one seemed to know why or where. Johnny had half an idea: those letters, the visits home—reminders of the life Mitch could now never have . . .

Then his brother Mickey wrote to him, told him Janice had said to tell him she was going out with Barney Mee. And Johnny hadn't gone home after that for a while, had found other places to be when he was on leave, writing lies home so his father and brother wouldn't suspect, coming to think of the army as his home now . . . the only place he could be understood.

Drifting further in his mind from Cardenden and the friends he'd once had, and the dreams he'd once thought were within his reach . . .

45

It was dark and Cary Oakes was hungry and the game still wasn't over.

In prison, he'd been given lots of good advice about evading capture, all of it from men who'd been caught. He knew he needed to change his appearance: easily achieved with a visit to a charity shop. A new outfit of jacket, shirt and trousers for less than £20, topped off with a flat tweed cap. After all, he couldn't suddenly make his hair grow. When he saw his likeness in the newspaper, he made further adjustments, shaving himself scrupulously in a public convenience. He found a few stray carrier bags and filled them with rubbish. Examining himself in a shop window, he saw an unemployed man, a little bitter but still with enough money to buy the shopping.

He found the places where the down-and-outs spent their days: drop-in centres in the Grassmarket; the bench beside the toilets at the Tron Kirk; the foot of The Mound. These were safe places for him. People shared a can and a cigarette and didn't ask questions he couldn't make up answers to.

He was shivery and achy, made soft from his stay in the hotel. The windswept night on the hills had skimmed off some of his strength. It hadn't played the way he'd wanted it to. Archibald was still alive. Two spirits needed cleansing from his life: both were still to be dealt with.

And Rebus . . . Rebus had turned out to be something more than the "wild operator" described by Jim Stevens. The way the reporter had talked, Oakes had expected Rebus to turn up naked to do battle. But Rebus had brought a whole goddamned army with him. Oakes had escaped by

dint of good fortune and the weather. Or because the gods
wanted his mission to succeed.

He knew things now would be difficult. In the centre of
the city, he could remain anonymous, but further out
there'd be more danger of discovery. The suburbs of Edinburgh remained places where strangers did not go undetected for long. It was as if people sat with their chairs at
their windows in a constant state of alert. Yet one such
suburb was his ultimate destination, as it had been all along.

He could have taken a bus, but in the end he walked. It
took him well over an hour. He passed Alan Archibald's
bungalow: 1930s styling with a bow window and white
harled walls. There was no sign of life within. Archibald
was in a hospital bed, and—according to one newspaper—
under police guard. For the moment, Oakes had scratched
him from his plans. Maybe the old bastard would die in
hospital anyway. No, he was heading uphill and along another winding road into East Craigs. He'd been here just
twice before, knowing people would get suspicious if he
suddenly started frequenting the area. Two trips, one at
night, one in the daytime. Both times he'd taken taxis from
the foot of Leith Walk, making sure he was dropped off a
few streets from his destination, not wanting the cabbies to
know. In the dead of night, he'd walked right up to the
walls of the building and touched trembling fingers to the
stonework, trying to feel for a single life-force within.

He knew he was in there.

Couldn't stop shaking.

Knew he was in there, because he'd called to ask, identifying himself as the son of a friend. Asked if he could
keep his call a secret: he wanted his visit to be a surprise.

He wondered if it *would* be a surprise . . .

Now, he was level with the car park. He sauntered past,
just another tired worker on his way home. From the corner
of his eye, he checked for police cars. Not that he thought
they'd have guessed, but he wasn't going to underestimate
Rebus again.

And saw instead a car he thought he recognised. Stopped
and put his bags down, making to change hands, making
out they were heavier than they were. And studied the car.
A Vauxhall Astra. Numberplate the same. Oakes bared his

teeth and let out a hiss of air. This was too much, the bastards were determined to wreck his plans.

Only one thing for it. He fingered the knife in his pocket, knowing he'd have to do some killing.

He had ditched the carrier bags and was lying beneath the car when he heard footsteps. Turned his head to watch them coming closer. He reckoned he'd been lying on the ground for a good hour and a half. His back was chilled, and the shivers were starting again. When he heard the clunk of the locks disengaging, he slid out from his hiding-place and tugged open the passenger door. Seeing him, the driver made to get out again, but Cary Oakes had the knife in his right hand while his left grabbed at Jim Stevens's sleeve.

"Thought you'd be pleased to see me again, Jimbo," Oakes said. "Now close the door and get this thing moving." He took off his jacket, tossed it on to the back seat.

"Where are we going?"

"Just drive, man." His shirt followed.

"What are you doing?" Stevens asked. But Oakes ignored him, loosed his trousers and threw them into the back too.

"This is all a bit sudden for me, Cary."

"A man who likes a joke, huh?" As they left the car park, Oakes realised he was sitting on something. Pulled out the reporter's notebook and pen.

"Been working, Jim?" He opened the notebook, and was disappointed to see Stevens had used shorthand.

"Why'd you go see him?" Oakes asked, beginning to tear each page of the notebook into four.

"See who? I was visiting an old neighbour of mine, and—"

The knife arced into Stevens's side. He took his hands off the wheel, and the car veered towards the kerb. Oakes straightened it up.

"Keep your foot down, Jim! If this car stops, you're a dead man!"

Stevens examined his palm. It was wet with blood. "Hospital," he croaked, face twisted with pain.

"You'll get a hospital *after* I've had my answers! What made you go to see him?"

Stevens hunched over the wheel, taking control again. Oakes thought he was going to pass out, but it was just the pain.

"I was checking details."

"That all?" Ripping at the notebook.

"What else would I be doing?"

"Well, that's why I'm asking, Jim-Bob. And if you don't want knifing again, you'll convince me." Oakes reached for the heater switch, slid it to full.

"It's for the book."

"The book?" Oakes narrowed his eyes.

"I don't have enough material with just the interviews."

"You should have asked me first." Oakes was silent for a minute.

"Where are we going?" Stevens had one hand on the steering-wheel, one pressed to his side.

"Turn right at the roundabout, head out of town."

"The Glasgow road? I need a hospital."

Oakes wasn't listening. "What did he say?"

"What?"

"What did he say about me?"

"Probably what you'd expect."

"He's *compos mentis* then?"

"Pretty much."

Oakes wound down the window, scattering the scraps of paper. When he turned round again, Stevens was scrabbling on the floor with his hand.

"What are you doing?" Oakes brandished the knife.

"Paper hankies. I thought I'd a box somewhere."

Oakes examined his handiwork. "Just between you and me, Jim, I don't think paper tissues are going to do the job."

"I feel faint. I've got to stop."

"Keep going!"

Stevens' eyelids looked heavy. "See if they're in the back."

"What?"

"The box of hankies."

So Oakes turned in his seat, pushed his clothes around. "Nothing here."

Stevens was rooting in his pockets. "Must be something . . ." Eventually he found a large cotton handkerchief, eased it inside his shirt.

"Take the airport exit," Oakes commanded.

"You leaving us, Cary?"

"Me?" Oakes grinned. "When I'm just beginning to enjoy myself?" He sneezed, spraying the windscreen with spittle.

"Bless you," Stevens said. There was silence in the car for a moment, then both men laughed.

"That's funny," Oakes said, wiping an eye. "You blessing me."

"Cary, I'm losing a lot of blood."

"It's all right, Jimbo. I've seen people bleed to death before. You've got hours left in you." He sat back in his seat. "So you were out there all by yourself, checking background . . . ? Who knew you were going?"

"Nobody."

"Not your editor?"

"No."

"And John Rebus?"

Stevens snorted. "Why would I tell him?"

"Because I made you mad." Oakes pushed out his bottom lip. "Sorry about that, by the way."

"Was it really all lies?"

"That's between me and my conscience, man."

The car hit a bump and Stevens grimaced.

"Know what they say about pain, Jim? They say it makes you see colour for the very first time. Makes everything really *vivid*."

"The blood certainly looks vivid."

"There's nothing like it," Oakes said quietly, "not in the whole world."

They were coming to another roundabout. Off to their left sat Ingliston Showground, unused for the most part of the year. Unused tonight.

"Airport?" Stevens asked.

"No, take a left."

So Stevens did, and found himself approaching a building site. Another new hotel was being thrown up, to complement the one at the airport exit. Around it lay farmland, the dwellings few and far between. There were no visible lights at all, not even from planes landing and taking off.

"No hospitals near here," Stevens said, dread over-coming him.

"Pull over."

Stevens did as he was told.

"They'll have a doctor at the airport," Oakes told him. "I'll need your car, but you can walk it."

"Better still, you could drop me off." Jim Stevens licked his dry lips.

"Or better yet . . ." Cary Oakes said. And his hand flew, and the knife went into Stevens' side again.

And again and again, as the journalist's words became twisted sounds, finding a new vocabulary of terror, resignation and pain. Oakes dragged the corpse out and dumped it behind a mound of earth. Searched in the pockets and found Stevens' cassette recorder. There wasn't much light, but he was able to prise it open, remove the tape. Left the recorder behind; took the tape. Little money in Stevens' wallet: credit cards, but he wanted neither to use them nor be caught with them in his possession. He bent down again, wiped the recorder on Stevens' jacket, getting rid of prints.

The wind was cutting through him. If he tried concealing the body, he might die of hypothermia. He raced back to the car, got into the driver's seat and headed off. The heater wouldn't go any higher. The blood was sticking his underpants to the seat. He could feel it against his skin. Couldn't put his clothes on yet: had to keep them clean. Couldn't go wandering around Edinburgh with bloodstained clothes.

Another trick from prison. Maybe his fellow inmates hadn't been so stupid after all.

On the way back into town, he stopped in a deserted supermarket car park, threw the tape into a bin.

Then he was on his way. Knew he had at least one night before the body was found. One night when he'd have some shelter, courtesy of Jim Stevens' car.

46

Anything out west was a Torphichen call, but news travelled fast. Roy Frazer drove Rebus out to the scene. The whole drive, Rebus only said one thing to the young man.

"You screwed up about Eddie Mearn. It happens. Best to have it happen young when you can still learn from it. Otherwise you get intimations of infallibility, which translates to your colleagues as 'smart-arse.'"

"Yes, sir," Frazer said, frowning as though trying to memorise the advice. Then he reached into his pocket. "Message from DS Clarke." He handed over the note. Rebus unfolded the piece of paper. At first he didn't take it in. His brain was overloaded as it was. But eventually the words hit him with the force of electricity.

I did a bit of digging. Joseph Margolies wasn't just a doctor. He worked for the council for a time, had special responsibility for children's homes. Don't know if it means anything, but I get the feeling you had him down as a G P. Cheers, S.

He read the note half a dozen times. He wasn't sure if it *did* mean anything. But he could see definite connections beginning to appear. And connections could always be exploited . . .

The DI from Torphichen was Shug Davidson. He offered a brief smile as Rebus got out of the car.

"They say the culprit always returns to the scene of the crime."

"That's not funny, Shug."

"Way I hear it, you and the deceased weren't exactly bosom buddies."

"Maybe towards the end," Rebus said. "Have they moved him yet?"

Davidson shook his head. Work on the construction site had stopped. There were faces at the portakabin windows. Other workers milled around outside, wearing hard hats, drinking tea from their flasks. Their gaffer was complaining that work was a fortnight behind as it was.

"Then a few more hours isn't going to make much of a dent, is it?" Davidson said.

Rebus had ducked beneath the *locus* tape. The victim had been pronounced dead. They were photographing the body. Forensics had already completed taping it. Uniforms were spreading out from the *locus*, seeking clues. Davidson had the whole situation under control.

"Any ideas?" Davidson asked Rebus.

"One fairly big one."

"Oakes?" Rebus looked at Davidson, who smiled. "I read the papers too, John. Friend of a friend told me Oakes had dumped on Stevens. Next thing, Oakes is on the run after the attack on Alan Archibald." He broke off. "How is he, by the way?"

"Doing better than this poor bugger," Rebus said, moving closer to the body. Professor Gates was crouched—or as Gates himself liked to say, on his "cuddy-hunkers"—at Stevens' head. He nodded a greeting towards Rebus, but carried on with his initial appraisal of the scene. One of the forensics team held out a clear plastic bag, into which Jim Stevens' possessions were being dropped.

"No car keys?" Rebus asked. The forensics woman shook her head.

"No car either," Davidson added.

"Stevens drives a Vauxhall Astra."

"I know, John. It's being hunted."

"Must have been brought here in a car. Oakes doesn't have one."

"Probably lost a lot of blood en route," Gates said. "His shirt and trousers are soaked, but there's not that much lying beneath him."

"You think he was stabbed somewhere else?"

"That would be my guess." Gates turned to the forensics officer. "Let Inspector Rebus see the machine."

She lifted a small metal box from the bag. Rebus looked at it closely, but knew better than to touch.

"It's his recorder."

"Yes," Gates said. "And in his right-hand pocket, well away from the wounds and the blood."

"But there's blood on it," Rebus said.

Gates nodded. "And no tape inside."

"The killer took the tape?"

"Or it was important enough for the deceased to take time to remove it, even though by that time he'd already been stabbed and was probably entering a state of shock."

Rebus turned to Davidson. "Any sign of it?"

"That's what they're looking for." Davidson motioned towards the uniforms. "John, have you any idea what Stevens was up to?"

"Last time I spoke to him, he was going to look into Oakes's past."

"Wonder what he found."

Rebus shrugged. "Bringing in Oakes *has* to be the priority."

"After his attack on you, it already was."

Rebus stared down at the lifeless body of Jim Stevens. Stevens, who had been Rebus's shadow for so long, and who had come back into his life only recently.

"I'd only just started liking him," Rebus said. "That's the funny thing." He looked at Davidson. "I get the feeling the game's not over, Shug. Not by a long chalk."

One of Davidson's officers sprinted towards them. "Car's been found," he called.

"Where?" Rebus was first to ask.

The officer blinked, shook his head. "You're not going to like it . . ."

Jim Stevens' Astra sat on a single yellow line on a street called St. Leonard's Bank, just round the corner from St. Leonard's cop shop. St. Leonard's Bank boasted a single row of higgledy-piggledy houses, all of them facing a wrought-iron fence behind which sat Holyrood Park and Salisbury Crags. The car was parked outside a double-fronted three-storey house painted a vivid pink. The key was in the ignition. This was what had first alerted one of the neighbours. They'd gone next door to ask if anyone there had left their keys in their car. Heading out to investigate, they'd found the doors to be unlocked. On opening the driver's side, they'd noticed how wet and stained the seat seemed to be. Pressing fingers down into the fabric, lifting them away to find them stained viscous red . . .

"Is he taking the piss or what?" Roy Frazer said. A crowd from St. Leonard's had gathered, though more, it seemed, out of curiosity than from a desire to help. Rebus started shooing most of them away. He'd brought three of the forensics team with him; the rest would follow when they'd finished at the construction site. Chief Superintendent Watson came to gawp, and to make sure everything was "under control."

"It's Shug Davidson's call really, sir," Rebus informed him. "He's on his way."

The Farmer nodded. "Fair enough, John. But let's get the car moved ASAP, even if only into our car park. It's already been on Lowland Radio. Leave it much longer, we can start selling tickets."

It was true that the crowd around the car was swelling. Rebus recognised a few faces from Greenfield. The estate was only a short walk away.

Roy Frazer was repeating his question.

"He's taunting us," Rebus answered. He went to see how the forensics team was doing.

"Found this on the floor under the driver's seat," one of them said. Inside a plastic bag he had a cassette tape, unlabelled. There was a single bloody thumb print clearly visible on its casing.

"I need this," Rebus said.

"We need to print it."

Rebus shook his head. "The print belongs to the victim." He was managing to smile. *You clever bugger, Jim*, he was thinking. *He didn't get your tape . . .*

At least, that was what he hoped.

"Something else," another of the team said, pointing to show Rebus a spread of tiny spots on the windscreen. "These are on the inside. The way the pattern is . . . it's like someone coughed or sneezed. If it was the killer . . ."

"Is there enough for DNA?"

"It's a hell of a long shot, but you never know. Don't know if this is relevant." Now he pointed to a notebook on

the floor of the passenger side. It had a tin spiral holding
the loose-leaf pages in place. Shreds of paper clung to the
spiral, showing where pages had been torn out.

Rebus patted the man's shoulder. He didn't like to say
*It doesn't matter. I know who killed him . . . I may even
know why . . .* When he turned away, he was carrying the
cassette tape in its little poly-bag, for all the world like a
solemn kid who'd won a goldfish at the fair.

Because it was quieter there, Rebus used one of the interview rooms. He'd slotted the tape into one of the recorders,
being careful to hold it by its edges. No point destroying
trace evidence. He had a pair of Sennheiser headphones on,
and spread out in front of him the contents of Cary Oakes's
file, as well as cuttings of his recent newspaper interviews.
He'd telephoned Stevens' old employer, and they were fax-
ing over the unused portions of transcript. Every now and
then, a uniform would stick his or her head round the door
and hand him the latest fax sheets, so that the table became
covered.

Siobhan Clarke went so far as to bring him a mug of
coffee and a BLT, but otherwise left him to it, which was
just what he wanted. His mind was on nothing but the interview he was listening to.

"Little bugger came to us with his mum . . . my wife's
sister, she was. Right little runt he was." The man's voice
sounded old, wheezy.

"You didn't get on with him?" Jim Stevens' voice, making the hairs rise on Rebus's arms. He looked around but
Stevens' ghost was nowhere to be seen; not yet . . . Occasional background noises: coughs, voices, a television playing. An audience . . . no, spectators. Spectators at what
sounded like a football match. Rebus went through to CID
and dug in bins, looked through the papers sitting folded
and forgotten on window ledges, until he found one for the
previous day. Seven thirty: UEFA Cup action. That seemed
to fit the bill. He tore out the TV page, took it back with
him to the interview room, turned the tape on again.

"I hated him, to be frank with you. Bloody disruption,
that's all it was. I mean, we had ourselves sorted out, everything going smoothly, everything just so . . . and then the

two of them come waltzing in. Couldn't very well kick them out, being family and all, but I made sure they knew I wasn't happy. Oi, I'm watching that!"

Someone had changed channels. Studio laughter. Rebus checked the paper: a sitcom on the BBC.

Back to the sound of crowd and commentator.

"We had some high old ding-dongs, him and me."

"What about?"

"Everything: him staying out, him thieving. Money kept disappearing. I laid a few traps, but I never caught him, he was too canny for that."

"Did your fights ever become physical?"

"I should say so. Tough little runt, I'll give him that. You see me the way I am now, but back then I was fighting fit." He coughed loudly; sounded like his lungs were being turned inside out. "Give me that water, will you?" The old man took a drink, then broke wind. "Anyway," he went on, not bothering to apologise, "I made sure he knew who was boss. It was my house, remember." As if Stevens were accusing him.

"You were the boss," Stevens reassured him.

"I was and all. Take my word for it."

"And if you thumped him, it was just so he'd understand."

"That's what I'm telling you. And he was no angel, believe you me. Mind you, try telling the women that."

"His mother and her sister?"

"My wife, aye. She never saw any harm in anyone, did Aggie. But I'd have to say, even back then I knew there was badness in him. Deep-rooted badness."

"You tried knocking it out of him."

"I'd have needed a sledgehammer, son. Did use a hammer on him once, as it happens. Bastard was tough by then, ready to give as good as he got." Rebus thinking: *The poison passed from one generation to the next. As with abuse, so with violence.*

"Did he run with a gang?"

"Gang? Nobody would have him, son. What did you say your name was?"

"Jim."

"And you're with the papers? I spoke to some of your lot when he was put away."

"What did you tell them?"

"That he should've had the electric chair. We could do a lot worse ourselves than bring back hanging."

"You think it's a deterrent?"

"Once they're dead, son, they don't do it again, do they? What more proof do you want?"

There were sounds of someone bringing Stevens a cup of coffee or tea.

"Aye, they're good to me in here."

Nursing home . . . Cary Oakes's uncle . . . What was his name? Rebus found it in the notes: Andrew Castle. Alongside it, the name of his nursing home. Rebus got on the phone, found a number for the home and rang them.

"You've got a resident called Andrew Castle."

"Yes?"

"He had a visitor last night."

"He did, yes."

"Did you see him leave?"

"I'm sorry, who is this?"

"My name's Detective Inspector Rebus. Only Mr. Castle's visitor has turned up dead, and we're trying to trace his last movements."

There was a tapping at the door. Shug Davidson came in. Rebus nodded for him to sit.

"Gracious," the woman at the nursing home was saying. "You mean the reporter?"

"That's who I mean. What time did he leave?"

"It must have been . . ." She broke off. "How did he die?"

"He was stabbed, madam. Now, what time did he leave?"

Davidson, seated across the table from Rebus, turned some of the fax sheets round so he could read them.

"Just before bedtime . . . say, nine o'clock."

"Did he have a car with him?"

"I think so, yes. He parked it outside."

"Was anyone seen hanging around?"

She sounded puzzled. "No, I don't think so."

"Any suspicious sightings the past day or two?"

"Gracious me, Inspector, what's this about?"

Rebus thanked her for her time, said someone would be coming to get her statement. Then he put down the phone, checked the home's address against an *A-Z*.

"Shug," he said, "I've got Stevens at a nursing home near the Maybury roundabout, probably from around seven thirty last night till nine."

"Maybury's on the road out to the airport."

Rebus nodded. "I think Oakes was already there."

"Where?"

"The nursing home."

"Who was Stevens seeing there?"

"Oakes's uncle. The questions Jim used on the tape . . . I think he'd already talked to the uncle, already made up his mind about him."

"How do you mean?"

"The questions were angled a certain way, letting the uncle show himself as a sadist."

"You're going to tell me this uncle turned Cary Oakes into a psychopath?"

Rebus shrugged. "That's you talking, not me. What I *do* think is, Oakes has a grudge." He thought for a moment. *I have a date with my past. A date with destiny . . . with someone who wouldn't listen . . .* Oakes's words to Stevens at the end of their last interview . . . "Alan Archibald lives out that way." He opened the *A-Z* again, pointed to Archibald's street, then the cul-de-sac which housed the nursing home. They were barely half a dozen streets apart. "I thought Oakes went there to scope out Alan Archibald."

"Now you think different?"

"He came back to Edinburgh to settle old scores. There's none older than his uncle." He looked up at Davidson. "I think he'll try to kill him."

Davidson rubbed a palm over his jaw. "And Jim Stevens?"

"Was in the wrong place at the wrong time. If Oakes thought Jim was on to his plan, he'd have to deal with him. Oakes took the tape from Jim's recorder, only Jim had switched tapes. Then Oakes tore out the pages from Jim's notebook. He didn't want us knowing."

"But we were bound to find out where Stevens had been."

"Eventually, yes." Rebus tapped the tape machine. "But without this, it would have taken a while."

Davidson was starting to rise. "Long enough to let him carry out his plan?"

"Which means it's got to be soon." Rebus was on his feet too.

As Davidson reached for the phone, Rebus sprinted from the room.

47

They had undercover officers on the scene. It was difficult to blend in: most of the staff were middle-aged women. Young, wary-looking men with CID haircuts looked out of place. The officers came from the Scottish Crime Squad. Andrew Castle was confined to his room. There were two men in there with him: one participating in a game of cards—twopenny bets—while the other sat in the corner, affording the best view of door and window. The window was curtained. There was another man in a parked car outside.

"Would he try a sniper shot?" had been one of the questions at the briefing. Rebus had doubted it: he'd no known access to guns, and besides, it was personal with him. His uncle would have to know the why and the who before any killing could be done.

One of the other officers was pushing a mop up and down the corridor outside. Rebus and Davidson were satisfied.

Another question from the briefing: "What if all we do is scare him off?"

Rebus's response: "Then we've saved an old man's life . . . for now."

He'd listened once more to the whole tape, and didn't doubt that Oakes's uncle had been—and probably still was—rotten to the marrow, despite his senility and frailty. Now he had questions.

If Cary had ended up in a home where he'd been loved, would everything have been changed? Were people programmed from birth to become killers, or did other people—and sets of circumstances—conspire to make killers of them, turning the potential that was in most people into something more tangible?

They weren't new questions, certainly not to him. He thought of Darren Rough, the abused becoming abuser. Not all abuse victims took that road, but plenty did . . . And what about Damon Mee? What *had* made him leave home? His parents' failing marriage? Fear of getting married himself? Or had he been coerced away, forcibly stopped from returning?

And why had Jim Margolies died?

And would Cary Oakes walk into the trap?

My, my, my, said the spider to the fly . . .

Oakes had been the spider for far too long.

Rebus dropped into hospital to check on Alan Archibald. There was nothing for him to do at the nursing home. In fact, as one of the Crime Squad officers had succinctly put it, he was "a positive hindrance." Meaning that because Oakes knew Rebus, his presence on the scene could spoil everything.

"Soon as anything happens, we'll call."

Rebus had made the officer write his mobile number on the back of his hand. Then had handed him a business card anyway: "Just in case you wash it off by mistake."

Archibald was at the far end of an open ward, with a screen around his bed. Bobby Hogan from Leith CID was sitting bedside, flicking through a copy of *Mass Hibsteria*.

"Your team's going down, Bobby," Rebus told him.

Hogan looked up. "It's not mine." He waved the football fanzine at Rebus. "Someone left it on the ward."

The two men shook hands, and Rebus went to fetch

another chair. Alan Archibald was snoring gently, head propped up on three pillows.

"How is he?" Rebus asked. Archibald's head was bandaged and there was a gauze compress taped to one ear.

"Thumping headache."

"Well, his head *did* take a thumping."

"They did some tests, say he'll be fine." Hogan smiled. "They tried testing his memory, but as Alan said, at his age he's lucky to remember which day it is, dunt on the heid or no'."

Rebus smiled too. "You know him then?"

"Worked together years ago. That's why I asked for this detail."

"Were you with him when his niece was murdered?"

Hogan stared at the sleeping figure. "It took all the juice out of him, like his batteries were flat after that."

"He wanted it to be Cary Oakes."

Hogan nodded. "I think anyone would have done as far as Alan was concerned, but Oakes was the obvious choice."

"Still could be."

Hogan looked at him. "Not according to Alan."

"I wouldn't trust anything Oakes said. Everything in his world has to be twisted round."

"But he thought he was going to kill Alan . . . why bother lying to him?"

"To amuse himself." Rebus crossed one leg over the other. "That seems to be what he's been doing ever since he hit town, spinning stories . . ." And now Rebus was surplus to requirements; other officers would bring in Cary Oakes.

"Did you ever get anywhere with Jim's suicide?"

Rebus looked at Hogan. "I was beginning to. I got sidetracked."

"So what can you tell me?"

Alan Archibald grunted, and his lips started moving as though savouring something. Slowly his eyes opened. He looked to his left and saw his two visitors.

"Any sign of him?" he asked, voice dry and brittle. Hogan poured him some water.

"Do you want any more tablets, Alan?"

Archibald made to shake his head, then screwed shut his

eyes with the sudden pain. "No," he said instead. As Hogan trickled the water into his mouth, it dribbled either side of the plastic cup and down his chin. Hogan dabbed it with a napkin.

"He'd make a great nurse." Archibald winked at Rebus. His eyes looked unfocused; Rebus wondered what kind of painkillers they had him on. "They haven't caught him?"

"Not yet," Rebus admitted.

"But he's been busy, hasn't he?"

Rebus didn't know if it was pure instinct or whether something in his voice had alerted Archibald. He nodded, told Archibald about Jim Stevens, about the nursing home and Oakes's uncle.

"I remember the uncle," Archibald said. "I interviewed him a while back. I think he hated Oakes almost more than I did."

"You didn't happen to mention him to Oakes, did you?"

Archibald was thoughtful for a moment. "Not for a while. He might have been in one of the letters I sent." His eyes widened. "How did Oakes know where he was? You think I . . . ?" Pain coursed across his face. "I should have twigged. But I wasn't thinking like a copper, that's the bottom line. I had my own motives. I wasn't really interested in the uncle, only in what he could tell me about Oakes. There was that one question always at the back of my mind . . . that one question I needed the answer to."

"Yes," Rebus agreed.

"Everything I'd learned went out the window." Tears were welling in Archibald's eyes.

"Don't blame yourself," Hogan said, touching his shoulder.

Archibald was looking past him, towards the seated figure of John Rebus. "Whether he killed her or not . . . I'll never know for sure, will I?"

Tears dropped on to Archibald's cheeks and down his chin. Bobby Hogan dabbed at them with the already damp napkin.

"All these years not knowing . . . damned fool to think I could . . ." He closed his eyes, crying softly. In the other beds, no one stirred. Crying in the night maybe wasn't so unusual here. Bobby Hogan had taken hold of both the old man's hands. It looked like Archibald was squeezing with all his might.

Alan Archibald was in hospital because he'd become obsessed with an idea. Rebus, knowing what he knew now, was wondering if Jim Margolies had become obsessed too. With nothing else to do, he headed back to St. Leonard's. It took a couple of hours, several phone calls, and a lot of grudging help before Rebus got what he wanted.

He sat at his desk scoring through points on his notepad. The people he'd spoken to from the Health Board and Social Work had all asked if it couldn't wait till morning. Rebus had insisted it could not.

"It's a murder inquiry," had been his only line of attack. When pressed for details, he'd said he couldn't add anything "at the present moment in time," trying to sound like the sort of detective they'd expect him to be: a bureaucrat, a man following a preordained path of investigation where no overnight rest-stops could be taken.

In the end, he'd had to drive to the various offices himself to pick up the information he'd asked for. On each occasion, he'd been met by the official he'd spoken to on the phone. They'd all stared at him with ill-will and irritation. But they'd all handed over the documents. Which gave Rebus little to do but head back to St. Leonard's and plough through the field of information on Dr. Joseph Margolies.

Dr. Margolies had been born in Selkirk, and educated in the Borders and at Fettes. His medical degree was completed at the University of Edinburgh, with stints working in Africa for a Christian charity. He'd become a general practitioner, then had taken to lecturing, specialising in pediatrics. And eventually, as Siobhan's note had said, he'd been employed to "look after" the council-run children's homes in Lothian, a job which also took him into private homes licensed by the council—such as those owned and operated by churches and charities.

What his job meant in effect was that he checked the children for signs of abuse, and would be brought in to make a physical examination should any accusations of abuse be made. Also, some of the kids were classed as "difficult cases," and a medical prognosis would be part of their ongoing record. Dr. Margolies might recommend psychiatric consultation, or a move to some other type of institution. He could prescribe treatments and medication. His powers, in effect, were almost without limit. His word was law.

About halfway through his reading, Rebus began to get a queasy feeling in his gut. He hadn't eaten for hours, but didn't think that had anything to do with it. Nevertheless, he forced himself to get some fresh air, visited Brattisani's for a fish supper with buttered bread and tea. Afterwards, he knew he'd been away from the station for the best part of an hour, but couldn't recall any of that time: no faces, no voices. Brain busy with other things.

He remembered a recent case, a priest who'd abused children for years. The children had been in the care of nuns, and when any of them complained they were thrashed by the nuns, told they were liars, and made to attend confession—where, listening to them, would be the same priest they'd just accused of abuse.

He knew that oftentimes paedophiles were well able to hide their true natures for months and years as they trained for positions in children's homes and the like. They would pass all the checks and psychological tests, only later for the mask to slip. Their need was so great, they would go to extraordinary lengths to fulfil it. And sometimes it might have remained latent had they not encountered at some point a fellow traveller, each spurring the other on . . .

Like Harold Ince and Ramsay Marshall. Rebus could believe that either one, left in isolation, would never have found the strength to begin their eventual programme of systematic abuse. But together, working as a team, the effect had been to intensify their lusts and desires, making the eventual abuse so much more appalling.

Rebus looked back through all the paperwork on Dr. Joseph Margolies, until he was sure of what he saw.

That Margolies had been attached to the city's children's homes at the time of the Shiellion scandal.

That he had retired soon afterwards—and prematurely—on "health grounds."

That he was considered courageous by those he worked

with for the way he'd kept going following his daughter's suicide.

Rebus didn't find much about the daughter. She'd killed herself at fifteen, hadn't left a note. She'd been a quiet child, withdrawn. Adolescence had done her few favours. She'd been worried about upcoming exams. Her brother Jim had been devastated by her death . . .

She hadn't leapt from some high spot. She'd slashed her wrists in the bathroom of her home. Her father had kicked open the door and found her there. It was believed she'd done the deed in the dead of night. Her father was always the first to rise in the morning.

Rebus put a call through to Jane Barbour. By dint of white lies and stubbornness, he secured her mobile number. When she picked up, he could hear loud music and cheering in the background.

"Good party, is it?"

"Who's this?"

"DI Rebus."

Another wave of cheering behind her. "Hang on, I'll just take this outside." The sounds died away. Barbour exhaled noisily. She sounded drunk. "We're at the Police Club."

"What's the celebration?"

"Take a guess."

"Guilty verdicts?"

"On both the bastards. Not a single juror went against us."

Rebus sat back in his chair. "Congratulations."

"Thanks."

"Cordover must be seething."

"Bugger Cordover. Petrie pronounces tomorrow. He'll stick them away for ever and a day."

"Well, congratulations again. It's a hell of a result."

"Why don't you come down? We've enough booze here—"

"Thanks all the same. But it's a coincidence, I'm phoning about Ince and Marshall."

"Oh?"

"Indirectly anyway. Dr. Joseph Margolies."

"Yes?"

"You know who he is?"

"Yes."

"Was he called to give evidence?"

"No, he wasn't. Christ, it's so mild out here tonight."

Rebus wondered if she was on anything other than a natural high. "Why wasn't he called?"

"Because of the facts of the case. It's true a few of the Shiellion kids made accusations at the time, but they weren't believed."

"There'd be a medical check, though."

"Of course, carried out by Dr. Margolies. I interviewed him several times. But the boys were known to be gay, insofar as they worked as occasional rent boys around Calton Hill. If they ran from Shiellion, that's where everyone knew to find them. So you see, evidence of anal sex was not in itself evidence of abuse—I'm quoting the Procurator Fiscal's line. To my mind, these kids were underage and in care, and anyone who had sex with them was guilty of abuse." She paused. "End of rant."

"Sooner you're free of this case the better."

"So why are you dragging it all up again?"

"I'm trying to get a fix on Dr. Margolies."

"Why?"

"When you talked to him, was he helpful?"

"As much as he could be. He said himself the kids had been caught lying before, so who was going to believe them next time? And a lot of the abuse claims referred to oral sex and masturbation . . . not many medical tests for those, Inspector."

"No," Rebus said thoughtfully. "So he didn't give evidence?"

"Not in court. Fiscal said it would be a waste of time. Might even have harmed our case by casting doubt in the jury's mind."

"In which case Cordover might have wanted the doctor as a witness."

"Yes, but he didn't, and I wasn't about to give him a hand." She paused. "You think Margolies was involved in a cover-up?"

"What makes you ask?"

"I wondered about it myself. I mean, chances are there were people working at Shiellion who had a good idea what was happening. But nobody stuck their head above the parapet."

"Afraid to cause trouble?"

"Or warned off by the Church. It's not been unknown in the past. Of course, there's an even worse scenario."

Rebus dreaded to think what it might be. But he asked anyway.

"Just this," she said. "People knew it was happening, but they just didn't care. Now if you'll excuse me, I'm heading back indoors to get blisteringly drunk."

Rebus thanked her and rang off. Sat with his head in his hands, staring at his desk.

People knew . . . they just didn't care . . .

Just as during their actual trial, Ince and Marshall were being held in Saughton Prison. The difference was, now they'd been found guilty they were no longer on remand. As remand prisoners, they'd been able to wear their own clothes, phone out for food, and go about their business. Now they'd be getting used to prison garb and all the other comforts of the prison regime proper.

They were being held in separate cells, with an empty cell between so there was less chance of them communicating. Rebus didn't know why anyone bothered: they'd probably end up in the same sex offender programme.

He had a difficult choice to make: Ince or Marshall? Of course, if one failed him, there was nothing to stop him trying the other. But that would mean going through the same process again, asking the same questions, playing the same games. The right choice might save him all that grief.

He chose Ince. His reasoning: Ince was the elder, with the higher IQ. And though early on in the relationship, there was no doubt that he'd been the leader, the pupil had soon become the master. In the courtroom, Marshall had been the one who'd scowled and grunted and played to the gallery; the one who'd looked as though the trial had nothing to do with him.

The one with no visible show of shame, even as his victims told their stories.

The one who'd fallen down the stairs a couple of times on his way back to the cells.

Yes, Marshall had learned a lot from Harold Ince, but he'd added ingredients of his own. He was the more savage, the more amoral, the less penitent. He was the one who thought it was the world's problem, not his. At the trial, he'd tried quoting Aleister Crowley, to the effect that only *he* had the right to judge his actions right or wrong.

The court hadn't thought much of that.

Rebus sat in the visitors' room and smoked a cigarette. He'd called Patience, got the machine: a message telling callers to try her mobile. He did so, found she was at a friend's. Another woman doctor, off on prenatal leave.

"I might stay the night," Patience told him. "Ursula's offered."

"How is she?"

"Sick."

"Oh dear."

"You misunderstand: she's sick she can't drink. Never mind, I'm drinking for two."

Rebus smiled. "I'll go to Arden Street," he said. "If you're going home, let me know."

"You think I should stay away?"

"It might be an idea." He meant until Cary Oakes was caught. When he rang off, he got through to St. Leonard's, who confirmed that the patrol car was now stationed outside Patience's friend's.

"Safe as houses, John."

So he sat in the visitors' room and smoked a cigarette, defying the sign on the wall, flicking ash on to the carpet. The uniform brought Harold Ince in. Rebus thanked him, told him to wait just outside. Not that Rebus expected anything from Ince: no violence, no escape attempt. He looked resigned to his fate. Since Rebus had seen him at the trial, his face had grown longer and thinner, the pallid skin hanging from it. His stomach bulged, but his chest seemed to have caved in, as though the heart had been removed. Rebus knew that at least one of Ince's victims had committed suicide. There was a smell from the man: sulphur mixed with Germolene.

Rebus offered him a cigarette. Ince, slumping into a chair, shook his head.

"You gave evidence, didn't you?" The voice was thin and reedy.

Rebus nodded, flicked ash. "Your lawyer tried carving me up."

The brief flicker of a smile. "I remember now. Didn't work, did it?"

"And now you've been found guilty."

"Come to rub it in?" Ince's eyes found Rebus's for the briefest moment.

"No, Mr. Ince, I've come to ask for your help."

Ince snorted, folded his arms. "Yeah, I'm well in the mood to help the police."

"I wonder if he's already made up his mind?" Rebus asked, as if wondering aloud.

Ince's forehead creased. "Who?"

"Lord Justice Petrie. He's a tough old buzzard."

"So I've heard."

But soft on his kids, Rebus thought to himself. *Or is he . . . ?*

"My money's on Peterhead for the pair of you," he said. "You'll be there a long time. That's where they take the sex offenders." Rebus sat forward. "It's also where a lot of the real hard cases are kept, the ones who rate kiddiefuckers slightly lower than the amoeba on the evolutionary ladder."

"Ahh . . ." Ince sat back, nodded. "So that's it: you've come to scare me. Let me save you the effort: the guards at the trial told me what I could expect, whichever jail I'm sent to. A couple of them said they'd be coming to see me themselves." Another glance at Rebus. "Isn't that thoughtful?"

Behind the show of bravado, Rebus could tell Ince was terrified. Terrified of the unknown. Every bit as scared as the kids must have been, every time they heard him approaching . . .

"I don't want to scare you, Mr. Ince. I want you to help me. But I'm not stupid, I know I have to offer something in return."

"And what would that be, Inspector?"

Rebus stood up, walked over to where the video camera covered the room.

"You'll notice I'm not taping this," he said. "Good reason for that. This stays off the record, Mr. Ince. Anything you tell me, it's for my own satisfaction only. Nothing to do with building a case. If I ever tried using it, it would be my word against yours: inadmissible."

"I know the law, Inspector."

Rebus turned towards him. "Me too. What I'm saying is, this is strictly between us. I could get into trouble just for making you an offer."

"What offer?" Sounding interested now.

"Peterhead, I know a few of the villains up there. I'm owed favours."

There was silence while Ince digested this. "You'd put in a word on my behalf?"

"That's right."

"But they might choose not to heed it."

Rebus shrugged, sat down again, arms resting along the edge of the desk. "It's the best I can do."

"And I only have your word that you'd do it anyway."

Rebus nodded slowly. "That's right, you do."

Ince was studying the backs of his own hands, his fingers gripping the desk.

"Well, I must say, that's a very generous offer." A touch of humour in the voice.

"It could save your life, Harold."

"Or it could be totally meaningless." He paused. "What is it you want to ask me?"

"I need to know who the third man was."

"Wasn't it Orson Welles?"

Rebus made himself smile. "I mean the night Ramsay Marshall brought Darren Rough to Shiellion."

"Long time ago. I was on the drink back then."

"You made Darren wear a mask."

"Did we?"

"Because of the other man. Maybe it was his idea. Didn't want Darren recognising him." Rebus lit another cigarette. "You'd been drinking. Maybe with this man. Chatting about this and that. Eventually telling him your secret." Rebus studied Ince. "Because you thought you could see something . . ."

Ince licked his lips. "What?" Said so quietly it was barely above a whisper. Rebus lowered his own voice.

"You thought he was like you. You could see a potential. The more you talked, the clearer you saw it. You told him Marshall was bringing some kid along. Maybe you suggested he stay."

"You're making this up, aren't you?"

Rebus nodded. "Insofar as I can't prove any of it, yes, I'm making it up."

"This potential you speak of . . . I'd contend it's in every one of us." Now Ince looked at Rebus, and his eyes seemed harder. He held Rebus's gaze, returned it. "Do you have any children, Inspector?"

"I've a daughter," Rebus admitted, knowing the danger of letting Ince into his personal life, letting him inside his head. But Ince was no Cary Oakes. "She's grown up now."

"I bet at some point in your relationship you've thought about what it would be like to bed her, to have sex with her. Haven't you?"

Rebus could feel the pressure behind his eyes: anger and revulsion. Strong enough to make him blink away the smoke.

"I don't think so."

Ince grinned. "That's what you tell yourself. But I think you're lying, even if you don't know it. It's human *instinct*, nothing to be ashamed of. She might have been fifteen, or twelve, or ten."

Rebus got to his feet. Had to keep moving, otherwise he'd pound Ince's head into the desk. He wanted to light another cigarette, but was only halfway through the current one.

"This isn't about me," he said. Even to his ears, it sounded weak.

"No? Perhaps . . ."

"It's about Darren Rough."

"Ah . . ." Ince leaned back on his chair. "Poor Darren. They had him down on the list of witnesses, but didn't use him. I'd have liked to see him again."

"Not possible. Someone murdered him."

"What? Before the trial?"

Rebus shook his head. "During it. I've been trying to find a motive, only now I think I was looking in all the wrong places." He rested a hand on the desk, leaned down over Ince. "I had a look at the charge sheets, the evidence. Just you and Marshall; none of the other victims mention a third abuser. Was it just that one night? Someone who tried it just the once . . . ?" Rebus sat back down in his seat. He'd finished the cigarette at last; lit himself another from its stub, chain-smoking now. "I found Darren at the zoo. Found out where he lived. It leaked to the newspapers. This third man . . . he knew you weren't going to mention him in court. I don't know why, but I can guess. But the one thing he was scared of was Darren. Which was fine—as far as he knew, Darren Rough was well out of things. Then suddenly he reads that Darren's here, and he can guess why: Darren's helping with Shiellion. There's half a chance he saw something or heard something, maybe without knowing it. There's half a chance our third man's picture might end up in the paper after the trial, and Darren will recognise it.

"Suddenly there's danger. So he has to strike." Rebus blew a thin column of smoke at Ince. "We both know who I'm talking about. But for my own satisfaction, I'd be happier to hear a name."

"That's why Darren died?"

Rebus nodded. "I think so."

"But you've no proof?"

Rebus shook his head. "And I'm unlikely to find it. With you or without you."

"I'd like a mug of coffee," Harold Ince said. "Milk, two sugars. If you order it, it might come *sans* saliva."

Rebus looked at him. "Anything to eat?"

"I'm partial to a chicken korma curry. Nan bread, no rice. Sag aloo as a side dish."

"I can phone out for it."

"Again, I'd prefer it unadulterated." There was confidence in Ince's voice now. He'd made a decision.

"And meantime we'll talk?" Rebus asked.

"For your own peace of mind, Inspector . . . yes, we'll talk."

Rebus sat in the darkness of his living room, sipping from a glass of whisky and water. The street outside was night-time quiet, interrupted by the occasional dull crunching sound of car tyres passing over the setts. He didn't know how long he'd been sitting there, maybe a couple of hours. He'd put a CD on, but hadn't bothered getting up to change it. It had been on the repeat function for three or four plays. 'Stray Cat Blues' had never felt so sordid. It affected him more than the literate and well-mannered "Sympathy for the Devil," which had an air of desperation to it. There was no desperation in "Stray Cat Blues," just the certainty of underage sex . . .

When the phone rang, he was slow to answer. It was Siobhan, relaying a message. Patience's flat had been broken into.

"Did they get anyone?"

"No. A couple of uniforms are still there. They're waiting for someone who can deal with the alarm . . ."

Rebus called St. Leonard's, and a patrol car arrived to take him to Oxford Terrace. The driver could smell whisky on Rebus's breath.

"Been out partying, sir?"

"Your basic party animal, that's me." Rebus's tone ensured no more questions came from the front of the car.

The alarm was still ringing. Rebus went down the

steps and pushed open the front door. The two uniforms were in the kitchen, far away from the noise. They'd made themselves tea, and were searching the cupboards for biscuits.

"Milk, no sugar," Rebus told them. Then he went back into the hall and used his key to disable the alarm. One of the uniforms handed him a mug.

"Thank God for that. It was driving us mental."

Rebus was at the front door, examining it.

"Clean job," the uniform said. "Looks like they had a key."

"More likely he picked it." Rebus went back into the hall. "But he couldn't pick the alarm box . . ." He walked from room to room.

"Anything missing, sir?"

"Yes, son: some hot water from the kettle, two tea-bags and a spot of milk."

"Maybe the alarm scared him off."

"If he picked one lock, why not another?" Rebus thought he knew the answer: because the very fact the alarm was set had told the intruder something.

Told him no one was home.

And he wanted *someone* to be home—Rebus or Patience—that was the whole point of the exercise. Cary Oakes hadn't broken in with the intention of stealing anything. He'd had other plans altogether . . .

When they left, Rebus reset the alarm and made sure the mortice lock was engaged as well as the Yale.

In the trade, it was known as shutting the stable door.

He got the patrol car to take him home by way of Sammy's. Not that he went into her flat—he just wanted to see everything was OK. She wouldn't be on her own; Ned would be sleeping beside her. Not that Ned would give Oakes many problems . . .

"Do me a favour, will you?" Rebus asked the driver. "Arrange for a car to come past here once an hour until morning."

"Will do, sir. You think he'll try it again?"

Rebus didn't even know if Oakes knew Sammy's address. He didn't know if Stevens had known it. He used the car's two-way to talk to the nursing home.

"Quiet as the grave here," he was told.

Then he tried the hospital, got one of the night staff, who assured him there was someone with Mr. Archibald and, yes, they were wide awake. From her description, Rebus guessed it was still Bobby Hogan.

Everyone was safe. Everyone was covered.

The patrol car dropped him off, and he climbed the stairs to his flat. Unlocking the door, he thought he heard a sound on the stairwell below him. He peered over the banister, but couldn't see anything. Mrs. Cochrane's tabby probably, rattling the cat-flap as it went in or out.

He closed the door after him, didn't bother with the light in the hallway. He knew it well enough in the dark. Switched the light on in the kitchen and boiled the kettle. His head was thick from the whisky. He made tea, took it through to the living room. Too late for music, really. He walked over to the window and stood there, blowing on the tea.

Saw a shape move. On the pavement across the road. The outline of a man. He cupped his hands to the window, put his face between them, trying to block out the light from the streetlamp.

It was Cary Oakes. He was swaying slightly, like he could hear music. And he had a huge smile on his face. Rebus turned from the window, looked for his phone. Couldn't see it anywhere. He kicked books across the floor. Where the hell was it?

His mobile then: where was that? He'd forgotten to take it with him; probably in a coat pocket. He went to the hall cupboard: no sign of it. Kitchen? No. Bedroom? Not there either.

Cursing, he ran back to the window to check if Oakes had gone. No, he was still there, only now he had his hands raised, as though in surrender. Then Rebus saw he was holding two small dark objects. He knew what they were.

His cordless phone and his mobile.

"Bastard!" Rebus roared. Oakes had been in the flat; picked the stairwell Yale and the front door.

"Bastard," Rebus hissed. He ran to the door, yanked it open. He was halfway down the stairs when he heard the main door creaking open. Had it been locked? If so, Oakes had dealt with it quickly.

Suddenly Oakes was there at the foot of the stairwell, backlit by a single bulb on the wall. All the walls were painted a weak-custard yellow, making his face seem jaundiced. His teeth were bared, mouth open to expose his tongue. He dropped the phones on the stone floor, reached into his waistband.

"Remember this?"

He was holding the knife. Purposefully, eyes on Rebus, he started climbing the steps, his feet making the sound of sandpaper on wood.

Rebus turned and ran.

"Where you going, Rebus?" He was laughing, not worried about keeping his voice down. The neighbours were students and old-age pensioners: he probably fancied his luck against the whole lot of them.

Mrs. Cochrane had a telephone. Rebus thumped on her door as he passed, knowing it to be a futile gesture. She was stone deaf. The students on his landing: would they have a phone? Would they even be home? He ran in through his own door, shut it after him. The Yale clicked, but he knew it would take more than that to keep Oakes out. He slid the chain across, knew a good kick would probably smash it and the Yale both. Where was the key for the mortice? It was usually in its lock. He looked on the floor, then realised Oakes must have taken it. He'd studied the locks, known the mortice would keep him out . . . Rebus put his eye to the spy-hole. Oakes's face appeared from nowhere. Rebus could hear what he was saying.

"Little pigs, little pigs, let me in."

Lines from *The Shining*.

Rebus went into the kitchen, opened the cutlery drawer. He found a twelve-inch-long Sabatier with a riveted black handle. He didn't think it had ever been used. He ran his thumb over its blade and cut himself.

It would do.

Rebus had come up against knife attackers before. But he'd been able to reason with most of them. The others, he'd been able to deal with . . . But that was then and this

was altogether different. Back out in the hall, he decided
to take the fight to Oakes. With the carving-knife in his fist,
he slid the chain off, threw open the door. He was expecting
an immediate attack, but none came. He craned his neck,
couldn't see Oakes on the landing.

"Piggy going walkies."

Oakes's voice: halfway down to the first landing. Rebus
was out of the door, not hurrying, trying to keep calm. Eyes
boring into Oakes's, peripheral vision fixed on Oakes's
knife.

"Ooh, that *is* a big one," Oakes mocked. He was moving
backwards down the stairs, seeming sure of himself. "Let's
take it outside, Rebus. Let's give it some air."

He turned and jogged out of the tenement. Rebus
thought for a moment. His telephones were lying there. He
should pick up his mobile and call in, get officers here
pronto. Then he thought of Alan Archibald and Patience
and Janice . . . and of his parents' grave. Of Jim Stevens.
Time to end it. He had to keep Oakes in his sight, couldn't
let him slip away again.

He reached down, pocketed the mobile, and headed for
the door.

Oakes was standing on the pavement, nodding.

"That's right. Just the two of us."

He started walking. Rebus followed. The pace was brisk,
without either man ever breaking into a jog. Oakes kept his
head angled back towards his pursuer. He looked pleased
that things were turning out this way. Rebus couldn't see
the logic, but he was wary. So far, Oakes had done nothing
without good reason. Bouncing around Rebus's head, the
words *Finish it! This is the last round* . . .

"Good for the arteries, an early-morning constitutional.
Helps make up for the Scottish diet. I looked in your fridge,
man. I had more food in my fucking cell back in Walla
Walla. Whisky by the chair in the lounge, though: I have
to give you credit for that." He laughed. "What are you,
Sam Spade or something?"

Rebus said nothing. Oakes was a lot younger than him,
and fitter too. Last thing Rebus wanted was to tire himself
out yapping.

They were crossing Marchmont Road, heading along

Sciennes and past the Sick Kids Hospital. Rebus cursed himself for living in such a quiet area. The pubs had all emptied; the chip shops were closed. There were no clubs, not so much as a massage parlour. Then, on the other side of the road: two young men walking home, knees just locking and no more—the end of a good night's drinking. One of them was demolishing a kebab. They looked at the strange pursuit. Oakes's knife was in his pocket, but Rebus brandished his.

"Call the police!" he called out.

Oakes just laughed, as if his buddy was drunk and joking, waving his rubber dagger around.

One man grinned; the other, the one with kebab sauce on his chin, stared, still chewing.

"I'm not joking!" Rebus shouted, not caring who he woke up. "Call the cops!"

He couldn't stop to show them ID, couldn't risk letting Oakes out of his sight: there were too many potential victims out there. And he couldn't take his eyes off Oakes for a second.

So they kept moving, leaving the two young men far behind.

"By the time they get home," Oakes said, "they'll have forgotten the whole thing. It'll be drinks from the fridge and Jerry Springer on TV. That's how it is these days, Rebus. Nobody gives a shit."

"Nobody but me."

"Nobody but you. Ever wondered why that is?"

Rebus shook his head. He didn't mind Oakes talking: while Oakes was talking, he was using up energy.

"You never think about it? It's because you're a fucking dinosaur, man. Everyone knows it—you, your bosses, the people you work with. Probably even your doctor friend. What's with her: she likes to screw prehistoric things?" Oakes laughed again. "In case you're wondering, I kept fit in the pen. I can bench-press your ass. I can keep this pace up all day and night. How about you? You look about as fit as something extinct."

"Sometimes all you need is attitude."

They were cutting through narrow passageways now, coming out on Causewayside.

"Where are we going?"

"Nearly there, Rebus. Wouldn't want to tire you out . . . what's the Scots word again: puggle?" He laughed. There were cars on Causewayside. Rebus made sure they saw him holding the knife. Maybe they'd stop at a phone box or flag down a patrol car. But he knew the odds weren't good— not many patrol cars round here. Probably no foot patrols either. They'd drive home, and then *maybe* they'd phone to report it.

And *maybe* someone from St. Leonard's would come to investigate.

It would be too late. Whatever was being played out, he got the feeling it was coming to its conclusion right now. For some reason, it had to do with . . . no . . . he knew where they were. The far end of Salisbury Place: they were at the junction with Minto Street.

"It was here, wasn't it?" Oakes asked, stopping because Rebus had stopped too. "She was crossing the road or something?"

Sammy . . . crossing the road when the driver hit her. Twenty yards down Minto Street.

Rebus stared at Oakes. "Why?"

Oakes just shrugged. Rebus was trying to focus again on *this* moment. This was what counted; he could think about Sammy later. He had to stop letting Oakes *play* with him.

"He sent her flying, huh?" Oakes was saying. He had his hands in his pockets, as if they were just stopping to chat. Rebus couldn't remember which pocket the knife was in. His own weapon hung from his right hand, useless for the moment. Crossing the road and she . . . she never had a chance.

He realised he hadn't been here since the day after the collision. He'd been avoiding the place.

And somehow Oakes had known the effect this place would have on him. Rebus blinked a few times, tried clearing his head.

"You've been to check on her, haven't you?" Oakes asked.

"What?" Rebus narrowed his eyes.

"You went to your girlfriend's flat, knew I'd been there.

Next thing you did was go to your daughter's. But you didn't go in, did you?"

It was like staring into a devil's eyes. "How do you know?"

"You wouldn't be here otherwise."

"Why not?"

"Because I've *been* there, Rebus. Earlier tonight."

"You're lying." Rebus's voice was dry, his throat acrid. *Trying to get you off your guard, same trick worked with Archibald . . .*

Oakes just shrugged. They were at the corner. Diagonally across from them, two cars had drawn up side by side at a red light. Taxi on the inside lane; boy racer revving beside him. The taxi driver was watching what looked like a fight about to break out: nothing he hadn't seen before.

"You're lying," Rebus repeated. He slipped his free hand into his pocket, brought out the mobile. Used his thumb to press the digits, holding the phone to his face so he could watch it and Oakes at the same time.

"She didn't need her legs anyway," Oakes was saying. The phone was ringing. "There's no answer, is there?"

Sweat was trickling into Rebus's eyes. But if he shook his head to clear the drops, Oakes would think he was answering his question.

The phone stopped ringing.

"Hello?" Ned Farlowe's voice.

"Ned! Is Sammy there? Is she all right?"

"What? Is that you, John?"

"*Is she all right?*" Knowing the answer; needing to hear it anyway.

"Of course she's—"

Oakes flew at him, the knife emerging from his right-hand pocket. Missing Rebus's chest by centimetres. Rebus stepped back, dropped the phone. He had the longer reach. The taxi driver had his window down.

"Cut that out, the pair of you!"

"I'll cut it out all right," Oakes hissed. "I'll dice it and slice it." He made another sweep with the knife. Rebus tried to kick it away, almost lost his footing. Oakes laughed at him. "You're no Nureyev, pal." A quick thrust took the knife into Rebus's arm. Rebus felt his nerves go dull: prelude to agony. *Finish it*.

Rebus took a step forward, feinted with the knife, so that Oakes had to move position. On the edge of the pavement now. Rebus saw the traffic lights behind Oakes were changing. Oakes leaned forward, slashed at his chest. Thin whistling sound as Rebus's shirt split. Blood warm on his arm, more blood trickling from the fresh wound. Red to red/amber.

To green.

Rebus charged in with his foot up and hit Oakes solid in the chest with his sole. Oakes got in a swipe before he was propelled back into the road, where the boy racer, oblivious to the fight, radio on full-blast and his girl with her arm around him, was showing off his car's acceleration from a flat start. The car clipped Oakes, sent him flying, breaking his hip and, Rebus hoped, a few more bones to boot. The car screeched to a halt, the young man's head appeared through the window. He saw knives. He pulled his foot off the clutch and roared off.

Rebus didn't bother to catch the licence plate. He stood on Oakes's knife-hand, forcing the fingers open, then lifted the knife and pocketed it. The taxi driver was still at the lights.

"Phone for police assistance!" Rebus called to him. He held his injured arm to his chest.

Oakes was rolling on the ground, hand to his thigh and side, teeth bared not in a grin now but in a grimace of pain.

Rebus stood up, took a step back, and kicked him in the groin. As Oakes groaned and retched, Rebus gave him another kick, then crouched down again.

"I'd like to say that was for Jim Stevens," he said. "But if I'm being entirely honest with you, really it was for me."

Rebus spent an hour in the casualty department—four stitches to his arm, eight to his chest. The arm wound was deepest, but both were clean. Oakes was somewhere nearby, being treated for breaks and fractures. Six of Crime Squad's finest on guard detail.

A patrol car took Rebus back to his flat, where he retrieved his cordless phone—didn't want any of the students
pocketing it—and had a mouthful of whisky. Then another
after that.

The rest of the night he spent at St. Leonard's, typing
his report one-handed, giving an additional verbal briefing
to Chief Superintendent Watson, who'd been summoned
from bed and whose hair sported a cow's-lick which
flapped when he moved his head.

There was little certainty that Oakes could be charged
with Jim Stevens' murder. It would depend on forensic
evidence: fingerprints, fibres, saliva. Stevens' cassette had
been bagged and handed over to the white-coat brigade.

"But he'll go down for the attack on me and Alan Archibald?" Rebus asked his superior.

Farmer Watson nodded. "For the Pentland attack, yes."

"What about the attempted murder of three hours
ago?"

The Farmer shuffled paperwork. "You've said yourself,
most of the witnesses will have seen *you* with the knife,
not him."

"But the taxi driver . . ."

The Farmer nodded. "He'll be crucial. Let's hope he gets
his story straight."

Rebus saw what his boss was getting at. "Sir, you do
believe I acted in self-defence?"

"Of course, John. Goes without saying." But the Farmer
wouldn't meet his eyes.

Rebus tried to think of something to say; decided it
wasn't worth his breath.

"Crime Squad are pissed off," the Farmer added with a
smile. "They hate an anti-climax."

"I might not look it, but inside I'm crying for them."
Rebus turned to leave the room.

"No going back to the hospital, John," the Farmer
warned. "Don't want him falling out of bed and saying he
was pushed."

Rebus snorted, went downstairs and into the car park. It
would be growing light soon. He dry-swallowed some more
painkillers, lit a cigarette and stared in the direction of Holyrood Park. They were there—Arthur's Seat, Salisbury

Crags—it was just, you couldn't always see them. It didn't mean they weren't there.

Easy to lose your footing in the dark . . . Easy for someone to come up behind you . . .

Rebus left the car park and headed into St. Leonard's Bank. Stevens' car had been taken away for examination at Howdenhall. At the end of the road, there was a gap in the fence, allowing passage into the park itself. Rebus headed down the slope towards Queen's Drive. Once across it, he started to climb. Away from the street-lighting now, his steps were more tentative. He sensed more than saw the starting-point of Radical Road, above which loomed the irregular rockface of the Crags themselves. Rebus ignored the path, kept climbing until he was on top of the Crags, the city spread out below him in a grid of orange sodium and yellow-white halogen. The beast was definitely beginning to awake: cars heading into the city. Turning round, he saw that the sky was a lighter shade of black than the mass of rock below it. Some people said Arthur's Seat looked like a crouched lion, ready to pounce. It never did pounce, though. There was a lion on the Scottish flag too—not crouched but rampant . . .

Had Jim Margolies come up here with the express intention of leaping off? Rebus thought he knew the answer now. And he knew because of the Margolies' dinner engagement that evening, across the park from where they lived.

That, and the fact of a white saloon car . . .

50

Dr. Joseph Margolies lived with his wife in a detached house in Gullane, with an uninterrupted view of Muirfield golf course. Rebus didn't play golf. He'd tried a few times as a kid, dragging a half-set of clubs around his local course, losing half a dozen balls in Jamphlars Pond. He knew some of his colleagues had taken up the game thinking it would help their careers, making sure to concede defeat to their superiors.

That didn't sound like a game to Rebus.

Siobhan Clarke parked the car, and switched off the radio news. It was ten in the morning. Rebus had managed a couple of hours' shut-eye in his Arden Street flat, and had phoned Patience to let her know Cary Oakes was behind bars.

"Stay in the car," he told Clarke, manoeuvring himself out of the door. Not easy with one arm strapped up and his chest giving him grief every time he stretched.

Mrs. Margolies answered the door. Close up, she resembled her son. Same flat chin, same narrow eyes. She even had the same smile.

Rebus introduced himself and asked if he could have a word with her husband.

"He's in the greenhouse. Is there a problem, Inspector?"

He smiled at her. "No problem, madam. Just a couple of questions, that's all."

"I'll show you the way," she said, standing back to let him in. She'd glanced at his arm, but wasn't going to comment on it. Some people were like that: didn't like to ask questions . . . As he followed her down the corridor, he glanced through open doorways, seeing domestic order everywhere: knitting on a chair; magazines in a paper-rack; dusted ornaments; gleaming windows. The house dated from the 1930s. From the outside, it seemed to be all eaves and gables. Rebus asked her how long they'd lived there.

"Over forty years," Mrs. Margolies replied, proud of the fact.

So this was the house Jim Margolies had grown up in. And his sister too. From the notes, Rebus knew she'd committed suicide in the family bathroom. Often, in a situation like that, the families elected to sell up and move somewhere new. But he knew other families would elect to stay, because something of their loved one still remained in the home, and would be lost forever if they abandoned it.

The kitchen was tidy too, not so much as a cup and saucer drying on the draining-board. A message-list had been fixed to the fridge with a magnet in the shape of a teapot. But the list remained blank. Mrs. Margolies asked him if he'd like some tea. He shook his head.

"I'm fine, thanks anyway." Still smiling, but studying her. Thinking: *The wife often knows . . .* Thinking: *Some people just don't ask questions . . .*

Outside the kitchen door was a short hall with two walk-in cupboards—both open to display garden tools—and the back door, which also stood open. They stepped outside and into a walled garden, obviously much worked-on. There was a rookery, and next to it some flowerbeds. These were separated by a trimmed lawn from a long, narrow vegetable bed. Towards the bottom of the garden were trees and bushes, and tucked away in one corner a small greenhouse with a figure moving around inside.

Rebus turned to his guide. "Thank you, I'll be fine."

And he walked across the lawn. It was like walking across luxury Wilton. He looked back once, saw Mrs. Margolies watching him from the doorway. In a neighbouring garden, someone was having a bonfire. Smoke crackled over the wall, white and pungent. Rebus walked through it as he neared the greenhouse. A black labrador pricked up its ears at his approach, then pushed itself up to sitting and gave a half-hearted bark. Its nose and whiskers were grey, and it had about it a pampered look: overfed and, in its declining years, underexercised. The door of the green-house slid open and an elderly man peered through half-moon glasses at his visitor. Tall, grey hair, black moustache—just the way Jamie Brady had described him: the man who'd gone to Greenfield looking for Darren Rough.

"Yes? Can I help you?"

"Dr. Margolies, I'm Detective Inspector John Rebus."

Margolies held up his hands. "You'll forgive me for not shaking." The hands were blackened with soil.

"Me too," Rebus said, gesturing to his arm.

"Looks nasty. What happened?" Not sharing his wife's reticence. But then maybe she'd had half a lifetime of biting back questions. Rebus leaned down to rub the labrador's head. Its heavy tail thumped the ground in appreciation.

"Got into a fight," Rebus explained.

"Line of duty, eh? We've met before, I think."

"Hannah's competition."

"Ah, yes." Nodding slowly. "You wanted to speak to Ama."

"I did then, yes."

"Is this something to do with her?" Margolies was re-treating back into the greenhouse. Rebus followed, and saw that the old man was potting seedlings. It was warm in the greenhouse, despite the day being overcast. Margolies asked Rebus to close the door.

"Keep the heat in," he explained.

Rebus slid the door shut. Most of the available space was taken up with work surfaces, trays of seedlings laid along them in rows. A bag of potting compost lay open on the ground. Dr. Margolies was scooping a black plastic flowerpot into it.

"How does it feel to get away with murder?" Rebus asked.

"I'm sorry?" Margolies took a seedling, pushed it into its new pot.

"You murdered Darren Rough."

"Who?"

Rebus took the pot from Margolies' fingers. "It's going to be a devil trying to prove it. In fact, I don't think it will happen. I really do think you've got away with it."

Margolies met his eyes, reached to take his pot back.

"I'm sorry," he said. "I haven't the faintest idea what you're talking about."

"You were seen in Greenfield. You were asking about Darren Rough. Then off you drove in your white Mercedes. A white saloon car was seen in Holyrood Park around the time Darren was killed. I think he went there for sanctuary, but you found it an ideal site for a murder."

"These riddles, Inspector . . . Do you know who I am?"

"I know exactly who you are. I know both your children committed suicide. I know you were part of the Shiellion set-up."

"I beg your pardon?" A slight trembling in the voice now. A seedling slipped from parchment fingers.

"Don't worry, Harold Ince is going to keep his side of the bargain. He talked to me, but it wouldn't be admissible, and he won't tell anyone else. He told me you were at Shiellion that night. Ince had talked with you often, had come to know you. He'd told you what he did to the kids in his care. He *knew* you wouldn't say anything, because the two of you were alike. He knew how useful it would be to him if a doctor, the man responsible for examining the children, were part of the whole enterprise." Rebus leaned close to Margolies' ear. "He told me *all* of it, Dr. Margolies."

The after-hours drinking, loosening up the doctor. Then the arrival of Ramsay Marshall with a fresh new kid, Darren Rough. Making the kid wear a blindfold so he wouldn't recognise Margolies—this at the doctor's insistence. Sweating and trembling . . . knowing this night changed everything . . .

And afterwards: self-loathing perhaps; or maybe just fear of exposure. He hadn't been able to cope, had feigned ill-health, opting for early retirement.

"But you could never loose Ince's grip on you. He'd been blackmailing you, him and Marshall both." Rebus's voice was little more than a whisper, his lips almost touching the old man's ear. "Know what? I'm so fucking *glad* he's been sucking you dry all these years." Rebus stood back.

"You don't know anything." Margolies' face was blood-red. Beneath the checked shirt, he was breathing hard.

"I can't *prove* anything, but that's not quite the same thing. I *know*, and that's what matters. I think your daughter found out. The shame of it killed her. You were always the first one awake in the morning; she knew *you'd* be the one to find her. And then somehow Jim found out, and he couldn't live with it either. How come *you* can live with it, Dr. Margolies? How come you can live with the deaths of both your children, and the murder of Darren Rough?"

Margolies lifted a gardening fork, held it to Rebus's throat. His face was squeezed into a mask of anger and frustration. Beads of perspiration dripped from his forehead. And outside, the billowing smoke seemed to be cutting them off from everything.

Margolies didn't say anything, just made sounds from behind gritted teeth. Rebus stood there, hand in pocket.

"What?" he said. "You're going to kill me too?" He shook his head. "Think about it. Your wife's seen me. There's another officer waiting for me out front. How will you talk your way out of it? No, Dr. Margolies, you're not going to kill me. Like I say, I can't prove anything I've just said. It's between you and me." Rebus lifted the hand from his pocket, pushed the fork aside. The black lab was watching through the door, seemed to sense all was not well. It frowned at Rebus, looking disappointed in him.

"What do you want?" Margolies spluttered, gripping the work-bench with both hands.

"I want you to live the rest of your life knowing that I know." Rebus shrugged. "That's all."

"You want me to kill myself?"

Rebus laughed. "I don't think you've got it in you. You're an old man, you're going to die soon enough. Once you're dead, maybe Ince and Marshall will rethink their loyalty to you. You won't be left with any reputation at all."

Margolies turned towards him, and now there was clear, focused hatred in his eyes.

"Of course," Rebus said, "if any evidence does turn up, you can be assured I'll be back here at the double. You might be celebrating the millennium, you might be getting your card from the Queen, and then you'll see me walking through the door." He smiled. "I'll never be very far away, Dr. Margolies."

He slid open the greenhouse door, manoeuvred his way past the dog. Walked away.

It didn't feel like any sort of victory. Unless something turned up, there'd be no justice for Darren Rough, no public trial. But Rebus knew he'd done what he could. Mrs. Margolies was in the kitchen, making no pretence of doing anything other than waiting for him to return.

"Everything all right?" she asked.

"Fine, Mrs. Margolies." He headed down the hall, making for the front door. She was right behind him.

"Well, I just was wondering . . ."

Rebus opened the door, turned to her. "Why not ask your husband, Mrs. Margolies?"

The wife often knows, never brings herself to ask.

"Just one thing, Mrs. Margolies . . . ?"

"Yes?"

Your husband's a cold-blooded murderer. His mouth opened and closed, but no words came. He shook his head, started down the garden path.

Clarke drove him to Katherine Margolies' house, in the Grange area of Edinburgh. It was a three-storey Georgian semi in a street half of whose homes had been turned into bed-and-breakfast establishments. The white Merc was parked in front of the gate. Rebus turned to Clarke.

"I know," she said: "stay in the car."

Katherine Margolies looked less than thrilled to see him.

"What do you want?" She seemed ready to keep him on the doorstep.

"It's about your husband's suicide."

"What about it?" Her face was narrow and hard, hands long and thin like butchers' knives.

"I think I know why he did it."

"And what makes you think *I'd* want to know?"

"You already do know, Mrs. Margolies." Rebus took a deep breath. Well, if she didn't mind them talking like this on her doorstep . . . "When did he find out his father was a paedophile?"

Her eyes widened. A woman emerged from the neighbouring house, preparing to walk her Jack Russell terrier. "You better come in," Katherine Margolies said sharply, eyes darting up and down the street. After he walked in, she closed the door and stood with her back to it, arms folded.

"Well?" she said.

Rebus looked around. The hall had a grey marble floor veined with black lines. A stone staircase swept upwards. There were paintings on the walls: Rebus got the feeling they weren't prints. She didn't seem to have noticed his arm, had no interest in him that way.

"Hannah not home?" he asked.

"She's at school. Look, I don't know what it is—"

"Then I'll tell you. It's been gnawing at me, Jim's death. And I'll tell you why. I've been there myself, standing at the top of a very high place, wondering if I'd have the guts to jump off."

Her face softened a little.

"Usually it was the booze doing it," he went on. "These days, I think I've got that under control. But I learned two things. One, you have to be incredibly brave to pull it off. Two, there's got to be some crunch reason for you not to go on living. See, when it comes to it, going on living is the easier of the two options. I couldn't see any reason why Jim would take his life, no reason at all. But there had to be one. That's what got to me. There *had* to be one."

"And now you think you've found it?" Her eyes were liquid in the cool dimness of the hall.

"Yes."

"And you felt it worth sharing with me?"

He shook his head. "All I need from you is confirmation that I'm right."

"And then you'll have contentment?" She waited till he'd nodded. "And what right do you have to that, Inspector Rebus? What gives you the right to sleep easy?"

"I never find sleep very easy, Mrs. Margolies." It seemed to him then—and maybe it was a trick of the light—that he was seeing her at the end of a long dark tunnel, so that while she stood out clearly, everything between and around them was a blur of indistinct shading. And things were moving and gathering on the periphery: the ghosts. They were all here, providing a ready-made audience. Jack Morton, Jim Stevens, Darren Rough . . . even Jim Margolies. They felt so alive to him he could scarcely believe Katherine Margolies couldn't make them out.

"The night Jim died," Rebus went on, "you'd been out to dinner with friends in Royal Park Terrace. I wondered about that . . . Royal Park Terrace to The Grange."

"What about it?" Looking bored now more than anything. Rebus thought it was bravado.

"Easiest route is to cut through Holyrood Park. Is that the way you drove home?"

"I suppose so."

"In your white Mercedes?"

"Yes."

"And Jim stopped the car, got out . . ."

"No."

"Someone saw the car."

"No."

"Because something had been making his life hell, something he'd maybe just discovered about his father . . ."

"No."

Rebus took a step towards her. "It was bucketing down that night. He wouldn't have gone out walking. That's your version, Mrs. Margolies: in the middle of the night he got up, got dressed, and went out walking. He walked all the way to Salisbury Crags in the rain, just so he could throw himself off." Rebus was shaking his head. "My version makes more sense."

"Maybe to you."

"I'm not about to go shouting from the chimney-tops, Mrs. Margolieses, I just need to know that that's how it happened. He'd been talking to one of the Shiellion victims. He found out his father was involved in the Shiellion abuse and he was afraid it would come out, afraid the shame would rebound on to him."

She exploded. "Christ, you couldn't be more wrong! It had nothing to do with that. What's any of this got to do with Shiellion?"

Rebus collected himself. "You tell me."

"Don't you see?" She was crying now. "It was Hannah . . ."

Rebus frowned. "Hannah?"

"Hannah was his sister's name. Our Hannah was named after her. Jim did it to get back at his father."

"Because Dr. Margolies had . . ." Rebus couldn't bring himself to say the word. "With Hannah?"

She rubbed the back of her hand across her face, smudging mascara. "He interfered with his own daughter. God knows whether it was just once. It might have been going on for years. When she killed herself . . ."

"She did so knowing who'd be first to find her?"

She nodded. "Jim knew what had happened . . . knew why she'd done it. But of course nobody ever talks about it." She looked at him. "You just don't, do you? Not in polite society. Instead he tried shutting it out, accepting that there was no remedy."

"I'm not sure I understand." But he understood something, knew now why Jim had beaten up Darren Rough. Displaced anger: he hadn't been hitting Rough; he'd been hitting his father.

She slid down the door until she was crouching, arms hugging her knees. Rebus lowered himself on to the bottom step of the staircase, tried to make sense of it: Joseph Margolies had abused his own daughter . . . what would have made him turn to a boy like Darren Rough? Ince's insistence, perhaps; or simple lust and curiosity, the thought of more forbidden fruit . . .

Katherine Margolies' voice was calm again. "I think Jim joined the police as another way of telling his father something, telling him he'd never forget, never forgive."

"But if he knew all along about his father, why did he kill himself?"

"I've told you! Because of Hannah."

"His sister?"

She gave a wild, humourless laugh. "Of course not." Paused for breath. "Our daughter, Inspector. I mean Hannah, our daughter. Jim had . . . he'd been worried for some time." She took a deep breath. "I'd noticed he wasn't sleeping. I'd wake in the night and he'd be lying there in the darkness, eyes open, staring at the ceiling. One night he told me. He felt I ought to know."

"What was he worried about?"

"That he was turning into his father. That there was some genetic component, something he had no control over."

"You mean Hannah?"

She nodded. "He said he tried not to have the thoughts, but they came anyway. He looked at her and no longer saw his daughter." Her eyes were on the pattern in the floor. "He saw something else, something to be desired . . ."

Finally Rebus saw it. Saw all Jim Margolies' fears, saw the past which had haunted him and the expectation of recurrence. Saw why the man had turned to young-looking prostitutes. Saw the dread of history. *Not in polite society.* If families like the Margolieses and the Petries represented polite society, Rebus wanted nothing to do with it.

"He'd been quiet all evening," Katherine Margolies went on. "Once or twice I caught him looking at Hannah, and I could see how scared he was." She rubbed the palm of either hand over her eyes, looked up to the ceiling, demanding something more from it than the comfort of cornice and chandelier. The noise that escaped from her throat was like something from a caged animal.

"On the way home, he stopped the car and ran. I went after him, and he was just standing there. At first, I didn't realise he was at the very edge of the Crags. He must have heard me. Next thing, he'd vanished. It was like a stunt, something a stage magician would do. Then I realised what it was. He'd jumped. I felt . . . well, I don't know what I felt. Numb, betrayed, shocked." She shook her head, unsure even now what her feelings were towards the man who had killed himself rather than give in to his most feral craving. "I walked back to the car. Hannah was asking where her daddy was. I said he'd gone for a walk. I drove us home. I didn't go down to help him. I didn't do anything. Christ knows why." Now she ran her hands through her hair.

Rebus got up, pushed open a door. It led into a formal dining room. Decanters on a polished sideboard. He sniffed one, poured a large glass of whisky. Took it through to the hall and handed it to Katherine Margolies. Went back to fetch another for himself. He saw the sequence now: Jane Barbour telling Jim that Rough was coming back to town; Jim dusting off the case, becoming intrigued by the third man. Knowing his father had been working in children's homes. Wanting to know, quizzing Darren Rough, his world collapsing in on him . . .

"You know," his widow was saying, "Jim wasn't scared of dying. He said there was a coachman."

"Coachman?"

"He took you to wherever it was you went when you died." She looked up at him. "Do you know that story?"

Rebus nodded. "An old Edinburgh ghost story, that's all it is."

"You don't believe in ghosts then?"

"I wouldn't say that necessarily." He raised his glass. "Here's to Jim," he said. When he looked around, there wasn't a ghost to be seen.

A week later, Rebus received a phone call from Brian Mee.

"What's up, Brian?" Rebus already guessing from the tone of voice.

"Ah, shite, John, she's left me."

"I'm sorry to hear that, Brian."

"Are you?" There was a hint of disbelief in the laugh that followed.

"I really am, I'm sorry."

"She told you, though?"

"In a roundabout sort of way." Rebus paused. "So do you know where she is?"

"Cut the crap, John. She's at your flat."

"What?"

"You heard me. She's biding with you."

"First I've heard of it."

"She doesn't know anybody else over there."

"There are bed and breakfasts, rooms to rent . . ."

"You're not putting her up?"

"You've got my word for it."

There was a long silence on the line. "Christ, man, I'm sorry. I'm off my head with worry here."

"Only to be expected, Brian."

"Think it's worth my while coming to look for her?"

Rebus exhaled. "What do you think?"

"I think she used to love me."

"But not any more?"

"She wouldn't have left otherwise."

"True enough."

"Even if she finds Damon, I don't think she's coming back."

"Give her some time, Brian."

"Aye, sure." Brian Mee sniffed. "Know something? I used to like it that folk called me Barney. I know how I got the name, you know."

"I thought you said you didn't?"

"Oh aye, but I know all the same. Barney Rubble. Because folk thought I was like him. Somebody said it to me once, not just 'Barney' but 'Barney Rubble.' "

Rebus smiled. "But you liked the name anyway?"

"I didn't say that. I said I liked that I had a nickname. It was a sort of identity, wasn't it? And that's better than nothing."

Rebus's smile stretched. He was seeing Barney Mee, the tough little battler, wading in to save Mitch. The years separating the present from that long-ago event seemed to fall away. It was as if the two could live side by side, the past a ghostly presence forever of the here and now. Nothing lost; nothing forgotten; redemption always a possibility.

But if that was true, how could he explain that Dr. Margolies would never see a court of law, his crimes known only to the few? And how to explain that the Procurator Fiscal seemed able to prosecute Cary Oakes only for the attempted murder of Alan Archibald? All the forensic evidence connecting him to Jim Stevens could be explained away: fingerprints and fibres in Stevens' car—Oakes had ridden in it before. Hell, three police officers had watched him being driven away from the airport in it. The Stevens file would be kept open, but no one would be investigating. Everyone knew who'd done it. But short of a confession, there was nothing they could do.

"Let's stick to our strongest suit," the fiscal depute had said. This meant discarding the attack on Rebus, too, even though the taxi driver had been willing to testify.

"Too many possible arguments for the defence," the fiscal depute had said. Rebus tried not to take it personally. He knew prosecution was a game all to itself, where the best player might lose, the cheat prosper. He knew it was the job of the police to investigate and present the facts. It was the job of lawyers like Richie Cordover to then twist everything around until they could persuade juries and witnesses that Celtic fans sang "The Sash" and Cowdenbeath was an ideal holiday location.

"Hey, John?" Brian Mee was saying.

"Yes, Barney?"

Brian laughed at that. "What about coming through some weekend, just you and me, eh? Double-act at the karaoke, and see if we can dust off some chat-up lines."

"Sounds tempting, Barney. I'll give you a bell some time." Both men knowing he wouldn't.

"Right then, that's you on a promise."

"Cheers, Barney."

"Bye, John. It was good to catch up with you . . ."

Another paedophile had been released from prison, this time in Glasgow. GAP had organised a bus and headed off for Renfrew, where he was rumoured to be holed up. Some of the younger males in the company had gone for a night on the town, which had ended with a full-scale battle raging through the streets.

It was hoped, at least in some quarters, that the resulting negative publicity would sound the organisation's death knell. But Van Brady was still giving interviews and getting her picture in the papers, still applying to the Lottery for funding. Journalists liked that she talked almost exclusively in sound-bites, even if half of them had to be toned down for publication.

There was a memorial service for Jim Stevens. Rebus went along. He suspected that in his day Stevens had prob-

ably fallen out with at least three-quarters of the mourners.
But there were eulogies and sombre faces, and Rebus
couldn't help feeling that Jim wouldn't have wanted it that
way. Afterwards, he held a little wake of his own in the
Oxford Bar's back room with three or four of the loudest,
rudest, and funniest hacks around. They drank till well after
midnight, their laughter almost drowning out the music
from the ceilidh band in the corner.

Rebus stumbled down the road to Oxford Terrace,
dumped his clothes in the washing basket and had a shower.

"You still reek," Patience told him as he climbed into
bed.

"I'm keeping up traditions," Rebus said. "Edinburgh's
not called 'Auld Reekie' for nothing."

He thought it curious that Cal Brady should want to speak
to him. Cal was out on bail, awaiting trial for various
offences against the person on the night of the Renfrew
stramash. The morning phone call was so unexpected,
Rebus walked out of the station without telling anyone
where he was going. They met up on Radical Road. Cal
had wanted somewhere not too far from home, but not a
cop-shop, somewhere they could talk without anyone
hearing.

The wind was flying, stinging Rebus's ears. There were
occasional blasts of sunshine as the fast-moving clouds
broke, only to blot out the sun again moments later. Cal
Brady had deep bruises beneath both eyes, and a burst lip.
His left hand sported a bandage and he seemed to limp ever
so slightly as he walked.

"Bad one, was it?" Rebus asked.

"Those weegies . . ." Cal shook his head.

"I thought it was Renfrew?"

"Renfrew, Glasgow . . . all the same, man. Mad bastards,
each and every one. Their idea of a square go is to rip your
face off with their teeth." He shivered, pulled his denim
jacket tighter around him.

"You could button it up," Rebus told him.

"Eh?"

"The jacket . . . if you're cold."

"Aye, but it looks stupid when you do that. Levi jackets

are only cool when they're open." Rebus had no answer to that. "I hear you got a bit of a scrape yourself."

Rebus looked at his arm. No sling now, just a taped compress. Another week or so, the stitches would dissolve. "What did you want to see me for, Cal?"

"These fucking charges."

"What about them?"

"I'll probably end up going down, record I've got."

"So?"

"So, I could do without it." He twitched a shoulder. "Gonny help me out?"

"You mean put in a good word?"

"Aye."

Rebus stuck his hands in his pockets, as if relaxing. In truth, he'd been on his guard ever since arriving at the meeting-point five minutes before Brady: on the lookout for traps or a possible ambush. Lessons learned from Cary Oakes. "Why should I do that?" he asked.

"Look, I'm no fucking snitch, right?"

Rebus nodded agreement, as seemed to be expected.

"But I hear things." He paused. "Try not to, but sometimes I can't help it."

"Such as?"

"So you'll put a word in?"

Rebus stopped walking. He seemed to be admiring the vista. "I could tell them you're one of mine. I could make you sound important."

"But I wouldn't *be* your grass, right? That's the crux."

Rebus nodded. "But you've got something to trade?"

Cal looked around, as if even here he might be overheard. When he lowered his voice, Rebus had to move close to him to hear what he was saying over the noise of the wind.

"You know I work for Mr. Mackenzie?"

"You're his enforcer."

Brady prickled at that. "Sometimes he's owed money. Happens to a lot of businesses."

"Sure."

"I make sure his debtors know the risks they're taking."

Rebus smiled. "A nice way of putting it."

Brady looked around again. "Petrie," he said, like this would explain everything.

"I know," Rebus said. "Nicky Petrie owed Charmer money, got beaten up in lieu of a final reminder."

But Brady was shaking his head. "It was his sister owed the money."

"Ama?" Brady nodded. "So why thump Nicky?"

Brady snorted. "She's a cold, hard bitch. Maybe you haven't noticed. But she likes her little brother. She *loves* little Nicky . . ."

"So you were sending the message to her?" Rebus thought about it, remembered something Ama had said to him at the beauty contest: *Who do I owe money to?* "Why didn't she get the money from her father?"

"Story is, she wouldn't ask him for the time of day, and he wouldn't give it to her if he'd a watch on either arm."

"I still don't know what this has to do with me."

"That flat of theirs."

"What about it?"

"*She* lives there. The blonde you were looking for."

Rebus stared at Brady. "She's in that flat?" Brady was nodding. "What's her name?"

"I think it's Nicola."

"How do you know all this?"

Brady shrugged. "They can't help talking, that little gang."

Rebus thought of the scene on the boat . . . the way the drunk had been about to say something until warned off by Ama Petrie . . .

"They know about this Nicola?"

"They *all* know."

Which meant they'd all lied to Rebus . . . including the brother and sister, Nicky and Ama.

"Is she Nicky's girlfriend?"

Brady shrugged again.

"Or Ama's maybe?"

"I don't get involved," Brady said, waving his hand as though to cut the discussion dead.

"How about you, Cal? Still living with Joanna?"

"Nothing to do with you."

"How's Billy Boy? Don't you think he'd be better off with his dad?"

"That's not what Joanna wants."

"Has anyone asked Billy what *he* wants?"

Brady's voice rose. "He's just a kid. How's he supposed to know what's best for him?"

"I bet when you were his age you knew what you wanted."

"Maybe," Brady conceded after a moment's thought. "But I'll give you odds-on I didn't get it." He laughed. "Maybe I'm *still* not getting it. Know what I think about that?"

"What?"

"Just watch."

And Rebus did watch, as Cal Brady unzipped his fly, took out his penis, and began to urinate off the edge of Radical Road. Standing well back from the performance, it seemed to Rebus that he was pissing on Holyrood and Greenfield and St. Leonard's, pissing in a giant arc over the whole city.

And if Rebus had been able, at that exact moment he might have joined him.

Returning to St. Leonard's with Siobhan Clarke after a call-out, Rebus made a detour to the New Town. Clarke knew better than to ask why: he'd tell her in his own good time and not before.

It was late afternoon, and he sat kerbside, indicators flashing, wondering about Nicky Petrie. To pay a visit, or not to pay a visit? Would the girlfriend be there? Would Petrie string together another series of lies and half-truths? Clarke was about to open her mouth to say something when she saw his hands tighten on the steering-wheel.

A woman was coming down the steps from Petrie's building. Rebus saw for the first time that a taxi was waiting. She stepped into it. He'd caught only a glimpse of her: tall, willowy. A blonde pageboy cut. Black dress and tights beneath a billowing black wool coat. Rebus switched off the indicators, made to follow the cab, started explaining the situation to Clarke.

"Where do you think she's going?"

"Only one way to find out."

The taxi headed towards Princes Street, crossed it and crawled up The Mound. Through traffic lights at the top and took a right down Victoria Street. Grassmarket was the destination. Nicola paid the driver, got out. She looked around, somewhat uncertainly. Her face was like a mask.

"Bit heavy on the make-up," Clarke commented. Rebus was trying to find a parking space. Finding none, he left the car on a single yellow line. If he got a ticket, it could join the others in the glove compartment.

"Where did she go?" he asked, getting out of the car.

"Down Cowgate, I think," Clarke said.

"Hell does she want down there?"

While Grassmarket itself had been gentrified, the area immediately to the east was still Hostel City: a place the city's dispossessed could, for the moment, call its own. Things would doubtless be different once the politicians moved in down the road.

They stood on street corners, or sat on the steps of disused churches—baggy-trousered and grim-bearded, with too few teeth, and stooped backs. As Rebus and Clarke rounded the corner, they saw that the woman was walking with exaggerated slowness through a phalanx of admirers, only a smattering of whom bothered asking her for spare change and cigarettes.

"Likes to show off," Clarke said.

"And not too fussy with it."

"Just one thing bothering me, sir . . ."

But Nicola had turned to acknowledge a wolf-whistle, and as she did so she saw them. She turned again quickly and upped her pace, keeping a tight hold of her zebra-skin shoulder-bag.

"Not the world's greatest surveillance," Clarke said.

"She knows us," Rebus hissed. They broke into a trot, ran along the pavement below George IV Bridge. She wore flat-heeled shoes, ran well despite the tangle of her long coat. She found a gap in the traffic and darted across the road. Cowgate was horrible: a narrow canyon, with high-sided buildings. When traffic built up, the carbon monoxide had no place to go. The stitches in Rebus's chest slowed him down.

"Guthrie Street," Clarke said. That was where Nicola was headed. It would bring her up on to Chambers Street, where she could more easily lose her pursuers. But as she turned into the steep wynd, she bumped into someone. The collision sent her spinning. Something fell to the ground, but she kept running. Rebus paused to scoop it up. A short blonde wig.

"What the hell?"

"That's what I was trying to tell you, sir," Clarke said. Ahead of them, Nicola was tiring, holding the wall for support as she hauled herself up the incline. Limping, too, an ankle twisted in the collision. Eventually, just as she reached Chambers Street, her hair short and merely fair now rather than blonde, she gave up, stood with her back to the wall, panting noisily. Perspiration was streaking the make-up. Behind the mask, Rebus saw someone he knew only too well.

Not Nicola, Nicky. Nicky Petrie.

Petrie's words: *Straitlaced old town, how else are we going to get our thrills . . . ?*

Rebus's heart was on fire as he stopped in front of him. He could hardly get the words out.

"It's story time, Mr. Petrie." He slapped the wig down on Nicky Petrie's head. Petrie, with a show of disgust, re-moved the wig, held it to his face. It was hard to make out now what was sweat and what was tears.

"Oh God, oh God, oh God," he kept saying.

"Where's Damon Mee?"

"Oh God, oh God, oh God."

"I don't think He's in a position to help you, Nicky."

Rebus looked at the clothes. They could belong to Ama Petrie: brother and sister were of similar build, Nicky slightly taller and broader. The black dress looked tight on him.

"This is what you like to do, Nicky? Dress up as a woman?"

"No harm in it," Clarke added quickly. "We're all different."

Nicky looked at her, blinking to refocus his eyes.

"You could do with a makeover, sweetheart," he said.

She smiled. "You're probably right."

"Who does your make-up, Nicky?" Rebus asked. "Ama?"

He straightened up. "All my own work."

"And then you head for this side of town? Walk up and down and soak up the admiration?"

"I don't expect you to—"

"Nobody's asking what you expect, Mr. Petrie." He turned to Clarke. "Go fetch the car." Handed her the keys. "We'll need to take Mr. Petrie here to the station."

Petrie's eyes widened with fear. "Why?"

"To answer a few questions about Damon Mee. And to explain why you've been lying to us all along."

Petrie made to say something, then bit his lip.

"Suit yourself," Rebus told him. Then, to Clarke: "Go get the car."

Rebus questioned Nicky Petrie for half an hour. He made sure that anyone who wanted to gawp had the chance to come into the interview room. Petrie sat there with his head in his hands, not looking up, while a parade of CID and uniforms commented on his shoes, tights and dress.

"I can get you some trousers and a shirt," Rebus offered.

"I know what you're trying to do," Petrie said when they were alone. "Humiliate me all you like, this lady's *not* for talking." He managed a small defiant smile.

"I'm sure your dad will come riding to the rescue anyway," Rebus commented, pleased to see some of the colour leave the young man's lips.

"I don't need my father."

"That's as may be, but we'll need to contact him. Best for us to do it rather than the papers."

"Papers?"

Rebus barked a laugh. "Think they'll let something like this pass them by? No, sir, you're going to be cover-boy for a day, Nicky. Congratulations. Bit of pan-stick and a wig, they might even pay you for the privilege."

"They don't need to know," Petrie said quietly.

Rebus shrugged. "Cop-shops are like sieves, Nicky. All these people who've seen you here . . . I can't promise they won't talk."

"Bastard."

"If you like, Nicky." Rebus leaned forward. "All I want to know is where I can find Damon Mee."

"Then I can't help you," Nicky Petrie said, with all the defiance he could muster.

Plan Two: Ama Petrie.

She flew into the station like a whirlwind. Cal Brady was right: she had a soft spot for her little brother.

"Where is he? What have you done with him?"

Rebus looked at her with a façade of utter calm. "Shouldn't those be *my* questions?"

She didn't seem to understand.

"Damon Mee," Rebus explained. "Nicky met him at Gaitano's, took him to the boat where you were having one of your parties. That's the last time he was seen alive, Ms. Petrie."

"It's got nothing to do with Nicky."

They were seated in the same interview room, Nicky Petrie having been taken down to the cells. It was also the same interview room where Harold Ince had first been questioned. Ince had been sentenced to twelve years, Marshall to eight, the bulk of both sentences to be served at Peterhead. Had Rebus known anyone there, he might have put in a word for Ince. But he didn't know a single damned soul . . .

"What's got nothing to do with Nicky?" he asked.

"It's my fault, not his."

Rebus understood: she thought Nicky had talked, had

somehow incriminated himself. She was underestimating him. The chink in her armour which Cal Brady had detected: she loved her brother too much.

Rebus sat back, knew how to play this. He asked her if she wanted anything to drink. She shook her head violently.

"I want to make a statement," she blurted out.

"You'll probably want a solicitor, Ms. Petrie."

"Bugger that." She stopped suddenly. "Is Nicky here? In this station?"

"Safely in the cells."

"Safely?" Her voice trembled. "Poor Nicky . . ." She was dry-eyed but her face was tense.

"Did Damon Mee know Nicky wasn't really a woman?"

"How could he not?"

Rebus shrugged. "Your brother's pretty convincing."

She allowed herself a brief smile. "He always said he should have been the girl and I the boy."

Rebus knew Nicky had run away from home aged twelve. He'd been running ever since . . .

"So what happened on the boat?"

"We'd all been drinking." She looked at him. "You know what parties are like."

She was trying to win him round to her side. Too late for that, but he nodded anyway.

"Then Nicky brought this piece of rough below decks."

"Piece of rough?"

"As in rough and ready. I'm not being a snob, Inspector."

"Of course not. I take it all of you knew Nicky's . . . preferences?"

"The gang of us, yes. A few couples were up dancing. Nicky and this Damon joined them." Her eyes went unfocused; she was picturing the scene. "Nicky had his head on Damon's shoulder, and just for a moment our eyes met . . . and he looked so *happy*." She screwed shut her eyes.

"Then what happened?"

She opened her eyes again, staring at the desk. "Alfie and Cherie were one of the other couples. Alfie was as drunk as I've ever seen him. For a joke, he leaned over and snatched Nicky's wig. Nicky chased him round the room.

And Damon just stood there, like he was thunderstruck. He looked . . . it really seemed hilarious at the time. His face was a picture. Then he ran for the stairs. Nicky saw what was happening and went after him . . ."

"They had a fight?"

She looked at him. "Is that what he told you?" She smiled. "Dear Nicky . . . You've seen him, Inspector. He couldn't hurt a fly. No, by the time I came up on deck, this Damon person had Nicky down on the ground. He was strangling the life out of him, at the same time thumping his head against the deck. Lifting it . . . thudding it back down. I grabbed an empty wine bottle, swung it at the side of his head. It didn't knock him cold or anything. The bottle didn't even break, not like in the films. But he let go of Nicky, staggered to his feet."

"And?"

"And seemed to lose his balance. He fell over the side and into the water. It's funny . . . the deck's not that high above the water line . . . he hardly made a sound as he fell."

"What did you do?"

"I had to make sure Nicky was all right. I took him back down below. His throat hurt, but I got a brandy down him."

"I meant, what did you do about Damon?"

"Oh, him . . ." She thought it over. "Well, by the time I went back up, there was no sign of him. I assumed he'd swum ashore."

Rebus stared at her. "Are you quite sure that's what you assumed?"

"To be honest . . . I'm not sure I thought anything at all. He was gone, and he couldn't hurt Nicky, that was all that mattered. That's all that ever matters to me. So you see, whatever Nicky's told you, he only did in order to protect me. I'm the one you should put in the cell. Nicky should go home."

"Thanks for the advice."

"You will let him go, won't you?"

He stood up, leaned across the desk towards her. "I know Damon's family. I've seen the way they've been suffering. Your precious brother doesn't know the half of it."

She glowered at him. "And why should he?"

He thought of a thousand answers, knew she'd rebut every one of them. Instead, he told her he'd need a written statement. He'd send someone in to take it. He made for the door.

"And then you'll let Nicky out, won't you, Inspector?"

His one little victory: he left without saying a word.

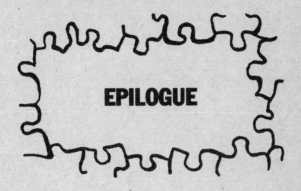

EPILOGUE

Later that night, he found himself in Cowgate again, further to the east this time, past the mothballed mortuary, walking towards the building site on Holyrood. Behind it, he could make out a couple of the Greenfield tower-blocks, and behind those Salisbury Crags. The sun had set, but it wasn't quite dark. The twilight could last an age at this time of year. Demolition work had stopped for the day. He couldn't be sure where everything would go, but he knew there'd be a newspaper building, a theme park, and the Parliament building. They'd all be ready for the twenty-first century, or so the predictions went. Taking Scotland into the new millennium. Rebus tried to raise within himself a tiny cheer of hope, but found it stifled by his old cynicism.

No longer twilight now. Darkness had fallen. Shadows seemed to rise all around him as a bell tolled in the distance. The blood that had seeped into stone, the bones that lay twisting in their eternity, the stories and horrors of the city's past and present . . . he knew they'd all come rising in the digger's steel jaws, bubbling to the surface as the city began its slow ascent towards being a nation's capital once again.

Forget it, John, he told himself. It's the Old Town, that's all.

Cary Oakes sat in the visitors' room at Saughton Prison. They hadn't put any cuffs on him, and there was just the one guard. One guard was almost demeaning. Then the door opened and his solicitor walked in. That's what they were called here—solicitors. Cary smiled, bowed his head in greeting. The lawyer was young, looked eager but flustered. First time, probably, but that was OK. Youngsters, working hard to make the grade . . . they'd put in the hours for you, go the extra yard. Cary had nothing against fresh blood.

He waited till the guy was seated and ready, notepad out, pen held in his right hand. Then he began his spiel.

"I'm innocent, man, so help me. And you've got to do that: you've got to help me. Between us, we can prove I didn't do anything." He leaned forward, rested his elbows on the table. "It'll make your career. You're my man, I can sense it."

Gave a big open smile.

Read on for an excerpt from Ian Rankin's

SET IN DARKNESS

Now available from St. Martin's Paperbacks!

Darkness was falling as Rebus accepted the yellow hard hat from his guide.

"This will be the admin block, we think," the man said. His name was David Gilfillan. He worked for Historic Scotland and was coordinating the archaeological survey of Queensberry House. "The original building is late seventeenth century. Lord Hatton was its original owner. It was extended at the end of the century, after coming into the ownership of the first Duke of Queensberry. It would have been one of the grandest houses on Canongate, and only a stone's throw from Holyrood."

All around them, demolition work was taking place. Queensberry House itself would be saved, but the more recent additions either side of it were going. Workmen crouched on roofs, removing slates, tying them into bundles which were lowered by rope to waiting skips. There were enough broken slates underfoot to show that the process was imperfect. Rebus adjusted his hard hat and tried to look interested in what Gilfillan was saying.

Everyone told him that this was a sign, that he was here because the chiefs at the Big House had plans for him. But Rebus knew better. He knew his boss, Detective Chief Superintendent "Farmer" Watson, had put his name forward because he was hoping to keep Rebus out of trouble and out of his hair. It was as simple as that. And if—*if*—Rebus accepted without complaining and saw the assignment through, then maybe—*maybe*—the Farmer would receive a chastened Rebus back into the fold.

Four o'clock on a December afternoon in Edinburgh; John Rebus with his hands in his raincoat pockets, water

seeping up through the leather soles of his shoes. Gilfillan
was wearing green wellies. Rebus noticed that DI Derek
Linford was wearing an almost identical pair. He'd probably phoned beforehand, checked with the archaeologist
what the season's fashion was. Linford was Fettes fast-
stream, headed for big things at Lothian and Borders Police
HQ. Late twenties, practically deskbound, and glowing
from a love of the job. Already there were CID officers—
mostly older than him—who were saying it didn't do to
get on the wrong side of Derek Linford. Maybe he'd have
a long memory; maybe one day he'd be looking down on
them all from Room 279 in the Big House.

The Big House: Police HQ on Fettes Avenue; 279: the
Chief Constable's office.

Linford had his notebook out, pen clenched between his
teeth. He was listening to the lecture. He was *listening*.

"Forty noblemen, seven judges, generals, doctors, bank-
ers . . ." Gilfillan was letting his tour group know how important Canongate had been at one time in the city's
history. In doing so, he was pointing towards the near future. The brewery next door to Queensberry House was due
for demolition the following spring. The parliament building itself would be built on the cleared site, directly across
the road from Holyrood House, the Queen's Edinburgh residence. On the other side of Holyrood Road, facing Queensberry House, work was progressing on Dynamic Earth, a
natural history theme park. Next to it, a new HQ for the
city's daily newspaper was at present a giant monkey-
puzzle of steel girders. And across the road from that, another site was being cleared in preparation for the
construction of a hotel and "prestige apartment block." Rebus was standing in the midst of one of the biggest building
sites in Edinburgh's history.

"You'll probably all know Queensberry House as a hospital," Gilfillan was saying. Derek Linford was nodding,
but then he nodded agreement with almost everything the
archaeologist said. "Where we're standing now was used
for car parking." Rebus looked around at the mud-coloured
lorries, each one bearing the simple word DEMOLITION.
"But before it was a hospital it was used as a barracks. This
area was the parade ground. We dug down and found ev-

idence of a formal sunken garden. It was probably filled in to make the parade ground."

In what light was left, Rebus looked at Queensberry House. Its grey harled walls looked unloved. There was grass growing from its gutters. It was huge, yet he couldn't remember having seen it before, though he'd driven past it probably several hundred times in his life.

"My wife used to work here," another of the group said, "when it was a hospital." The informant was Detective Sergeant Joseph Dickie, who was based at Gayfield Square. He'd successfully contrived to miss two out of the first four meetings of the PPLC—the Policing of Parliament Liaison Committee. By some arcane law of bureaucratic semantics, the PPLC was actually a *sub*committee, one of many which had been set up to advise on security matters pertaining to the Scottish Parliament. There were eight members of the PPLC, including one Scottish Office official and a shadowy figure who claimed to be from Scotland Yard, though when Rebus had phoned the Met in London, he'd been unable to trace him. Rebus's bet was that the man—Alec Carmoodie—was M15. Carmoodie wasn't here today, and neither was Peter Brent, the sharp-faced and sharper-suited Scottish Office representative. Brent, for his sins, sat on several of the subcommittees, and had begged off today's tour with the compelling excuse that he'd been through it twice before when accompanying visiting dignitaries.

Making up the party today were the three final members of the PPLC. DS Ellen Wylie was from C Division HQ in Torphichen Place. It didn't seem to bother her that she was the only woman on the team. She treated it like any other task, raising good points at the meetings and asking questions to which no one seemed to have any answers. DC Grant Hood was from Rebus's own station, St. Leonard's. Two of them, because St. Leonard's was the closest station to the Holyrood site, and the parliament would be part of their beat. Though Rebus worked in the same office as Hood, he didn't know him well. They'd not often shared the same shift. But Rebus did know the last member of the PPLC, DI Bobby Hogan from D Division in Leith. At the first meeting, Hogan had pulled Rebus to one side.

"What the hell are we doing here?"

"I'm serving time," Rebus had answered. "What about you?"

Hogan was scoping out the room. "Christ, man, look at them. We're Old Testament by comparison."

Smiling now at the memory, Rebus caught Hogan's eye and winked. Hogan shook his head almost imperceptibly. Rebus knew what he was thinking: waste of time. Almost everything was a waste of time for Bobby Hogan.

"If you'll follow me," Gilfillan was saying, "we can take a look indoors."

Which, to Rebus's mind, really was a waste of time. The committee having been set up, things had to be found for them to do. So here they were wandering through the dank interior of Queensberry House, their way lit irregularly by unsafe-looking strip lights and the torch carried by Gilfillan. As they climbed the stairwell—nobody wanted to use the lift—Rebus found himself paired with Joe Dickie, who asked a question he'd asked before.

"Put in your exes yet?" By which he meant the claim for expenses.

"No," Rebus admitted.

"Sooner you do, sooner they'll cough up."

Dickie seemed to spend half his time at their meetings totting up figures on his pad of paper. Rebus had never seen the man write down anything as mundane as a phrase or sentence. Dickie was late thirties, big-framed with a head like an artillery shell stood on end. His black hair was cropped close to the skull and his eyes were as small and rounded as a china doll's. Rebus had tried the comparison out on Bobby Hogan, who'd commented that any doll resembling Joe Dickie would "give a bairn nightmares."

"I'm a grown-up," Hogan had continued, "and he still scares me."

Climbing the stairs, Rebus smiled again. Yes, he was glad to have Bobby Hogan around.

"When people think of archaeology," Gilfillan was saying, "they almost always see it in terms of digging *down*, but one of our most exciting finds here was in the attic. A new roof was built over the original one, and there are traces of what looks like a tower. We'd have to climb a ladder to get to it, but if anyone's interested . . . ?"

"Thank you," a voice said. Derek Linford: Rebus knew its nasal quality only too well by now.

"Creep," another voice close to Rebus whispered. It was Bobby Hogan, bringing up the rear. A head turned: Ellen Wylie. She'd heard, and now gave what looked like the hint of a smile. Rebus looked to Hogan, who shrugged, letting him know he thought Wylie was all right.

"How will Queensberry House be linked to the parliament building? Will there be covered walkways?" The questions came from Linford again. He was out in front with Gilfillan. The pair of them had rounded a corner of the stairs, so that Rebus had to strain to hear Gilfillan's hesitant reply.

"I don't know."

His tone said it all: he was an archaeologist, not an architect. He was here to investigate the site's past rather than its future. He wasn't sure himself why he was giving this tour, except that it had been asked of him. Hogan screwed up his face, letting everyone in the vicinity know his own feelings.

"When will the building be ready?" Grant Hood asked. An easy one: they'd all been briefed. Rebus saw what Hood was doing—trying to console Gilfillan by putting a question he could answer.

"Construction begins in the summer," Gilfillan obliged. "Everything should be up and running here by the autumn of 2001." They were coming out on to a landing. Around them stood open doorways, through which could be glimpsed the old hospital wards. Walls had been gouged at, flooring removed: checks on the fabric of the building. Rebus stared out of a window. Most of the workers looked to be packing up: dangerously dark now to be scrabbling over roofs. There was a summer house down there. It was due to be demolished, too. And a tree, drooping forlornly, surrounded by rubble. It had been planted by the Queen. No way it could be moved or felled until she'd given her permission. According to Gilfillan, permission had now been granted; the tree would go. Maybe formal gardens would be recreated down there, or maybe it would be a staff car park. Nobody knew. 2001 seemed a ways off. Until this site was ready, the parliament would sit in the Church of Scotland Assembly Hall near the top of The Mound. The committee had already been on two tours of the Assembly Hall and its immediate vicinity. Office buildings were being turned over to the parliament, so that the MSPs could have somewhere to work. Bobby Hogan had asked at one meeting why they couldn't just wait for the Holyrood site to be ready before, in his words, "setting up shop." Peter Brent, the civil servant, had stared at him aghast.

"Because Scotland needs a parliament *now*."

"Funny, we've done without for three hundred years . . ."

Brent had been about to object, but Rebus had butted in. "Bobby, at least they're not trying to rush the job."

Hogan had smiled, knowing he was talking about the newly opened Museum of Scotland. The Queen had come north for the official opening of the unfinished building. They'd had to hide the scaffolding and paint tins till she'd gone.

Gilfillan was standing beside a retractable ladder, pointing upwards towards a hatch in the ceiling.

"The original roof is just up there," he said. Derek Linford already had both feet on the ladder's bottom rung. "You don't need to go all the way," Gilfillan continued as Linford climbed. "If I shine the torch up . . ."

But Linford had disappeared into the roof space.

"Lock the hatch and let's make a run for it," Bobby Hogan said, smiling so they'd assume he was joking.

Ellen Wylie hunched her shoulders. "There's a real . . . atmosphere in here, isn't there?"

"My wife saw a ghost," Joe Dickie said. "Lots of people who worked here did. A woman, she was crying. Used to sit on the end of one of the beds."

"Maybe she was a patient who died here," Grant Hood offered.

Gilfillan turned towards them. "I've heard that story, too. She was the mother of one of the servants. Her son was working here the night the Act of Union was signed. Poor chap got himself murdered."

Linford called down that he thought he could see where the steps to the tower had been, but nobody was listening.

"Murdered?" Ellen Wylie said.

Gilfillan nodded. His torch threw weird shadows across the walls, illuminating the slow movements of cobwebs. Linford was trying to read some graffiti on the wall.

"There's a year written here . . . 1870, I think."

"You know Queensberry was the architect of the Act of Union?" Gilfillan was saying. He could see that he had an audience now, for the first time since the tour had begun in the brewery car park next door. "Back in 1707. This," he scratched a shoe over the bare floorboards, "is where Great Britain was invented. And the night of the signing, one of the young servants was working in the kitchen. The Duke of Queensberry was Secretary of State. It was his job to lead the negotiations. But he had a son, James Douglas, Earl of Drumlanrig. The story goes, James was off his head . . ."

"What happened?"

Gilfillan looked up through the open hatch. "All right up there?" he called.

"Fine. Anyone else want to take a look?"

They ignored him. Ellen Wylie repeated her question.

"He ran the servant through with a sword," Gilfillan said, "then roasted him in one of the kitchen fireplaces. James was sitting munching away when he was found."

"Dear God," Ellen Wylie said.

"You believe this?" Bobby Hogan slid his hands into his pockets.

Gilfillan shrugged. "It's a matter of record."

A blast of cold air seemed to rush at them from the roof space. Then a rubber-soled wellington appeared on the ladder, and Derek Linford began his slow, dusty descent. At the bottom, he removed the pen from between his teeth.

"Interesting up there," he said. "You really should try it. Could be your first and last chance."

"Why's that then?" Bobby Hogan asked.

"I very much doubt we'll be letting tourists in here, Bobby," Linford said. "Imagine what *that* would do for security."

Hogan stepped forward so swiftly that Linford flinched.

But all Hogan did was lift a cobweb from the young man's shoulder.

"Can't have you heading back to the Big House in less than showroom condition, can we, son?" Hogan said. Linford ignored him, probably feeling that he could well afford to ignore relics like Bobby Hogan, just as Hogan knew he had nothing to fear from Linford: he'd be heading for retirement long before the younger man gained any position of real power and prominence.

"I can't see it as the powerhouse of government," Ellen Wylie said, examining the water stains on the walls, the flaking plaster. "Wouldn't they have been better off knocking it down and starting again?"

"It's a listed building," Gilfillan censured her. Wylie just shrugged. Rebus knew that nevertheless she had accomplished her objective, by deflecting attention away from Linford and Hogan. Gilfillan was off again, delving into the history of the area: the series of wells which had been found beneath the brewery; the slaughterhouse which used to stand nearby. As they headed back down the stairs, Hogan held back, tapping his watch, then cupping a hand to his mouth. Rebus nodded: good idea. A drink afterwards. Jenny Ha's was a short stroll away, or there was the Holyrood Tavern on the way back to St. Leonard's. As if mind-reading, Gilfillan began talking about the Younger's Brewery.

"Covered twenty-seven acres at one time, produced a quarter of all the beer in Scotland. Mind you, there's been an abbey at Holyrood since early in the twelfth century. Chances are they weren't just drinking well-water."

Through a landing window, Rebus could see that outside night had fallen prematurely. Scotland in winter: it was dark when you came to work, and dark when you went home again. Well, they'd had their little outing, gleaned nothing from it, and would now be released back to their various stations until the next meeting. It felt like a penance because Rebus's boss had planned it as such. Farmer Watson was on a committee himself. Strategies for Policing in the New Scotland. Everyone called it SPINS. Committee upon committee . . . it felt to Rebus as if they were building a paper tower, enough 'Policy Agendas,' 'Reports' and 'Occasional Papers' to completely fill Queensberry House. And the more they talked, the more that got written, the further away from reality they seemed to move. Queensberry House was unreal to him, the idea of a parliament itself the dream of some mad god: "But Edinburgh is a mad god's dream/Fitful and dark . . ." He'd found the words at the opening to a book about the city. They were from a poem by Hugh MacDiarmid. The book itself had been part of his recent education, trying to understand this home of his.

He took off his hard hat, rubbed his fingers through his hair, wondering just how much protection the yellow plastic would give against a projectile falling several storeys. Gilfillan asked him to put the hat back on until they were back at the site office.

"You might not get into trouble," the archaeologist said, "but I would."

Rebus put the helmet back on, while Hogan tutted and wagged a finger. They were back at ground level, in what Rebus guessed must have been the hospital's reception area. There wasn't much to it. Spools of electric cable sat near the door: the offices would need rewiring. They were going to close the Holyrood/St. Mary's junction to facilitate underground cabling. Rebus, who used the route often, wasn't looking forward to the diversions. Too often these days the city seemed nothing but roadworks.

"Well," Gilfillan was saying, opening his arms, "that's about it. If there are any questions, I'll do what I can."

Bobby Hogan coughed into the silence. Rebus saw it as a warning to Linford. When someone had come up from London to address the group on security issues in the Houses of Parliament, Linford had asked so many questions the poor sod had missed his train south. Hogan knew this because he'd been the one who'd driven the Londoner at breakneck speed back to Waverley Station, then had had to entertain him for the rest of the evening before depositing him on the overnight sleeper.

Linford consulted his notebook, six pairs of eyes drilling into him, fingers touching wristwatches.

"Well, in that case," Gilfillan began.

"Hey! Mr. Gilfillan! Are you up there?" The voice was

coming from below. Gilfillan walked over to a doorway, called down a flight of steps.

"What is it, Marlene?"

"Come take a look."

Gilfillan turned to look at his reluctant group. "Shall we?" He was already heading down. They couldn't very well leave without him. It was stay here, with a bare light-bulb for company, or head down into the basement. Derek Linford led the way.

They came out into a narrow hallway, rooms off to both sides, and other rooms seeming to lead from those. Rebus thought he caught a glimpse of an electrical generator somewhere in the gloom. Voices up ahead and the shadow-play of torches. They walked out of the hallway and into a room lit by a single arc lamp. It was pointing towards a long wall, the bottom half of which had been lined with wooden tongue-and-groove painted the selfsame institutional cream as the plaster walls. Floorboards had been ripped up so that for the most part they were walking on the exposed joists, beneath which sat bare earth. The whole room smelt of damp and mould. Gilfillan and the other archaeologist, the one he'd called Marlene, were crouched in front of this wall, examining the stonework beneath the wood panelling. Two long curves of hewn stone, forming what seemed to Rebus like railway arches in miniature. Gilfillan turned round, looking excited for the first time that day.

"Fireplaces," he said. "Two of them. This must have been the kitchen." He stood up, taking a couple of paces back. "The floor level's been raised at some point. We're only seeing the top half of them." He half-turned towards the group, reluctant to take his eyes off the discovery. "Wonder which one the servant was roasted in . . ."

One of the fireplaces was open, the other closed off by a couple of sections of brown corroding metal.

"What an extraordinary find," Gilfillan said, beaming at his young co-worker. She grinned back at him. It was nice to see people so happy in their work. Digging up the past, uncovering secrets . . . it struck Rebus that they weren't so unlike detectives.

"Any chance of rustling us up a meal then?" Bobby

Hogan said, producing a snort of laughter from Ellen Wylie. But Gilfillan wasn't paying any heed. He was standing by the closed fireplace, prying with his fingertips at the space between stonework and metal. The sheet came away easily, Marlene helping him to lift it off and place it carefully on the floor.

"Wonder when they blocked it off?" Grant Hood asked.

Hogan tapped the metal sheet. "Doesn't look exactly prehistoric." Gilfillan and Marlene had lifted away the second sheet. Now everyone was staring at the revealed fireplace. Gilfillan thrust his torch towards it, though the arc lamp gave light enough.

There could be no mistaking the desiccated corpse for anything other than what it was.

IAN RANKIN

"This is crime fiction at its best."
—*Washington Post Book World*

"A brilliant series . . . The work of a master."
—*San Francisco Chronicle*

*Don't miss these spellbinding Inspector John Rebus
novels from the acclaimed, award-winning author*

KNOTS AND CROSSES

Rebus's city is being terrorized by a baffling series of murders, and he isn't just a cop trying to catch a killer—he's the man who holds all the pieces of the puzzle . . .

TOOTH AND NAIL

Sent to London to help catch a vicious serial killer, Rebus must piece together a portrait of a depraved psychopath bent on painting the town red—with blood . . .

MORTAL CAUSES

A young man's tortured body is found in a medieval cellar far beneath the Edinburgh streets, and to find a killer, Rebus must travel from the city's most violent neighborhood to Belfast, Northern Ireland—and make it back alive . . .

HIDE AND SEEK

In an Edinburgh housing development, a junkie lies dead of an overdose, his body surrounded by signs of Satanic worship. Rebus knows it was no accident. Now, to prove it, he's got to scour the city and find the perfect hiding place of a killer . . .

STRIP JACK

When a respected MP is caught in a police raid on an Edinburgh brothel and his wife Elizabeth suddenly disappears, John Rebus smells a set-up. And when Elizabeth's badly

beaten body is found, Rebus is up against a killer who holds
all the cards . . .

LET IT BLEED

Two suicides and a murder just don't add up—unless John
Rebus follows a trail to the truth that snakes through Edinburgh's stark alleys and sad bars. But he's up against a
murderous conglomerate that's leeching the life and soul
out of his city and, if it can, him too . . .

BLACK AND BLUE

A murdered oil-rig worker. A copycat serial killer. A re-
opened case that doesn't bode well for John Rebus. Rebus's
Scotland is riddled with trouble. Now he's got to tie up the
loose ends if he wants to save his job—or live to see another dark Edinburgh day.

HANGING GARDEN

Organized crime is fighting for a hold on John Rebus's
peaceful Scotland. But when his own daughter is mortally
injured as a gangland warning to him, even a dedicated cop
like Rebus might make a deal with the devil to find the
culprit. Not for justice. For revenge.

**AVAILABLE WHEREVER BOOKS ARE SOLD
FROM ST. MARTIN'S PAPERBACKS**